I0642233

The Diamond of the Gods

Book 1

The New Guardians

Dachs Aldman

© 2017 Dachs Aldman
All rights reserved.

ISBN: 0692064648
ISBN-13: 978-0692064641

Chapter One
The War of the Gods and of
Orrlick the Sorcerer.
— translated from the Ancient Writings of
Vilhum

In the beginning, when the galaxy was new, the Gods lived together in peace. This was when the race of man were all one, living side by side, each content. Saebourg, the baby of the Gods, was beloved by the Ice Men. He chose to live among them instead of lording over them, for he loved and cherished his people, and they lived well and excelled with his love, protection, teachings, and guidance. This was the same with the other Gods. Each had his followers, those who worshipped and respected him. Each God in turn loved, protected, and cherished his followers. This was as a good God should. Much like a proud parent. Only with a very large family.

As with most things in the galaxy, there was an exception to this rule. Saebourg's firstborn brother, Zerak, was God to no one. He chose to live alone, apart from his siblings and their followers. This suited him, and he left his siblings to their lives and they to his. Oh, he did poke his nose in occasionally to see what was going on in the rest of the world and to say hi to his family. The Gods welcomed their distant relative and enjoyed his visits, understanding that in time he would return to his solitary life.

In life, things tend to change over time. Sure enough, his solitary life changed one day. A bastard child came looking for him. No one knows who the boy's parents were or had been. Just like no one knew why or how the boy knew of Zerak. Or how the boy found the solitary God. Only that the boy went looking for him and found Zerak.

Once the child found Zerak, somewhat to the God's surprise (contrary to legend, Gods don't always know all that will happen—just most things), the child asked to be a man of Zerak. This surprised him even more, which is amusing, as surprising a God is quite an accomplishment. After some thought, Zerak agreed, and he took the boy for his follower. This being the first, Zerak asked what the boy wished. Having searched him out instead of going to one of his siblings, there must have been a reason. The boy asked to be taught the secrets of the galaxy and the spirit. He wished to learn the meaning of many things. Zerak agreed, having seen his brothers teaching their followers many things. He saw that this was good for man and followed his family's example. The boy learned quickly and grew, as boys do. Over time, he became a wizard. Some people knew him as a sorcerer. Regardless of the title, all knew him as Orrlick. Neither bothered the man; he simply thought of himself as a follower of Zerak. Once Orrlick reached manhood, time had no effect on Orrlick, as it had no effect on those whom had reached adulthood and choose to follow him in searching out the God Zerak. The followers of Zerak became known as a clan of ageless followers, having learned from Zerak how to stop time from affecting them.

One day Zerak was wandering through the ice at the top of the world and came across a perfectly round diamond about the size of a dumpling. Zerak did like dumplings, specially apple ones. With honey. And sweet cream. Cinnamon too. He took the Diamond, since it hadn't been found by anyone else, and he wondered what to do with such a beautiful, perfectly clear diamond. Besides just looking at it. Or through it at times. Even if it was pretty, it should have something more than just beauty. Over time the decision was made for him in a way. The diamond acquired a soul from being carried around by the God. This was a surprise, not only to Zerak. After all, who had ever heard of a diamond having a soul? He found that now that the Diamond had a soul, he could do miraculous things with it. His followers were awed by this and bestowed it with the name the Ice Diamond of the God Zerak. No one said they were all that creative, maybe a bit long-winded at times. Over time the name was shortened to simply Zerak's Ice.

Now, as in most families, not all of Zerak's siblings were alike. Where Zerak was solitary and quiet, his brother Arrah was almost the total opposite. Arrah was so handsome he was almost beautifully pretty. (Zerak thought of him as something of an over-primped-up pretty boy.) Arrah called his followers the Mulsins. He rejoiced in his followers making sacrifices, which they usually burned for him on delicately carved altars. Beheadings were enjoyable at times too, just to keep things changed up. The pretty God was called the God of all Gods by his followers. He was addicted to their words of love and adoration for him. The sacrifices became almost a drug for him, their scent sweet, their screams musical. No matter what was burned as an offering, he craved the smell. The beheadings became mesmerizing music. He relished his followers, looking down on them as deserved more than earned. His days were good, bathing in his followers' love for him. Until his brother ruined it. That damn diamond. When he heard of it, it was the last time he could enjoy anything as he had before. This made his life miserable. He didn't like being miserable.

Miserable had to stop.

To end being miserable, he went to his brother and asked, "Brother, it isn't right that you choose to stay away from your family's advice and companionship, is it? Perhaps the Diamond has corrupted and twisted your mind, leading you even farther from us. Perhaps you should give up the ice."

This uncharacteristic concern for anyone other than himself puzzled Zerak at first. It made him wonder what his sibling was really thinking and what he wanted. Arrah almost always wanted something if he was acting nice. Zerak looked into his brother's heart, as unpleasant as that could be, and seeing his brother's true motive, he answered Arrah.

"Don't you have more than enough to make you content, if not happy? Your followers present you with sacrifices, many heartfelt words of praise, even calling you the God of Gods. Your family allows this, even though we know better. You have lands, people, peace. This should be more than enough for you. For any God. Why covet my diamond? Be wary of it, as it can kill you. God or not."

Arrah was not used to being told no. He wasn't used to heeding good advice from other Gods either. He was not used to being made to look a fool, even if his brother meant no harm, only warning. He wasn't used to being walked away from. This was just too many things he wasn't used to—and more importantly, things he didn't like.

What Arrah was used to was getting what he wanted, when he wanted it, from whomever he wanted. Arrah was also used to giving in to his implosive nature and his short and sometimes violent temper.

As Zerak turned and walked away from his jealous brother, Arrah raised his hands and, in great rage, struck Zerak down. After striking his brother, Arrah took the Diamond and ran.

When Zerak's other brothers found out, they asked Arrah to return what he had taken to Zerak followers. They knew that no good could come from what he had done. Arrah said no. Why should he? So much for the theory that being nice will get you further. They then told him to return it. Again, Arrah refused. Along with his other shining qualities, he was stubborn.

His stubbornness led to man finding out what had happened, and they left the peaceful lives they had shared behind. The race of man, regardless of what God they followed, declared war on Arrah. His Mulsins were attacked and hunted.

This was how the war of the Gods had spilled over to their followers. The holy war continued for many years. One day the wars, those fought between the Gods and those fought between men, grew across the world until they reached the holy places of Aban. Arrah became desperate. He took the Diamond, whose soul was a good-natured soul, preferring peace, and after a long struggle forced the Diamond to change the earth. Many men died. All the Gods lost followers that day — the day the mountains disappeared and were replaced with the great waters.

Seeing this, Zerak and his brother Saebourg joined their power and channeled the great waters into borders to hold the water so that it wouldn't drown the entire world. This separated men from one another though. It also forced men from their Gods. Not just Arrah, but all the Gods.

Arrah was furious that two of his brothers would stand against him. "How dare they stand against the God of Gods!" he roared as he raised Zerak's Ice again. He would force it again to do as he wished, never thinking that the Diamond could, or even would, fight back. After all, he was the God of Gods, his followers all agreed. Ask any of them. Well, any left alive. The diamond, though, was not one of his followers; he didn't think of that.

Arrogantly thinking he would get what he wanted, as he usually did, he advanced on to where his brother's diamond lay. He would make it do his will again, and in doing so the earth would do as he wished. Who could refuse him? He was a God—and a handsome one. This time, however, the Diamond's mother, the Earth, fought back. Being made from the earth, the Diamond joined with its mother and laid a trap. While the Diamond lay in the open, looking innocent and helpless, the earth around it was filled with danger. As Arrah walked toward the Diamond, he crossed an invisible barrier. This tripped a spell, one laid by Mother Earth to protect the Diamond. The combined power of the Diamond and Mother Earth made the earth begin to glow a deep red. The red began to turn brighter until it was the color of a sun.

While Arrah hadn't noticed the tripping of the spell, he couldn't help but notice the changes in the earth. After all, it was glowing very brightly. It was also putting off such power as Arrah had never felt, and he was unable to control it. Then, about the time that he realized he couldn't control the power, the earth erupted all around him. His right leg was torn from his body at mid-thigh; his left was blown off from the knee down. Had he been standing he would have suddenly fallen. As he was already flying through the air from the force of the explosion, he didn't notice the loss of his legs. The pain of the amputations was just added to the pain of the side of his face getting similar treatment as his legs. His all-too-handsome face was blown apart: flesh, bone, blood, and even teeth were mangled in the explosion. So, surprised by the power and blinded by the pain, he never noticed the damage to his hand that he had been stretching out toward the Diamond. The power here had an even more devastating effect on his hand. It just…vanished. His last thought before landing with a sickening thud on his back and sliding across the ground was: how he wished the pain would have vanished with it.

Despite all that, the Earth complied to a certain extent with Arrah's will. In his fury, pain, and surprise, he lost control for a very brief period, and this led to his will expanding beyond his first thoughts. The earth's crust broke apart as though it were nothing more than a flaky crust of a pie. Following the breaking of the earth's crust came the leveling of mountains. As the great waters returned, they crumbled the mountains like so many sand castles on the beach at the rising of the tides.

Arrah fled as best he could with his injuries. Even Gods need time to heal. As he crossed the great ice at the top of the world, he let out a bone-chilling cry, one that came from the depths of the soul, oddly distorted by the damage to his face and mouth, the sound of which none had ever heard before. Arrah fell upon the ice, rolling in the snow, trying in vain to numb his wounds. It was all in vain. The pain stayed; his once-handsome (some thought softly pretty) face was forever ruined. He felt his limbs begin to heal. He knew that they would never return as fully as they had been before the explosion. He could walk, just never with the grace or arrogance he once had.

Once he had somewhat numbed the pain, he rose from the ice and snow, and all saw that his wounds would never fully heal. Stop hurting to some degree, yes. Heal fully — not even close. Not even a God could fight such power and fully recover. His followers averted their eyes from the wounded God.

In an anger filled with shame, sadness, and more than a little bit of embarrassment, none of which he took responsibility for, Arrah rose, gathered his worshippers, and left for the south. Here he settled them into what became a city called Gorinkail and had them build him many temples. One overshadowed them all though: a stone, iron, and wood tower. Its twin spires and domed roof rose into the sky to such a height that on cloudy days, the clouds would hide the top. It was here that his followers had enshrined the Diamond, much to its distaste. Maybe the Diamond didn't like heights? The holy shrine was built from blasted pure white marble that ran with veins of gold and housed in a room at the top of the temple. This shrine entirely encased the Diamond. The blocks were massive to keep Arrah from giving in to his longing to look upon and use the Diamond again. For all knew that if that came to pass, Arrah would not survive. While he could live with his injuries from the last attempt, there would be no second attempt. On clear, calm nights, you could hear Arrah sobbing as he stood and looked at the massive blocks containing is prize, sometimes caressing the cool marble with the stump of his arm. He sobbed openly for having impulsively attacked his brother. Each time he would flee, terrified, from the tower.

As the years turned to centuries, the world of the Mulsins began to change. One change came slowly, and Arrah became not only their God, but also their ruler. Their God King.

While all this was taking place in the south, to the north, Saebourg was leading his followers all the way to the ice at the top of the world. These men were the hardiest and most warrior-like of the earth, living hard yet honorable lives. Saebourg taught them not only how to stay warm in the frozen world they lived in but also how to make and use swords, axes, and bows. How to heal and read and write. Some say he also filled these hard warriors with hatred for all Mulsins. Others say that they learned this on their own. After all, Mulsins followed the God King, who had taken their God's powerful and loved diamond. Arrah having attacked their God and stole from him didn't help their view of the Mulsins. That was just mean-spirited in their minds. So in the years that followed, these hardy northern warriors wandered their world in search of their blood enemies of long ago. The Mulsins. In time the Mulsins sometimes wondered if they should have spent less time building pretty temples, brushing their hair and making sacrifices to Arrah and put more effort into learning to make and use swords and other weapons. Such is hindsight.

Chapter Two

Around this time, Dagnour White Bear, who had become the greatest king of the men of the north, saw that the way south was open and that the signs and stars were right for returning what had been stolen. He decided to travel to the cove of Zerak. He went looking for Orrlick the Sorcerer. He planned to ask Orrlick to help his people take the Diamond from Ol' Scary Face and return it to their God, from whom it had been stolen in the first place. This was just wrong, in his way of looking at things. He was sure returning it would make it and Orrlick much happier. After all, you should keep your God happy. Happy Gods were usually good Gods.

At this point in time, Gia, who was married to Orrlick, was well along in her pregnancy, and he wasn't eager to leave her. After time, though, Dagnour convinced Orrlick to come with, and they left one day. Orrlick did leave a note for his loving wife, though, telling her he was going on a trip with Dagnour and that Dagnour's sons might join them and that she wasn't to worry. After all, what could happen with fast-footed Ziggy Wolf Paw, Rishgar Owl Claw, and the powerfully huge Selgouth Sea Lion with them?

Now they picked one of the hardest winters to make this trip. It felt as though the ice had even colder ice forming on it, if that was possible. At night, the tundra sparkled and shone, almost as though lit from beneath. Its cold, white, fluffy snow shone light gray as it reflected the light of the stars and moon. If the moon and stars came out. This was one night the moon was hiding; the stars, though, still shone like sparkling ice flakes in the dark sky. It was as though the moon thought it was foolish to be out in this cold. To see through the darkness, Orrlick drew upon his knowledge and powers, creating a white snow owl that glowed a soft silvery light to guide them and allow them to see their way. The owl slowly floated a few feet above their heads over the frozen tundra and guided the group through towering trees, some of which were reduced to splinters from the cold. The owl's feathers became coated in delicate, lacy frost, and being connected to its creator by both will and magic, Orrlick's gray hair and beard also became the color of frost. He didn't mind; after all, it wasn't cold, just a color change.

They traveled for many miles through the cold, snow, ice, and wind—at times, all of them at once, which even the hardy men thought was a little cruel of Mother Nature to do. One or two at a time, sure. All at once though? That was bordering on just spiteful of her. They finally crossed into Khanikstran. Land of the Mulsins. It became warmer as they came closer to Gorinkail.

Once they arrived at Gorinkail, they sought a secret way into the city. After all, the Ice Men couldn't just walk in the front gates. They looked nothing like the Mulsins and would stand out like an Elsaar bear in a pigeon coop. Besides, the gates were closed for the night, and they all agreed it would be rude to wake up the sleeping guards by knocking on the gates. One must be polite when visiting someone else's city.

After finding a way in, while not exactly the cleanest, biggest, or best smelling, the group found their way to the ironwood and marble tower where the ice diamond lay. They stood and admired the tower; after all, it was well built and designed. They all agreed they should give credit to the builders. Even if they were measly Mulsins, they had built the tower that had lasted for so many years. That meant something had been done right.

When they decided to climb the ancient stairs, they all hesitated a bit. The stairs hadn't seen a human foot for many centuries, and the stairs had been designed for a much smaller-built man. Even Ziggy, who was the lightest of the bunch, was heavier than all but the heaviest Mulsin. Who knew if those stairs would hold the Ice Men after so many years of neglect? Would the stairs have held them when they were first built?

After eyeing the stairs and making a few comments about their strength or possible lack thereof, Dagnour looked at the group, looked at the stairs, and decided to lead by example, just as he had done in his kingdom. He started up the stairs, stepping on each stair cautiously and quietly. There was no point in running up them and taking unnecessary chances with the stairs disappearing from under the big men or in waking someone up. Besides, he had left his wife a note saying he would be safe. The rest took his lead and followed, leaving some space between them. The stairs, for their part, held, even if they creaked from time to time.

After a long climb, they reached the sleeping chamber of Arrah. They stopped and looked about for any unpleasant surprises such as trip wires or, in Orrlick's case, hidden spells. Finding nothing, they cautiously and a little fearfully slipped through the chamber. At one point, they all came to a sudden stop and watched as Arrah tossed and moaned in his sleep; the carved wooden mask he had taken to wearing to cover his disfigurement had an eerie look in the soft starlight that filtered through his white-sand-washed silk curtains. The pain never really left him or let him rest. His mind would never let him forget the explosions either, giving him haunting nightmares that made him toss and turn in his sleep. Once he settled again, the group continued through to their objective: the Shrine of the Diamond.

Dagnour motioned for Orrlick to open the marble shrine and remove the Diamond. Orrlick quietly refused though. "Before the God-maiming explosion, the Diamond enjoyed being touched by both man and God. Arrah went and made it angry, though, and in response to the abuse he had done to it, it has hardened itself. Now it would not welcome me touching it; for me to touch it would mean I would suffer a fate many times worse than Arrah has suffered. Not being a God, I doubt I would survive this. You must understand: the Diamond can see the true soul, the deepest of hearts, of a man. Now only someone of pure heart and soul who bears no ill will or evil intent toward his fellow man may handle the Diamond. All others, no. Very big no," he explained while shaking his head.

This perplexed Dagnour. *This was something that would have been good to know before getting here*, he thought yet didn't say it aloud. Maybe they could have brought along the babe of a holy man. What babe had an ill thought? Those were learned feelings and thoughts brought on by life. Well, could have, should have, and would have didn't do them much good right now, did it? He was thinking of what to do, as were the others, when his son Rishgar surprised them all and walked over to the shrine. He looked at the beautiful marble slabs and then leaned his pack against a wall, took off his weapons, and quietly set them with his pack. The rest looked at him quizzically. What was he doing? Rishgar then leaned into the slab on the top and heaved against it, pushing it to one side. He then reached into the shrine and gently picked up the Diamond. He lifted it out of its marble prison and held it carefully in his hand, close to his broad chest, almost like he was holding a week-old puppy. It pulsated a soft glow, which almost looked happy. Had it been a puppy, it would have been licking his face in happiness. It had been a long time since it had seen anything outside of the marble box, and it was dark in there. Why couldn't they have made it of crystal? At least then the Diamond could have looked at the sun passing the windows. Being in complete darkness, this can get rather boring after a few minutes. Rishgar had a softly content look on his usually hard and chiseled face, almost angelic in the soft light from the Diamond.

Orrlick was the first to recover from the surprise. Looking at Rishgar, he said, "Seems there is one among us who is pure of heart and soul. This could be his death, possibly all of his descendants' deaths as well. Still, it now rides with him and his descendants to carry and protect the Diamond. It is not something I would have wished on anyone, for it is a great burden. It now rests on him though."

Rishgar's father sighed somewhat sadly. Yet his heart swelled, for he was immensely proud of Rishgar. While he didn't wish to see his son die because of his good heart, he was proud to have been blessed with such a son. They all looked at the big man; each had his own thoughts on this development.

Selgouth stood and looked at this younger brother with a thoughtful look on his scarred face. He was somewhat in awe, for here was the boy who had fought with him in the dirt and snow, like all brothers are wont to do when young. Well, sometimes when they are grown as well. Although those times were usually after one or three too many mugs of the strong brew of the Ice Men that had accompanied a friendly argument over who was the prettiest girl in the village or who had the fastest dog. Yet looking back on those days, when they were covered in snow or dirt from wrestling over who had hit the rabbit with their arrow, or who had tagged who first with their wooden swords, he couldn't remember a time when Rishgar had ever fought with him out of meanness or with hateful intentions. When he won, he was the first to offer a hand and smile, sometimes through busted and bleeding lips, to the loser. If he was the loser, he never held a grudge to be left festering and brought up later. When they were done, it was done. Dagnour stepped over to his younger brother. "If it becomes such a burden, then his brothers and

I will stand by him and help him for as long as he carries the Diamond."

Orrlick quietly coughed. "This is touching; however, we have been here too long. Unless we wish to explain to Mr. Wooden Face why we are playing with his prized possession, we should leave. No?"

Rishgar picked up his pack and weapons. Then he set the Diamond in a pocket inside his shirt. It didn't feel as heavy as he thought it would, and it rested quietly against his chest. After settling his kit on himself, he followed the others in creeping quietly out through the sleeping chamber, down the creaky stairs, and out of the city through the same way they came in. After emerging from the city, they looked at the wasteland before them for a moment, then set off.

After the Ice Men had set off into the wasteland, Arrah came out of his fitful and nightmare-filled sleep. He looked about his chambers, more than anything to reassure himself of being someplace other than his horrible dreams. His mask itched; the sweat from his sleep seemed to aggravate his skin, making it feel as though ants were crawling all over his face. After removing the mask and rubbing his face and it with a soft cloth, he replaced the mask and stood. He shuffled into the room of the shrine to stand by the marble-encased Diamond. It took a few moments for him to overcome his surprise and the ice-cold terror that came from seeing the top of the marble shrine open. Had the Diamond decided to take revenge on him for its being imprisoned for so long? Had it escaped to finish what it had started all that time ago? Would Mother Earth swallow him up with the help of the Diamond? All these thoughts shot through his scarred and now-terrified mind. Still, he woodenly walked to the shrine and looked into it. (Perhaps if Rishgar had replaced the lid, Arrah would never have known the Diamond was gone, and things would have gone on as they had for so long with him not knowing the Diamond was taken. He hadn't, and Arrah did know.) Upon seeing that the Diamond was no longer there, his terror changed to something else. The formerly pretty-faced God of Gods was now not happy. Very not happy. Unhappy Gods were not good Gods. Unhappy spoiled Gods were even worse.

Bad Gods could do bad things in big bad ways.

And Arrah did.

He snatched up his great two-handed sword, and in a fit of rage he dropped to the base of the tower and threw all his power into a swing that brought down the entire tower in one blow. The tower collapsed in an explosion of dirt, dust, and debris, taking the dome and second tower with it. The roar from the destruction woke his city of followers. They woke to their God floating over the city — something that they had never seen before. The anger in his voice as he screamed at them just added to their surprise and terror.

Arrah screamed in fury at the citizens, "You have lost the privilege of living here in this city I have built for you! For becoming lazy and naive and letting a thief" — there were actually more than one; so much for the God of Gods knowing everything — "steal what I paid for in blood, pain, and beauty" — he really was vain — "you shall be cast out of your fair city! You shall be without a city until you return the Diamond to me!" In his fury he began destroying the city even before all his followers could escape into the wasteland. He raged through the city, wildly swinging his great sword, randomly destroying entire buildings with a single swing. For other buildings, he called down lightning and watched in dull satisfaction as they exploded. Still others he left to burn or to collapse under those he destroyed with sword or lightning. At length, the city was little more than smoking and burning rubble. Its former occupants stood at a distance and watched in horror and sadness as their homes and businesses were destroyed. They had no idea who had stolen the Diamond, where it might be, or even where they would sleep the next night. How were they to return the Diamond? Their God seemed to have finally succumbed to his injuries from the Diamond and its mother, Earth.

Leagues away to the north, Orrlick and the others heard the destruction of the city and the wails of its citizens. Well, former citizens. They could feel the rumbling of the earth through their boots, and the still night now had a strong breeze coming from the direction of the city. They all came to the same conclusion: Old One Hand was awake, and he had noticed his prized possession was missing. Oops.

Orrlick was the first to speak as he turned to continue north. "I'd say he will want it back. From the sounds of it, he will want it back in the worst way too. Can't think of anything that can compare to an angered God, and he is plenty angered."

Rishgar thought for a few steps, then said, "The diamond can protect us, no? Look at what it did to Arrah in the past. Do you not think it will protect us from him and his followers?"

Orrlick thought for a few moments. Then he nodded and smiled at the young man's intelligence. "Yes, I believe it will. It will be the only thing that can protect us from his mob of followers. When they catch up to us, Rishgar, hold the Diamond up for them to see. That should work to protect us from their fear and Arrah's fury."

Shortly after that, the mob of followers fell upon the small band of men. Arrah was leading the horde; the fury and insane rage shone bright in his eyes, manically showing from behind his mask. The men turned to face their pursuers, forming a line to either side of Rishgar. When the mob was a short distance from the men, Rishgar gently removed the Diamond from inside his clothes and held it over his head for all to see. He thought the sight of it alone, being held by a mortal man, would stop the God and his followers and turn them back. The Diamond had much different ideas though.

Making a God mad was one thing. Making the Diamond mad was something else entirely. And Arrah had made it very mad. The Diamond knew who Arrah was, what he had done. The Diamond remembered the countless minutes that felt like years stuck inside total darkness. It remembered what Arrah had done to his brother God. The God who had been kind to the Diamond after finding it. The God who hadn't hidden it away in cold stone. The good God who meant no man harm.

The Diamond decided to protect those who had removed it from its cold, dark tomb. For that was how it saw the shrine, a tomb. Maybe all that time in the cold dark had made the Diamond a little…off.

Whatever the reason, the Diamond let its hatred rule its thoughts at that moment. The sky turned bright white, even though it was still the deep of night. It was so bright even Rishgar closed his eyes and covered them with one hand to protect them. Yet he stood strong and kept the Diamond aloft in his other hand. Arrah screamed in pain and fear, turned away, and fled back to his once-great city. The first lines of the horde that had come to attack the small group of Ice Men were vaporized; they just vanished into the light. Dark places on the ground from their shadows were all that remained of them. Those farther behind managed to stop, turn any direction other than the way they were originally heading, and sprint away into the night. All thoughts of getting back what their God had lost vanished. If their God wanted it back that bad, he could go get it, seemed to be the new ruling thought in the horde's mind. After all, even their God fled in the face of the Diamond's revenge.

The Ice Men looked at one another in amazement. They had no idea the Diamond would react in such a way. Orrlick felt bad about the Mulsins that had been killed. Well, at least until he remembered they were going to take the Diamond back and kill him and his friends. Probably in very creative and unpleasant ways. He figured Gia wouldn't like that. At those thoughts, he didn't feel bad about the dead Mulsins anymore. *Good Diamond, bad Arrah*, he thought. Bad Arrah for taking his anger out on his followers, for that was no way to treat a God's followers. Good diamond for protecting Orrlick and his friends. As though reading his thoughts, the Diamond seemed to glow happily.

Rishgar overcame his surprise and horror of the vaporized Mulsins in a similar way. He reverently stroked the glowing diamond, turning it slowly in his scarred, powerful big hands. He then softly replaced it to his pocket, turned, and resumed walking north. His companions quietly followed, each with his own thoughts, as they left Khanikstan for their home to the north to return the Diamond to where it had once happily lived.

Now all of this didn't go unnoticed by the other Gods. Destroyed city? That might bring some attention. Angry mobs? They tend to be loud and light fires. Yes, those things they would notice. They were hard to miss. They all gathered and discussed what had happened and what it meant for the future of the world and themselves. At length Zerak spoke to them. "I don't think joining the Diamond in declaring war upon Arrah is the best course of action. This would destroy the world and all who live on it. I cannot see how that is right. Why should the entire world pay for what Arrah has done? I can only see one way for the world to survive. That is for all of us to remove ourselves from the world of man."

This was meant with murmurs and some quiet outbursts from the other Gods. For they enjoyed their followers and the earth. Some did not want to leave. Others saw the wisdom of Zerak's words.

One of these was Franzil, Lion God of the Gurns. He also saw the side of not wanting to leave the world of man entirely. After a few moments of thought, he had an idea. "Could we leave the world of man in flesh yet remain in spirit so as not to abandon our followers? In this way Arrah wouldn't be able to find us and do battle with us and, in doing so, destroy the earth. In spirit, we could still guide and shelter our followers, yet Arrah wouldn't be able to cause much trouble with us. And as long as Rishgar and his descendants hold the Diamond, Arrah cannot take over the entire world. With it in the world, and with a safe protector, Arrah cannot conquer the world. Do we not agree on this?"

This was met with a more positive round of murmurs. They were not happy, as the Gods were saddened by having to leave the world they loved. They agreed, though, that this was the best for their followers and the world.

The Gods said farewell to their followers. It was a sad occasion, yet it left their followers in a positive mood, knowing that their Gods were still there in spirit. They would not be alone. All save one God then left the world.

Arrah.

Arrah remained and had to live with the knowledge that the Diamond, which had once been in his possession although not really his, was held by Rishgar, and this prevented Arrah from taking the entire world for his. For Arrah this festered like an infected knife wound in his soul. It irritated and angered him; gradually, it poisoned his soul, spreading slowly to consume him.

As the Gods took their physical leave of the world of man, Orrlick sat and spoke with Dagnour. He wore a serious and somewhat worried look on his sun-worn face as he spoke. "You understand that the Diamond must be protected, despite all of its power. Perhaps because of its power. Either way, you and your sons must begin to plan and prepare for Arrah's return and his rage at us for having re-stolen the Diamond." He chuckled a little at the last part, then the serious look returned to his face, and his tone wasn't so light. "I have spoken to your sons and told them how to make these preparations. They will go their ways. Unfortunately, this means the end of the Ice Country. Not the Ice Men though. They will keep the Diamond from Arrah. This we shall do as long as one Vilhumite lives."

After this, Orrlick raised his voice, loud and clear he yelled out; "The Diamond that you so covet will be protected from you, and in doing so the world will be protected from you as well! Do you hear me, Stumpy? You shall not possess it again. You shall not touch it with your remaining hand! I will watch you, Arrah Wood Head, and if needed will go to war against you. This I will do to the end of time."

Arrah heard.

Arrah heard and was seriously pissed off by it. He thrashed around the wasteland, taking his anger and frustration out on rock, sand, and any living thing not fast or smart enough to get away from him. Boulders, rocks, sand flew in a hurricane of debris. He knew that Orrlick spoke the truth and that the truth was that his pretty and powerful diamond was forever out of his reach.

Orrlick heard the terrible storm; from a distance it looked like a bad sandstorm. He knew he and his friends had angered a God, one who was also spoiled. He shrugged. They had accomplished their goal, and maybe it was about time that this God learned he couldn't have anything he wanted.

After watching the storm from a distance for a while, each man lost in his own thoughts, the group turned to one another and said their farewells. Somehow, they knew they wouldn't see one another any time soon, if ever in this lifetime.

Selgouth made his way north, traveling for many months until he came to a hilly land bordered by craggy mountains to one side and, on the other, a strong river and rolling fields filled with black fertile soil from the flooding of the river in times past. Here he stopped traveling and settled in, building a great hall for himself. Over time this became a town that became a city. He called it Culuth. He and his children and their children through the ages became a strong and powerful people. Their men were typically brave, cunning, strong, and great warriors. Much like Selgouth had been. Here, in this rough yet beautiful land, these battle-hardened warriors stopped the attacks from the southern enemy. Time and again they destroyed their enemy, growing stronger and smarter each time. The gray-bearded warriors taught those who barely had peach fuzz the tricks of battles past. In turn, the young warriors took the lessons to heart. Then they thought up new and fun ways to improve on those old tricks and tactics. Well, fun was dependent on which side of the fight you asked. These descendants often joked about how slow the southern people were to learn. Or they had short memories—either one was amusing. This was because it seemed southerners in each generation felt they were powerful enough to attack and win. Well, they had the first part correct. That was also the easy part. After all, a mouse can attack a snow lion if the mouse has the courage. Or a total lack of self-preservation. The second part, though, winning—that seemed to confuse them greatly. They had mastered the art of dropping their weapons and running away though. Or dying. They were good at that too. Every army must have something they are good at.

Now Ziggy, he worked his way southward. Not into the ruined lands of Arrah though. Why would he wish to live there? All that sand that got into everything. Chafing in places that were hard to reach. Ruining meals. Making your eyes scratchy. No thank you. Besides, Arrah had ruined most of the land. Instead he wandered until he found broad, flat fields that seemed to run to the end of the earth. The fields were covered with thick grass and, in places, wild wheat fields. On these fertile grasslands, he found great herds of animals. Some were stout and thick-furred with short, stumpy legs ending in sharp hooves. Others were herds of horses: long-legged, strong-necked horses. Often, they had finely sculpted heads and flowing manes and tails. He and his people learned to tame and ride these horses. (He often wished they had had these horses when they went on the quest to reclaim the Diamond. It would have saved a great deal of walking on their part.) Like Selgouth, his children and their children became great warriors. One great difference between the two was that Ziggy's people took full advantage of the horses of their prairie and became great mounted warriors—a first in the history of man. They learned to shoot bows with great accuracy and speed from their horses. And what bows they were too. Made from horns and sinew, the bows were shorter than those made from ash wood, yet the shorter bows were just as powerful or more so. More importantly, they could easily be wielded on horseback. They also invented and used lances: long handled weapons with wicked tips and often steel caps on the butts of the lances. After all, sometimes you missed with the pointy end and had to hit your opponent with the other end. Or the tip would break off if it was a really bad day. While they could fight on the ground, all the warriors learned to fight with empty hands; then the knife, sword, and other weapons were mastered. All before moving to horses. They much preferred to fight mounted. This made chasing down the enemy so much easier than on foot. And they didn't wear out their boots so fast. A good, comfortably broken-in pair of boots was something to keep as long as possible. This land became known as the Vadotans, and Ziggy's descendants became nomadic people.

After watching his sons depart, Dagnour sadly began his long journey home and returned to his kingdom. He was sad, for he was now alone. He missed his sons yet was proud of them. He took to building large ships made for speed and battle. These he built and used to wander the great waters. He protected his allies and defeated his enemies. Like his sons, his people became masters of being warriors in their environment. The ships and their crews became a welcomed or not-so-welcomed sight, depending on which side of that coin you fell.

Of the group, the one with the longest and most difficult journey was Rishgar. The youngest brother and holder of the Diamond took his people and headed west, making the long and difficult journey to the coast opposite his father. Here Rishgar built great ships as well. There was a big difference in them though. His ships were built for long journeys with great cargo as opposed to mainly battle. They sailed for many weeks until they hit—almost literally, for it was very foggy when they found them—the islands that became known as the Cloud Islands. Their name coming from the fact that they often seemed as though they were in the sky, surrounded by clouds instead of on the earth and surrounded by water. Here he and his people settled onto the islands, turning their great ships into great halls and building a great rock wall around the city, the smooth, black, almost mirrored rock making a thick and sturdy wall behind which the fortress was protected. The city drew its name from the wall of black rock, which was called Black Stone. Within Black Stone there was a fortress, the Hall of Rishgar.

Shortly after Black Stone was finished, Saebourg caused two meteors to fall near the city. Rishgar dug these up and forged a blade from a deep, dark one with veins of blood red weaving through it. In firelight the blade looked to be alive, as though small red snakes were moving along its length. The blade would cleanly slice a piece of paper dropped onto its edges, it was so sharp. The second, smaller meteor Rishgar turned into the hilt of the sword, carefully fitting it to not only his sword, but also to the Diamond he was entrusted to protect and care for. He set the Diamond into the hilt, leaving about half the Diamond showing, the rest safely and carefully protected by the worked meteor. At first the hilt was like the blade, almost ink black with red veins through it. Once Rishgar set the Diamond to it, though, these red veins turned almost the color of lightning. After seeing this, Rishgar had the grip made of dark ray skin with a blue leather wrapping over the ray skin. The guard was a stout and strong piece of folded metal that was etched and soaked in acid to turn it a deep royal blue, almost purple. From a large sheep, a sheath was made with carved decorations on the hard leather outside. The soft fleece was left on the inside, allowing the natural oils of the fleece to protect the magnificent blade. Once finished, the sword was of such a size that only Rishgar could wield it. The Diamond was happy with its new home, lending an almost warm feel to the sword's blade and handle. Rishgar kept the Diamond, sword, and sheath beside his throne, having had a special rack carved into the throne for the sword to rest in where he could see it and be reminded of the great responsibility he had undertaken. Privately, he also thought the Diamond enjoyed seeing the goings on in the throne room from its stand over the throne. When Rishgar sat upon his throne, the Diamond became one with its stand, so none except Rishgar could pick the sword from the stand. Whenever Rishgar drew the sword, it would pulse in an angry deep-red glow. In his hand, it felt as though the blade were alive, almost craving battle.

Upon completion of the sword, even thousands of miles away, in the wasted lands of the desert, Arrah felt something new. Something that lent an almost coppery taste to his mouth and an icy-cold feeling deep in his soul, a sinking-rock feeling in his stomach. These were new and rather unpleasant feelings for him. He had never felt or tasted fear before. He knew it now.

In time Rishgar grew old and knew he would be passing the sword and its Diamond to an heir. He knew the proper protector of the Diamond would be chosen by the Diamond, and the protector would be marked in some way. When one son was born with pure gray, almost white eyes, rather than the usual various shades of blue that his other children shared, Rishgar knew the next protector was born. He carried his infant son and future protector to the sword where it rested in its stand. As he came close, the Diamond began to pulse softly, and the child reached for it, wrapping his small hand around the Diamond

as much as he could once he reached it. This became the tradition for all protectors born: their gray eyes being handed down through the generations and their fathers carrying them to the sword so it could strengthen the bond between Rishgar's lineage and itself. Some said the Diamond enjoyed the time with the babies before they grew.

Let's not forget Orrlick. After watching his friend and his sons departing, Orrlick hurried home. (In hindsight, he wished he had had one of the horses from the prairie as well.) While the fast pace of his travel home tired him, he was happy and eager to get back to his wife and to meet his child. Well, children. His loving and devoted wife had given birth to twins. Two girls. His happiness at having two beautiful daughters was severely dampened by hearing his wife had died in childbirth. He visited her grave and sat sadly for many days, neither eating nor moving from his vigil. At length, he drew himself up and slowly walked back to his home and his daughters. He knew his departed wife had no desire to meet him in the afterlife just yet. He had to raise their daughters.

He spent several days with his daughters, thinking over what to name them. Finally, after much thought, he named the elder one Elsa. She had bright-red hair and almost pure white skin that felt like warm cream to the touch. When Orrick picked her up, she cried out, and he saw her left hand grow three small interconnecting circles on its tiny palm. He knew it was the mark of a witch. This added a troubled feeling to his sadness. She was the first female who had been chosen to be a witch. This could be very good or very bad. Only time could tell. He hoped for the first. Either way, he loved her greatly.

His second daughter also had the soft cream-colored skin of her sister. While her sister had thick, straight red hair, hers was a bright golden color, thick and full of waves. While she was a child, it seemed to always be a rat's nest of tangles. She never minded; she seemed to enjoy the time spent with her father as he brushed it out, talking with her and her sister about whatever came to mind. Orrick named her Natasha.

Now Natasha was deeply loved by Orrlick and her older sister. This sometimes led to the two competing for her attention. Why? Who knows, as she loved her father and older sister the same, having seemingly endless and pure, innocent love for them both. Not that she wasn't above sometimes using their love for her to get an extra dessert after supper, just for fun. Or because the cook had made her favorite. This was never done with malice. She just liked desserts. Who doesn't?

The years passed quickly, and soon the girls reached their sixteenth year. Now Orrlick had a bad dream. He blamed this on Zerak interrupting his usually sound and dreamless sleep. Zerak was a God, though, and could interrupt one of his followers' sleep if he wished, especially to pass along an important message. Even if it left Orrick sleepy and sad in the morning. He was sleepy because the bad dream woke him and he couldn't get back to sleep. He was sad because he had been asked to choose a daughter to send away to be married to Rishgar. While he knew Rishgar to be a good man, and one he would be glad to call a son-in-law, Orrick didn't wish to lose one of his beautiful daughters so soon after losing his loving wife. (It still hurt to think of her, like she had just died the day before even after all these years.)

Zerak wished to have Orrick's family married with Rishgar's so they could keep Arrah from ruining the world of man. (Arrah was still not happy, and now he knew fear. A pissed off and scared God was not something to trifle with.) Zerak knew that joining the two families would ensure hope against the darkness of Arrah.

After waking from this dream and request, he slowly made his way to his wife's well-tended grave in the dark. He sat on his usual rock and spoke to her — well, to her headstone — about what he had been asked to do. Boiled down: pick a daughter to send away and possibly never see her again. As he sat there with tears of pain and a little frustration running down his weathered and rosy cheeks to his whiskers, he knew in his heart he should send Elsa. Knowing what lay ahead for whichever he chose, for he knew the heavy responsibility that lay upon Rishgar and his children, Orrlick chose his other daughter, Natasha. While Elsa might be the stronger willed daughter, Natasha would actually enjoy what lay ahead for her. Elsa would just see it as a job, and not one she wanted.

After watching the sun rise with his wife, he slowly walked to his home and after having their first meal of the day with his daughters, he asked them to sit down with him, and he explained that he had been asked to send one to be a queen, how hard it had been to choose, and that great responsibility would come with it. They all cried and held one another for a long while after he explained it all to them and whom he had chosen.

After Natasha had left on her journey to her new and, as she saw it, exciting life, Orrlick and Elsa cried for a long time. Not only because she had lost her sister, but because she knew Natasha was not to live as Elsa would. Natasha would grow old and die in time, and Elsa would lose the time she would have liked to have with her sister when Natasha left their home.

After time passed, Elsa and her father grew close and understood and comforted each other. They studied and shared their powers, for she was a powerful witch, as he was a powerful wizard. Together they found purpose in keeping an eye on Arrah, for he needed watching. He was a bad God. Some men thought this would be a mission for them for all eternity. No one could say for sure. No man seemed to want to poke at that with a sharp stick either—no sense in tempting fate.

Part One

BRASSEL
Chapter One

Memories that stay with people through their lives are often some of their first memories. For Joran, it was the humid warmth that carried the smells of fresh bread, cooked meat (and sometimes burned, depending on who was cooking), and fresh-from-the-oven sweets such as cookies, cake, and sometimes pies. He felt comfortable and safe, sometimes even young again, whenever he was in a kitchen, smelling the smells of childhood. No matter where he went or what he achieved, being in a kitchen would take him back to his days of the VonRiches' kitchen. The heavy soot-and-grease-stained beams set in the low ceiling of their kitchen held the smells and heat close, seeming to amplify them to the senses. Or maybe that was just his memory making childhood feelings bigger than they had really been. Either way, he sometimes caught himself staring at a fire in the deep ovens and remembering how he had played under the work tables or would sit and watch the dancing flames on the freshly washed pots, enjoying how the insides of the iron pots gave the flames a colder look than the copper pots, which lent their copper color to making the flames seem warmer and hotter than he knew the flames were. He had learned how hot the flames were once, having dropped a toy soldier into the cook fire and, without thinking, reaching in to grab it back before the fire consumed it. He got off lucky, just some redness and a few blisters. And a serious yelling at by the head cook. He learned to keep his fingers out from under the feet of the kitchen help in much the similar way. Not playing with kitchen knives was learned after they lent a few scars to his hands and one to a foot. These were accompanied by a few more admonishments from the head cook. Usually at a very loud volume. He did learn a few good lessons from the knives though. One was how to keep them sharp and well maintained. This was useful later in life for swords. The second was that the sharp end wasn't supposed to go into you. That hurt. Pointy end in the enemy. Or fresh bread.

When he had trouble sleeping, thinking of those good times spent in the kitchen — and sometimes falling asleep to the fire dancing off the post and hearing the crackle of wood in the fires and the spitting of meat roasting over those fires — would help him drift off.

Of course, he couldn't think of the kitchen from his childhood without remembering how his aunt was the center of everything going on there. Even with all the kitchen help, Elsa with her red hair seemed to be everywhere. She refused to let even a loaf of bread leave the kitchen without her approval. She seemed to bring something special to a roasting pig or somehow made a honey loaf just that much sweeter. Joran had stolen enough of these to know which ones Elsa had made and not made, even without seeing her make them. Nothing seemed to be below her interest in the kitchen. She had a gift of knowing what to add or, sometimes more importantly, not to add to each dish. He had a memory of her having a soft, soothing, and sweet glow around her. Maybe that was just his mind embellishing childhood memories again. He didn't mind this, even if it brought with it memories of her "nudging" him out of the way of other kitchen staff or away from the sweet cakes or cookies. Sometimes that nudge was a little more like a hard shove with her foot or hand, accompanied by a knowing smile from her. If he didn't get the hint and came back for a toy or a second try for a treat, that gentle shove became a little more…encouraging the second time. There was never a third. Even when he wound up skidding across the floor on whatever body part landed first from her second encouragement, he would pick himself up, giggling or even laughing out loud over having been caught again. Elsa would smile, no menace in her heart toward him. After all, boys would be boys. The two of them treated it as a challenge: Could he get away with sneaking a honey loaf or bit of pie without getting caught? In all the years of trying, he couldn't remember ever getting away clean. He still loved her and would often smile at these memories.

In those innocent childhood years, all Joran knew was that his aunt was the most perfect and important woman in all the earth. Even with her usually serious and sometimes stern look, she reserved her soft loving smiles for him only, it seemed; she was beautiful. He sometimes wondered if her soft and mousy, smooth red hair was filled with magic; it seemed to dance with the flames from the cooking fires. Except for the pure white patch. She typically wore her long hair in a thick braid over her shoulder. Sometimes it was a plain, simple braid, like what she sometimes did with loaves of bread. Other times it was an intricate and wondrous work of art. At night, when she would put him to bed in his soft-yet-sturdy bed near hers, he would often touch her lock of white hair. It seemed to tingle his small fingers with magic, just adding to his awe and love of his aunt. After being put to bed, he would sleep soundly, knowing all was right with his world, as he had his aunt looking over him. Sometimes when he thought back on those days, he would agree: getting old was icky. Sort of how he used to view green vegetables. He knew she probably agreed with the getting old part. Not so much the vegetables part.

The kitchen of his childhood memories was near the center of Brassels, an often rainy and foggy land that had the Dark Water Sea on one side and the White Straights on the other for neighbors. Some said the White Straights were named for Dagnour White Bear. Others said they were named for their waters, which were often rough white-capped waves. The Dark Water Sea had no such confusion. All knew why it was called that. The waters were always dark. Sometimes they seemed unnaturally so.

The farm itself was built as most of the farms in that part of the world were built: with solid, well-fitted beams and logs. Instead of making just one or two individual buildings that were spread apart, they built them around a central courtyard and facing inward, creating one big square building. There were windows to the outside of the buildings and a few doors. These windows were usually smaller, and the doors would often lack any kind of latch to the outside. Often the doors looked like they were just a part of the solid walls. The second-story balconies and large windows were reserved for the inside of the buildings. Every building the farm needed was included in the structure around the central courtyard, from the barns to chicken coops. The only break in these buildings was the central gate: a massive, solid piece of work made from oak and iron. It could open to allow four horses through at a time. When closed and locked, though, a mouse would have trouble getting in.

The main floor was made up of areas that functioned as dining rooms, the kitchen, slaughter and meat processing area, stables, etc. The second story was made up of rooms, some great and intricately decorated, others more utilitarian and plain. The farmhands, who helped raise the crops in the rolling fields that stretched in all directions from the central buildings, raised livestock, built and maintained the farm, and worked in the home and kitchen, lived on this level. As did the VonRiches. Mr. VonRich himself lived and kept his office in a square room on a corner, over the kitchen and general dining room. It was in this dining room that his workers were welcomed three times a day for meals. There they enjoyed Elsa's cooking and discussed the day's events and what work would be done in the future, the exception being those working the fields. They would come for their first meal, then leave to the fields with a packed lunch. They would return and enjoy supper with the rest of those who lived and worked on the farm — after cleaning themselves up, no matter how hungry they were. Elsa was fussy that way.

VonRich was unique in that he not only ate with his farmhands, he also tried to treat them with fairness and kindness, as opposed to viewing them as little more than farm animals that talked, whom he would get the last bit of work from them regardless of their well-being. Instead, the tall, almost lanky yet powerfully built man paid attention to his farmhands' health and overall well-being. While he seldom was seen with a smile on his lips under his misshapen nose (there was much speculation as to what had happened to it), all his fifty-some-odd workers respected and liked the kindly man who often pitched in and helped with the work about the farm and seldom raised his voice to any of them. His sons were expected to work the same as the hired hands. Work they did; after all, someday they would be the farm's owners and would need to know what end of a shovel to hold or the difference between soy and wheat. Some even thought of him as their sweet older uncle as opposed to an overbearing master of the farm, as many of the farmers in the area were. Seldom a day went by that he didn't have dirt on his hands and a sweat-stained shirt to toss in the laundry.

He was a deep believer in the Gods, and before each meal he thanked the Gods with his head bowed over his work-hardened, scarred, large folded hands. Everyone on the farm knew this gave the farm owner a sense of peace, and in respect to this, they would enter the hall quietly and attempt, most of the time, to make it orderly. There was no set seating; all were free to pick where they sat for the meal, the exception to this being the head and foot chairs. These were always occupied by Elsa and Mr. VonRich. After the thanking of the Gods, everyone dug into the wonderful food. It was hard to control this, as Elsa made sure it was always wonderful, and hard work built up healthy appetites. This all added to the controlling and calming effect Mr. VonRich had from the head of the heavy-slabbed and worn table in the dining hall. The older workers liked how this kept the younger ones in line and taught them self-control and patience. Well, most of the time.

Now, while VonRich was the owner of the farm and probably the most important man on the farm, some would argue that at times Sladvick bumped the owner out of number one, as he kept the men armed, the plows fixed, and the horses shod. Sladvick was the blacksmith on the farm. He was plain-looking, neither tall nor short. As far as looks went, there were a few things that set him apart from most men on the farm. One was his constantly ruby-red face, from all the time in front of the heat of his forge. This was plainly seen, as he kept his beard shaved, for a good day could go bad if a large ember from the forge or a piece of slag got caught in his beard. His scarred, ruby-cheeked face was quick to smile, making his eyes almost twinkle in happiness. The other thing that set him apart from most men was his immense strength. Like most men in his trade, he was exceedingly strong. To someone just meeting him, this was deceiving, as Sladvick wasn't as physically massive as many blacksmiths. To be sure, he was bigger than the average man; he just wasn't the size of a fully grown bull. It wasn't uncommon to see him pick up a full-size maul by the end of the long wood handle and swing it like most men swing a nail hammer. Yet he wasn't stupid. Many seemed to think that strong physically meant weak mentally. With this intelligence came a healthy sense of humor; after all, life was too short to be serious all the time. Granted, there were times to be serious. He seemed to know things about steel that were impossible to know. Sladvick wore a heavy leather apron that was split below the waist like a pair of pants, each leg having a pair of ties that fastened behind the thigh. This allowed freer movement yet kept the leather in place. The apron ran to the middle of his powerful calves. He also wore a sleeveless leather shirt under the apron; it had a higher collar than a normal shirt to keep the embers and slag from going down his shirt. It laced in the back to keep the leather laces from getting in the way and to prevent anything going through the lace holes. The shirt and apron were well worn and blackened in places from the fire and hot metal. His powerful hands and arms had scars from years of burns from the fire and metal. These stood out as smooth, almost shiny lighter-colored skin against his tanned skin. If the light caught these just right, they looked like stars against the darkness on a clear night. On his legs, he wore loose-fitting light cotton or wool pants, depending the season. Keeping them loose again helped protect him from burns. The ember or slag might burn a hole in the pants, but if they were loose, there was a good chance the embers wouldn't burn into his skin, as opposed to skin-tight pants that would let the embers do just that. His boots had soft soles and just about reached the bottom of his apron. Unlike most men's boots, though, his had a double leather layer on the top, again to protect himself from the slag and embers of his trade.

Now Sladvick's forge was filled with wondrous things, not the least of which was the pulsating glow of hot metal that was almost mesmerizing to watch, especially in the dark. Then it seemed to almost come alive. Once Joran grew too old to stay inside and be watched over all the time, the forge was one of the first places he was drawn to. After finding the dirtiest places to play, he had found the forge. Not that the forge was spotlessly clean. Organized, yes. Clean? No.

At first Sladvick was wary of having the young boy exploring his forge, and for a while the only words really exchanged between the two were warnings. Do not put your little fingers on that, or keep away from this. Now Sladvick would never have intentionally hurt Joran or let him hurt himself seriously, for Sladvick had a kind heart that was the biggest part of his body. He did know that sometimes boys needed to learn from experience, and they didn't get that experience from being told not to do something, then being stopped from doing it. This was a life lesson for Joran. He was used to the women of the farm telling him something was sharp, hot, or dangerous and not to do it or touch it. They would do just about anything short of hanging him from the rafters in a flower sack to keep him from hurting himself. On the other hand, Sladvick, like most men, would keep a watchful eye on the boy and warn him not to touch or do this or that, yet unless the boy was about to do something that was very dangerous, they let him touch or do this or that which they had just warned him about. Life experience was a good teacher. And yes, that piece of metal might not have looked hot, but the blister on his fingers said otherwise. Through these experiences, Joran learned to respect not only Sladvick, but the forge in general.

Over time, the two became friends, and their conversations grew past "Joran, I wouldn't touch that, I was you" sometimes followed by, "*Ouch!*" in a high squeal and a muttered word or two around a finger stuffed in the mouth. Usually those words sounded suspiciously like something the farmhands would use. Words Joran wasn't supposed to know. Who could be certain, though, when they were being uttered around hurt fingers?

One bit of advice Sladvick instilled in Joran was, "If you start a job, you should finish it. Leaving things half-finished is the mark of a lazy and thoughtless man." That led to another lesson: "If you start working metal, don't forget about it and let it cool, then come back to it days later. It is bad for the metal, and your sweat will be for a poor finished product, while if you keep at it, you will sweat less and have a better finished piece."

Joran looked thoughtful for a bit after hearing about the metal not cooling and asked what all children ask, often to the exasperation of their parents, "Why?"

Sladvick continued working the piece he had on an anvil, and between hammer blows he explained how the makeup of the metal breaks down from cooling and heating and cooling, heating and so on. After a time that will make the metal brittle and weak. Then it should be melted down, and the blacksmith must start from scratch.

Another time he told the inquisitive boy, "If you set out to do a job, do the best you can. It only takes a little more effort to turn an OK job into a good job." This was said while he was fitting a nail in a horse's shoe.

Joran understood that shoes were important to the horses; he didn't see why the fuss with making it look good though. This led to the age-old question, "Why?"

"Because I will know it wasn't done as well as I could do it."

"That's on the bottom of the shoe, though; no one will see it, and it is in the dirt all the time anyway. Why waste time on it after it is fitted?"

"Well, like I said, I will know it wasn't done as well as I could have done it. Call it pride, and seeing that horse will remind me that it wasn't as good as I could do. I will see that horse every day; I don't need that every day." He stood and patted the mare's shoulder. "And besides, you know how females are: she likes to look pretty." He smiled and winked at Joran. The mare just turned her head and looked at him with her ears up as though she knew he was talking about her.

Over time, Sladvick taught the boy at the forge. Not only did Joran learn about metals, heat, oils, horses, salt, and wood, he also learned about things not related to metal or horses. He was smart enough to know not to repeat those lessons in front of Elsa though. One lesson he did learn and take to heart, though, was the value and satisfaction of doing a job from beginning to finish – doing a good job at it too. He learned about manners, patience, and self-control. The last he thought was odd at first, as the blacksmith could easily pick up almost any man and break him like kindling for a fire. Yet Sladvick taught him it is often best to let blowhards search for someone else to prove themselves with. This wasn't to say Sladvick wouldn't stand and fight if needed – he was a skilled and vicious fighter – he just was very controlled and didn't see the point in fighting every drunk who came looking for a fight. Joran also learned to be thrifty and stand by his word. If he said he would or wouldn't do something, it meant he was going to honor that. These things were the backbone of the society of their land.

At first Elsa was worried about Joran being at the forge. Not only was she worried he would get hurt – she already knew how men were when it came to letting little children learn after being warned – she didn't want the boy to get in the way of Sladvick doing his work. One day when she took a pot out to be repaired, she told Sladvick, "I hope Joran isn't becoming a pest and interfering with your work. If he is, send him back to the house, and I will busy him with other things."

Sladvick caught the scared looked on Joran's face behind his aunt's back. He knew the boy enjoyed learning the trade and talking to the blacksmith. "He isn't a problem, ma'am. He is smart and keeps out from underfoot. He is a help to me at times, helping me clean up and such. He is welcome here — not to worry." Sladvick winked at Joran and smiled as he said it. Joran relaxed and smiled. His friend had not only paid him a man's compliment, he had kept him outside and at the forge.

"You are sure? I know he asks questions nonstop. Even after having a dozen answered, he seems to have two dozen more right behind it."

"Aye, you are right, ma'am. That he does. It is the way of boys, though, and it shows he is intelligent enough to be curious. Besides, he is good at sneaking me sweets from your kitchen from time to time."

Elsa burst out laughing at that; her rich full laughter filled the forge for a moment. Both Joran and the smith smiled, knowing it was sometimes more than a few sweets. They weren't about to share that though.

Sladvick inspected the pot she had brought him. "I remember when I was his age I asked questions of the master journeyman smith I was apprenticed to all the time. You don't have girls in the kitchen asking you questions day and night?"

Elsa smiled. "Yes. I do."

"It would reflect poorly on the kindly man who taught me if I didn't treat the boy here as my master journeyman treated me when I was learning; I don't think he ever chastised me for asking something, even if I had asked it several times before." He was selecting a bar of iron to fashion a new handle for the pot from, setting it in the glowing coals. Joran was quick to start the bellows. He had held his tongue through the conversation, seeming to know that it was best to be quiet, so as not to jeopardize his freedom at the forge with his new friend.

After the repair was done and Elsa was walking across the hard-packed, rich black earth to the kitchen, Joran happened to look over to Sladvick and saw something he hadn't seen before. The kind smith had a faraway look on his face as he watched her walk away. Joran thought it was almost sad. Then he felt like he was seeing something he wasn't meant to see. That no one was meant to see. He looked away quickly yet couldn't get the look out of his mind. He was smart enough to say nothing to the kindly man about it, even if it started to grow into an idea in his young and innocent mind. After a while it grew to the point he was about to burst if he didn't talk to someone about it.

One night, not long after that day, Elsa was cleaning him up. She seemed to find more dirt on him, no matter how hard he tried to get it all.

"Ummm...Elsa?"

"Yes?" she said absently as she continued to wash his hair for the second time. *Where do boys get this much dirt?*

"Do you love Sladvick?"

She dropped the soap and stopped, stunned. "Well, he and I have been friends for a long time; I guess you could say I do love him." *Where is he getting this? Better yet, where is he going with it?*

"That is good. Why don't you get married then? I think he loves you, and you two make each other happy."

"And you think this is a good idea?" Her voice had gone from absent to bordering on just cold and hard.

Wow, that went out onto thin ice and fell through in a hurry, Joran thought. Even so, he had come this far. Might as well keep going, finish the job, so to speak. *See, I do pay attention.*

"Isn't that what people do when they love each other? Get married and make each other happy for the rest of their lives?" He managed to sound ignorant of her change in tone.

"Where did you come up with this? Did Sladvick say something to you? He put you up to this? You talk this over with him already?" There was no more playing dumb about her tone this time.

Uh-oh . . . this is not going the way I thought it would. A job started should be finished though.

"No, he didn't say anything; I came to the conclusion myself. I haven't said anything to him about it. I wanted to talk to you about it first." It all kind of tumbled out of him in one long breath. *What did I do wrong? Never seen her like this.* "He does like you though."

His head was yarked (that was a technical term, according to the smith) around by his hair little too quickly. *I should get one of the kitchen girls to give me a haircut*, he thought. Then he saw the look on Elsa's face, and all thoughts of technical terms or haircuts vanished.

"The only good part of this idea you somehow got into your head is you talked to me about it first. Do you hear me?" Her face was a mask of pure anger; her usually kind and happy eyes burned hotter than his friend's forge. He had never seen her like this. *So much for sliding onto thin ice and falling through. I just jumped off a cliff.* "You are to leave thinking about those topics to the adults. I don't want you talking to him about this. You don't bring this up to anyone else either. You understand?"

He went to nod his head and got a painful reminder that his hair was a much-too-convenient handle for her to grab. She relaxed her grip at his attempted nod. Not being able to nod and wanting to be sure she knew he understood, he croaked out a "Yes, Elsa."

After hearing that and seeing the look on his face, she let go of his hair and gave him a big hug. "You're a good boy; just sometimes you have to be careful with ideas that you get. Do you understand?"

He just nodded again; it seemed safest to agree with her right now. In his young mind he thought, *I hope I never see her mad like that again. Especially not at me.* He never thought to ask why she got the way she did.

Well, at least not right then. Sometimes he was a little slow with the right questions.

It wasn't until a few days later that he thought of a different way to come at the question.

He had just gotten into bed for the night. He heard Elsa get into her bed, and he waited a few moments. Then he tried a different way to get to the answer he wanted.

"Elsa, who would you like to marry?" he asked into the darkness of their room.

At first, he thought she hadn't heard him.

"Joran." Then silence.

"Yes?"

"Joran...go to sleep," she said in a tired voice. *He certainly is stubborn at times.*

"No." Saying that to her surprised both of them.

OK, stubborn is an understatement for him.

"Why is it such a secret? You aren't being fair about this with me. Or with Sledvick."

He certainly is grown-up in his thinking at times.

The room was quiet for a little bit.

Hope she isn't coming over here to grab my hair again—got to get that cut tomorrow.

"Joran! Sleep!"

And off the cliff I go again.

"OK...OK. Still don't think it is nice of you," he said as he rolled over and burrowed into his blankets.

He is right. I shouldn't snap at him like this. He meant no harm—just the opposite. He was trying to look out for those he loves and admires.

"Joran, I have never even thought of getting married. There is too much for me to take care of for me to ever get married. I know you think that isn't fair or right or kind of me when it comes to your friend. It would be even more wrong of me to marry him and then be a poor, inattentive wife for him. Do you understand?"

There was silence for a bit.

"I think so. It would be like lying to him if you did get married. Right?"

He is smart. Sometimes he uses it.

"Yes, Joran; that is a way to look at it."

He mulled this over in his mind. He didn't like the feeling he had that Elsa was lonely, even if she didn't want to admit it.

"When I get big, will I get married? Or will I grow up to be like you, a very important person who takes care of others their whole life?" His voice wasn't sad, just curious.

"You'll be married," she said. *Oops, maybe I shouldn't have said that just now.*

Joran shot upright in his bed, all thoughts of his warm blankets forgotten. "I will? Who is she? Is she nice like you? Does she bake pies like you do? Could you teach her to make sweet buns like yours? Do I know her already?" he demanded. In his mind, he ran through all the girls he knew. Not that the list was that long at his age.

Elsa smiled in the darkness, and it came through in her answer to the boy. "Well, that is something for later. Now sleep; it's late."

He sat there silent in the darkness, thinking of marriage and weddings. Then a sad thought came to him.

Without thinking about it, he blurted out a question. "I can't get married. I don't know where my mother is or who she is. She has to be at the wedding." A tear silently slid down his cheek, yet there was no quiver to his voice, just sadness. "My father wouldn't be there either."

She heard him laying back down, pulling the covers up, and then silence. Just his steady breathing. Not the steady, deep breathing of sleep though.

Her heart ached. So much had come up in one night. *Why did he have to be so inquisitive?*

"Joran," she said softly as she got out of her bed and went to sit on the edge of his. "She passed away." She gently stroked his hair. *I can't lie to him about it; he deserves the truth. I am only surprised he hasn't asked sooner than now.*

The only response to this was the quiet squeaking of his bed as he burrowed under his blankets and sobbed. Not the wailing loud sobbing that sometimes comes from children who get bad news like that. No, this was the quiet sobbing that is sometimes worse. The kind that you know comes from a soul deeply hurt. The kind that almost needs the tears to heal itself.

He wasn't the only one to shed tears just then. She felt a tear slide down her face, slowly at first, then faster as it worked its way down over her cheeks, picking up speed like a ball of snow coming off the peak of a mountain. The first tear didn't surprise her; after all, she had known his mother and knew she was a good woman who had deserved to live to raise her son. No, it was those tears that followed that mildly surprised her. After all, she was a grown woman who had lived through very rough times. *Then again, what can be harder than telling someone his mother is dead?* she thought to herself. *Especially a small boy.*

After what felt like hours, even though it was only a few minutes, she quietly went to him, sat on the edge of his bed, and softly, tenderly rested her hand on the covers that muffled his tears. He started at the touch, then came out from his cave of bedclothes and grabbed her in a hug with such strength it surprised her. He buried his tear-streaked face in her night clothes. *He seems almost desperate to hold on to someone real. Does he think that holding tight to me will keep me from dying too?*

She leaned over and held the boy with the big heart, which at this moment was broken.

She knew he needed the time to let out the pain before he could start to heal from this. Yet she felt she should try and console him.

"She was a good woman—hardworking, smart, quick-witted—who spoke well of others," she said softly into the darkness. "She had a heart bigger than the sun, always positive and encouraging of others." She could feel him slowly stop shaking; the tears still came though. *Did tears hurt more when shed for someone you never knew?* She didn't know. "Most importantly, though, she loved you with her whole heart. More than anyone can know." It was after softly saying these words that she noticed he had gone quiet, even though his small hands were still latched on to her. He had drifted off to sleep, listening to the kind words about his mother.

She gently pulled his hands off her clothes and laid him back on his pillow and covered him for the night. *That hurt; it is done finally though*, she thought, feeling something like a sad relief. Now he knew and could work on healing that part of his life and hopefully move back to being his usually happy, if mischievous, self.

Joran had help getting back to his usually happy self. The blacksmith wasn't his only friend, even though he and the strong man had a special friendship. There were children around his age, some older than others, with whom he was at the very least friendly with, if not good friends with. These other children would not only smile and wave; if their hands weren't full of something or another, they were known to take a few minutes to play with him if possible. Even as children, they had chores on the farm. According to the adults, chores built character and instilled in children a good work ethic. Sometimes the children thought this was a cartload of cow dung. They didn't voice those thoughts though; adults seemed to think a cuff to the back of the head built character, too, sometimes. Joran understood that chores were important and sometimes followed along with the older boys, helping if he could, lending an extra set of hands to pump water or breaking up kindling for the kitchen. After all, no fires for the ovens, no pies and cakes. Pies and cakes were important to a small boy.

There were a couple who were close to his age though. The oldest boy of these was named Berhard. He was a year or two older than Joran and quite a bit taller. This made him popular, since he could reach the higher shelves in the kitchen. Or boost Joran up on his shoulders to reach them. That was where the cooks usually hid the cakes and sweet rolls to cool. Now since he was the tallest and oldest of the group, he was the natural pick for being the leader. Ordinarily, he would have been the leader since he was the eldest of the children. This was one of those exceptions to the rule though. Berhard was a Gurn; this meant he was a little slow on the uptake at times. Like a typical Gurn, he made up for this in courage, almost to a fault. Now don't think these traits affected his personality negatively. Just the opposite. He had a cheerful personality and an easy smile. He also had a special affinity for animals. He once found an abandoned puppy in the fields. He carefully carried it home in his big hands, keeping it under his coat. For the next few months he tenderly nursed it to health, hand feeding it warm cow's milk from a thin reed until it could eat on its own. When it came to the group of children, though, he often stood back and let the younger and quicker-witted children take the lead. They usually led him to fun things, and he liked having fun. So did his faithful and ever-present dog.

The next boy that Joran often was seen playing with was the physical opposite of Berhard. Drazen was small; even though he ate with a healthy appetite, he never seemed to grow much. Up or out. Some adults said it was because the little chipmunk was always running, only stopping when he had to. This had brought about his nickname. He never minded; after all, chipmunks were cute. His mind, mouth, and feet all seemed to be connected to some invisible chain, and if one of those three were still, the other two had to keep running to make up for the part that wasn't moving. He seemed to have an excited, if sometimes almost nervous, energy about him. Thoughts seemed to run straight to his mouth, never slowing to be thought through. Sometimes his mouth didn't seem capable of keeping up with his mind. Thoughts would be started, then midsentence his mind would come across a shiny new thought, and his mouth would follow his brain and run off on the new thought, the previous one forgotten. One farmhand commented on his short attention span once, "Not only does he run like a chipmunk, he has the attention span of one." He had chuckled. No one ever meant any ill will to the little two-legged chipmunk, for even though he almost constantly spoke, no one could remember ever hearing him say a bad word about someone else. Now he did sometimes forget his manners, and a salty word would fly out of his quick mouth before he realized it. This was usually followed by one of those character-building cuffs on the head from an adult—if Drazen was standing still, that is. Even if the adult was often trying to keep a straight face while correcting the little fella.

Now while Joran usually played with the boys, there were also girls on the farm. The one who seemed to run with Joran and his two friends the most, though, was a black-haired, green-eyed girl named Geeta. Now while she often made up wild tales for the boys, keeping them enthralled, she was far from an innocent and sweet little girl. For when she wasn't entertaining the boys with stories, she was causing them all kinds of trouble, whether it was convincing them to run off into the orchards and steal fruit from the VonRiches' trees and vines or working them against one another to the point where they were rolling in the dirt over something they couldn't remember when the dust had settled, just that Geeta had started it somehow. Even after all this, they seemed to give in to her each time. She liked to lord over them like a little queen, pulling strings of commoners just for her amusement. The more trouble she caused, the more she seemed to enjoy it, often tossing her long black hair in laughter while the boys rolled in the dirt. None of the boys understood her. Some of the adults, though, would look on and wonder what would become of the manipulative girl.

Joran and his friends would spend the winters playing in the snow. They made snow forts, sometimes digging them out of the deep snow piles, other times making them on the snow, cutting blocks of snow and attempting to build castles of snow that would shine with a crystal-like brilliance in the cold winter sun. Snowball fights would usually follow the building of the castles. Other days were filled with thrilling rides down the snow-covered hills on carefully fitted wooden sleds made by their parents. Joran, having no father to build him a sled, rode a finely made one by his friend Sladvick. Each night after riding it, Joran would carefully wipe off the snow and rub down the runners with beeswax to keep them smooth and fast in the snow.

A special treat that all the children would eagerly wait for was the day that VonRich would declare the ice on the small lake safe. Then they would spend their days gliding around the ice on the skates that either Sladvick or a previous blacksmith at the farm had made; some had been handed down through three or four siblings. These skates were treasured by the children, who would carefully stone the blades until they were almost a mirror and rub oil into the straps that held the blade to their boots until the leather was soft and water would bead up and run off it. Parents joked that this was the only chore that the children looked forward to. The ice covering the small lake just north of the farm's buildings was covered in scratches and scuffs from the blades almost all winter. If it became too bumpy or if it hadn't frozen smooth that winter, some of the men would go down and punch a hole in one corner of the ice and would auger water out of the hole until most of the small lake was covered in water. Overnight, the lake would freeze smooth and even for the children.

Now if the weather was too cold for even the hardy children to go out all bundled up in their thickest fur coats and boots, or the snow and ice had become slushy messes in the summer, the children had the hay barns to play in. There were old ropes hung from the rafters in some of the hay barns. These sturdy and still-strong ropes had hung there so long that they had soaked up the deep sweet smell of the hay. Some say that VonRich had hung them himself when he was just a boy. No one knew for sure, though, as he would never answer, just smile, when asked. This made no difference to the children, who loved swinging on the ropes and then falling into the deep piles of hay. Sometimes they played a game of king of the ropes, which involved climbing up the ropes and then swinging at one another and trying to knock one another into the hay. Last one on the ropes was the king of the ropes. Now, as with most things, the ropes came with a rule. While they were allowed to swing on the ropes, they were told not to climb all the way to the rafters and play in those. No matter how tempting those rafters looked, the children weren't to go climbing around in them. Not opening the big doors and swinging outside of the hay barn was the other rule. Usually the children followed these two rules carefully.

The hay barns weren't the only entertainment the children would find in the spring. There were birds' nests to find in the trees and baby ferrets to watch play in the fields. Fresh fish to be caught where they had skated the winter away.

Now things weren't always quiet and happy. Remember those rules about the hay barns? Geeta got it into Drazen's head one day to not only disobey the rafter rule, but to ignore the rule about swinging out the door flying over the yard. This, of course, ended badly for Drazen. Breaking the first rule went OK for him; Geeta had decided to talk him into climbing up to the rafters and jumping off to catch the rope and swing out over the barnyard through an open hay barn door. She watched with gleaming green eyes as he jumped from the rafter and caught the rope. Drazen swung out the doors so fast it seemed he was flying. Until he started to swing back toward the barn. Not the barn door, the barn. It seemed that the way the ropes were hung, they didn't swing out the doors in a straight line. Looking back on things, the boys decided this was part of the reason why they were told not to swing out the doors. The ropes didn't let you swing back in. The other reason became painfully clear to Drazen when he hit the barn wall and fell to the ground, where he promptly broke his leg. There was no soft hay to land in. Somewhere between him leaving the barn door and then hitting the barn wall, Geeta disappeared.

While the little chipmunk lay in the dirt stunned, one of the few times he was speechless and motionless, Joran realized he would have to help his friend, since Geeta was nowhere to be seen, despite this being her idea. She would, of course, deny it if asked, like she usually did with her innocent look.

Joran stood with a concerned look on his face and considered his options. First, Drazen had broken two rules. At the very least, he would get into trouble for that. OK, that was a minor issue at this point, since his leg was clearly broken. No leg was supposed to look like that. Drazen was an unhealthy pale white under his usual tanned skin as well. Joran figured the sweat wasn't from the warm weather. To his credit, Drazen wasn't crying or screaming in pain. Rather, he was biting his lip and just gutting it out.

At this point Joran caught movement from the corner of his eye. He turned and saw a huge horse standing some ways off. On the horse's back was a tall rider. Joran knew that sometimes the draft horses were ridden; usually, though, it was bareback. Just from the pasture up to the barns. This horse and rider clearly had traveled a long way with the man riding the huge animal. The saddle gave it away to Joran. The rider was wearing a dark-green cloak with a deep hood. Even with the distance and the hood, Joran could tell the man was watching him and his friends with a thoughtful and intense look. Seeing this, Joran suddenly felt cold. Not the kind of cold that come from a breeze coming up. No, this was a deep, bone-chilling cold, almost fear. It was a new feeling for the boy. As fast as it had come, it passed and left him momentarily confused. Even though the rider never spoke or approached them, Joran thought he had seen the rider before.

His mind came back to the important thing at that moment, helping his hurt friend. He turned his back on the horse and rider and began to deal with the issue at hand. He removed his and Drazen's belts, then sent Berhard to find some straight wood to set the broken leg. After using their sturdy leather belts to fix the boards to the broken leg, as he had seen the field hands do once, Berhard and Joran lifted Drazen into an empty cart they found around the corner of the barn.

Berhard let out a little laugh.

Joran looked at him quizzically. "What's so funny?"

"Just thinking how glad I am that it wasn't me flying out the barn door and falling down like this."

"Gee, that is big of you."

"No, it's not that I want Drazen to be hurt; it's that I can see you and him trying to get me into this cart. You two can't lift me and would probably wind up dragging me across the farm by my arms like an old feed sack or something."

Joran had to admit that it was kind of a funny thought, all things considered right now. That brought him back to the big horse, and the man riding it made Joran mad when he realized the man hadn't bothered to help. That soured his personality quickly.

"Fine, just sit there and watch. Don't help us," he muttered under his breath.

Berhard heard him even so.

"What are you talking about? Geeta isn't around, as usual," he said bitterly. The funny image of being dragged across the farm was gone. Usually her meddling led to some wrestling in the dirt, maybe some bruises or a torn shirt. This time it had broken many of the rules of the farm. Not just the two big ones about the barn.

"The guy on the big horse. He could at least have come over and offered to help us get him in the cart or pull it with his horse."

"Huh? No one's around."

"Over ther—" Joran stopped midsentence as he turned to point at the horse and rider that he had seen. His friend was right; no one was there.

"Maybe you two could stop talking about a mystery horse and its rider and get me some help?" Drazen had found his voice again, even if he wouldn't be running around any time soon. Maybe he would find an interest in board games.

"Never mind; let's go," Joran said as he leaned into pushing the cart toward the big house and the kitchen.

When Elsa saw the two boys pushing the cart toward her, she knew the third one had been hurt. If they were doing chores, there would be a horse pulling the cart, not Berhard and Joran pushing it. When they arrived, she looked at the crude splint and had the two boys half carry, half drag their friend over to a low table with help from two of the kitchen maids.

"Gently lay him on there," she said calmly.

"Yes, ma'am," they said quietly, knowing sooner or later they were going to have to explain how this had happened. The severity of the situation was finally sinking in.

As they set the now-trembling, pale, and clammy friend on the table, taking care not to bang his leg on anything, Elsa began mixing up a hot tea from herbs stored in old glazed jars at the back of a cupboard. It wasn't the cupboard that had the sweet tea and hot chocolate either.

She sent a kitchen maid to get some better splint material, blankets, and a pillow while the tea brewed. While waiting on the tea and the maid to return, she pulled a small, short, thin bladed knife from its delicately worked sheath on her belt. The carved bone handle had once been brilliantly white. It was now a yellowed white color. She carried the beautifully made knife everywhere and used it for just about everything from cutting errant strings that she came across on clothes to peeling apples when she sat out back and watched the sun set. The knife effortlessly slid through Draven's pant leg, revealing the now swollen and deformed leg. She frowned at it; this was going to take some doing. It didn't look too badly broken, not that there really is a good broken bone. But this looked to be more of a fracture than a total break. She didn't see any bone sticking out through the skin, which was a plus too. Still, this was going to be difficult.

Shortly the maid returned. She set him up on the pillow and covered him with the blanket, leaving his bum leg exposed. Checking to be sure the tea had cooled enough to drink, she poured a cup full of the foul-smelling tea and handed it to Drazen. She then laid out the splint materials next to him.

"Drink," she said.

He took the thick earthenware cup and screwed up his face at the smell. He was used to her handing him good things to drink. Not this.

"It stinks," he said.

"Drink it anyway," she said with a little more authority.

"Will it fix my leg?"

"Well, it won't suddenly turn to hot chocolate no matter how long you sit there holding it. Drink," she said, a little irritated now.

Drazen eyed her a second or two and then took a little sip, barely more than sticking his tongue in the cup to taste the foul-smelling brew.

"Yuck!"

"Didn't ask you if you liked it. Medicine isn't supposed to taste good. Drink it, or we will have to deal with your leg in a different manner," Elsa said, even more irritated.

"Oh?" he asked hopefully. Maybe there was a good option to the gross concoction she had made him. Hadn't he been punished enough? This was just cruel now.

His curiosity changed to horror as he watched Elsa walk purposefully over to a rack of knives on the wall. Without hesitation, she selected two knives. One, a large, heavy bladed, wood-handled cleaver. Its razor-sharp edge caught the firelight like a mirror. The other, a long-bladed bread knife with a rolling toothy cutting edge. Its wood handle matched the cleaver's handle. The boys all knew that both knives were razor sharp. Drazen had images of the cleaver, which to him now looked like an ax that the woodsmen used to split logs. In his mind he saw it effortlessly slicing through great hunks of meat. Unfortunately, those hunks of meat were attached to him at the time. The bread knife, with the rolling toothy edge, no longer promised fresh bread soaked in honey. Rather it now looked like a woodsman's crosscut saw.

Elsa saw his horrified look as she walked back over to where he lay on the table and critically examined his leg. *There's more than one way to get him to drink tea, and this will be less painful than having him held down while I pour it down his throat. Somewhat more fun too,* she thought ruefully. She then took the big cleaver and pointed to a spot about two thirds up his calf. Much too close to Drazen's boy bits for his liking. Not that he liked the idea of losing the leg; losing more than that, though, really didn't appeal to him.

"Well, the other option is we cut off the broken part," she said seriously. "Right about here should do it. Shouldn't hurt much worse than what you have now. Then when it heals, you can ask the woodworkers to make you a peg leg. I am sure they can make something that you can put a shoe on and a matching crutch to hobble around."

Drazen went even whiter, if that was possible. This time his eyes got in on the act and bugged out almost as though someone was pushing them out of his head from behind. Easy choice. He chugged down the foul-tasting tea in big, desperate gulps, swallowing even the dregs of the tea at the bottom of the cup without stopping to breathe between gulps. These made him choke a bit, bringing tears to his eyes. He didn't stop though. *She's serious. Must drink foul-tasting concoction before she lops off my leg with that meat ax.* This was the only thing going through his mind at that point. He set the cup down, almost dropping it, and leaned back to catch his breath. *I drank it. Goal achieved. Umm. Now what?* he wondered.

He didn't have long to wait for the answer to that question.

After a few minutes, he felt his eyelids getting very heavy; his head drooped to the side; his breathing relaxed and became deep and regular.

Well, that wasn't so hard now, she thought to herself as she replaced the knives to the rack. She noticed the relief on his young friends faces. *He has good friends; he is lucky.*

He screamed in his drugged sleep only twice while she set the break and then kept it in place with the wood and cloth. It would hold while he rested and let his bone start to knit back together. Hopefully it wouldn't cause him too much trouble. *Well, he will know when the weather is going to change for the rest of his life. I hope that is the only problem it causes him,* she thought after inspecting her work. *If it were winter I would pack it with snow to work the swelling down.*

Her thoughts were interrupted when Joran gently tugged on her shirtsleeve.

"Will he walk again?" he asked. His face showed great concern and worry.

"He should—and even run again if he is lucky," she said gently.

"You won't have to cut off his leg then? Really?" His eyes darted to the knife rack and back to hers.

OK, maybe that was a little too far, she reproached herself.

"If he doesn't get an infection, and he rests like I tell him to, he should be fine in time," she assured him. "Now about how this happened."

"Geeta got him to swing in the hay barn, out past the doors," Joran said softly, looking at his feet. *I don't want to get him in trouble,* he thought. *She will find out sooner or later, though, and it's best to tell the truth now.* He had learned that over the years.

"Oh?" *I should have known she was in on this somehow.* "And where is the instigator now?"

Joran knew that tone. It didn't mean anything good was coming.

"Don't know," he mumbled, unsure where this was going, only knowing he didn't want to get involved in wherever it was going.

"Go get her."

"I don't know where she is." *Maybe that will get me out of this mess, and it is true—no idea where she went this time.*

"Young man, I didn't ask if you knew where she was. I told you, not asked you, to go get her. Find her and bring her here. Now." Her voice left no room for argument or any way to wiggle through doing what he was told.

He ran out of the kitchen to find Geeta. *Not sure how I am going to bring her to the kitchen when I find her though. Guess I'll figure that out once I find her. First things first though. Find her*, he thought as he ran out the door. It started to dawn on him that she did this every time something went sideways, leaving the boys to take the brunt of whatever it was.

He found her a little while later playing with her dolls under an old cart that was missing a front wheel. She seemed happy to go with him. *She has something up her sleeve again,* Joran thought as he walked with her back to Elsa. He didn't trust her to go straight to Elsa on her own.

"What happened in the hay barn?" Elsa asked Geeta as soon as she and Joran walked into the kitchen.

"The boys were playing," she said innocently. "Why?"

"Why? Look at Drazen's leg and tell me they were just playing." Elsa pointed at him sleeping on the table. There was a hard and angry edge to her voice.

"I saw him fall, didn't look like he was hurt that bad," Geeta answered with a slight quiver to her voice. *Uh-oh…This isn't going as it usually does,* she thought.

"You didn't stick around long enough to see how bad he was hurt after you talked him into swinging out past the door!" Joran yelled at her. "Elsa was going to cut his leg off because of you!" He had tears of anger running down his cheeks now.

Elsa looked at Joran and saw the anger and hurt in his eyes. *He is a good and loyal friend, only this time the best way to help his friend is to let me take care of this.*

"Joran, would you give Geeta and I some privacy, please?" she asked softly.

Joran looked at her, shot an angry look at Geeta, and stomped out of the kitchen.

"You, *sit!*" she yelled at Geeta as soon as the door was closed behind Joran.

More out of surprise than anything, she sat heavily on the stool near her. Her eyes went wide.

Not as wide as poor Draven's when I said his leg would have to come off if he didn't drink the tea though, Elsa thought.

While Joran had done as Elsa had told him to do and left, he didn't go far. He wanted to see if Geeta had gotten away with it again. So he sat on a pile of wood across the yard from the kitchen door and waited. He always wanted to help Draven. He couldn't do that until Geeta and Elsa were done though.

Surprisingly, he didn't have long to wait on things. About fifteen, maybe twenty minutes later, Geeta flew out of the kitchen door as though dragons were on her heels. Tears streamed down her face as she sobbed.

Wow, that is a first, Joran thought, watching her go with a bemused look on his face. *Maybe she got thrashed for a change.*

He cautiously approached the kitchen; Draven was still in there after all.

Elsa was putting cool compresses on Draven's head when Joran peeked around the door.

Good sign: she looks calmer.

As much as he wanted to know what had happened to Geeta, he didn't ask. Rather, he asked about his friend. "Will he wake up soon?" he asked as he approached the opposite side of the table from Elsa.

"Yes, he has a slight fever; it will pass though," she said and replaced the compress with a new one.

The two stood quietly for a bit, both lost in their thoughts and watching over Draven.

Finally, Elsa looked at Joran, knowing he wanted to know what had happened. *He is a curious boy after all.* "No, I didn't take a switch to her," she said.

"She had it coming this time. After what happened to Draven," he said, not exactly angry, more disappointed than anything. *She gets away with everything.*

"Girls don't get switched," Elsa said.

"Not switching her hasn't worked with her. She had it coming this time," he said defensively, unwilling to let it pass.

"Joran, why don't you find some men to make up a gurney to carry your friend to his room to rest?"

"What did you do to Geeta then?" He wanted to know what punishment she had gotten.

"Should I find other things for you to do too?" she asked with a raised eyebrow.

Joran went out and found some farmhands to help him. In the end, they simply picked up the top of the table and carried Draven on that rather than move him off it, then moved him into his bed. This way he was only moved once. *Huh, why didn't I think of that?* Elsa thought when she saw the men gently pick up the top of the table. A short time later, the tabletop was returned. All cleaned off too.

At supper that night, she noticed not only was Draven missing, Joran was too. When asked, one of the kitchen girls said that when she had taken some broth up for Draven in case he had woken up, she saw Joran sitting by Draven's bed. He was changing the compresses and talking to his friend, who was still sleeping. She had made Joran a plate and taken it up for him as well, since it didn't look like he was going to leave the bedside anytime soon.

Draven steadily improved through the spring and summer.

In light of how things started that spring, the rest of the spring and summer were quiet. Draven spent it healing up, more than a little irritated he couldn't get up and go riding or play in the fields or fish or do much of anything with the boys. Instead he spent more time than he liked shucking corn, peeling potatoes, or having to do lessons.

Geeta always seemed to find some place to run off to or something to do other than playing with the boys anymore. Whatever Elsa had said or done to her seemed to have stuck. At least for now.

Now while Joran and Berhard were good friends, it wasn't as much fun to hang out alone with him all the time. It wasn't that he wasn't a nice guy to hang out with or wasn't up to doing fun stuff. It was that Berhard never seemed to think of anything to do, leaving it to Joran to come up with things to do all the time. That could get old. Drazen had often been the one to come up with new things to do.

That led the boys to the fields at times, just to watch the workmen and listen to them talk. Sometimes there were great stories to listen to. Other times, the men were just talking about boring things going on at the farm or in town. If it was the former, the boys would spend the day listening to the stories. If it was the latter, the boys would usually wander off to find something more interesting. After all, hearing what happened in town wasn't all that exciting when compared to the legends and stories of old times.

This one fine summer day the men began talking about what could be said was the most important event in the history of man. It was an epic battle fought off in a land far away from here. The boys decided this was going to be a good day to stay and listen to the men tell stories.

They listened as the men spoke of the Battle of Stutgath while they worked. The boys listened, mesmerized by the story of the huge battle. Over the course of the day, they heard how it had started, how Arrah had swarmed out into desert over six hundred years earlier. But who really knew how long ago it had been?

According to the men, it had started when great numbers of Vibaions, Colaans, and Rackians all decided for some reason to flood across Culuthious. It might have had something to do with the Khanikstranns who came after them. Who could say? Maybe the Khanikstranns had seen the other groups heading off somewhere and decided to follow out of curiosity. Who could say? They weren't around to ask nowadays.

What was known was that after the great lands of Culuthious had been destroyed in a brutal and excessive fashion, as was the Mulsins' usual way of doing things, the Mulsins had moved off to the great fortress of the Ziggyian Fort. Now while Culuthious had gone under the hordes easily enough, and the Mulsins had pretty well blown up, knocked over, or basically broken everything in the city, they decided to go break things in the same fashion at the Ziggyian Fort.

Unfortunately, someone seemed to have forgotten to send the script they wanted the Ziggyians to follow Ziggyians in the massive fort. This led to things not going as they had before.

After looking at the walls of the fort from the outside for five years, Kal Arrah finally ran out of patience with the defenders. He decided they just weren't going to play nice and let him have his fun breaking things inside their fort. Disgusted with their poor hospitality, he packed up his army and left to find a more accommodating playmate. Or it might have been because his followers were dying from the arrows being shot out of the fort from time to time. Either way, he packed up his toys of war and left.

About this time, the other kingdoms realized the invasion wasn't just aimed at the Ice Men, but against all their kingdoms. Upon realizing this, the rulers decided to join forces against Arrah and went to meet him and his followers. They met one another on the plains just outside Stutgath. Now had you asked the residents of Stutgath, they would probably have agreed that they would have preferred to have this meeting take place someplace else. Preferably a long way off.

They hadn't been asked though.

The battle started with the united kingdom's attacking from all sides. The most famous charge seemed to be the one made to the front of Kal Arrah's army by the Tra Gurns. The battle went on for hours, at times raging furiously, at other times ebbing as the soldiers became fatigued yet continued to fight, taking a slight breather before picking up things again. Finally, at the center of the armies, Kal Drath attacked Arrah himself. These two fought, each knowing that this two-man battle would decide how the entire battle would come out. Looking back on it, just sending those two out into a field to fight, winner take all, would have not only been

easier. It would have saved thousands of lives as well. While Drath would probably have been all for this option, Arrah would almost assuredly have preferred the armies beat on each other instead. Ironically, he wound up fighting one on one with Drath anyway. Things just didn't seem to be going his way at all.

Now you would think that after so many generations having passed since the fight between the two, their fight would have faded from their memories or have changed so much through the ages that the battle would be unrecognizable to those who had been there. Not this battle. Not only had it been passed down through the generations, it had been done so in great detail and accuracy. This ensured it was fresh in the minds of the farmhands, as though they had seen the battle themselves yesterday. In great detail, they described each blow, parry, block, and strike landed. The boys could almost hear the clanging of the swords as they sat there listening to the men talk.

Then the workmen came to the pivotal part of the battle, where Drath was sure to lose. He was down, tired, and injured, and his sword felt like a blacksmith's anvil. Barely able to raise his sword, much less his shield, he turned his chest toward Arrah. Once he saw Arrah was looking at him, Drath unlatched his breastplate and let it fall to the ground, displaying his tunic. At the sight of Drath's tunic, Arrah fumbled his sword, shocked by the tunic. It was at that moment that Drath summoned his remaining strength and killed Arrah with a mighty, adrenaline-fueled, all-or-nothing two-handed blow. Had he missed, he knew he wouldn't have been able to stop the movement of the sword, as he had his whole body behind the blow. The momentum would carry him around in a circle, giving Arrah his back, and Drath would lose. The blow landed solidly into Arrah, sinking the blade of the sword deeply into Arrah, almost creating two little Arrahs.

The story made Joran question certain aspects of the battle and the story. His friend had just enjoyed the story and was all worked up and excited after hearing it.

"What was on his tunic that was so special?" Joran asked the farmhand who had been telling the story.

"I don't know. I just know that it was something that got into Arrah's head and made him lose. Everyone who tells the story agrees on that part at least," the man replied matter-of-factly. "And storytellers seldom agree on parts of a story like that."

"Who cares?" Berhard asked. "The good guys won, and it was a great battle." He was excited and didn't want the good feelings ruined by silly questions; at least he saw them as insignificant questions. What difference did it make what was on the tunic?

Joran, however, didn't share his view.

"Was it a magic tunic?" he asked, just not willing to let it go with an explanation of "everyone said so."

"Well, it may have been," the field hand replied. *If I agree with him on an explanation, maybe he will stop questioning a good battle story.* "All I know is that when the tunic was uncovered, Arrah fumbled his sword and all but forgot about his shield. That is what gave Drath the opportunity for a second to sink his sword into Arrah, almost cutting him in two. Or so people say. That part may be a little exaggerated. Who can say?"

Joran sat thoughtfully for a bit. "No, there has to be a reason that something like a tunic, not even a piece of armor, would make Arrah fumble his weapon like that. Drath had to have some form of magic on the tunic."

"Perhaps. No one has ever asked why or how the tunic worked. Maybe it was just a shock to see his enemy take off his armor during a battle that made Arrah do what he did. Odd things sometimes happen in the heat of battle. Men become blood drunk; others just freeze up. Who can say?" the farmhand replied. *I gotta hand it to him; he is persistent.*

The two boys thanked the farmhands for the story and wandered off to let them work.

A few minutes after leaving the workmen, Berhard stopped in the middle of the farm road and cocked his head to one side, a thoughtful look on his face. This was a surprise to Joran, who couldn't remember when he had seen Berhard with that look on his face. Confusion sometimes, sure. Anger, occasionally. A big smile that would light up his eyes? All the time. Thoughtful though? Nope. This was new.

"I have an idea: let's do the duel from the story. One of us can be Arrah, the other Drath. We can get some old broom and pitchfork handles for swords," he said happily.

Well, that does sound like fun. This is a good first idea of his. Joran laughed to himself.

The boys ran off to find what they could for swords (forgetting about the shields and armor part of things). Shortly afterward they were happily, if clumsily, going at each other with some homemade wood swords, one made from a broken broom handle and one from an old hoe. They had affixed cross guards to the broken handles with some old nails they had pulled out of an old broken wagon and then straightened. Well, made a little less bent at least. Once armed, they gleefully declared war on each other.

This went on for three or four days, and the two boys had started to accumulate a collection of bruises and a goose egg or two on their heads. Around this time, Joran decided that they were missing something that would make this new game much more enjoyable. Something to protect themselves with was sounding more important each time one of them landed a blow on the other. Berhard agreed wholeheartedly, and he was the bigger of the two. Maybe the knights of old knew a thing or two after all. Shields and armor were more than just for show. After some thought they snuck into the kitchen and "borrowed" two pot lids — old ones — and some head-size old metal pots. After Berhard rang the pot that Joran was wearing on his head the first time, they put the game on hold again and made a slight change to their helmets. An old blanket was cut in half and stuffed into each of their helmets. Much better. They then happily returned to beating each other with their wooden swords.

Things were progressing nicely; the boys had started to get the hang of using their swords and shields. They hadn't been able to figure something out for breastplates though. It was a farm after all, not a castle where they might have found old armor plates to use. Old flour sacks and twine didn't do much to protect their chests. They didn't mind at all; a sort of unspoken agreement had grown between them concerning the lack of breastplates: you don't hit me there, I won't hit you. Besides, this was fun.

The fun continued until one day Berhard got a little carried away, and Joran didn't duck fast enough and caught a blow to the face. Berhard felt terrible about it. He never meant to hurt his friend. Joran was usually fast enough to duck swings to the head or else take the blow with his pot helmet with the blanket padding. This time, though, Joran took the wooden blade squarely across the left side of his face, just under his eye. He landed hard on his back on the ground with a cloud of dust rising from where he lay.

Joran didn't notice the blood that was freely running down his face from the ragged tear on his cheek. He was seeing stars — *odd, it's the middle of the day*, he thought — and had a high-pitched ringing in his ears from the blow. He shook his head, trying to clear things up as he stumbled to his feet. Suddenly a new feeling poured through his body. He suddenly felt like he could run forever and not get tired. That was the last thing he remembered.

Berhard later filled him in on what happened. Well, he filled him in on what he could, after he could talk again. You see, Joran beat him into a bloody mess while screaming words that Berhard had never heard; they didn't even sound like any language he had heard. For his part, Joran just remembered seeing a scarred and horrible face where Berhard's usually friendly and open face had been. When he had seen that face, something inside him made him attack the face in a blood-drunk fury.

Afterward, Joran felt terrible. Especially when he saw what he had done to Berhard's usually open and friendly face. There was also a feeling of...satisfaction buried under all the other feelings rolling in his poor head. He hated that feeling and couldn't understand where it had come from. He knew he shouldn't feel that way. Even a little bit. Berhard was his friend after all.

Once he got his head back on straight and saw what he had done, he had helped his friend to the kitchen. Joran knew that was the best place for his friend's injuries to be looked after. All thoughts of wooden swords and ancient battles were forgotten. Elsa could help Berhard. All thoughts of his own injuries were forgotten. He didn't even notice that his cheek was swelling up and in turn forcing his eye to close.

Elsa took one look at the boys and had one of the other kitchen girls help her with patching them up. *Boys will be boys*, she thought when she saw them. Nothing looked to be broken, and bruises and cuts healed.

After some cold compresses and some evil-tasting concoctions, which both boys drank down without argument, she looked at the cut on Joran's face. He didn't like how she was eyeing it. He really didn't like what was coming when one of the serving girls brought over some heavy leather straps. Elsa laid him on the table and, with the help of the other girl, strapped him down, paying special attention to his head.

"OK, this is going to hurt," she said as she took a needle and fine silk thread in hand. "That gash won't heal if I leave it. And it might become infected. So you get some needlework. Try to hold still for this."

Joran was really not liking where this had gone. *Well, nothing to be done about it now. Just suck it up and gut it out. At least she is being honest; it will hurt,* he thought bravely. *Duck. Next time, duck,* he chided himself.

He still screamed when the first few stitches were put in. After that, his face seemed to go numb. Maybe Elsa had put something on the needle? Who cared? The stitches didn't hurt. He could feel the odd sensation of his skin being pulled together — no pain though. It was kind of nauseating, but he kept it down. The tears running down his cheeks were beyond his control though. *Maybe she won't notice the dented pots and lids. She won't put anything on that punishment to make it hurt less.*

Once it was over and the boys had gotten their lecture over ruining good cookware, they got ready to leave. Joran was walking past Elsa with Berhard.

"Well, at least I beat Kal Arrah." Joran chuckled to Berhard as he scratched at his bandage.

Before Berhard could respond, Elsa had Joran by the ear and was pulling him back to the table he had just left.

"*Ouch!*" he squeaked at the unexpected pain. *At least it is the other ear, not the one on the side with the stitches.*

"Who told you about Arrah?" she asked sharply. Her face was set hard. Joran and Berhard knew that look. No messing around with her when she looked like that. Berhard was thinking maybe he should have kept going out the kitchen rather than following his friend.

Joran looked at her, confused. *What did I say wrong? First a clot to the head, then stitches. Now this?* "Elsa, it's Kal Arrah. Not Arrah. So—" That was as far as he got before Elsa slapped him. Both boys were stunned. She had never raised a hand to either of them like that. Ever. It wasn't a hard slap, just unexpected, and it surprised them. "You are never to speak that name again. Do. You. Understand?" He nodded slowly.

"Now where did you hear that name?" she asked quietly yet still angry.

Joran looked at her in a whole new light. *Damn.* "Ummm…Some of the workers in the fields told us about the great battle and how Ar…he was defeated in a sword fight. Berhard and I were playing at that, the sword fight between them. I was Drath this time. Only I didn't get to drop my breastplate. Not that we really have any of those; we just use some old flower sacks and string to hold them on with. This time, though, we didn't get to that part. Berhard rang my bell pretty good, and I beat him without needing to drop the breastplate."

Both boys watched Elsa for her response to this, as they could see she was not happy about something, and it wasn't just the stitches on Joran and Berhard. They just didn't know what it was.

Elsa sat and thought for a moment. "You listen to me closely, Joran," she said quietly, talking just to Joran as though Berhard weren't there anymore. He wished he weren't there, yet he was too curious to slip away.

When she was sure she had all of Joran's attention, she continued. "Joran, this is very important. Understand? Good. You are never to speak of Arrah again."

Why does she keep leaving off the Kal part? Joran wondered.

"I mean it. You have to promise me that you won't speak of him again, ever," she said. Her face had softened some and even looked a little worried around the edges. Like she was trying to hide it. This made Joran nervous; he had never seen her like this.

"I promise," Joran said, his tone somewhat hurt.

"You sure? Your life depends on this. I mean it."

"Yes ma'am," he said with a little more conviction in his voice as he raised his head and looked her in the eye. "It was just a game," he added.

Any signs of worry left her face as she sat back and looked at him with reproach. "A stupid one. Look at the beating you gave Berhard; you could have killed him. Do you want to kill your friend? Didn't think so."

"Hey! I'm the one with the stitches!"

"You weren't the one in danger. Berhard was. Now off you two go. Might want to go rest after all that. Don't forget your promise. Never mention that name again. Ever."

The two boys wandered off. She figured they would wander off to the hay barns and take a nap, especially Joran. The tea he drank had a slight sleep herb in it, but it was not enough to knock him out if he didn't let it.

Sure enough, the boys had wandered off to their favorite hay barn and dozed off in the sweet-smelling hay. Berhard slept peacefully, even though his bruises still hurt.

Joran, on the other side of the coin, tossed and turned, dozing fitfully and having strange dreams. When he woke later, all he could remember were bits and pieces of them. Something about Elsa saying he was much too young, too innocent for this to happen yet. Then in another part, which seemed to happen later in the dream, she sadly called for her father. He had never thought of her having a father, which was odd. Of course she had one. Everyone had one.

Those were welcome memories of the sleep though. The blackness was what he remembered the most, with fear that bordered on terror. It never took a real form, seeming to float like a dark cloud, sometimes appearing to be a horse and rider, then slowly turning into a horrid face. The one constant was the feeling of dead animosity that it exuded toward him. Sometimes it felt like the darkness was curious. Always watching him. He never told Elsa about it.

Chapter Two

Childhood doesn't last forever, and it wasn't long after Joran had left his behind that the storyteller came back to VonRich's farm.

The storyteller was known to arrive at the gates of VonRich's farm -- no set schedule, just from time to time he would come. He was always welcome though. In truth he was a homeless wanderer who made his way through life and the world with his ability to tell stories. His voice seemed to have a certain magic to it that made the old stories seem new and to come alive as he told them. The clang of swords in a battle sounded real when he spoke, almost leaving the ringing sound in your ears. The roar of an angry bear? That would leave chills in your spine. He could also sound like the wind through a bird's wings, soft and whispery. Bird songs? He could imitate them so well, the birds themselves would come to listen to him. No matter how many characters there were in a story, each had a different and distinct voice, and not just the male characters. He could sound like a little girl one moment and, in the next breath, be a huge knight with a deep bass voice and gravely laughter. Now all of this paled in comparison to the storyteller's ability to make you actually hear rain. All different kinds of rain. Heavy downfall? You wanted a cloak, even if you were indoors. All of this would keep his audience enthralled for hours.

Appearance-wise, the storyteller looked more like a disrespectable old man of questionable ethics. His apparent lack of a proper name didn't help with the respectability level. He was just known as the storyteller. When Joran saw him this time, the man was wearing what appeared to be a relatively new, deep-red wool cloak complete with a hood. The wool was a heavy, thick wool too. He wore the cloak open to reveal his odd-looking long-sleeved tunic underneath, the likes of which Joran had never seen. It was clearly from lands far from here and looked like it had been made from several different tunics. The multicolored silk was faded and worn, with food and wine stains here and there. Probably a few ale stains too. It had a deep, loose-fitting, bright-blue hood over a bright-red yoke that covered the shoulders, chest, and back to about a third of the way down his torso. Under the yoke, the rest of his tunic was bright green, almost mint-leaf green. It tied at the neck with three holes on one side and the black chord going through one hold on the right side. The tunic fell to the tops of his thighs and was belted with what looked like an old cinch from a saddle, complete with the original brass cinch buckle. A heavy knife was hung from the belt in a sheath made from fine bridle leather dyed a deep brown. It was well oiled yet showed years of use and care. If you looked closely at the sheath, you might be able to see some old tooling on it. The knife's handle, a plain light-colored wood, was angled across the storyteller's stomach, where it could be drawn with either hand. His brown cotton pants were worn in the knees. The lower legs were splattered with dirt and mud from the road, and the cuffs were tattered. They hung low over his mismatched shoes. One was a dark-brown leather and laced with what looked like was once white satin ribbon. The other shoe was made of faded black leather and laced up with an old piece of brown leather. Despite this, the shoes looked comfortable. All his clothing had been patched or resewn here and there. Joran was especially taken with the man's cloak. *That looks warm and well made,* he thought. He'd never had such a fine-looking cloak.

The man's ancestry was a mystery; his thick, straight white hair was worn midlength to just above his shoulders. The close-cropped white beard and sharp features of his weathered angular face gave no real hint of any one land, almost as though it was from an ancient people who had long ago ceased to exist. In spite of this, it was a kindly face. He still stood straight and tall. Clearly, he was still a strong man, yet not prone to violence. The most striking feature, though, were his eyes. They were strikingly bright blue and still held a happy, mischievous, young look to them. They would light up even more when he smiled, which was often. His straight, if somewhat tobacco- and coffee-stained, teeth were still all there and straight.

He and Elsa seemed to have some history. She called him the Hungry Mutt, not unkindly. Actually, the opposite: she would say it with something like affection. In return, he would compliment her profusely. Which, of course, she secretly enjoyed. After all, what lady didn't enjoy compliments? Even if was from someone who was raiding her beer stocks. His visits to the farm would signal the resumption of what seemed to be a long-running competition between the two. The competition seemed to center on what he could pilfer from her kitchen and wine cellars, even though he was always offered his fill of things. Pastries, roast ducks, and wine were the main targets of opportunity. He could slice both drumsticks off a fresh roast duck with his knife and make them disappear before anyone seemed to notice. The only things in the kitchen safe from him were the fish. Even when Elsa had him in her sight, there were plenty of people who would provide him with fresh loaves of whole grain bread and honey in exchange for one of his stories.

Joran was no exception to this. If anything, he was the biggest supporter of it.

Elsa would feign being upset with the two of them, chasing them from her kitchen, armed with whatever happened to be at hand. Anything from brooms to mostly-empty flour sacks would be transformed into arms used to defend her kitchen from the two thieves. She would chase them to the door, often beating the pair with hard blows. The broom would sting—not enough to make them stop laughing though. The flower sacks just made them look like ghosts by the time they reached the door. Once outside, they would look at each other and laugh at the state of themselves. Then they would go off to enjoy the cakes they had managed to stuff in their pockets before being so rudely removed from the vaults of heavenly food. Joran's reward for the beatings from Elsa were stories. And hearing her laugh. The storyteller would enthrall and amuse Joran with stories from the distant past, often while enjoying a bottle of beer or wine from the most recent of raids on Elsa's cellars.

Even though Joran knew the best stories were told in the dining hall for all to hear, he enjoyed the ones he earned from the storyteller in private best.

As it was VonRich's farm, he was allowed the first request of the evening.

Being deeply religious, he would ask for stories of old, the time of the beginning and of the Gods.

"Such serious and deeply thought stories" was the storyteller's response when asked for those stories.

Elsa laughed. "You seem to find most subjects serious and thought-provoking," she said as she brought him a freshly drawn black beer.

He accepted the thick earthen mug of beer with a dramatic smile and wink for her and set it down to settle. "Ah, m'lady, bringer of great gifts. Sadly, it is a danger of my chosen profession."

Seeing that his beer had settled with a deep, thick foamy head, he drank deeply with a thoughtful look on his weather-worn face. Once he set the mug down again, he did something totally unexpected and different in the hall. He leaped from his chair, snatched his cloak from the back of it, and whirled it around his body as he stood to his full height.

From deep within his hood, a deep yet soft voice floated out, reaching everyone in the hall.

"In the deepest darkness at the beginning of time, the Gods pulled together the earth and planets, setting the sun in the center with the stars to fill the heavens at night. They then took one of these newly formed balls and began to fill it with things. First, air and water and earth. Then they added creatures and plants to the earth and water." His voice seemed to soothe and mesmerize those in the hall. Half-drunk mugs of beer and glasses of wine were forgotten, resting in his audiences' slack hands. He slowly looked around the hall, peering at his audience from the depths of his cloak.

Seeing that all were transfixed on his words, he said, "Then the Gods each created a people to call their own. Save Zerak, hiw people searched him out. All of the Gods had an equal share of followers. They were named the Saebourg, …" He continued listing the original tribes of man.

Joran was just as transfixed as the rest of those in the hall, even though he and the rest had heard the story before. Everyone in Brassel was familiar with the story, or a close variation of it. What held everyone's attention so tightly, was they had never heard it told in such a way as tonight. Joran's mind let his imagination run wild, going in directions he had never explored or even knew he had. At times he thought he could see the Gods of old actually making the world and tossing the stars into the night sky. Then there was the one thing that Elsa had made him promise all those years ago to never bring up or even think about. Arrah. Here the storyteller was bringing up that long-forgotten name. With it, cold chills and bad memories came back.

Despite his promise to Elsa, Joran listened closely as each God and his people were described in deep detail. Even Arrah's.

The storyteller worked his way through Saebourg, God of the Ice Men; Issa, God of the Dinesians; and so on until the last God, Arrah. This brought another cold chill to Joran.

With that, he looked around at the others in the room, wondering if they were having the same reaction to the story and, more importantly, to the name Arrah.

Everyone seemed to have a different reaction to the story. While they were all rapt with attention, Sladvick's eyes were wide in awe and wonder. By contrast, VonRich had gone pale, and his eyes had tears standing in them. Others had their hands clasped tightly before them on the table or were ringing them in their laps. Elsa was standing in the door to the kitchen with her shawl wrapped around her shoulders. Even though it wasn't cold, she gripped the shawl

tightly over her breasts.

Is she is getting the chills too? Or is she just making sure no more pies disappear today? Joran wondered.

His attention was brought back to the story when the man mentioned the Diamond. "As time came and went, a God named Zerak made a Diamond that resembled the earth. Only much smaller. Zerak made it round and as smooth to the touch as fine satin. He looked to the stars for inspiration, putting the light and twinkle of the brightest stars inside the jewel. These he mixed with the northern lights, blending the lights of the stars with the greenish white lights from the north. To finish the jewel, the God put an enchantment on it. With this enchantment, Zerak could see things. Past, present, and future were opened to the God."

Joran quietly gasped, realizing he was so caught up and entranced in the storyteller's tale that he had forgotten to breathe. He took a deep breath and relaxed, feeling himself return to the great hall. He continued to listen, though, entirely transfixed with the storyteller and his story of how Arrah had stolen the Diamond. His eyes grew wide with awe as he listened to how the other Gods had declared war on the their Arrah. How Arrah had fought back, forcing the jewel against its will to flood and destroy the lands. He leaned forward to hear how the jewel had finally fought back against Arrah. How it had mangled the God who had forced it for so long to do the God's evil will. Joran almost fell off his seat when the old man paused to empty the stein of beer he had. *When did I lean that far forward?* he thought as he reseated himself farther back on the chair, hoping no one had seen his clumsiness.

While Joran was getting himself resituated, Elsa came forward to refill the storyteller's stein. Her movements looked different somehow, more regal, more defined. Her eyes had a fierce light in them, seeming to mirror her movements.

While the storyteller took a moment to take a long pull of the fresh beer, there were quiet, almost reverent murmurs throughout the hall.

"Never have I heard this story recounted as this was," Sladvick said, almost to himself, in awe.

He started a little when Joseph replied, his tone just as hushed as Sladvick's. Sladvick hadn't realized he had actually spoken aloud.

"No, only kings have heard this story from the book of ancients. I worked for a man once, many years ago, who heard it while at court in Brassel. He remembered parts of it, not all of the story though. This is the first I have heard all of the story."

Both men returned to silence when the storyteller resumed his story. His voice carried to the far corners of the hall, so all could hear how Orrlick the Sorcerer had gone to retrieve the Diamond from Arrah. How Orrlick had taken his allies Dagnour and his three strong sons with him. The people in the hall sat in rapture as they listened to how the lands were protected against the renegades of Arrah and how the Gods had left the earth to the humans, leaving Rishgar to safeguard and care for the Diamond in his fortress.

Joran found the part about the specially forged two-handed sword with the Diamond set in its hilt especially fascinating. *That must be a magnificent work of deadly art,* he thought. *Long way from the stick swords we used as small boys.* Then he remembered the beating that he had given his friend that fateful day so long ago. *Probably best we only had sticks.* He almost missed the part about how the ancestors of Rishgar continued to occupy the throne and keep Arrah in check, much to Arrah's maddening frustration.

The girls in the room paid special attention to how Orrlick sent his cherished daughter to Rishgar to become the mother of all future protectors of the Diamond. How he kept his other daughter with him to teach her the arts of sorcerers and fulfill her destiny of being marked.

This brought the story to its conclusion, the old storyteller gradually and softly lowering his voice to a dramatic tone, bringing everyone in the hall even further under his spell of the story. "Orrlick and his gifted daughter Elsalia cast spells across the lands to alert them against the coming of the evil Arrah. Some men say that these spells are still among us and will be until the end of days. Always here to protect man against the foretold day of the return of Arrah, when he will come back to the lands and retake the Diamond that had maimed him so dearly. For in Arrah's mind, this meant he had paid for the right to call the Diamond his own. Arrah's return and attempt to take the Diamond will bring about the battle of all battles, which will decide the fate of the world."

At this, the storyteller fell silent. He did so in such a subtle way that it took those listening a moment to realize he had stopped talking. Only when he let his cloak drop onto the chair's back did they realize he was done. Even then, the silence drew on. The sounds of night creatures filled the silence in the hall. Crickets accompanied bullfrogs in an odd music. The crackling of the dying logs in the hearth added to the soft music of the night.

After what seemed like a long time, VonRich coughed softly and stood. The scraping of his heavy oak chair against the stone floor sounded unusually loud in the great hall. With his voice slightly choked with emotion, he faced the storyteller. "My old and good friend, I would like to thank you, not only on my behalf, but on behalf of all of us here tonight for the great honor you have given us, sharing such a story. This is something that is rarely given to us common subjects. Thank you." He slowly sat back down; the creaking of his chair was heard throughout the hall.

The storyteller was slightly taken aback. In all the years he had known VonRich, he couldn't remember ever hearing the man say so many words at once, and never with such emotion. Still, his eyes were bright like stars as he kindly grinned. "Oh, it has been many years since I have been in the presence of royalty, much less long enough to share an old story. Kings these days are much too busy to listen to the ancient stories. They can't be bothered to appreciate the old tales. Stories are like songs: people must hear them from time to time for them not to be lost." He took a drink from his stein, then continued with a mischievous tone, "And who knows? A king may be hiding anywhere these days. Who can say?"

This brought a laugh to those in the hall. A king here in the hall? And there may be gold coins falling from the skies in the morning. With that, the hall started to empty. While they may not have known where a king would hide, they did know when the sun would come up. And it would be coming up early tomorrow. Story time had come and gone; it was now time for sleep.

After almost everyone had left and the kitchen girls had cleared the tables, the storyteller walked to Joran.

"Will you help me to my place to sleep tonight? Elsa didn't tell me where I was to sleep this time. Pretty sure it isn't to be in the kitchen." He winked, knowing she would never leave him alone in the kitchen.

Joran happily hopped off his stool. "Sure. Thank you for the great story," he said as he went to the kitchen and grabbed a circular black hammered-iron lantern that he lit with a stick from the banked fires.

When Joran returned to the great hall with the lantern, he saw VonRich talking quietly with the storyteller. This isn't what caught Joran's eye though. It was the odd look that seemed to pass between the storyteller and Elsa, who stood at the back of the hall. Her shawl was still wrapped tightly around her.

"Ready to show this old man to his warm bed?" the storyteller asked as Joran walked up.

"Yes, and it looks like you're ready to get some sleep." With that, Joran turned and walked off. As he led the old man down a hall toward the guest quarters, Joran's curiosity got the better of his tongue.

"You didn't finish the story. What happened when Arrah and the protectors of the Diamond finally met? Was it an epic battle with Arrah losing? Was the magnificent, great sword used to kill him?" The questions poured from him.

"Oh, that is another story for another time." The storyteller chuckled as he removed a bottle of wine from his cloak. Joran noticed it was one of Elsa's better bottles, usually reserved for winter Yule time or weddings. *That ol' thief; wonder how he got to that,* Joran thought with a bit of a laugh.

"I would like to hear that story; would you trade one of Elsa's fresh-baked wild berry pies for the story?" he asked hopefully, knowing how sought-after her wild berry pies were.

After taking a long drink of the fine wine, the storyteller looked at Joran for a moment, amusement in his eyes. "I can't tell you that story yet."

"Why not?"

"Well, you see, they haven't met yet. Can't tell a story about something that hasn't happened, now can I?" He chuckled. "I have to wait for those two to meet, and then I can share what happened."

Joran wasn't to be put off with this. After all, he had already picked the berries for the pie that afternoon. He wanted a good return on his investment of pricked fingers.

"You can make up what happens in a story: who wins, who loses. After all, it is just a story. No?"

"Not all stories are just stories, and not all stories are based on real events. Who can say when facts and actual history are hidden behind the title of story?"

At this, Joran could feel the traits of his race beginning to come to the surface: hardheadedness and just plain old stubbornness. "Now you are just having a joke with me. It is just a story. People don't live that long, and whoever heard of real magic?"

"Oh, Orrlick wouldn't like you saying things like that. He will be celebrating his eight thousand and fifth birthday soon. Granted, they don't do a candle for each year anymore; they just don't fit on the cake. How would you light them all if they did all fit? And all that melted wax on the frosting? Yuck. They do still have cake; after all, it is a birthday, and cake is important." He smiled. "Especially the icing."

"What?" Joran exclaimed. "No one can live that long. It's impossible."

The storyteller gave Joran a thoughtful look. "How old are you?"

"Not eight thousand," he shot back sarcastically. "I'll be ten soon."

"Hmm. And in those ten years, you have learned all that is possible in the world? Heard all that is possible? All that has happened?"

Joran bit off the quick remark he was about to make; his steadfast confidence in what he thought was shaken a little. A little unsure of himself now, he thought for a second. "Well, the oldest man I ever met was the man from Kreigers Farm, and he is over ninety years old. He is so old, his beard is white like new snow. He is the oldest man in the county," Joran said a little defensively, trying to regain his footing in the conversation.

"Hmm. And the county is a big place, no?"

Rather than answer him, Joran took another tact.

"How old are you?"

The storyteller chuckled at the change in tact and question. "Older than you, boy. Don't you see the white beard?"

Damn, that didn't work, Joran thought.

"I still say it is just a story. One that you don't want to finish," Joran said, and he stalked along through the courtyard.

"Oh, there are lots of men who would take your side in this discussion, saying that they only believe in what they can touch, see, feel, and smell. And they aren't bad people for believing this." The old man stopped and looked at the stars, a wistful look on his face. "Men will go their whole lives believing this way, seeing the world through a set of laws that they set up for themselves to help them understand the world around them. They don't wish to accept or simply can't fathom a world outside the one we see and live in every day. In the other world, things that can't even be imagined in this one are common and accepted as facts. Now imagine if the door between those two worlds opened? Just a crack. What is to say that things can't change? Perhaps the old man at Kriegers Farm is now considered young?" He looked down at Joran, standing next to him with the lantern in his hand.

The boy had an almost confused look on his face for a bit. Then he set his features, giving his face a look of conviction. "I like this world. The other side of the door sounds dangerous, with all the questioning and changing of the laws of nature as we see them here."

"You think there is always a choice about what world we live in?" he asked patiently. "Sometimes life is chosen for you, and you are given a great task to complete. Noble things to do. What if this other world were to choose you to do such things?"

"Me?" squeaked Joran as he opened the door to the room for the storyteller to have for the night.

"I have seen stranger things. Just think on it. Now head off to bed; rest well. I am going to sit here and enjoy a pipe and finish this wine with my friends, the stars," he said.

"The stars are your friends?" Joran looked up as he asked. *Maybe he has spent one or five too many nights alone with a bottle,* he thought. Instead he said, "If you don't mind me saying so, you are rather odd sometimes. I still like you; you're a good man nonetheless."

"I am a little odd, I guess, probably the oddest you will ever meet. Thank you for the compliment; it's nice to know that others think of you in such a light. Now head to bed. Elsa will be looking for you and will be worried," he lightly chided him.

Joran walked back to the main house in the starlight; he had left the lantern with the storyteller. Since he was familiar with the way, he thought the old man would appreciate having the light.

After crawling into bed, he was suddenly exhausted. He tossed and turned, clawing at his bedclothes. His dreams were filled with a dark figure; the evil of it seemed to radiate off the figure like the heat from the blacksmith's forge. Monsters chased him, grabbing at him if he slowed as he fled across a mutated landscape — one that he had never seen or imagined before. As he ran, the landscapes and monsters began to merge with familiar things from his world, then changed back into something from another place. Those from the other place relentlessly tried to claim him.

Chapter Three

It was a few days later when the storyteller began getting dirty looks from Elsa, usually when he was innocently walking near the kitchen. He saddled up his horse after one such look and said he had an errand over in the next county to do.

"You mean I can stop wondering where my pastries, wine, and beer have gotten to for a while?" Her tone was somewhat unforgiving.

With an almost childish gleam in his eyes, he bowed to her deeply. "Would m'lady care for her humble servant to gather anything for her while he is away?"

She thought for a moment. "Yes, as a matter of fact, if you would, bring me some seasonings from the Thysion dealer at the county market. It is just past the Three Taps Tavern. I am sure you will have no trouble finding the tavern," she said with a laugh.

"M'lady, I am sure their cooking will not stand a chance when compared to yours, nor will their serving girls be nearly as radiantly beautiful as you. Yet the trip will be long and lonely. This will build up a thirst not only for beer, but for someone to talk with."

"Talk to your horse," she sniffed, not unkindly.

"Oh, he listens well enough." He gently patted the horse's nose while he answered her. "It is his replies that are lacking. Perhaps you could spare the boy for a while?"

Joran's ears perked up at this. *Please say yes, please say yes* kept running through his mind, almost willing Elsa to agree. He held his tongue though.

"I don't think so. You seem to be a poor influence on him, teaching him to steal from my kitchen for you," she said smartly. "I would prefer him not having these bad habits expanded upon."

"M'lady, how can you say such a thing?" the storyteller asked with an angelic look while he slipped a pastry into his pocket without even thinking. "Don't you agree a growing boy should get out and see the world some? Learn about the wide world and its wondrous lands?" He slipped a bottle of wine into the cloak as he finished.

Joran held his breath now. *Please say yes* raced through his mind again.

"I think he has seen more than enough of the wondrous lands, and he's seen them with much more responsible supervision than you will give."

Damn. So much for that, Joran thought as his heart sank.

"That being said, I know I can count on him to remember the seasonings and where to get them more than I can count on you to do that. He won't get so smashed to the point of blindness on wine and beer that he confuses cinnamon with pepper. Or sugar with flour. Perhaps it is best he goes with you. I see him being the more responsible one between the two of you." She smiled, seeing Joran's excitement, his face beaming. "Just don't go visiting the ladies of pleasure or any of the fighting pits with him," she added.

"M'lady!" the old man said in mock hurt. "I would know nothing of such places or even where to find them if I did."

She raised an eyebrow and just looked at the storyteller.

"I shall avoid all such places if I think I see them." He chuckled.

"That's a good man; see that you do. I will be back shortly with a list of seasonings and things that the kitchen is low on." With that, Elsa disappeared into the kitchen.

"Well, Joran, I see we are to have a little trip together. That requires horses. Shall we see which ones we could borrow from the stables?" With that, Joran and the storyteller set off to get horses.

Shortly after picking two horses, Joran and the old man were trotting down the road to town. The day was clear-skied and sunny. A light breeze tugged at their clothes from time to time; otherwise it was still. Both were happily munching on fresh cookies from the kitchen. Joran had reasoned that a trip should have snacks and had snuck back into the kitchen to get some. Finding freshly baked maple nut cookies, he snatched a cloth and wrapped some in it. He then found a skin of wine for the old man and an earthenware jug of milk for himself. They would get thirsty on the road too. After a few hours, though, Joran's legs were getting sore, and the ride was getting boring to him. Being his first real trip off the farm, he was learning the hard way just how far things could be from home. "Sir, how much longer?" he asked again.

"Now Joran, I told you the last time you asked it was going to be past lunch before we arrived. Is the sun past midday yet?" the old man replied patiently.

"I don't remember it taking so long the last time I was in town," Joran said. "Then again, I was barely able to walk back then. I seem to remember it was a grand town though."

The old storyteller smiled quietly. "I am sure it was to a small boy on his first time. It is much like any other village though," he said. Joran noticed the old man seemed to have his thoughts elsewhere.

Thinking a story would be a nice way to pass the time, Joran decided to see if his traveling companion could be coaxed into a tale of some sort to help make the ride pass faster. After thinking for a minute about how to get one, he started asking questions.

"Can I ask a personal question?" Joran asked.

"Um, huh? Oh yes, of course," the old man stammered. Clearly, he had been thinking of other things.

"I never hear anyone call you anything other than the storyteller or old man. Do you have an actual name?" Joran asked.

Chuckling, he replied, "Of course I do. Over the years many people have called me many things. Some I won't repeat though. Especially in front of a young boy." He winked at Joran before continuing. "One name works as well as another for the most part."

Joran looked down at his horse's mane. "I'm just Joran. Nothing more," he said sadly.

"Come now, that is the only one you have right now."

"What? Aren't you given your name when you are born?" Joran asked, confused.

"Right now, you only need one. Joran works just fine right now," the old man said. "Over the years, you will earn or just be given others."

"Why is that?"

"Well, over time you outgrow one or it just doesn't fit you like it should. Do you still wear the same boots or socks you did when you were younger?"

Joran shook his head.

"See, names can be the same. Sometimes there comes a time to change one or add to it. You will get there in time. If not, you will have a strong and true name for your whole life." The old man smiled at him.

Thinking for a moment, Joran said, "Elsa calls you Old Mutt or Hungry Mutt sometimes."

Laughing, the old man replied, "Yes, she does. Not sure why though. Maybe I sleep too much, like an old dog. She and I are old acquaintances. Who can say why women do half of what they do?" He chuckled.

"Well, I guess that means I should call you Mr. Hound then. Since that is what is polite, yes?" For some reason Joran found this very important. The old man not having an actual name had always seemed wrong to Joran. Like no one cared enough to call him anything other than the old man or the storyteller. Since the old man was so kind, that just seemed to be very wrong in Joran's mind.

The old man turned and looked at Joran thoughtfully for a minute, then smiled. "Well, now. That is very polite and I rather like it. Thank you, Joran."

Joran smiled and said, "I guess that settles that, Mr. Hound."

"Thank you, Mr. Joran," the storyteller replied while bowing in his saddle.

"You know, a story would help the miles go by," Joran said with a twinkle in his eyes, changing the subject quickly. He wanted to get as much from this trip as he could, and time alone with the storyteller was precious.

The storyteller smiled, enjoying the fact that his traveling companion enjoyed his stories. He spun tales of monsters, orcs, fairies, dragons, battles, and defeats. Sure enough, the miles seemed to slip by unnoticed beneath their horses' hooves.

After one story in particular that centered on civil wars of many centuries ago, Joran had a puzzled look on his face.

"What are you thinking so hard about?" the storyteller asked, somewhat amused. He hadn't thought there was much to think that hard about in the last tale. Just a tale about the Gurnish civil wars. One side won by killing the other side's warriors and breaking all their toys. The other side had lost. They hadn't killed the other warriors, nor had they broken all their toys. It was not that confusing.

"Why are the Gurns that way?" Joran asked after the horrific tale of battle was finished.

"Oh, that is what has you curious? Why a people are the way they are?"

"Yes, it is."

"Well, I think it is that the Gurns are a very stubborn, proud, and virtuous people. Unfortunately, the second and third traits can lead people to do things for odd or unclear reasons. At least they are that way to those watching from the outside. The first trait can make them stay with the decision, even if they later realize it is wrong or not the best decision to follow," the man said, leaning back and watching some birds fly around a bush near the road.

Joran seemed to chew on this mentally for a while. "I have a friend who is a Gurn," he said. "He seems to be a little…bogged down when it comes to thinking. If you know what I mean. Like a horse in knee-deep mud. He will get to the other side sooner or later. It is just usually later."

The storyteller chuckled. "You mean Berhard? Yes, I had noticed that. He seems a good-hearted boy and loyal friend nonetheless."

"Why is he like that?" Joran persisted.

"Well, since the Gurns spend so much time thinking on how to be proud and virtuous, they don't give a lot of thought to anything else really. Your brain can only do so much at a time."

About that time, they came to the top of a gradual hill. From the top of that rolling hill, they could see a long plane stretching out before them, and in the distance, they could see the edges of Northern Holtsville.

As they drew closer, Joran felt a pang of disappointment. For to him, the small, tightly grouped stone houses seemed a letdown from what he expected. He wasn't sure what he was expecting exactly; this wasn't it though. The houses were built from stone, some a weathered dark gray and others a dark creamy color. All had either black or gray ceramic tiled roofs. The tiles were fitted so tightly, Joran wasn't sure if some were all one size or if they had been made different sizes and then fitted together. The windows in the houses were filled with thick panes of wavy glass, some with bubbles in it. The doors were made from thick planks of wood, some faded and weatherworn, others covered in paint.

Between these sturdy, if smaller than expected, houses were winding streets and alleys. The main two roads met in roughly the middle of the town with smaller winding streets branching off them. Alleys were here and there, some barely big enough for two horses to walk side by side. In the far distance, Joran could see the jagged mountains, their peaks still covered in snow.

While Joran was taking this all in, their horses trudged along down the hill, kicking up the dark reddish-gray dust of the road. These little dust clouds would engulf the horses' hooves, then be blown away in the breeze. Before long, the dirt road gave way to the cobbles of the village, and the little dust clouds changed into soft clanging of horseshoes on stone.

The townspeople paid the two country folk no mind; at most, they gave them a quick look and then went back to rushing about on their business. Joran was amazed by the wild array of colors that the people wore, from the fancy gowns (they couldn't really be called dresses) that the women wore to the soft silly-looking hats and tight pants that the men wore. The city folk all seemed to look down on the farmers and country people in the town. Joran noticed that those not dressed in the odd (and to him impractical) way of the city people were expected to step aside or wait for the other to pass, yet weren't afforded the same courtesy in return.

They sure seem to be rude and think highly of themselves, Joran thought as he looked at the rather arrogant looks on the villagers' faces.

"They sure are a colorful lot, aren't they? All dressed up like they are," the storyteller commented, watching Joran's expressions and seeming to read his mind.

"Well, they seem to view themselves as special, even if those clothes aren't worth a broken shovel when it comes to doing real work," Joran replied, trying to keep his tone neutral.

"Let us find something to eat, shall we?" The storyteller decided it was time to change the subject, and his belly was telling him it was time to eat. Fresh cookies did not replace an actual meal.

Until then, Joran hadn't noticed that he was hungry. He agreed, looking from the oddly dressed people to the storefronts, hoping to see something that looked good to eat. Granted, right now he would have settled for a two-day-old loaf of bread, he felt so hungry.

"Is there a place here that will let us in?"

"There are many taverns and specialty food dealers to buy a meal from here." The storyteller chuckled, seeing the look of concern on Joran's face.

The look of concern changed to a look of confusion. "Buy food? Those who come to the farm at meal time are given a meal out of common decency, courtesy. I don't think VonRich has ever thought to charge someone for a meal from Elsa's kitchen. Even if those meals are delicious."

"Things are different here. Not just in how they dress and act, but also in how things get done. Did you not know that VonRich sells a part of his fall harvest to people here? The baker buys a great deal of his grain from VonRich, often paying extra to have it milled before delivery by the farmhands. The brewer buys his hops from the farm as well. Where did you think all of the fall harvest went?" he asked.

Joran thought for a moment, having never given it a thought, knowing that the beer was brewed on the farm and all bread and meat prepared in the kitchen from the stores were held in the barns. *Well, now that he points it out, that is a lot of food we harvest each fall. Never thought it was more than we used on the farm though. Just thought it was stored away until we ate it.*

Then Joran had a horrifying thought. "I have no money to buy food with," he blurted out.

"I have plenty for both of us, don't worry. Can't let a growing boy go hungry, now can we?" The storyteller chuckled as he reined in the horse in front of a low, cream-colored stone building just one story high. In front, above a heavy set of double doors, a sign was hanging off two thick chains and sticking out from the building. On the sign was a carved picture of two beer steins with an apple between them. Above and below the pictures were words. Joran couldn't read though.

"I can recognize those as letters," Joran said, pointing to the sign. "I don't know what they say though. Would you tell me what they say, please?"

"Oh, they say we will get good food and drink here if we have coin to pay for it," the storyteller said with a wink. Then his face turned pensive. "You mean you can't read? Or write?"

"Oh, I am sure I can. I just haven't learned yet," Joran said with a little smile on his face. "I can make quills for writing very well; my friend the blacksmith even made me a special knife for making them. I know VonRich can read and do numbers. Even big numbers he can do in his head quickly and accurately. I think the blacksmith can do numbers as well, although not always in his head. I know because I see him scratching numbers in the dirt sometimes. Don't know if he can read. Never asked. I was always busy learning other things from him. They are the only ones I know of on the farm who can do that, and they all seem too busy to teach me."

"Well then. Elsa has been dropping the pie, so to speak. She should have started teaching you reading and numbers years ago. I shall have to speak with her on that when we get back," he said, somewhat irritated.

"Elsa can read? And do numbers?" Joran exclaimed, surprised.

"Well of course she can. Have you never seen her cookbooks? Or how do you think she learned all that medicine she knows? She can read very well. She should have been teaching you how to do so as well." He seemed very upset having learned that Joran couldn't read or do numbers.

Joran's attention was quickly off the reading topic and firmly planted in the tavern topic. The low, thick-beamed ceiling with its smoke-darkened oak held his attention now. It was a large and open room with a rough stone floor worn smooth from years of boots and chairs being slid over it. The heavy tables and chairs were haphazardly spaced around the open room. In the front and back, along the stained stucco walls, were large hearths, unlit now with the summer heat. Their chimneys were made from dark red brick, with heavy wrought-iron candleholders set into them. Overhead, three large wrought-iron candleholders hung from the ceiling on heavy chains, giving off a soft light from the candles. Along the wall to the left of the doors, bottles of beer were stacked neatly along the shelves behind the heavy, roughhewn dark wood of a long bar top. In the middle were several handles sticking up from the bar, their brass handles polished smooth from years of use and cleaning. He was curious what those did. The smell was a mix of cooked meat, stale beer, the sweet tang of wine, sweat, rich tobacco, stale perfume, and deeply tanned leather. It was a new and not all unpleasant smell to Joran.

The storyteller guided Joran to a table near the bar, amused by the look of wonder on the boy's face.

"Bartender, what is there to eat today?" asked the storyteller of an old, fat, and unkempt man behind the bar.

Wiping his hands on his stained cotton apron, he replied with a bored tone, "We have some stew that was cooked fresh yesterday and some venison cooked two days ago. The bread was delivered only four days ago. We also have three kinds of beer and one kind of wine," the man said, gesturing to the shelves behind the bar.

"Well then, we shall have two bowls of the stew, heated up, a loaf of bread with honey, and I will have a stein of your darkest beer on tap and the boy will have a stein of cold milk."

The bartender looked at them skeptically. "And how will you be paying for all this?"

The storyteller shook the purse on his belt. The coins made a heavy clinking sound.

This seemed to have a magical effect on the bartender. He suddenly was less surly-looking and disappeared into the back of the tavern.

After seeing the bartender leave, Joran looked around the tavern some more. For the first time, he noticed a figure lying across a few chairs pushed against the wall. The figure was snoring loudly.

"Is that man over there sick?" he asked, gesturing toward the snoring figure.

"He will be when he wakes up" was the dry reply from the storyteller.

"Why is that? He didn't go to sleep sick?" Joran was confused.

"He was drunk when he went to sleep. When he wakes up his head will be pounding, his stomach will be rolling, and bright lights will make things worse. If he mixed beer and wine, or something stronger, the night before, he will be even sicker," the man replied knowingly.

"Shouldn't someone take care of him?"

"I would say he doesn't wish to be taken care of."

"Oh. You know him?"

"No. Not him specifically. I know of others like him. And I have been in his shoes personally from time to time."

"You have?"

"Yes."

"What made you want to drink so much wine, beer, and whiskey to make yourself sick in the morning?" Joran asked. He had never seen anyone get that drunk. Even on winter solstice celebration, he couldn't remember anyone getting so drunk that they were sick the next morning.

"It seemed like a good idea at the time."

"What would make that a good idea?"

"Usually a celebration." He paused, then muttered, "Or a woman."

At that moment, much to the storyteller's thankfulness to have the subject changed, the food and drink were brought out. Joran's attention was focused on the food now. The stew was greasy, overly seasoned, and only slightly warm, with tough meat, while the bread was hard and stale. Nothing like the fresh loaves Elsa or the girls in the kitchen cooked daily. Joran didn't notice this, though; he was just hungry and dug into the food. Using the bread to soak up the remains of the stew helped soften it and clean the bowl. After finishing his meal and emptying his stein, Joran sat quietly as he had been taught and waited for the man to finish his second stein of beer.

After a bit he commented on the meal, "Well, that was…" – he searched for a word to describe the meal honestly yet not negatively – "filling." This whole trip wasn't really living up to his expectations of things. Northern Holtsville wasn't living up to the image he had had in his mind at all.

"I'll go with average. Tavern food the world over is all pretty much alike in quality. Have yet to be in one that I would whip a horse to get back to for its food." With that, he laid some coins on the table, which vanished into the bartender's thick fingers before they had a chance to even stop spinning. He led Joran out the doors and back into the sunlight.

Seeing the sun had started to set, Joran reminded the old man about the seasonings and such.

"We can take care of her shopping and then find some lodging for the night and for the horses. Sound good?" he said as he unwrapped the reins from the pole outside the tavern.

They wandered away from the tavern, walking beside the horses. After crossing a few intersections, they found a small, narrow three-story building with painted glass windows; the painting of a small jar was framed by more letters that Joran couldn't read.

The storyteller stopped, though, looking through the window into the display of various open sacks of brightly colored spices and seasonings. Over the open sacks hung dried plants, neatly arranged by size.

What caught the old man's eye, though, were the heavy-bodied, dark-skinned men standing at the counter inside the shop. They were dressed in loose, flowing robes and pants of light-green cotton, with sturdy leather sandals on their feet. At their cloth belts were broad, curved swords, the grips made of an odd rough-looking leather. Each also carried a dagger at the small of their backs. They eyed everyone with a look of bored disinterest. Outside the shop were two small horses. They had odd-looking saddles with what looked like armor plates on them. *Cute horses, just not worth much as workhorses,* Joran thought as he looked at their delicate heads and tiny hooves.

The storyteller gently guided Joran past the shop, then stopped a few shops past the spice dealer, turned, and looked back.

"Why didn't we go in?" Joran asked. "I think that was the shop Elsa wanted us to visit." It certainly smelled like the right place.

"Rackians."

"Huh?"

"Inside the shop were two Rackians. Haven't seen any of them in a while. Usually they act as transporters for the Vibaions."

"Huh?"

That seems to be his new favorite word, the old man thought.

"They are the people from Vibaion. Hence, Vibaions. Southern Mulsins," he answered shortly. His eyes focused on the street behind them.

"Oh, the ones we defeated in battle," Joran said, happy he had remembered the old stories.

"Yes."

"What are they doing up here? Especially in a small town like this?"

"They are now traders. It's just very odd to see them this far north and so far off their major trade routes."

"We can't go inside if they are there?"

"We will; I just wanted to see if there were any more of them. We can act like we were just tying up the horses and getting our coin. When we go in, don't say anything and stay near me. Understand?"

"Yes." Even though he didn't totally understand, it was best to go along and do as the man asked him to do.

They walked back down to the shop, setting off the little bells over the door as they walked inside. Joran liked the bright tinkling sound they made.

Joran was fascinated by the shelves of spices and seasonings. He could name some, only a few though. When he walked past the sugars, he was amazed to see that there were different kinds: white, brown, dark brown, thick grained, and fine grained. One glass jar was filled with what looked like a pure white powder. He guessed it was sugar as well, since it was with all the other sweet-smelling sacks and jars.

The owner of the shop was a short man, thinly built with long gray hair that he wore braided down his back. *Only girls do that*, thought Joran when he saw the man's hair. He was dressed in a bright-red shirt that hung to just above his knees. It was belted at the waist with a delicate-looking belt with silver fittings and intricate workings. From the belt hung a small knife and two pouches. His legs were covered with loose brown velvet pants that were tucked into highly polished black boots that reached mid-calf.

Before the owner was a scale on the counter; he was carefully weighing small, oiled pouches that held various spices. After weighing each pouch, he wrote something down in a thick book and moved on to the next pouch. The two men on the other side of the counter watched him closely.

Upon hearing the bells, the little man turned and addressed Joran and the storyteller, "Thank you for coming in. If you will please wait, I will be with you shortly. These gentlemen were here first, and once we have finished our business, I will be happy to help you." His speech was very different from anything Joran had heard before, almost lisp-like.

"Thank you, good sir, there is no hurry though," the storyteller responded. Only this time his voice was very different: scratchy and old. Weak. Joran turned to see what was the matter and was stunned to see the old man stooped over, hanging his head and shaking it from side to side.

What happened? Joran wondered as he went to help his friend.

"No, take care of the old man and his son now; our business will take some time," said one of the big men at the counter.

"No need to interrupt your business for us," the storyteller said, still in his odd voice.

"I don't like to feel rushed when I do business, and this will take time. Get what you came here for and be gone." The politeness was gone from the man's voice this time. He too had a strange accent, which made his tone that much harder.

"Why thank you; you're a kind man," the storyteller responded. "My master wrote down what he wishes; I have a list here somewhere." He made a show of patting his pockets and looking through his coin purse. Finally, he found it and handed it to the shop owner, his hand shaking a little. "I hope you can read it; my master's handwriting isn't the best, and I can't read."

Can't read? What? Again, Joran held his tongue. While he didn't understand why the storyteller was putting on such a show, he knew how to follow directions from an adult.

The merchant took the list, glanced at Elsa's flowing handwriting, and disappeared into the store.

The Vibaion stood at the counter, staring at the old man and Joran. He nodded to the old man and eyed Joran coldly. "What's your name, boy?"

Well, until this very moment, Joran had always told the truth. He had been a truthful and honest boy his entire life. At this moment, though, he saw a totally different world, one that was filled with shadows and deception. Somewhere in his brain, a little voice was telling him to follow the lead of the the story teller. This meant responding truthfully to the man's question was not a good idea. The little voice warned him that this was dangerous. So he lied. "Berhard, sir," Joran muttered and looked at his feet nervously.

"Gurnish name for a boy who doesn't look a bit like a Gurn?"

Oops. Why did I have to pick Berhard's name? The man is right; we look nothing alike.

"You're not pure-blooded Gurn, are you?" the man asked. His face had changed to a more intent look; he eyed Joran closer.

Joran shuffled his feet and sought an out for the mess he had backed himself into. The little voice wasn't helping much. It was silent. *Thanks, tell me to lie and then don't help me out of the mess the lie creates*, he thought.

Then in a fit of inspiration he came up with an answer that he thought would get him out of this box that he didn't want to be in.

"My mother was a Gurn. People say I favor my father though."

"Your mother *was* a Gurn? She is dead?" the man with the scarred face asked, his voice soft yet curious.

Joran still didn't trust this man with the odd sword.

"Yes," he said, letting a little quiver creep into his voice as he looked down. "She died in a fire. It was a long time ago. I was still a baby."

The Vibaion turned back to the counter, losing any interest in the boy. Half turning, he tossed a copper coin at Joran. It fell short, though, landing a short distance before the story teller. "The all-merciful and powerful God Arrah's face is on it. While he can't bring you back your mother, perhaps he can bring you some good fortune. Or some sweets." The man winked at Joran.

Before Joran could react (he had never had coins before), the old man bent and quickly snatched up the coin, turned to Joran, and handed it to him. Only the one that Joran found in his hand was a common penny from the village. "Thank the kind man," the story teller said, lightly cuffing Joran upside the back of his head.

"Thank you, sir," Joran sputtered. *Ouch! Was that really needed? I was getting to thanking him; I was trying to figure out why he switched coins on me.* He kept the coin the story teller had given him closed in his hand, as though someone would steal it.

About this time the spice merchant returned with several cloth packets. He handed them to the old man, who paid him and thanked him, and then the two left the shop.

After walking a few buildings away, toward their horses, the storyteller eyed Joran.

"What?" Joran asked somewhat defensively.

"You took a very dangerous gamble back there."

"You clearly didn't want them knowing who we were. What with all that 'can't read or write' and a different voice. Figured I best follow along with your lead," he explained. "Wasn't I supposed to? That was wrong of me?"

"It was very quick thinking of yours—and very perceptive of you to realize what was expected of you. I think you fooled them nicely," he said as he winked at Joran.

They were quiet until they reached the horse.

"Why did you change the coin though? A copper coin is the same here as there, isn't it?"

"Usually they are. Sometimes, though, Arrah coins are best not picked up. Now let's get going; we have a long trip ahead of us."

"Huh? The inn is just down the street."

"That changed; we are heading back tonight. Besides, Elsa may reward us with bringing her seasonings back quickly with a pie or plate of cookies," he said with a grin.

"I like that idea. She bakes really good grain and nut cookies."

The horses didn't seem to share their enthusiasm of heading back in the night. It had been a long ride out to the village that morning, and now it would be a long ride back without any real rest. They didn't like the night anyway; dangerous things lived in the night. Despite that, they moved slowly back toward home.

"May I at least see the coin the Vibaion gave us?" Joran asked. He had never seen a coin from another place.

"Joran," the old man said with quiet conviction in his voice. "The world isn't filled with good people like Elsa and VonRich. There are a great many in this world who don't deserve your trust. Among those people are the Mulsins. Especially the Vibaions. Besides, I think it best you don't have or see anything with Arrah's face on it. He is so ugly you might get nightmares from it," he chided Joran.

"The battles between the west and the Mulsins ended hundreds of years ago though," he countered.

"Not all men feel that it is over. Some still think it is being fought."

"Oh."

"Now cover up with that cloak from the saddlebag. Elsa will be less than happy with either of us if you come back with a cold."

Joran reached back and pulled out a middleweight cloak, a plain dark-brown one, and put it on. He didn't feel at all cold; the night air felt good to him. He didn't argue though. His friend was right: Elsa wouldn't be happy if he came back sick. It would also involve some of her foul-tasting teas to make him better.

After a while, Joran quietly asked, "Mr. Hound, did you ever meet my parents?"

"Yes" was the soft reply.

"Are they both dead?"

"Yes."

"Wish I had some memory of them. You know, of before they…" He couldn't finish the thought. "I have tried to remember them. Really tried. I can't think of anything about them."

"You were a baby when they died. It is understandable that you don't remember them."

"Do you remember them?"

"Yes."

"What were they like?" Joran asked hopefully.

After shifting in the saddle and looking at the stars, the old man replied, "They were quiet, everyday folks. No one really paid them any interest. If you walked past them in the market, no one would turn their head to look twice at them."

This angered Joran. "Elsa said that my mother was very beautiful," he said with a hard edge in his voice.

"Oh, your mother was a beauty. No arguing that."

"Then where do you get the idea she wouldn't turn heads in the market?" Joran had seen how men looked at pretty women, and turn their heads men did.

"What I meant was, neither of your parents were royalty or highborn merchants. They were quiet, hardworking village folk. People don't pay those kinds of people any mind. If they did look twice, all they saw were a young couple with a newborn son. No one looked closer than that, and that was how it was supposed to be."

"How it was supposed to be?"

"Life is complicated."

Switching thoughts, Joran asked about his father. "What was he like?"

"Hmm.... medium build and thick muscled, coarse light-blond hair. Powerful hands. He was quiet, not prone to lots of words. Very hardworking. Could outlast two or three draft horses a day."

"Was he a good man?"

"Yes. A very good man. I liked him. Miss him," he replied with deep sadness in his voice.

"Did he love my mother?"

"Oh, did he love her. More than life. She was his whole world. Until you came along; then you both were his world."

"What kind of home did they have? Where did they live?" Joran asked, his curiosity aroused. No one ever really spoke about his parents.

"Well, let's see. Your father built the house himself. He was very talented with his hands. Did I tell you they were very powerful hands? Yes, I did, didn't I? Well, he built a very solid house for your mother. He then filled it with sturdy, well-made furniture for her. The table he crafted for the kitchen was beautiful and solid. Your mother made it into a home for them, making blankets and such for the home and filling it with the smells of fresh bread and carefully cooked meat. I used to stop in and visit them when I was in the neighborhood. Your father was a master tradesman, talented in several trades. He reached master journeyman in two of them." The storyteller rambled on, telling Joran about the fine dark earth and how his father had planted a small orchard behind the house. He described the roses his mother would grow each summer, some as large as plates. Joran listened intently, soaking up every word from the storyteller. He never noticed he fell asleep to the slow steady rocking of the horse and the hypnotic sound of the man's voice and the creak of the saddle.

Much later, he felt himself lifted off the horse and carried softly into the house, up the stairs, and into his bed. He'd never noticed how strong the old man was until now.

He could smell that Elsa had joined them; she had a sweet, comforting smell that he would know even in the dark rain.

"Set him there," she said softly, and then she covered him with a soft old blanket. "Why did you two come back in the dark? The inn isn't that bad in the village."

"We ran into someone that he shouldn't be near."

"Who? The villagers are sometimes arrogant; they aren't dangerous though."

"A Vibaion."

"Here? Are you certain? We've never had them this far out from their homelands," she said, surprised.

"Yes, I am certain. His speech, dress, weapons, manners, and physical appearance all laid testament to his heritage."

"And the coin?"

"I swapped it out for a different one before he saw it. I will give it to the blacksmith; I am sure he can make something from the copper."

"Good idea."

"If he was a Jahagi, I will let him follow me away. He might find some enjoyment in seeing this part of the country. Perhaps I can even find some entertainment in his following me." The old man smiled. "Socerors like him games."

"I take it you are leaving us then," Elsa said sadly. She really did like the old man.

"Yes, time to move on. I have places to be and a great deal I must do in the coming years. Besides, when Jahagi sorcerers start showing up this far out, I get nervous for his safety. You and I have a great responsibility to carry with us. We can't get lazy or foolish now."

"So you will be gone for years this time." She sighed resignedly.

"Yes."

"Well, you do have a great deal to do," she said softly. "I will miss you."

This surprised the old man. He laughed good-naturedly. "You have started getting soft, being so sentimental. Hardly seems like you at all."

She not-so-softly swatted his arm. He faked serious injury. "You know what I mean: I know nothing about children or raising boys. Yet you and the others have assigned me with this task of such great importance."

"I would say you are doing a fine job." He smiled, then turned serious. "With the exception of his reading, writing, and numbers. You should really have taught him those by now."

"Should have known you would notice that," she sniffed.

"Oh, and be careful. He can lie with the best con artist."

"Joran? Lie?" She was stunned.

"Yes, and well. He lied to the Jahagi so well I thought he was telling the truth. And under great pressure too."

"Never. He won't even lie to get out of trouble."

"Yes. His parents came up as well. He is curious and asking about them."

"Did you tell him anything?" she asked, worried.

"Only basic things and that they were both dead. I see no reason in ruining his childhood with things that he probably can't cope with right now anyway. He is a good boy; let him enjoy life a while longer."

To Joran, who was mostly asleep, their voices sounded like a dream that he was floating through on a warm cloud. He let sleep take him then, carrying him through to late morning.

When he awoke, he didn't remember much of the night before, and what he did remember he thought was just a dream.

When he awoke, the kind old storyteller was gone.

Chapter Four

The years rolled past. Winter gave way to spring, and spring gave way to summer, with its lush fields and bright days. Summer relented, and autumn readied people for the coming winter, with its brilliant white coat of snow over the sleeping fields and biting yet invigorating winds.

In the never-ending wheel of time, Joran grew, as did his friends. Well, except for little Drazen. No matter what he ate, and he ate a lot, the little fella never seemed to grow. Sometimes people referred to him as the little squirrel: some because he was usually eating everything yet never growing bigger, others because he was usually scurrying here and there. Still others (these would be the girls of the farm) because they thought he was cute. In his usual good humor, Drazen never minded.

In contrast to the squirrel, Berhard grew like the fabled Sequoia trees in lands far away. He grew tall and strong. Even though he was still considered a boy, he was as strong as any field hand, and stronger than many. He enjoyed competing with the men in contests of strength. His favorite was seeing who could split a log with one blow of the ax. Even when he lost, he enjoyed it. Yet he had a gentle way about him at times that belied the immense strength he had. Anyone who saw him around a litter of puppies would have thought he couldn't lift a feather. Or a newborn foal, helping it to stand for its first time while its mother patiently watched.

Geeta grew as well, and while she didn't grow as tall as the boys, or as strong, she grew in ways the boys found appealing nonetheless.

Joran was somewhere in between the two boys. While he didn't stay small like Drazen, he was far from as big as Berhard. Some thought he would start growing to his full size later in life. In true adolescent boy fashion, the idea that he would grow a little later was almost not to be tested. Like most boys, Joran was prone to doing some things that might not be considered the best of life choices. On one such occasion involving a cart of sorts and a steep hill, things almost came to very short and abrupt ending for him.

The three boys had spent some time watching one of the men build a cart. OK, a very short time watching the man fit the boards and wheels and so on. They decided to build one of their own and race it down the hill on the far side of the farm. After a few badly mangled attempts at building one that stayed together, they had a cart to race down the hill with. Had they paid more attention to the building of a proper cart, theirs probably wouldn't have been as exciting. It liked to lose wheels at random times or fly apart once it had some speed. The fact that they hadn't bothered with a brake of some sort lead to some interesting times as well. Since the road they used the cart on was straight and ran to a gradual incline, they usually just let the cart slow itself.

Well, one splendid summer afternoon, Joran was showing off. While standing on the seat rather than sitting on it and steering, he broke the rope he was using to steer. While it was not the first time this had happened, it was the first time the driver wasn't sitting where he could use his feet to sort of keep it going straight down the hill. This change was how Joran found himself flying over the edge of the road and into large stream that bordered the road. This also brought to light an overlooked part of Joran's education. Swimming. Upon hitting the water, Joran managed to hold on to the cart, or rather what was left of it after it hit the water. Realizing he couldn't swim to shore, he caught one of the boards before it floated off and used it as an oar of sorts to paddle himself toward shore while he sat on a couple of other boards. Being properly motivated, he began quickly paddling toward shore. His thinking was, he could make it before the boards he was sitting on could float away, leaving him in the water with nothing to hold on to. While this was a good idea on the drawing board, so to speak, his paddling hastened the decision of the boards to go their separate ways. Before long he was barely holding on to the last bit of the cart with his legs and trying to make shore while tipping over into the water. Just before he hit the water, he saw the familiar figure of the dark-robed rider standing on the shore.

Despite all his frantic paddling, he started sinking into the quick-moving stream like a rock. A rock with wildly flaying arms and legs. He sunk to the bottom. He felt the smooth river rocks against his feet and the river plants along his legs as he was pushed along the bottom by the current. After a few seconds that felt like hours, he managed to brace his legs and push himself up toward the surface. While not graceful, he did manage to get his head above the water for a moment. He gasped for air while purging his lungs of the water he had swallowed and had shot down his nose on the way to the bottom of the stream. He also noticed time seemed to slow, and he noticed things in what seemed a clearer light that let him see details he had never noticed before. This was overshadowed by hearing his friends screaming for him as they ran along the bank. What he really thought was odd, though, was that the horse and rider, who didn't move to help, also didn't show any sign of a shadow, even though they were in the sunlight. Then he sank below the water again.

If I can grab a part of the cart, I can at least keep my head above the water and then float toward the bank, he thought, shoving himself upward again. Or what he thought was up. Rather, it was more of an upward direction at a slight angle. One that ran him right into a rock. All thoughts of, well, anything left his head in a bright light and painful clacking of his closing teeth. And then he just floated in blackness.

The next thing he remembered was more pain from his head, only this wasn't so much on the inside of his brain as coming from his scalp. And then he saw a figure that looked vaguely like Sladvick's back. While holding on to Joran's hair with one powerful hand, as his hair was the first thing Sladvick could get ahold of, he swam toward shore with the other. His strong strokes pulled the two to the muddy shore in short order. While keeping a good grip on Joran's hair — it really made a nice handle — he pulled the boy out of the water. Once they were on the shore, Sladvick rolled Joran onto his back and shoved hard, just below his rib cage, with upward pushes. On the second one Joran shot water out his mouth and nose, gasped, and did it again a few times. Sladvick then rolled the boy onto his side, started pounding his back, and let him finish spitting and sputtering to clear his lungs as he got his breath back.

"OK, OK, Sladvick, I'm good." Joran half croaked and half puked to get the pounding on his back to stop.

He rolled over and sat up, blowing his nose to clear it. *Ugh, I hate throwing up and having it come out my nose,* he thought as he wiped the blood from several cuts on his head out of his eyes. He spit the coppery-tasting blood out of his mouth and looked around, dazed and trying to focus his eyes. He was looking for the horse and rider. When he turned his head, though, he passed out, falling backward into the soft mud of the bank.

"Eh, he will live through that," Sladvick said as he picked up Joran and carried him toward the big house. "It's Elsa that he might not survive." He chuckled as he walked down the road with Joran's limp body in his arms.

Later, when Joran awoke in his bed, he felt dizzy and had a terrible headache. He reached up to rub his head and found it wrapped in bandages. *Oh, that can't hurt any more than it does now,* he thought, slowly and carefully sitting up.

"You idiot!" Elsa yelled at him when she saw he was awake.

Nope, was wrong, it can get worse, he thought, wincing at her loud voice.

"What on earth were you thinking?" she demanded.

Oh…She must stop yelling.

"Riding the cart we built," he said carefully and quietly. Oh, quiet was important right now.

"When did you decide that carts were meant to go in the river?" she demanded even louder this time.

Oh God. Head. Hurts. Stop yelling. Please.

"I didn't plan on it being in the stream. It just sort of wound up there," he said as he slowly laid back into the soft pillow. *Soft. Good. No pain. Quiet.*

"And who gave you permission to race a cart down a hill like that? If you could call that thing a cart!" she yelled.

Oh, pain again. When did she get such a loud voice? Can't she ask questions quietly?

"Well, we sort of just decided…"

"Decided what?" she yelled again.

"To build it one day. We saw some of the men building one and thought it would be fun to ride one down the hill." He opened one eye slowly, almost experimentally, and looked at her helplessly. *OK, answered her question. She will be quiet now. Yes?*

He was ready for another question or for her to yell at him again, and he steeled himself for the pain in his head that would come from it.

He was not ready for her to grab him in a tight hug and start to cry.

Well, that was unexpected, he thought, trying to keep his stomach from rolling from the sudden and unexpected movement. For some reason he would have preferred her to yell at him more; her tears seemed to hurt more than her yelling. He sat there quietly, listening to her sobbing for a while. Then he remembered the rider who cast no shadow. He almost asked her about him, telling her what he saw and what it might mean. Then the little voice in his head spoke up, telling him that the rider was something to keep to himself. It was something deeply private. Not to be shared with anyone. The rider was someone whom he would have to face later, by himself. He did not wish to involve Elsa in that, for he somehow knew that she would intervene on Joran's behalf with the rider. This felt wrong to him, so Joran said nothing. He would deal with the rider himself when the time came.

"Elsa, it wasn't that dangerous. We raced the cart down that hill many times." He left out how many times it fell apart though. "Just this time it decided to play at being a raft. I was sort of figuring out the theory of swimming, you know, keeping my head above water. Breathing. Then something hit me in the head, and I wasn't doing so good anymore."

"The something that hit your head would be a rock," she said tartly as she released him and dried her eyes.

Good, she isn't yelling. Head doesn't hurt so bad now.

"Ah, that makes sense. I thought maybe it was part of the cart. I would have been OK in a minute or two. I was getting pretty good at floating," he said lamely.

"Sure, you were; that is why Sladvick had to pull you out of the water by your hair."

He smiled a little at that.

"And what is so funny about that?" she demanded.

"Just remembered a time when you used my ears as a good handle and was thinking it was probably a good thing you didn't pull me out."

Elsa stood up, surprised. She still wanted to be angry with him, but she couldn't. She smiled at the memory. "True, you would look funny without your ears."

Once he could get out of bed, Elsa took control of his every waking moment. He was assigned the barns in the mornings, mucking out stalls and feeding horses and cows. Once that was done, he was back in the kitchen, where he became intimate friends with soap, water, and lots of dishes. From there, it was to the mill stone to carry the grain sacks in to be milled to flour. Then he got to carry the grain out, only this time as flour. Then he went back to the kitchen carrying the friendly sacks of flour for the kitchen girls to make bread with. Then he went back to the stalls and then back to the kitchen for the dishes. After a week, he hated every minute of it and began wondering if he could get away with running away.

This continued all summer. As he saw it, his imprisonment was never-ending.

As the fall colors started to come in, the weather confined the other children to the main house more and more, and Joran found things more enjoyable. He could at least play with his friends a little bit between chores. Well, except for Berhard — his size earned him more work. More so than even Joran. At least Berhard was allowed out into the fields and woods; Joran barely saw the outside of the main house and stalls. While he missed his friend, he thought of him as lucky.

While he could sometimes slip away and play with Geeta and Drazen, they had reached an age where playing tag in the barns or swinging on ropes in the hay rafters didn't hold as much enjoyment. Adults also seemed to notice this idle time and found productive things for the children to do. More and more they found themselves sitting someplace out of the way and talking among themselves. Well, Geeta and Joran would sit and listen while Drazen talked and bounced around on his feet. Much like his nickname, Drazen seemed to be always full of energy and completely unable to sit quietly, or even sit still longer than a meal. A short one anyway. Elsa had made sure he, like all the children, learned their manners. Joran once joked to Geeta that if he painted a face on a stick and leaned it in the corner in front of Drazen, Drazen would talk to it for hours and never notice it wasn't talking back to him. Geeta had laughed and agreed, adding that if you handed Drazen a rusted horseshoe, he would talk for hours about it.

One such afternoon, the three of them were sitting in the corner of the barn on some old feed sacks.

Geeta looked at Joran's arm. Pointing at the long, rectangular, almost white mark running down the outside of his forearm, she asked, cutting off Drazen's running voice, "What's with the mark on your arm?"

Before Joran could even register what mark she was referring to, Drazen switched topics midsentence and quickly answered her. Sort of. "I've seen that too. Since you grew up in the kitchen, didn't you, Joran? I figured it was from a hot stove or pot when you were little and didn't pay attention to what was going on around you. Elsa probably scolded him out terribly for being scalded like that. Didn't she, Joran? You know how she can get in a heartbeat. Goes from sweet ol' Elsa to angry wet cat Elsa before you can blink. Never saw anyone like that. Even a cat gives you a second or two to..."

"Dunno," Joran said, cutting off Drazen. *How can he talk that fast and long without even taking a breath?* He chuckled to himself. "It has been on my arm as long as I can remember." He eyed it closely for the first time, never really having paid it any attention before. It did look like a scar from a burn, kind of shiny and lighter than the skin around it. Now that he was thinking about it, he didn't remember ever seeing it tan either, even with the hours he used to spend in the sun. Always a kind of glossy pale-white color.

"Birthmark?" Geeta asked while she looked at it closely.

This started the squirrel off again, like a horse taking off across a field after having its rump slapped. "It could be a mark from a previous life, a battle scar. I saw a man with a birthmark once; it made this dark wine-colored mark on his neck, as though someone had poured wine on him and it stained his skin. I thought he had been hit in the neck or something, like with a board, 'cause I thought it was a bruise. Except one of the adults around — don't remember if it was my mom or not — told me it wasn't a bruise. They told me it was a birthmark, and I didn't get what they meant by that, since everyone is birthed, yet I had never seen a mark on them like that. Why did he have one? No one could tell me."

The conversation wandered off into other things, mostly whatever popped into Draven's active head and out his active mouth that seemed to be trying to keep up with his brain. And losing.

After finishing the pots and dishes again, Joran was looking at the mark intently as he walked out of the kitchen.

"Elsa? Where did I get this?" he asked as he walked past her while she was cleaning up one of the tables.

"Get what?" she asked without looking up.

"This," he said as he walked over to her and held his arm out, pointing at the mark.

Glancing at it, she said, "Oh, that. Don't pay it any mind," and went back to wiping down the table.

"Oh, wasn't really worried. Just was wondering if it was a birthmark."

"Well, something like that."

"Ah, OK. Did any of my parents have it?" he asked, thinking it was something that would be passed down to him. For some reason, that thought became very important to him. To have something of his parents.

She sighed a little. "Yes, your father had one similar. It has been in the family a long time." Then she walked over to put the rag in the wash basket.

Joran looked intently at the mark, then looked up as she walked back across the kitchen. As she came close to him, a thought suddenly hit him. "Is it like your hair? Something passed down from your mother?" He reached out and touched her white hair.

As soon as he felt her soft, silky hair, he became light-headed, and the mark on his arm felt cold. Not the whole arm, just the mark. Like someone had held a piece of ice against it. Only this cold went deep into the arm. At the same time, his head was filled with…things. Not like visions so much as feelings of memories. Like he had experienced and lost things that made him feel incredibly sad. A never-ending feeling of pain. This gave way suddenly to people. He saw all different kinds of people, with one thing the same. All of them seemed to be laid over the face of the kindly old storyteller. Then, just as suddenly, he felt inhuman power course through his brain. This was accompanied by the comforting knowledge of an unstoppable will. Elsa shivered slightly and gently pushed his hand away.

He instantly lost the cold feeling in his mark, and his light-headedness left him. He felt slightly disoriented.

"Wow. What happened?" he asked in awe.

"It's an old trick I learned a long time ago."

"Teach me?"

"Not tonight. Perhaps another time. It's time for sleep now. Unless you would like to get started on the wash tonight," she said, looking at the basket of rags.

"I'll head to bed," he said as he turned and slowly walked away. A feeling of fear crept over him.

"Elsa?"

"Yes?"

"Will you never leave?" he asked, almost scared at the answer he might get.

"No," she said softly, walking with him to his bed.

Joran felt better hearing her soft answer. Once he reached his bed, he changed into his night clothes and fell into a deep, dreamless sleep as soon as his head hit the pillow.

For the rest of the summer, Joran didn't have much time to contemplate or even see the odd mark on his arm. He was too busy, and often too dirty, to think about it. Or even see it.

With the ending of summer, people turned their thoughts to the most important celebration in the land. Well, all lands really. For everyone celebrated Yule. Yule was the day that all the Gods had decided to sit down and create the world and all that was in it. The celebration of Yule took place midwinter and had grown from a single day of celebrating to a full week of feasting, festive decorations, lots of scented candles, presents, plays, songs, and stories of the Gods. To VonRich, the last part was the most important.

Even with all the happiness that those on the farm had at Yule, there was a downside. Like most things, there was some bad with the good. In this case, it was VonRich's daughter, Catryna. She had gone and left the farm as soon as she could; however, she didn't intend to lose what she saw as her reward for putting up with the farm life her first sixteen years. Marrying a minor lawyer, who was a junior associate of some small firm in the village, had been her ticket out. VonRich thought his son-in-law was an overdressed, weak little man who had no idea which end of a shovel to hold on to or what an honest hard day's work was. While his daughter tried to conceal it, he also knew she

only came out once a year to remain on speaking terms with him, and in doing so, insure her inheritance of the farm. VonRich knew that if he left the farm to her, she would sell it the day his body was buried. She cared nothing about the farm or her ancestors who had worked the land, building what was there today. All of those who lived on the farm knew this and looked at her with something of quiet scorn when she lowered herself to visit.

They didn't allow this to overshadow the festivities though. A small annoyance like Catryna and her husband could easily be overlooked with everything else going on. As one farmhand said once, "Enough beer and wine, and you don't notice them at all."

As though copying his daughter's mood about the visit, the weather that Yule was on the gray and unhappy side. Instead of the nice champagne powder snow, this year the snow was mostly slush, more rain than snow when it fell, half melting during the day and turning to ice overnight, making walking around more than a little entertaining at times. Especially if you were carrying sacks of flour. Joran was doing just that one morning when he tripped in a rut of ice and fell into a half-frozen puddle. He managed to keep the flour from getting wet — at the cost of him getting soaked in the muddy ice water.

Well, I shouldn't have to take a scolding for ruining a sack of flour at least, he thought as he sloshed the rest of the way to the kitchen.

Joran had been pretty well confined to the kitchen all winter. He thought that this was taking the punishment for the cart accident that summer a little too far. He was missing out on the traditional pre-Yule anticipation he usually shared with his friends. In the years past he and his friends had eagerly anticipated the start of what they saw as a week-long party, even with the lousy weather. Instead, this year he was spending his pre-Yule time hunched over, his hair a mess, shuffling around with a sour look on his face.

Where the decorations usually made him smile and fill him with joy, this year they looked washed out and fake to him. In his eyes, the evergreen boughs looked like someone had made them out of twigs and straw, painting them to look green. The cranberries looked small and painted rather than full and ripe red from the sun. The tablecloth looked old and worn out. Even the candles irritated him. He thought this year they were overscented and didn't burn as well as in previous years. Such it was that he returned to his personal sullenness and moping around.

All this moping and shuffling around didn't go unnoticed by Elsa. She marched right up to him and put her hand on his head, checking for fever. After a few times, she disappeared into the back of the kitchen, coming back a few minutes later with the worst-smelling concoction Joran had ever smelled. It tasted just as bad. The little voice in the back if his head that was usually right, if no fun, told him he was bringing this on himself. If he only cheered up and stopped acting like a sick cow — Elsa's words — things would be much better. He ignored the little voice.

In spite of the foul tea and the little voice, this continued right up to the first morning of Yule week. That morning, things got a little more interesting. A Vibaion and two pairs of Rackians showed up with a team of horses and a wagon. Joran had learned a long time ago that no one would pay any attention to a boy who was quiet. This is how he listened to gossip and learned many secrets on the farm. And so this morning he was standing near the gate, toying with some insignificant item, trying to look busy yet quiet. He wondered what the unexpected visitors wanted.

He stole glances at the men: the Vibaion looked much like the one he had seen in the village the day he had gone to get herbs and seasonings with the storyteller. Much like the one in the shop, this one was carrying an odd-looking sword and kept his eyes moving, taking in everything. His glances were sometimes accompanied by quick turns of his head. While the Vibaion was alert and almost birdlike in the movements of his head, the Rackians were slow to move and looked bored. Lounging against the horses, they seemed barely awake in their heavy wool cloaks, with their hoods pulled up and their thick scarves wrapped loosely around their faces, protecting them from the biting winter winds.

VonRich approached the men in his finest clothes. After all, it was Yule. One must dress for the season. He had Catryna and her husband in his wake.

"Happy Yule," VonRich said happily when he was within earshot of the travelers.

All he received in response to his good cheer was a bored, "And to you."

"What can we help you with this fine day?" VonRich asked, ignoring the cold reply. "I have been told you have had an unusually good year with your goats and have done an exceptionally good job curing the meat. I have also heard you ask a fair price."

"Thank you for the compliments," VonRich replied modestly, bowing his head slightly at the man's words. "I take it you wish to purchase some of our meat?"

"Yes, I will buy all you have for sale," the Vibaion said, reaching for his concealed coin purse.

"We are a religious house, and it being Yule, we cannot offend the Gods by doing business during Yule. I would be happy to sell them to you in the morning."

The Vibaion stared at VonRich for a moment, clearly surprised at the response.

Before VonRich could reply, Catryna stepped in and said, "Don't be stupid; this man came out to our farm to do business in this terrible weather. Don't insult him by refusing to return the politeness. Sell him the meat already."

Her father turned to her, anger showing on his stubborn face, "You were raised better than this. We do not do business during Yule."

A squeaky and high-pitched voice, something one would expect to hear from a small boy, came from behind VonRich. "In the capital, we don't let foolish so-called holy days interfere with business. Sell the man the meat," Catryna's husband piped up, unasked for his opinion.

Without turning to look at his son-in-law, VonRich replied with a cold and determined tone, "That may be. Here, though, on my farm, we honor the Gods and observe Yule." "You would turn down gold?" his daughter squeaked out in horrified surprise as she raised her hand to her chest. "This is Yule. There will be no further discussion about this. If this gentleman would care to, I would be happy to have him join us tonight for the celebration and provide him and his companions rooms and stables for their horses. There is no shame or loss in honoring the Gods."

"I care nothing of your Yule or celebrations for Gods. My people do not follow in this way. If you have no interest in my gold, then I should find some other farmer who is. I will probably save some gold in the process, although it would cost me quality in meat," the man said coldly. VonRich looked at the man, almost with a sad expression. "I doubt you will find anyone around here willing to sell you anything. Yule is observed here by all, as it has been for many generations. I will gladly stand by my offer, though, of providing room and food for you and your men." Then with a small smile he added, "We have some of the best cooks and vintners here. You will surely have a fine meal and wine this evening. Please join us for our celebration. One can't always work. Take this evening to relax from your travels. After all, the meat will still be there in the morning."

After a few moments, the Vibaion sighed. "A good meal and half a day can't hurt. Provided you and I do business first thing tomorrow. Yes?"

VonRich smiled happily. "Yes. That sounds fine. Now please join us in the great hall for the feast. I will have the stable hands take care of your horses and the girls fix up some rooms for you and your men. Now please come this way."

Later, while carrying platers piled high with beef, lamb, and other food for the feast, Joran thought about how odd it was that the rule about no work during Yule seemed to be forgotten in the kitchen. Here, you would have thought that royalty was coming to visit. What with the way everyone ran around like chickens with their heads cut off. Well, maybe a bit more coordinated. With less mess too. Elsa oversaw everything, from the roasting turkeys to the presentation of the cakes for dessert. These seemed to be her real pride, over all else. Not a knife mark was to be seen in the icing. Each frosting tree had to be just so. Joran didn't care so much for how pretty they looked, just about how good they tasted. He knew the frosting was excellent, melting on his tongue like warm honey with vanilla. Elsa hadn't caught him sneaking a taste of it. If she had noticed, she hadn't said anything. Either way, Joran thought it was delicious.

Out in the great hall, the heavy tables almost creaked under the unusual weight of the food and decorations. Specially made pressed beeswax candles lined the middle of the table, giving a soft glow to the room. Along their bases were fresh-cut evergreen boughs decorated with clusters of red berries, giving the room a fresh smell. Along the walls more candles burned happily, adding to the light in the great hall. The large hearths in the hall were all piled high with merrily burning logs, and beeswax blocks added a sweet scent that wafted through the hall. When it mixed with the scents of cooked meat, roast turkey, fresh-baked breads, and the sugary smell of the frosting, it was hard not to drool in anticipation of the feast to come. Even Joran smiled in anticipation as he labored under the platters for the table.

Finally, all was ready, and they all sat at the table in their finest wear, specially cleaned and carefully prepared for this celebration. At the head of the table sat VonRich himself, a happy and joyous look on his face. His deep-red shirt matched the rosy color of his cheeks. He almost looked like a happy child, the way his eyes lit up and reflected the candles.

He rose from his chair, raised his wine goblet, and looked slowly around the table at each person seated in the hall. "My friends and guests. I dedicate this feast to the Gods. May they smile upon us and grant us another happy year, as they have done in the past."

All the farmhands raised their goblets and steins and said in respectful and solemn unison, "To the Gods."

At this, they all took a drink, set their drinks down, and turned toward VonRich. They knew a prayer would come before they could eat the delicious food set before them. They all knew it would be a short one; even VonRich knew cold food wasn't as good as piping hot. They also knew that he was uncomfortable speaking publicly. This caused him to forget the carefully worded prayers at the time they were to be recited and led to short, if very sincere and heartfelt, prayers to the Gods. Everyone one was sure the Gods understood and knew his heart was in the right place, even if he lacked the words.

Taking a deep breath and nervously folding his hands in front of his chest, he began with a strong voice, "Oh blessed Gods. We thank you for the bounty you have set before us. We thank you for the past year and the mercy you have shown us with good weather for the crops and strong livestock. We beg you for the same in the coming year, should you be so merciful. Thank you from your humble servants."

After this, with a smile, he raised his hands slightly and gestured to those around the table. "Please enjoy the meal before it grows cold." As he sat, everyone happily started in on the feast. Platters, bowls, and pitchers were passed around the table while they filled their plates with the delicious food.

Catryna and her husband would only join the farmers at this meal, having taken the rest of their meals either in their rooms or in the hall when the others were not there. Even with all those around, they only spoke with the Vibaion. He was the only one they felt deserved their attention. After all, the rest were just farmhands on what would be her farm.

Her husband started the conversation rather arrogantly, "My wife and I have often thought of visiting your lands. Learning more of your culture and lifestyle would help commerce and investment opportunities between our lands. Don't you agree?"

"My people and I prefer to keep to ourselves," the visitor replied politely yet with a cool tone.

"I am confused then," Catryna's husband continued in his high-pitched voice. "You are here now wanting to buy meat, presumably to take back and resell at a profit. Don't you think a contract for such future business would be useful?"

"My being here isn't totally by choice. I am here more from duty than from an interest in doing business with you," he said flatly. Then changing the subject abruptly, he turned to VonRich. "There are a lot of people who work on this farm; how do you manage to fit them all in this hall?" he asked. In doing so, he ignored Catryna and her annoying husband.

"Yes, we do," VonRich said, puzzled that the man was interested in something like that. Puzzled, the visitor looked around the table closely. "I was told there was an old man, stooped with a thick white beard and matching white hair. Yet I see no such man. Did he pass on from this life?"

"As you can see, I am the oldest here by a good many gray hairs." VonRich chuckled good-naturedly.

"An acquaintance of mine was sure he had met such a man from this farm while in the town here years back. A boy was with him—Gurnish if I am not mistaken."

Oh, this is bad. Very bad, thought Joran, who had been listening in. He managed to keep his face neutral and his eyes on his food, which now tasted like ash in his mouth. *This is why lying is bad: it always catches up to you and not to bring you flowers and cookies. What could they want with the storyteller and me?* He strained his ears, wishing they would change into those of a rabbit. *They can hear everything.*

"Do you have the boy's name? Or the old man's?" VonRich asked helpfully.

"I don't believe he ever mentioned either of their names, only their descriptions."

"I can't be of much more help, without more than a vague description. There are many old men around here."

"I thank you. It is true, with such a vague description it is difficult to find them, especially after so many years." The Vibaion lost interest in that topic and switched to another. "These cheeses are very rich in flavor, and their texture is excellent. Even the hard cheeses seem to melt in my mouth."

"Thank you, glad you are enjoying them," VonRich said proudly. "The man sitting across from you is the one who makes the cheese here. He's been doing it since he was a boy, following in his father's footsteps. Like his father did before him with his grandfather. We are fortunate to have him here."

The man across from the merchant smiled, and his cheeks seemed to turn a little redder at the compliments.

"Would you be willing to sell some cheese to go with the meat?" the Vibaion said slyly.

VonRich smiled, chuckling. "That was a nice try. We agreed no business today though. No?"

"Can't blame me for trying. And the food is delicious. You have some very good kitchen girls from the taste of it." The Vibaion smiled softly, seeming to enjoy himself.

VonRich raised his usually quiet voice. "Elsa, our guest from afar enjoys your cooking."

Elsa barely looked up from her plate, giving the merchant a brief glance. "Thank you. It is nice to hear others take pleasure in my cooking" was her cool reply. The Vibaion's eyes grew large at the sight of her when she glanced at him. Inclining his head to her, he said, "Truly, you're a magician with food."

Elsa had become short, cold even, with the guest. Very out of her character. "There is nothing magical about cooking. Just a desire to learn, an ability to learn from mistakes, and the patience to do both. Now magic, that is an entirely different book of learning."

"Some would say the same about magic: it takes time and persistence to learn. A great deal of making mistakes and moving on from them."

"That may be, but true magic though comes from the spirit, soul, and heart. Not from learning how to be quick fingered and knowing how to deceive people."

Elsa's eyes were hard, and she was not looking down at her plate any longer. Rather she was meeting the merchant's now-cold gaze. Neither seemed willing to look away, and it felt as though an unspoken message had passed between them and no one heard it in the now-quiet dining hall. Almost as though one had issued a test to the other, only neither of them knew who had issued it. Finally, the Viabion looked away and broke the trancelike look between them. Perhaps he wasn't ready for the test?

At that, things went back to being festive and cheerful in the hall. Once the last plate was removed from the tables, the next tradition of the farm started. While the tables were being cleared, several farmhands had snuck out and prepared themselves for the telling of the Gods. The masked and robed men came in slowly. They wore old, lovingly made masks and robes. The masks had hoods attached to the backs, both to hold the masks on the wearers and to completely cover them. The hoods flowed down into the old robes, which showed the folds from being stored in the heavy cedar-lined chests over the past year.

As they regally walked into the hall, they slowly made their way to the foot of the table that had VonRich seated at the head of it. Once assembled, each actor stepped forward and gave a much-abbreviated telling of what God they were dressed as. This followed an old pattern, a tradition followed year after year.

First there was Zerak. "The solo God, Zerak. For I live alone, and the future does my bidding. I control all to be" came the muffled voice behind the finely carved and painted mask.

Next, Vangarth A slightly deeper yet still muffled voice came forth. "I am Vangarth, a God who controls the worlds to come." And so it went until they came to Joran's good friend, the blacksmith. While the other Gods wore hand-carved and painted wood masks, Sladvick wore a highly polished metal mask that had been boiled in a special mix of acid salts until it was deep blue. It looked as though it were oily wet, even when dry. Even the cloak and hood were different. Where the other Gods' cloaks and hoods were different colors, ranging from deep greens to what had once been brilliant blues, Sladvick's cloak and hood were as black as possible. He even had black leather gloves covering his hands.

From behind the metal mask came Sladvick's calm and strong voice. It had an odd, almost far-away sound to it. "I am Arrah, God of the Mulsins. And I control the world to come." Joran noticed something rather odd happen to the visitors when his friend came to the table. The Vibaion covered his face with his hands. It looked almost like a reverent gesture from the man, as though looking at the mask of the God was a sin. Seeing this, Joran looked at the man's traveling companions. They surprised him even more. The Rackians looked terrified. They were almost cowering in their chairs, just short of crawling under the table to hide. Joran was puzzled. *Don't they know it is just a mask? They didn't cower like that from the other Gods' masks. These big men feared a mask on a blacksmith? Odd.*

Once Sladvick had finished his short speech, he joined the line of the other six at the foot of the table. With their arms bent, their hands raised to shoulder height, and their faces raised to face the heavens they began the final part of the Yule ceremony. In a low chant together, they spoke. "Each as one, and one as all, we control the world to come."

At this, VonRich stood, a little unsteadily — *maybe one too many steins of beer this year*, he thought — and replied to the Gods, "Gods of the world to come, you are welcomed to the home and farm of VonRich. We, those of us here at the farm, thank you for the bounty of the past year and beg of you for a good year to come."

"VonRich, we see you are a good and faithful man with a true heart. We seven place our blessing and protection on the house and lands of VonRich and those who live there. May you have a happy and full year to come." With that, they solemnly paced out of the great hall. The only sound was the swishing of their cloaks. Once they left, VonRich sat back down and looked around the hall at the eager faces. Once he had made them wait a bit, he laughed, and the hall erupted in laughter and cheerful voices. It was time for the presents. Each year VonRich gave each of his people a gift. These were carefully thought of during the year. It wasn't uncommon for him to lay in bed at night, staring at the whitewashed ceiling in his room, trying to think of a special gift for this person or that child. What was something they would really enjoy getting? Each year he seemed to pick just the right gift for each.

This year was no exception. There were a number of new cloaks and shirts, each made from heavy wool and well stitched. The field hands saw a good many pairs of heavy leather work boots and gloves, each made from deeply tanned fine leather. The craftsmen on the farm often saw a new tool or apron. The children usually were given a new toy or a much needed new bed or piece of clothing. Some were given highly treasured books. Not hand-me-downs either. New books from the printers in town. Each picked by VonRich himself. It made VonRich swell with happiness when he saw how happy a gift made someone: the tears of joy from a kitchen girl when she opened the leather cover of a new cook book or the look of pride of a field hand as he tried on his heavy-soled new work boots. To VonRich this was worth more than gold. His daughter did not agree. She saw it as throwing away her inheritance.

This year he had a special gift for Joran: something he gave to each boy when he reached a certain age. He handed Joran a silk-wrapped box. The red of the silk complimented the deep-green satin ribbon he had tied it with. Taking the gift from VonRich's old, strong, and calloused hands, Joran unwrapped the ribbon and silk. Inside he found a box made from white pine. The joinery was some of the finest. Opening the box, he found a dark-mahogany-colored tooled-leather sheath. Sticking out from the top was an ink-black ebony handle with fine metal pins holding it to the tang of the knife. The pins were highly polished and then bowled in the same acid salts as the mask Sladvick had worn. Their deep blue reflected the candlelight like a mirror.

"Mr. VonRich…" Joran croaked. He didn't know what to say.

"Joran, you are almost a full-grown man now," VonRich said, a solemn tone to his voice. "A man should always have a good knife. It will be useful for everything from daily work to eating and, the Gods forbid, protecting yourself or others if ever needed. Just remember, this will hurt more than an old rake handle to the head." He chuckled, remembering the time the boys had gotten carried away playing at knights. There were some chuckles from around the tables from those who caught the friendly joke.

Finding his voice, Joran thanked him. He then pulled the knife from the sheath. Its blade was highly polished and had a wavy look to it, much like the pond did when it had a light wind blowing across it. The deep, hot acid finish accented this more. Along the very edge, standing out in sharp contrast to the deep blue of the rest of the blade, was a highly polished silver edge. Joran looked at the gracefully curved cutting edge. Following it along its five inches, the tip cleanly flowed into the flat and file-worked spine of the knife. He then promptly sliced his fingernail off when he tested the edge. "Well, that was to be expected," Elsa said as she wrapped his bleeding finger in a napkin. It was unclear if she was referring to his growing up or his foolishness in slicing his finger open. Probably both.

The next day, VonRich met the Vibaion at dawn, as promised. Together the two men went through the meat lockers and the cheese rooms. Once the goods were loaded, the Rackians left with him. Later that day, Catryna and her husband packed up and left. With their leaving, things at the farm returned to everyday life. Winter wound along, as it does. Reluctantly it gave way to spring sunshine and chirping birds. This summer was slightly different. One of the young men had fallen in love and gotten married. Once married, he and his wife decided to move off the farm to a nearby house with enough land to start farming for himself. VonRich and the rest of those who lived on the farm wished them best of luck as they left in the wagon loaded with gifts and being pulled by two oxen. The oxen were a wedding gift to the couple from VonRich himself. As were a few words of advice and an open invitation to come visit whenever they wished.

This led to a new farmhand. Now while Joran tried to give people the benefit of the doubt, it was kind of difficult to do that with Rick. First impressions do speak volumes, and Rick's was volumes of ick. For starters, the man seemed scared of soap and water and was desperate to keep them separate from each other. Clearly, he rarely allowed the two to combine around him. This led to his stringy, unkempt oily hair and matted beard. The oily skin on his face did nothing to help the beard. His aversion to soap and water continued to his clothing. Joran wondered if the new man had ever washed his clothes. Getting caught in the rain didn't count, as far as Joran was concerned. The man's teeth, what few were left in his head, didn't help any either. They looked like they had been shoved in the gums by a bored child and stuck out in all directions. Overall Rick was a quiet man, keeping to himself for the most part. He worked hard enough, always carrying at the minimum his own weight, if not doing more than his share. Rarely did you ever hear him complain. He was just a quiet man who rarely smiled. After a few tries at talking with him and getting nowhere, Joran stopped bugging the man. This was made easier for Joran since he didn't have to smell the funk that seemed to follow Rick everywhere if he wasn't talking to him.

This summer was also different for another reason. Joran had new and different things wandering around in his head. One was Geeta. Until that summer, he had paid her little mind, thinking of her as an occasional playmate to swing in the barn with. Otherwise she was just something of a meddling annoyance to be tolerated. He much preferred to run with the other boys, Berhard and Drazen, and play at being knights, hunting, fishing, or building things. Even if they weren't that good at building things. The cart was still a sore spot for Elsa. This summer, though, for some reason beyond his comprehension, not that he really put all that much thought into it, he started to spend more time around Geeta, watching her and thinking how pretty she was. In the past he had thought of her as cute, if he thought of her at all. He also noticed the other boys were spending more time around her as well. He wasn't sure how he really felt about that. It was all new to him. He just knew he didn't like it when they were around her and he wasn't. For her part, Geeta drank up the new attention with abandon, flirting with any and all of the boys whenever possible, then giggling happily when the boys would stalk off from one another or, on rare occasions, wound up rolling in the dirt. While Berhard was kept away from her by having to work the fields, Drazen and his quick mouth were a different matter entirely, as far as Joran was concerned. Much of his time was spent with his overactive mind picturing the Drazen alone with Geeta. This led to Joran looking for any excuse, and sometimes just not bothering to look for an excuse, to wander the farm to put his worries at ease that Drazen wasn't alone with her.

Joran realized that the three of them, Drazen, Berhard, and himself, all had something that the others didn't when it came to Geeta. For example, Berhard was the biggest and strongest. Joran had heard some of the kitchen girls even call him handsome. Drazen was quick with his jokes and stories, often making girls cry from laughter. Joran for his part had the kitchen. While he himself had very limited cooking skills, he had easy access to the kitchen girls' cooking. He knew that Geeta liked sweets, whether it was cookies, sweet bread, or the hard candies Elsa sometimes made. Geeta liked them all. So rather than compete with Berhard's size or Drazen's golden tongue, Joran resorted to old-fashioned bribery for her affections. It was a simple deal: he brought her sweets; she gave him kisses. Joran thought this was fair enough, and it worked well for him.

All things, though, change sooner or later. The arrangement Geeta and Joran had changed the minute Elsa happened upon Joran collecting on one of his presents to Geeta behind the horse barn at the far end of the farm. While they were kissing, and possibly working up to more than that, Joran heard a voice he really would rather never have heard in such a situation.

"I made enough candies for you to each have one instead of sharing one between the two of you," Joran heard Elsa say flatly from the corner of the barn. In hindsight, it was rather funny to Joran; he had traded a cookie for this kiss, not candy. Right at that moment he found nothing amusing at all. Rather, he turned beet red and jumped away from Geeta.

"Joran was—" Geeta started innocently.

"I can see what he was doing," Elsa said, looking at Joran standing there turning even redder. "Joran. Follow me."

"Bu—"

She gave him a stern look, and he hung his head, wishing he could disappear into a hole until Elsa forgot the whole thing.

Sadly, at least in Joran's mind, Elsa had a long memory and an even more creative one. While he spent the rest of the summer well confined to the kitchen under her sharp eye, Drazen was free to wander as he pleased. The few times Joran saw him, he would smile happily, knowing that his only real competition for Geeta's kisses was stuck in the kitchen. This didn't help Joran's overactive mind either. Yet what could he do? He was stuck under Elsa's ever-watchful gaze. She even made sure someone else brought in flour.

Chapter Five

Toward late fall that year of kitchen confinement, as Joran thought of it, the storyteller returned. It was one of those crisp fall late afternoons, with a stiff breeze carrying the dead leaves across the fields and giving a hint of the smell of snow to come.
Joran was doing the one chore that Elsa let him do alone outside of the kitchen: slop the pigs. She seemed to know that Geeta would go nowhere near the pigs, which made it safe for her to leave Joran alone there.

Joran had just dumped the last of the kitchen scraps for the day into the trough when he looked up and saw a figure walking up the road toward the farm. It took a minute for him to recognize the storyteller, bundled up as he was against the crisp wind. His heavy cloak blew about him.
Once Joran realized who it was, he dropped the slop buckets and ran out to greet his friend. Once he was close enough to see the man's face, he realized the years hadn't been good to the storyteller. Hidden under the deep hood, his face lacked the childish happiness of before. Even the twinkle in his eyes was dimmed.
Still, Joran was happy to see the storyteller and wrapped him in a hug before walking next to him on the way back to the farm.

"My, you aren't so small anymore," the old man observed.
"Been a number of years since you last saw me." Joran laughed, not remembering how many years it had been just then.
"Yes, it has been a long time since I made it back here."
"Yes, it has been. You have been missed."
"Well, that makes an old man feel appreciated. How is everyone? Healthy and whole?"
"Yes. No lost fingers or anything. Not even a mild cold so far this year."
"Ah, it is good the good things stay the same."
"Well, not totally the same," Joran said, feeling a little guilty about giving his friend bad news.
"Oh?"
"Yes, there have been a few changes on the farm. One of the hands got married and moved out with his wife. They have a farm not far from here and seem to be doing well."
"Well, congratulations are in order for them then." He smiled as he said it. Some of the twinkle was coming back to his eyes.
"That it is. On the bad side, though, one of VonRich's prize dairy cows died this summer. Old age caught up to her."
"Well, age does like to collect its due from us all. Shame...I liked that cow. She was friendly and always gave good milk."
"I have to talk with Elsa," the old man said, switching the topic abruptly.
Caught off guard a little, Joran blurted out, "She is in a foul mood today. Maybe you would prefer to sleep in the hay barn. I could bring you some blankets, food, and water for washing. She should be in a better mood after a good night's sleep."

"No. I will talk with her as soon as we get there. Foul mood or not."

"You sure? No one wants to go near her today."

"Yes."

With this they walked the rest of the way in silence, stopping only long enough to collect the slop buckets Joran had dropped when he ran out to greet his friend.

When they reached the kitchen door, Joran slipped in quietly and put the buckets back where they were kept. He wished the storyteller had been as quiet; he might have gotten out of the kitchen before Elsa found the storyteller had returned.

"You're back already?" she snapped.

So much for getting out of here before she found out he was back, Joran thought as he set the last bucket down.

"Good day, mistress" was the charming reply.

"I don't have near enough food ready for you, so don't try and charm me into feeding you till you are full."

The storyteller bowed slightly and produced something from inside his cloak, showed it to Elsa, and returned it, all in one smooth, quick movement. While Joran hadn't seen whatever it was Elsa had been shown, he did see the reaction on her face. He also had a sneaking feeling he wasn't supposed to have seen any of the exchange at all.

Once Elsa had regained her composure, she noticed Joran was paying a little too much attention. She felt any attention was too much.

"Joran. Those buckets should have been scrubbed before returning them here. Look how filthy they are. Take them outside and scrub them."

"El —" he started to protest, knowing not only that he would miss out on what was shaping up to be an interesting time in the kitchen but that he would have frozen hands by the time the buckets were clean. The look she gave him ended that. Cold hands it would be. He gathered up the buckets and a brush. Then he walked out the door, letting it bang close behind him. That was as far as he went. While listening in on others was considered very bad manners, Joran knew that if he was chased out of a room, the conversation in that room would be very interesting. *OK, this is very bad manners. Since I am just listening in for my interest and not to spread gossip, this isn't too bad.* And in such fashion, good manners took a beating from curiosity.

At first Joran didn't hear anything. *Did they go to another room? That would just be mean of them.* Then he heard their soft voices.

"You have no idea where they went," Elsa was saying in a hushed yet intense voice.

"I have no need to know; I can follow it like a dog tracks a pheasant in the fields."

"Why would he take it? Better yet, where?"

"No idea." Joran could almost hear the old man shake his head as he said that. "I will take the quickest and easiest way toward where they will want it. They know things won't be complete until they have returned home with it."

"True. He has to return before he will consider it done. Wait, when did this happen?"

"Just a few weeks ago."

"That is too long for you to follow. It could already be back in the kingdoms of the north."

"Perhaps. Unlikely though. It is a very long way to travel in such a short time. If he has crossed into the other kingdom, follow him I will. Only then I will need your help."

"You know I must watch the boy. Yet you want me to leave?"

She has to watch me? Why? Not that I want her to leave. Well, it would give me more sweets time with Geeta if she did leave.

"Catching them is more important. Besides, this is safe."

"No, it isn't safe here."

"What do you mean? No one knows about the boy being here, how can they?"

"At Yule, there was a visitor, a Vibaion. He and his Rackians showed up out of the desert, no warning. He appeared as a business man, looking for meats from here. The thing was, he asked too many questions about an old man" — she gave him a sharp look — "and a boy. They had been seen together in the village some years ago."

They were quiet for a so long, Joran thought they had moved to another room to talk. Then he heard Elsa's voice. It was much quieter than before. "They may have recognized me as well."

"Things are much worse than we thought then."

"I can't be positive; he seemed to watch me closer than the rest here."

"I think it is time we moved him then. I have friends north of here, in the mountains. Stone cutters. He would be safe there."

"No."

"What do you mean, no? It clearly isn't safe here. He can leave with me in the morning."

"No. If he moves, I will have to go with. This will raise many more questions and suspicions than if he stays here and close to me. So no. He does not go anywhere."

"You are being foolish. Why would it require me to bring you?"
Elsa sighed. "He is at an age that requires close adult supervision. Responsible supervision," she added after remembering whom she was talking to.
"You're being overprotective. He is fine and will grow up to be a fine man. He doesn't need to be wet-nursed anymore."
Wow, the old dog has some teeth, talking to her like that, Joran thought in surprise.
"Overprotective or no, he stays. I was appointed his guardian until he is a grown man. Not just until he is close to it. Or, if you insist he leave, I go with him, suspicious or not." she said tartly. "Pick."
"Would you think and stop acting off your irrational feelings?" he snapped.

"I am not acting off irrational feelings." Her voice was cold, angry. "He would be safer in the hell that is Gorinkail all by himself than he would be here on the farm without me."
"You're being foolish," the old man scoffed.
"I most certainly am not. Just a few months ago I found him with a girl, alone. Who knows how far it would have gotten if I hadn't walked in and stopped things? That alone is proof he should be watched more. Not spirited off someplace else where who knows what will happen."

Yeah, thanks for nothing, Elsa. I, for one, would have liked to at least been able to get the kisses I had coming for the cookies. Maybe something else as well, Joran thought irritably as he listened.

The belly laughs from the old man cheered Joran up somewhat. "Wait, he is being a normal young man who is attracted to a pretty girl or two, maybe three? That natural way of things makes you that nervous for his safety?"

"How can you say that?" she snapped. "What would happen if you took him away and left him with some friends, only to come back a few years later and find him married with children? As it is right now, he is little more than a child himself."

"Oh, I doubt things have gone near that far." He chuckled.

No, they haven't, no thanks to Elsa confining me to the kitchen and pig trough, Joran thought bitterly. He missed Geeta's warm, wet, soft lips. And other warm, soft parts of her that he would like to explore. Without Elsa interrupting.

Elsa continued as though he hadn't spoken. "Not saying he wouldn't make an excellent stone cutter or farmer. I am certain he would make a great father as well. Do you really want to wait a couple of centuries again though? Perhaps longer before things are right again?"

"You really are serious about that."

"You are used to the cities; this is far from them. Here, it isn't Brassel. Here he was raised to do the right thing. Not what is convenient, as they do in the cities. Here, the greatest threat to things is a very pretty and well-developed, manipulative girl named Geeta. He has a great deal of interest in her, and she has a great deal of fun playing with not only his emotions, but every boy on this farm's emotions. Right now, I would like to keep her from playing with other parts of him."

"We have debated this long enough. Since you will not budge on this, fine."

In his excitement, Joran stood, taking his ear from the door. *I am getting to move someplace new and interesting,* he thought. All thoughts of Geeta and her soft, interesting places to explore evaporated in his excitement at his new life. Those thoughts disappeared just as quickly when Elsa opened the door. "I don't see clean buckets."

Maybe if I had kept listening at the door, I would have heard her walking across the kitchen, Joran thought while trying to cover up his hand-caught-in-the-cookie jar look.

"Well? Do those look clean?" she snapped at him.

Oops, she is mad. "I...Uh..." he stammered.

"The creek is that way," she said, pointing.

"I was going to use th—"

"Creek. Now. Clean."

OK, I kind of had that coming since I got caught. Just that using the well water wouldn't mean I have to stand in the creeks cold water and get cold feet as well as getting cold hands, he thought bitterly as he walked off to the creek. *Wouldn't have to walk so far either.* He thought miserably as he tromped off into the darkness.

Once he had scrubbed the buckets in the creek until they were spotless, or as close as he could figure in the dark, he walked back to the kitchen, his boots making a squish squish with each step. The buckets brushed his legs with each squish; he didn't bother holding them out from himself. He had gone from curious to just cold and tired now.

Upon reaching the courtyard, he saw Elsa walking up to VonRich's quarters. All thoughts of his cold feet and heavy buckets left his mind. Just as he was about to walk across the yard to leave the buckets in the kitchen and then slip over to see what he could hear VonRich and Elsa talking about, he saw a dark shape hidden in a shadow. Joran squinted at it, sure it was a person, just not who. *Who sneaks around the farm at night?* he thought as he slowly set the buckets down and then straightened up. He kept his eyes on the darker patch in the shadows. It just didn't look right. His suspicions were confirmed when he saw the shape slink along to the doorway to VonRich's.

Joran watched the figure; he still couldn't tell who it was, just that it was a person sneaking around the farm. *No one sneaks around here; there's no reason to,* he thought as he slid along in the shadows, careful not to pick his feet up all the way. The wet boots made too much noise. His mind raced with thoughts. What if the mysterious person meant to harm Elsa or VonRich? Both? With that thought, he carefully drew the present VonRich had given him for Yule. It felt cool in his hand, reassuring.

Joran was only a short distance from the figure hiding by VonRich's door when the figure suddenly turned and jumped quietly away from the door. Joran slid back into the shadows more, being careful to make no noise and keep the mystery figure in sight. When he saw it moving his way, he carefully brought up the knife. There turned out to be no need for it; the figure slunk past him, never slowing or even looking in his direction. That didn't keep Joran from figuring out who it was. The scent of the man gave him away. More accurately the stench. It was icky Rick: the new farmhand who was scared of soap and water.

The opening of VonRich's door brought Joran's attention away from Rick.

He saw Elsa silhouetted against the light inside. Her voice carried on the night air to Joran. "It is a very important personal matter."

"If it is money, I can will pay you more," VonRich pleaded with her.

"I have said this before: this isn't about money. It is a personal issue that I have to deal with." Her tone was kind yet firm.

"You'll come back when it is taken care of?" VonRich croaked, as though he had been crying.

I think he is in love with her, Joran thought, more than a little surprised. Not only with that thought, but that he had thought it to begin with. Sladvick wasn't the only one taken with her, Joran thought sadly.

"I don't think so. While you have been very good to me when I needed someone, I won't be coming back here. I am grateful beyond words for your kindness. I must leave though. I am sure the kitchen girls will keep you and those good people here well fed."

"You will be sorely missed," VonRich said, a tearful resignation in his voice.

"I will miss you as well. You are a good man with a good heart. If you could do me one last favor: don't mention I am leaving until tomorrow morning at the earliest."

"I can do that for you" was his sad reply.

"Don't be so sad; I will leave my recipes with the girls," she said softly.

With that, she turned and walked back to the kitchen to finish preparing supper.

Joran replaced the knife to its sheath; he had all but forgotten it while watching Elsa and VonRich. As he walked back to the buckets, he tried to work through the problem he now faced. Should he tell Elsa what he had seen? *And smelled,* he thought. *If I tell her that I saw Rick slinking around and eavesdropping, then I have to tell her how I knew that. That means I have to tell her and probably VonRich what I saw and heard. Those were things meant for no one but those two. OK, maybe Rick was just curious. He didn't seem to mean anyone any harm. Just like I didn't mean any harm.* Although he had to admit, he felt bad about what he had done. Maybe his little pastime hobby was one best left behind as he grew up.

He replaced the buckets in the kitchen and then went and took his place at the supper. As usual, Rick had a few open places around him; no one liked to sit near him at meal times. Oddly enough, it wasn't his table manners that drove them away; those were impeccable. It was his lack of hygiene. Regardless, Joran didn't see any difference in the man that would show his careful eavesdropping had let him in on anything life changing.

This evening, the only real change was the storyteller was with them. This brought anticipation of at least one story from him. Once the evening meal was served and the dishes were cleared, he stood. Looking at the shadows cast by the candles, he seemed to disappear into thought.

He then lowered his head, looking around the room slowly, taking in each person seated in the great hall. Taking a deep breath, he started his story.

"It is common knowledge, even this far away, that the Aborians walk this earth no more. This makes their God, Abori, cry with soul-deep pain. If you wander into their old lands, some say you can hear the God crying if you listen carefully in the darkest of nights. It is also common knowledge that if you look at your feet while listening for the crying God, you will see rocks turn to gems. Some say this is why the Aborians were wiped off the face of the earth, at least in their physical form. Others say it wasn't because of greed but because of their bloody sacrifices to their God and the eating of raw hearts. No one is sure if these were from animal or human sacrifice. Asking the sacrifices which they were- human or animal- after a ceremony was a little…inconvenient. To say the least. Putting all the parts back together proved challenging.

"Either way, war broke out, and the official reason written down in the histories was the bloodlust of their God. Most knowledgeable people, though, know it was over gems. When one country has such a coveted resource in rich supply and the neighboring one has none, it usually leads to envy. And envy can lead to fighting. Now if there had been no gems, the messy temple services would probably have been ignored.

"The war came though. The Aborians were wiped out. Greed is a powerful drug. The invading country had no wish to even share the wealth. They wanted it all. So they took it. All. Leaving only ghosts and a mournful God behind.

"People stayed away, not wishing to tempt the restless spirits or, worse yet, the sad God. Yet there were three young, and perhaps foolish, men. These men lived in the neighboring country and, like everyone there, knew of the riches just over the border. They laughed at the old wives' tales of ghosts and sad little Gods. If the God was that sad and unhappy with no one worshipping it, why didn't it make new followers? Pathetic little God. It couldn't even do that. If there was a God at all. Now there was something in the old wives' tales that they did pay attention to. Gems. Some as big as a goose eggs. You just had to sift through the dirt for them. Or walk the stream beds. Everyone knows gems like the water.

"So one day these men set out and traveled many turns of the wheel to reach the border of the haunted lands. Once there, they hid and watched the guards patrol the border between the two countries. After all, killing an entire nation was hard work. They didn't want to lose their reward for all that work. The gems. Hence, the border guards. Lots of them. After learning when it was safe to cross, the men snuck over the border, bags in hand to fill with gems and then bring back home. They slunk through the night, ignoring the sounds around them. After all, it was a windy night. Wind makes noises in the trees back home too, and no one says it is ghosts there. Different trees here, different noises.

"After crossing miles, listening to the wind in the trees, as they kept telling themselves, they could smell water. The morning breeze shifted and brought the crisp smell of water to the tired men. This reinvigorated them, and they started moving faster.

"At this point, one man stumbled and fell, dropping his bag. As he was picking himself up and reaching for his bag, he noticed gems sparkling in the early morning light, just barely catching the sun's rays as it came over the distant horizon. Deciding his cohorts weren't observant enough to see the gems around them and forgetting he had only noticed them after falling, then man slowed and let the others get ahead of him. Once they had hurried out of sight, he began running around, grabbing the gems like a spoiled child in a sweets shop grabs candy. He paid no mind to what was happening around him; he was only mindful of the treasure he had found.

"He continued, oblivious to everything, until he stopped to open a new bag to fill. That was when he heard something that wasn't just the wind. Thinking his cohorts had come back and caught him in the act of cheating them, he looked around and saw it wasn't them. After seeing it wasn't them, he wished it had been his friends. The last thing he saw before he was blinded was something only he could have described. Dropping his bags in a terrified panic, he ran blindly through the forest until he impaled himself on a low branch that had been broken off in a storm. Not seeing it, he ran into it so hard it punched straight through his head, leaving him hanging from it, still upright.

"His companions had no idea he was dead. They had fixated on the water, the smell fueling their imaginations of the wealth they would soon have. Like their friend, they didn't notice the change in the sounds around them until it was too late. One turned, curious at what it was he heard behind him. One look at the thing making that sound, and he ran. Terrified, he dove into the water. This might not have been so bad—it seemed safer than being on land—except that he didn't know how to swim. He drowned in a frenzy of thrashing arms and legs, screaming in horror between gulps of water.

"This left the third man. Seeing his friend sprinting into the water and thrashing about until finally drowning—he had kept his presence of mind to remember he couldn't swim either, and running into the water like that seemed foolish at best—the third man turned to see what had brought on such behavior. He was determined to remain calm and face whatever it was. After all, he had hunted. Animals tasted good; he'd just have to kill them first.

"Taking a deep breath and steeling himself, he turned and faced what had driven his two friends to insanity. He saw something horrible; there is no denying that. For the undead are far from pretty. Repulsed by them, he reassured himself that they couldn't hurt him though. He stood; his courage only left him when it was too late. Having been denied the first two for sacrifice, they made sure this one remained alive long after they started separating his body into neat parts.

"They kept him alive even after removing his heart, and true to the wives' tales and legends of old that he had laughed at, they ate it, passing it around like a ripe piece of fruit. The ghosts had left his ears, meaning for the man to hear them eat his heart, the tearing, wet sounds as they tore a piece and then chewed on it. He could feel it as they bit into his heart and chewed it. They didn't leave his eyelids, though, and he was powerless to stop watching them as he was dismembered before he was finally allowed to die."

At this, the storyteller stopped and took a long pull off his stein of beer. Looking around the room, he could easily see that the story was not what they had expected. Not at all.

One face, though, stood out. Rather than showing revulsion, it showed thoughtfulness.

"Something on your mind, Sladvick?" the storyteller asked him.

"I am not sure you have the story right. Not that I would say you have it wrong, just that it doesn't make sense."

Now it was the storyteller's turn to look thoughtful. "How so?"

"Well, ghosts are insubstantial, like the wind or mist. No?"

"True."

"OK, then how did they separate the last man's body? Where did his heart go when they ate it? How did they eat it in the first place? Mist and wind can't eat things if they have no mouth or teeth to eat with."

The storyteller stood there, his stein halfway to his mouth, and started to say something, then stopped. Finally, he lowered his stein and started to chuckle.

This annoyed the blacksmith, and it showed on his face. Then his face changed, and he laughed too. The joke had become clear to him; it just took a little bit for him to work it out. Finally, the rest of the hall started to join in as well, until everyone was laughing. Even VonRich himself was laughing.

Between gulping breaths of air and belly laughs, VonRich managed to say, "Very clever, very clever indeed. We can all learn from this." He gulped down another lungful of air. "Several things can be learned: greed and betrayal are bad. Fear is even more deadly. Finally, there are enough of the first three in life not to add angry ghosts to the mix."

The storyteller had stopped laughing when VonRich had started to make his point. He now spoke, evenly and without humor. "These are true and valid points, good sir. But there is much on earth that must be believed, as it can't be laughed off or reasonably explained."

At this point, those in the hall noticed that one person hadn't been laughing or even smiling. Rick. Sitting alone, as per usual, he had an angry, hurt look on his face. Almost as though he had been made the brunt of a bad and mean joke. He finally blurted out, "I don't see what is so funny about that. No reasonable man can believe in magic or ghosts that eat and carve up humans. It is only children or the addled in the head who can believe such idiotic things." And then he stormed out before anyone could say anything.

After all the dishes were cleared into the kitchen and Joran was cleaning them, he began to hear that little voice in his head. It kept bugging him, telling him that he should tell Elsa and the storyteller about Rick following Elsa. For a little while, he kept ignoring it, not wanting to get into more trouble. Finally, it seemed to yell at him that he best to tell them, as it might be very dangerous not to, trouble or not for Joran. He put down the pot he was scrubbing and walked over to Elsa and the storyteller. "Um, Elsa?"

"Yes? Finished with the pots?" she asked somewhat distractedly.

"No. It is about Rick."

Both the storyteller and Elsa turned to him with expectant looks on their faces.

"I…well…Earlier today when I was coming back from the creek with the buckets, I saw him following Elsa around by VonRich's door."

"You did?" she asked, paying full attention to Joran now.

"Yes. I saw him hiding by the door, and then once you had gone in, he went over and was listening at the door while you two were talking. Then he snuck away just before you came out."

The storyteller took a long look at Joran. "He is new; I don't remember him from my last visit here. When was he hired?"

"Just a few months ago, shortly after the other hand got married and moved to start his own farm," Elsa said, a little distracted. Clearly, she was thinking of something other than the newlyweds leaving. "It wasn't that long after the Vibaion was here," she said suddenly.

"Hmm. I think I will go have a chat with the new fella, explain to him that eavesdropping and sneaking around here is considered rude. I'll also ask him why he was doing it in the first place. Joran, where did VonRich assign Rick his room?"

Joran's pulse suddenly had gone through the roof. "It is the old room over the horses stables, by where we keep the wagons," he said in a rush.

"Show me."

Joran and the storyteller quickly left the warmth of the kitchen and headed over toward Rick's room. Quietly they slipped up the stairs, walking on the outsides of the treads to avoid making any noise.

"This one," Joran said, gesturing at the first door in the hall at the top of the stairs.

"The storyteller gently pushed Joran back against the wall behind him and softly touched the latch to the room. It opened easily, and the door slowly swung into the dark room, its finely fitted and well-oiled hinges making no noise. A stench of unwashed body, dirty clothes, and some other unpleasant things mixed in rolled out of the room to greet them. The storyteller slipped into the room and looked around in the moonlight at the mess that filled the room. Unmade bed, clothes strewn here and there, and a few personal items mixed. No Rick though. *Well, that is disappointing.*

Hearing no commotion, Joran peeked around the doorframe. Somehow, he knew that this wasn't just a mess from daily living. Rick had packed in a hurry and had left. Joran watched the old man. He seemed lost in thought, an empty look on his weathered face. Suddenly it was replaced with an urgent look. "Where are the other stairs to the stables?"

"Over there," Joran said, pointing to the other end of the dark hall.

With that, the old man sprinted from the room, moving much faster than Joran would have thought possible for an old man. Struggling to catch up, or even keep up, he took off after him. He caught up with him at the end of the barn, where Rick was trying in vain to get a horse to cooperate with him and stand still to be saddled. The horse wanted nothing to do with the smelly creature that was so rude as to wake it at this hour after a long hard day of work.
"Nice night for a ride," the old man said conversationally when he saw Rick and the horse.
Joran skidded to a stop, off to one side and just behind the storyteller. *You know, if he bathed more, he probably would have gotten away from us.*
Rick spun around, almost getting his legs tangled in the reins, and dropped the saddle. The horse shied away from him, glad to get away from the fowl human.
"Really, it isn't polite to just take someone else's horse like that," the old man said mildly. "And a saddle and bridle? Now that is just uncivilized of you."
"What is an old gray beard like you going to do about it?" Rick shot back, anger in his voice.

"Could make you wish you hadn't done that, for starters."

Rick fumbled for a short sword and yanked it from under his dirty cloak. "I'd like to see you two try," he roared at them, waving the rust-streaked and chipped blade at them.

Us? How did I get sucked into this? thought Joran. *I was just standing here watching; the storyteller was the one who was explaining things to Rick.*

"Joran, stay out of this," the storyteller said as he moved toward Rick.

"You should have followed your own advice, gray beard," Rick said as he lunged toward the storyteller, the old sword over his head.

Without thinking, and ignoring both good sense and the storyteller's order, Joran smoothly drew his knife blade down along his forearm with the edge facing out while stepping between his friend and smelly man with the sword. Later, he couldn't explain why he had done it or how he knew to draw a knife like that. It just...happened.

"Joran! *No!*" the storyteller bellowed as he watched the boy bring the knife up to ward off the blow.

Ricks next move was something totally unexpected. Something even he didn't expect. His head stopped dead, while his body and feet continued forward for a second before leaving the ground after realizing they were attached to the head. Then he was violently slammed to the floor. Sladvick had come up behind him, grabbed a handful of Rick's dirty hair, and tossed him to the ground. Picking up an old ax handle, Sladvick cracked Rick across the backs of his thighs as he started to struggle up. Rick roared in pain, rolled to one side, and kicked at Sladvick. His angry kick only found air though. "Now that isn't nice. You shouldn't kick at people," Sladvick said and promptly cracked Rick across the belly, just under the ribs, this time with some real feeling behind it from his powerful arms.

The air rushed from Rick's lungs, and he curled up into a ball, trying to get his breath back while his eyes watered. "That's better," Sladvick said, stepping back.

He then turned to look at Joran, who was slipping the knife back in his sheath. "Joran, that wasn't a smart thing to do."

Joran shuffled his feet and looked down, embarrassed. "He was attacking him, though, and he didn't have a weapon to defend himself, and I did."

"You two can discuss this later," the storyteller said. "And thank you, Joran, it was a noble, if somewhat foolish, deed." He then reached over, grabbed Rick's cloak, and pulled him onto his back. Searching through the man's clothes, he found a bulging purse made from fine double-thick silk. Upon opening it, he found it was filled with gold nuggets.

"Hey, that's mine!" Rick protested weakly from the ground, struggling to get up. Sladvick gently reminded Rick to stay where he was by putting the end of the ax handle on his forehead and shoving Rick back to the ground. Rick tumbled back to the ground and stayed there, a hurt look on his face.

"Awful lot of gold for someone like you to have. Been prospecting in your free time?" the storyteller asked.

For his part, Joran was stunned, seeing that much gold in one place. He had never seen so much, nor nuggets so large.

Rick just sat in the dirt, a sullen look on his face.

"Eh, don't bother answering that. Pretty sure where you got this. Nuggets this large only come from one place," the storyteller said, dumping the gold back into the pouch, tying it closed, and dropping it to the floor.

Rick looked at the pouch, his face an expression of hunger and desperation. When he saw that no one was paying him any attention, he grabbed the pouch of gold and rammed it into his trousers pocket and scurried back to a corner, away from the evil blacksmith and his evil stick.

"You know, had you just fought bare knuckles or rolled in the dirt, it wouldn't have been a big deal and I wouldn't have had to report it to VonRich," Sladvick said, looking at the man huddled in the corner. "Unfortunately, you had to go and pull a sword on someone. And a pathetic excuse for one at that," he said, shaking his head in disgust. Whether it was because of the low quality of the sword or that Rick had pulled it in the first place, Joran didn't know.

"I would appreciate it if you didn't say a word to him about this," the old man replied.

The other three all turned to him; their looks ranged from confusion on Sladvick's face to relief on Rick's. Joran was along the lines of just surprised.

"No? This is serious. He drew a sword and intended to use it. Poorly, he intended to use it though. No one does that on this farm. VonRich should know about it."

"True, it is serious. We have no time for this though. Joran, tie him up, and put him somewhere someone will find him sometime tomorrow." He turned to Sladvick. "Please, have I ever lied to you? If you wish, tell VonRich about this incident tomorrow. Right now, time is running short, and we must be going. Please help Joran stash that man someplace." With that, he left the two working on tying Rich up. He stopped struggling against them when Sladvick reminded him how the ax handle felt.

"We could stash him in the hay barn; it is warm enough he won't freeze, and we can use the chute we use for getting bales up there to get him up there," Joran said, ignoring the muffled screams of protest from Rich at the thought of being dragged up a ramp by a chain, like a bale of hay.

"Good idea, and the farmhands will find him when they come for the morning chores."

"Grab his shoulders; we can carry him over there."

"Well, that is unless they get hay from the other barn. Then he might be there a few days," Sladvick thought aloud. This brought new muffled screams from Rich and some tossing and attempts to kick Joran. With tied ankles, though, the attempts were pretty pathetic. "Now, now, that isn't nice. Keep that up, and we might stash you somewhere else. The chimney over my forge might work too; I think you would fit nicely there." The kicking and screaming stopped immediately. They were replaced with a wild-eyed look of horror.

While they were dealing with the smelly little bundle of joy called Rich, the storyteller hurried over to the kitchen to deal with a much better-smelling bundle of fun. Elsa.

"What did that smelly bag of rags have to say for himself?" she snapped before the man was even through the door.

"Well, hello to you too."

"Don't get smart with me. What did he say?"

"He was leaving when we caught up to him. We stopped him."

"By stopped him, you…" she asked, more worried now than demanding.

"We didn't kill him, if that is what you are asking. The fool pulled a sword—a rather cheap one at that. Sladvick had wandered by and decided to help us. Rich should only have some bruises. Sladvick played a nice game of whack an idiot with him. I think Sladvick was more offended by the low quality of the sword than by anything else." He chuckled. About this time, Joran walked into the kitchen and caught the last bit.

"And where were you during this?" Elsa asked, her tone a little too polite for Joran's comfort.

"I was with him," he answered, gesturing at the storyteller, hoping the questions would end there.

"Doing what with him?"

"Well, while that knife of his isn't what I would choose to go against a sword with, he was more than willing to defend me with it as best he could," the old man piped in. "No. Rick drew a sword, but Sladvick chanced to be nearby and knocked the belligerence out of Rick. The intervention was timely. Your cub here was about to do battle. That little dagger of his is a pretty thing but not much of a match for a sword. At least not without some training."

Damn. He couldn't have left that part out? Joran thought miserably.

"You did what?" she roared at Joran, who was quickly stepping into the shadows, behind the storyteller. The storyteller thought it funny that while Joran was more than willing to go up against a sword armed with a knife, he was more than willing to hide from Elsa.

"Now Elsa, the boy was only protecting me, and we really don't have time for this. Rick had a pouch full of black mine gold, the pretty colored nuggets. That means the Vibaions are watching this place. We had hoped to leave quietly with no one noticing right away. That isn't going to happen now. Elsa, go pack what you and Joran will need for the road. Pack light; we will have to travel fast. Sooner or later someone will find Rick, and then he will tell whomever he is working for what happened. I don't want them knowing what way we went."

Just as Elsa was about to leave and go pack, Sladvick walked in. He stopped in the middle of the kitchen, where he could look each of them in the eye. "For a simple storyteller and cook, you sure have attracted some mean enemies. Just who are you?"

"Umm, Sladvick, that would be a very good — and very long — story. Best saved for another time. I thank you for your help, and if you could,

keep Rick tied up here for a day or two longer. Maybe not literally, just don't let him leave the farm for a day or two. Give us a head start. Yes?"

Sladvick stood in the middle of the kitchen. First he looked at them. Then he looked down at his feet and seemed lost in thought for a minute or two. Then, drawing himself up, he turned to the storyteller. "I won't be able to do that for you," he said quietly, then continued in the same firm yet quiet tone. "I dunno what you all have gotten into, and I can't say I really care much. I just know it isn't the safest of things to be involved with, so I will be coming with you." He turned to Elsa. "Just to be sure you are safe, at least until you are a good long way from here." Elsa looked at him as though he had hit her between the eyes with an ax handle. Then she giggled. Then she laughed. "Sladvick, how can you protect us? You're no soldier."
Now that is just rude, mean, and ungrateful, Joran though, watching his friend's face. *He is a good man, strong and brave. Damn it, he took on a man with a sword using nothing more than a piece of wood. And won.*
Sladvick's face showed nothing except resolve. Even in the face of Elsa laughing at him, he showed no shame or humiliation. "I will go along as an escort nonetheless," he said calmly. "I won't allow you to leave without me."

"You? Won't allow?" she snapped at him. She stopped laughing abruptly.

"Sounds good to me; it would be nice to have you along," the storyteller cut in. A mischievous twinkle was in his eye.

Elsa turned on him in surprise. "You are out of your mind."

"Nope. I am not. He is a strong, practical, intelligent, and brave man. If nothing else, he can keep the horses shod along the way and give Joran and I someone to talk to. Elsa, your mouth has grown somewhat arrogant and snappish over the years, and miles of that will get old quickly," he shot back.

"You truly have drunk one too many steins of beer," she snapped at him.

"You see, that is a good example of what I was talking about. Now stop proving me right and go pack. Shoo! Time is running away from us here, and we should be the ones running."

"Thank you. I should pack as well; I didn't plan on going on a trip today. Kind of caught me unprepared," Sladvick said lightly as he walked back to into the night.

Joran was left standing off to the back of the kitchen; his mind wasn't keeping up too well with what was going on around him.

"Joran, doing OK? Scared?" the storyteller asked him gently. He seemed to be able to see that Joran's mind was running in ten different directions all at once.

"Um. None of it is really making any sense to me right now," he replied, hesitant.

"It is OK. Over the years to come, we will help you understand. I think it best that you don't totally understand what is going on though. OK? Try to understand a few big things though. I admit, there is some danger in what we are doing. Not extreme, like riding poorly made carts down hills near water." He winked at Joran, then continued, "There is some danger though. When thinking of that, remember that Elsa, Sladvick, and I are here to protect and guide you. For now, that is all you really need to understand or know. Does that help?" Seeing that Joran was calmer after processing that, the storyteller picked up a leather bag from a peg near the cupboard. "Come help me pack for the road."

Joran picked up a candle and led the way to the cellar, where the two proceeded to fill the bag with loaves of heavy grain bread, blocks of deep-orange cheese, bundles of seasoned and dried meats. Joran snatched up a bundle of Elsa's dense molasses cookies and slipped them in the bag as well. The storyteller disappeared around the corner to where Joran knew the special wines were stored. Reappearing, he had several bottles of the special sweet wine Elsa only used on special occasions. He put these in the bag as well, and then they slipped back upstairs and into the windy, dark courtyard.

They met at the main gates. Sladvick had unlatched them, and once they all had arrived, he slowly pushed them open. Even on the well-oiled hinges, there was a slight squeak, something Joran had never noticed during the day. As he went past the gate and into the night, the wind clawing at his cloak, Joran had a moment of deep sadness. Looking at the walls, he realized this was the only home he had ever known. This settled on him heavily. Then he realized he wouldn't get to trade Geeta for her soft kisses, or more, anymore. This sank into his heart like a sharp poker from the fire. It was too late now though. He was leaving. He was giving up everything that was familiar and special to him.

Wrapping his cloak tightly around himself and shouldering his pack to a more comfortable position, he followed Elsa and Sladvick up the road. Even with his friends, whom he realized he considered his family, he felt alone and cold. Scared. He admitted the last after a few steps. Once they reached the top of the rise, he stopped and looked back at VonRich's farm. In the distance, he could barely make out the walls around the courtyard. Turning with great sadness, he hurried after the others, his pack bouncing on his shoulders. The road before him almost seemed a dull silver in the weak moonlight. The fields and woods around it looked almost black..

Chapter Six

After who knows how many miles—Joran
certainly didn't know—he started nodding as he
walked. His legs burned with each step, and his
eyes watered from his constant yawning. The
tears were warm on his cheeks as they ran down
to soak into his scarf. His toes and knees hurt
from tripping over rocks, and sometimes
themselves, in the dark. All he wanted now was
sleep. Just to lie down where he was right now,
in the middle of the road, was fine by him at this
point. Even his hands felt tired, and they were
just hanging off his arms.
Their little party came to the crest of another hill.
*What is it with all these hills? Where did they all
come from?* Joran thought, having never noticed
there were so many before. Now there seemed
to be nothing but hills. Long rolling hills. Joran
decided he didn't like hills. At the top of this
one, they stopped, though, which to Joran came
as a nice surprise. Even with his exhaustion he
noticed the storyteller looking for something.
Then he set off, leaving the road behind and
heading into the dark woods.
*OK, the hills weren't that bad. I would rather do the
hills than wander off into a dark forest that could
have bandits hiding in it,* Joran thought, some of
the exhaustion leaving him. He wasn't happy
with what was replacing it though. Fear.
"Should we be leaving the road like this?
Sladvick asked, seeming to have read Joran's
mind.

"Yes, it is dark and no one should see us going this way" came the confident reply. "I doubt we will run into any thieves here either, and if the gold found in Rick's pouch had him spying on Elsa, I am sure there is more gold that would loosen someone's lips who might see us pass here in the daytime."

With that, they followed the old man into the field, toward the dark wood on the other side of it.

Joran had been thinking the road was difficult, what with its loose rocks and never-ending hills. The field, though, taught him that things can usually get worse. Here there was all manner of traps and things to fall over or into. The dirt itself seemed to be upset with him walking on it at this hour and kept trying to suck his boots off his feet. Add to it the rocks, rabbit, and gopher holes, and walking without falling all over the place like a drunk cow seemed an impossible dream.

After about a mile, Joran looked behind himself, thinking they had walked halfway across the kingdom. He wasn't impressed that it looked like they had traveled at most a mile from the road. He then looked forward and was dismayed to see a wall of black trees in front of him. Yep, things could get worse. If they could, they usually did.

"Just how do you propose we get through that and not get lost?" he asked between gulps of air while pulling his boots on once again.

The storyteller barely slowed down while answering Joran. "There is a game trail that runs through it. It isn't very far through to the other side. Just watch where you step; it is very dark under the trees. Just follow me, and things will be OK."

"How about I follow you for a bit, Joran?" Sladvick offered. "Your eyes are better, and I can just follow you down the trail." While Sladvick was smiling when he said this, Joran wasn't all that sure the big blacksmith was comfortable with this either. While Joran was happy for his friends' company, he wasn't sure if going down the trail would mean walking or falling down it. The field had been difficult enough.

Joran quickly found something good about being in the dark woods. It felt warmer; very little wind cut through the trees. Still, it was very dark, and Joran began to wonder if the old man really was following a path or just wandering through the woods blindly. This little seed of doubt quickly took root in Joran's fertile and sometimes overactive imagination and blossomed into a whole range of thoughts. While some were rather imaginative, none of them were good.

So when a deep gravelly voice came from the darkness, Joran's mind made the leap to hungry and angry giant. This brought out the fight-or-flight option buried deep in every man. Joran's courage decided to take a nap at this point; it had been working overtime all night, after all, leaving him the second option. Flight. Any thought of halting, like the voice had said to do, left Joran's exhausted mind when his courage rolled up in a ball and went to sleep. He turned and sprinted into the woods. During their walk in the woods, he had noticed that if you looked up, the trees blocked out the stars in such a way that you could avoid the trees simply by walking around the dark spots in the sky. It was a good theory, and one he intended to use to flee the giant. Like most theories, though, there were some things that hadn't been thought through all the way. If they were considered at all. One of these things came to play around the fourth step in his flight. While Joran wasn't the fastest sprinter on the farm, in this case he was properly motived, and his first two steps had brought him to a full-out sprint. The next two strides carried him to one of those things that aren't always thought of when a theory comes about. In this case it was in the form of a tree stump. One that was about the right height to slam into things that should never be slammed with a hard piece of wood. Ever. Joran, who was looking up and following the stars in the sky, was suddenly looking down and seeing a different kind of stars. The stump promptly showed a hole in his theory and put any future generations of little Jorans in jeopardy. It also brought him to a dead stop. Or a dead halt, depending on how you looked at it. He had stopped moving forward anyway.

Joran fell face first into the cold dead leaves, where insult was promptly added to his injury. A fairly hard rock kissed his forehead, taking his mind off the pain somewhat farther south on his body. In fact, it took his mind off pretty much anything as it knocked him pretty much senseless. No more stars even.

"Joran!" Elsa screamed. Don't ru — never mind," she muttered as she saw his flight end badly. Joran moaned and slowly rolled over, feeling the blood run down his face and the pain radiating out from where he had become intimate with the stump. He wiped the blood from his eyes and tried to clear his vision. For some reason, he thought shaking his head as he carefully rolled onto his knees would be a good idea. He regretted it as soon as he had started it. He couldn't decide what hurt more after that. About then he felt hands grabbing him. Not being able to see whose they were or what they were attached to, his imagination kicked in and added to his fear. They could be the giant's hands after all. All thoughts of headaches and hurt family jewels were forgotten. Escape at all costs became the overriding goal, and he clawed for his knife.

"Now, now, that is just uncivilized, little chipmunk." He felt his knife disappearing from its sheath. For some reason that made something snap in his exhausted and overtaxed brain. "Don't kill me...Don't kill me..." Joran started saying in a dead voice, almost a mantra to himself.

This caused him to turn from panic to confusion when he heard the voice attached to the strong hand holding him chuckle in reply. "Let's help you up—looks like you took a solid shot to the soft bits there." Once Joran was on his feet, more or less, he was helped—mostly dragged—back over to where Elsa was standing with a somewhat amused look.

Once he was back with Elsa and the others, they started moving among the trees, and Joran managed to clear his mind enough to think and see straight. His head had been bandaged, and the bleeding had slowed to almost nothing. He understood that he should be thinking of a way to escape. Sadly, his brain stopped there. He couldn't figure out a way to accomplish escape; walking so he didn't feel too much pain was taking up most of his brain's function at that point.

Through the trees, he saw a fire. When they got closer, he could see wagons around the fire and other people, who were just shadows at first. Once he, the storyteller, Elsa, and Sladvick came into the firelight, he could see the other man with them clearly. The one who caught and kept his attention, though, was a man whom Joran initially thought was a result of the rock to his head. The man wasn't big. He was massive. *His father must have been a giant.* This was the only thought Joran's addled brain could compose as he stared at the man sitting on the log. His sun-bleached blond hair was long and held in a thick leather thong at the base of his neck. Over his broad and heavily muscled chest was a well-worn, matte-black boiled-leather shirt with small interlocking squares of sand-washed metal. Rather than reflect the firelight, as most metal would, this seemed to soak up the light. The boiled leather and metal shirt went to midthigh. At the small giant's (as Joran had begun thinking of him) waist was an untooled, double-thick black leather belt. The buckle looked to have been made from the same metal as the squares on his shirt. At one side hung what Joran thought of as a two-handed sword; to the man, though, it was probably a hand, a hand and a half at best. Opposite the massive sword was an ax. The head was made of a gracefully curving blade; the butt of the ax was a blunt hammer head. This was mounted on a stout piece of wood about two thirds the length of a normal ax. The man's legs looked like stacked boulders wrapped in light-brown suede leather. Darker brown cotton cloth crisscrossed his legs, holding the suede together. His feet bore calf-high boots, the laces thick pieces of braided chord.

Joran just stared, rooted to the spot where he stood. The man who had caught up to him after probably the shortest foot chase in history was forgotten. The raspy voice of the little man holding his arm brought him back to Joran's mind.

"What a disappointing escape attempt that was," the man said, gently pushing Joran over toward Elsa and the others. "Was looking forward to a nice run in the woods this evening."

Elsa turned on Joran. "Why did you do that?" Without waiting for an answer or even giving him a chance to think of an answer, she stormed on. "You are not to even think of doing that again. Understand?" The last word might have sounded like a question, but Joran knew better than to even think of answering it.

Thankfully Sladvick slipped in before Joran could think of anything to say.

"Come on now, Elsa. Right now, his feet and legs are his best option. He hasn't learned to fight proper, nor has he grown enough to know how to stand and fight. Best for him to run at this point." He then chuckled. "Better yet for him to look where he is running, or he won't be running all that far."

While Joran turned red from embarrassment, he looked about the campfire and wagons. An unsettling thought formed in his mind. "Um, Sladvick? Did we just become captives of thieves?"

The storyteller burst out a short laugh. "Thieves?" He laughed harder. "I think that rock to your head knocked something loose. These are friends of ours. Not thieves." He seemed to forget that Joran had never seen these people before. How was he to know they were friends?

Joran looked around again, taking a second look at the mass of boulders in clothes across from him and the small man with the wicked-looking

sword who had dragged him into the camp. "Uh-huh." His voice didn't agree with the words.

The half giant started to laugh, a deep belly laugh, full of life and happiness. The laugh carried all the way to his dark-blue eyes, making them light up. "Mouse, your catch of the night isn't all that trusting."

Joran's suspicions showed clearly on his face as he eyed the two men. "I think you might have hit your heads too…"

The man who had brought them to the small camp didn't share his companion's laughter. Seeking to smooth things over and put Joran at ease, the storyteller stood and walked over to Joran and Mouse. "Joran, you've met Mouse," he said, gesturing toward the man next to Joran. "And this is Gunnarr," he said, turning to the half giant.

The half giant smiled and held his hand out toward Elsa. "Mouse, I would like to introduce you to m'lady Elsa. M'lady Elsa, this is Mouse." Mouse burst out laughing, surprising Joran, who took a step back from the strange little man. "M'lady Elsa?" He bent over laughing. "M'lady?"

Elsa squared her shoulders and turned her head up. "Yes. I am called that," she sniffed.

Mouse straightened up, wiped the tears from his eyes, and caught his breath. "Well, then, guess I should address you as such, m'lady," he said, trying to keep a straight face. He failed for the most part.

Once Mouse got himself over his laughing fit, Joran turned his attention back to Gunnarr. He had never seen a man from the kingdom of Dagnour. He was convinced this man was from the northern kingdom; only the men from the north were known to grow so large. All the stories, ones that he had thought nothing more than myth, came flooding back. Their reputation of being fierce warriors kept coming back to him. The callouses on the man's hands and the well-worn, sweat-stained handles of his weapons seemed to prove that.

Not to be left out, Mouse drew himself up to his toes, placed his hands behind his arched back, and affected a noble's airy voice. "Well, m'lady Elsa, I am Mouse. A simple and meager name, yes. It fits this humble jester though. I juggle and perform great physical feats." He dropped back to his heels with a bow.

"Would those physical feats refer to your spying and thieving?" Gunnarr chuckled as he slapped his knee with a massive hand.

"Well, no one is perfect now, are they?" Mouse chuckled. "Gotta have some not-so-good habits, no?"

Stepping back so all could see Sladvick, the storyteller continued his introductions. "This fine brave man is called Sladvick. He decided to join us on this trip." Sladvick smiled and raised his hand in a small wave to those around the fire.

"And I am called Mr. Hound," the storyteller said, taking a deep bow.

Mouse chuckled. "Mr. Hound? Such a friendly name."

"Oh, I am quite fond of it; the boy there gave it to me."

"Mr. Hound it is then," Mouse said, moving to the fire, pulling a knife from under his light-gray jacket and using it to lift the soot-stained iron pot off a rock in the middle of a pile of glowing coals. Setting it on the ground, he took the plates that Gunnarr handed him and started to pour stew into each plate. Handing them around, he said, "Eat. It has been a long day. There is bread in the back of that wagon." He pointed with his chin at one of the wagons around the fire.

Sitting on a log with his plate and a chunk of bread, Joran looked around the group. He was still uncomfortable with the new men, even though they clearly were friends of Elsa and the storyteller. Even Sladvick seemed to be relaxed around the oddly matched pair. Hearing that Elsa and the storyteller had used different names in the past did nothing to help Joran relax. Just the opposite: it shook his view of the world, and he felt a bit of his childhood disappear into the mists of time. This saddened him.

Turning his attention to the food, he found the stew of mystery meat, thick gravy, and badly cut-up vegetables delicious. Suddenly his stomach felt like an empty pit. The heavy thick-crusted bread soaked up the richly seasoned gravy.

After eating two plates and a good portion of a loaf of bread, Joran slid off the log he had been sitting on and rested his head against it. The food not only made his stomach feel better, it seemed to help his head hurt less as well. He was half-awake as he listened to Elsa and the storyteller.

"Well, you got us here. Now where?" Elsa asked the storyteller.

Taking a drink from the chipped beer stein, he swallowed and replied, "Well, I think the plan I came up with is brilliant in its simplicity."

"These oversize wagons have a part to play?" she asked, looking skeptically at the sturdy wagons.
"Yes. They are going to make us invisible." He smiled.

"You now do magic?" she sniffed.

"Well, at this time of year there are roads filled with wagons carrying harvests and goods between villages and cities. There are so many that a few more will be invisible with all the rest. We will go from being a cook and a storyteller to being freighters."

"W-w-w-what?" she stammered.

"Freighters. We move things from point A to point B. With wagons."

"And horses," Mouse piped in.

"I know what a freighter is and how it works. Do you have any idea how slow that is?"

"Well of course. About twelve leagues a day. It adds to the romance of the road and the hardiness of those who travel it."

"It will take us months to get anywhere."

"It is better to move slowly and be invisible than to move quickly and attract attention," he said, clearly finished with explaining this to her.

Elsa looked as though she wanted to reply; Mouse cut her off though. "Where are we headed first?"

"We will head north. I believe our prey is headed to Culuth."

"Fair enough. What will our bills of lading say we are carrying north?" Elsa asked, some sarcasm in her voice.

"Potatoes," Gunnarr said proudly.

"Potatoes?" Elsa asked. The expression on her face said much more.

"Yep. Wagons of potatoes. For those up north to make bread, pancakes, and that great clear spirit that puts fire in your belly and an ache in your head the next day. That's if you drink too much and fall down though," he replied cheerfully.

"We have that part of things taken care of," the storyteller said. He continued while looking at Gunnarr. "Now to look the part."

"And smell it," Mouse tossed in.

"Why are you two looking at me like that?" Gunnarr replied, suspicion in his voice.

"Boiled leather and metal-plate shirts aren't what the civilian freighters wear."

"And they stink."

"I feel naked without them though," he said sadly, looking down at his armor.

"Let us try something else, shall we?" Elsa said as she walked to a wagon that she had noticed a bundle of clothes in. She picked out a different cloak and shirt for him.

Gunnarr looked at the offerings with a hurt look. "I could just wear the cloak over the leather."

"Nope, you can still smell it from five wagons away," Mouse said.

"If I wash it, the leather gets soft and the plates rust. How about a perfumed cloak?" he asked hopefully.

"Nope. We all have to make changes we don't like," Mouse said. "And I don't know where I would get that much perfume."

Muttering under his breath, much of it something that should never be said in front of a lady, Gunnarr removed his leather and metal armor. The cream-colored cotton shirt under it was stained with sweat and rust spots. As he made a move to put the shirt over the stained shirt, Mouse stopped him. "Nuh-uh...Off with that shirt too. It smells as bad as the armor. Better yet, head down to the stream and take a bath before putting on the clean clothes," he said, tossing Gunnarr a block of yellowish soap and a towel. Gunnarr stripped off his shirt as well. Tossing it on top of the armor, he picked up the soap and towel and stomped off to the stream. Joran was stunned at the massive size of the man. Under his armor and shirt was so much muscle, the muscles looked like they had developed muscles.

After a bit, he came back, scrubbed clean. His freshly washed hair was pulled back again and tied in the thong of leather. The skin under his thick mat of hair on his chest was washed a light-pink color. Even the dirt under his nails was gone, as was his grouchy mood.

"Stars, you are a hairy one," Mouse observed from his seat on a log near the fire.

"*Oui*, can't help that." Gunnarr laughed. "Besides, it's cold where I come from. The hair helps keep me warm in the snow months."

"Cold in a lot of places. Looks like your family tree has a polar bear in there somewhere. Are you sure one of your father's from the long past didn't get lonely and decide a bear would make a nice bedmate?" Mouse teased.

"Takes a big man to take a bear like that," Gunnarr said shortly. "Takes a foolish man not to know when his mouth is going to get him into something his body can't handle," he added without a smile and looked at Mouse.

Mouse laughed good-naturedly, but before he could say anything back, the storyteller cut in. "This is all very interesting, discussing family and such; however, there are many reasons to get moving. No?"

"Why, there are. We can discuss this on the road." Mouse hopped up and moved to start harnessing horses and packing up camp. The rest followed suit, and soon the wagons were loaded and the horses were hitched.

"Let us walk the horses until we are out of these trees. Don't want anyone to get caught in the head by the branches," Gunnarr said.

As they started out, the big draft horses seemed almost excited to be on the move. Moving along the trail between the trees, they moved without any urging or encouragement. Once the small party reached the edge of the trees, Joran was sent ahead to poke his head out and see if anyone was about.

"Looks clear — not even a fox wandering around," he whispered when he got back to the group.

"Good, let's go," Elsa said, climbing up on a wagon before anyone could even offer to help.

"Sladvick, come share a wagon with me,"
Gunnarr said, reaching down to help the smith
up. "Mouse has let his mouth run too much of
late. Would be good to talk with a man such as
you."

"Would be happy to," Sladvick said, reaching
up and taking the bigger man's hand. He was
more or less hoisted up, barely touching the
wagon, before he was unceremoniously set on
the seat next to the smiling Gunnarr.

Picking up his staff, Mouse set off on foot,
leading the group toward the road that would
take them north. "Why don't Sladvick and
Gunnarr take the rear to dissuade anyone from
following us?"

"So we shall," Gunnarr replied, angling the
wagon to one side to let the storyteller and Elsa
move to the middle. In front of them, Joran
drove the lead wagon, following Mouse. Joran
was still getting over his short-lived flight
through the woods and was still getting
comfortable with their new companions.

The horse followed Mouse with no direction
from Joran, and the gentle rocking of the wagon
coupled with his lack of sleep over the past few
days and the filling meal he had eaten shortly
before led to his dozing off at the reins. For a
brief time, he listened to the little voice in his
head chastise him for not behaving admirably
back in the woods, where he got a lesson in tree
stumps. He was soon dozing, all thoughts of
trees long gone.

It was a change in the motion of the wagon that woke him a good while later. He slowly raised his head, noticing he now had a stiff neck, and looked around. The rocking of the wagon had ceased because the road had changed. Instead of the uneven dirt road, they were now on a well-fitted cobblestone road leading to a strange village.

Joran looked at the peaked roofs and narrow streets leading off the main road. Even the main road was narrow. He figured two wagons could barely pass each other on it. The oddly built homes near the road all had round doors and windows. *Must take a very skilled craftsman to make glass like that*, he thought in wonder. A white-and-orange cat crept out and eyed the party, then slipped back into the abandoned crate it was sleeping in. Otherwise, no one saw the group pass through the village.

Shortly after leaving the village and the stone road behind, the swaying of the wagon on the uneven dirt road lulled Joran to doze off again.

"There are other ways north. What if they haven't come this way?" Elsa asked quietly. Still, it woke Joran. He had a question of his own, one he figured he should have asked long ago. *What exactly are we after?* Thinking he might get the answer, he kept his head down and didn't ask, just listened to the hushed conversation behind him.

"If we sat around playing the 'what if' game, we would get nowhere" was the storyteller's annoyed response to her.

"I was just asking," Elsa said.

"If they haven't gone this way, then we will go on to the next city. The closer we get to the north, the fewer cities there are to pass through. Sooner or later we will find them." His tone led one to believe he was done discussing it.

Joran heard Elsa take in a short breath and waited for her to make a last remark. She just blew it out between her teeth though.

Shortly after that, the horizon began to change from inky dark to a deep purple, signaling the coming of a new day. The faint sunshine slowly slid across the sky, bringing an end to the windy night of adventure. One that Joran was still coming to understand. He had started off to find something, yet he had no idea what it was. Yet it was so important that in one night, his whole life was turned upside down.

Chapter Seven

After five days on the road, they came to Broonard, situated on the north coast. The first days had been good. Despite the wind and sometimes-biting cold, the weather was dry. The farms and villages they passed were well maintained. If a farmer was out and saw them, he or she always stopped to watch the party pass. Some waved; others just watched. Once they saw the wagons weren't stopping, they would return to their work. The same happened in the villages.

As the sun was starting to set on the first day, Mouse walked up a small hill covered with trees. At the top of the little hill was an opening, well sheltered from the wind. Here they unharnessed the horses, rubbed them down, and hobbled them for the night to graze. Once the horses were attended to, the group sat and ate the last of the food from VonRich's farm, then rolled up in their blankets and cloaks for the night. While the ground was hard, and the night air crisp, Joran let his imagination run about the adventure he was on. It helped him ignore the hard ground and cool air.

They woke the next morning to a fine mist with a faint wind moving through it. It wasn't long, though, until a steady drizzle replaced the mist, and the wind picked up a little. The rain brought out the earthy smell of the potatoes and soaked their cloaks. Mouse had joined Joran on the wagon. This was a lot less exciting than it had been the day before.

The horses, large and well-bred draft horses, had trouble with the slick mud and muck of the rain-soaked road. The wagons sank into the mud, making things even harder. Going up even a slight hill required everyone to get off the wagons and help push. The horses also required more frequent rests. The first day had seen them covering ten leagues; with the rain, they were lucky to cover six.

Elsa let it be known as well that they were traveling slower. Her temper was shorter than ever, and this went straight to her mouth. "I should have insisted we do this differently. This is just stupid," she snapped.

"Well, if you look at anything long enough, it is stupid," the storyteller responded lightly. This just seemed to irritated Elsa more.

"Wagons. What were you thinking? Slow, uncomfortable, uncovered, and smelly. An open carriage would be better. Faster too, with a team of four good horses. Or we could have all just ridden horses. No, wagons. Had to be wagons," she sniffed. Joran wasn't sure if it was from being cold or angry. *Probably both*, he thought, glad he didn't have to sit with her on the middle wagon.

"Well, we could have done that. Along with it would be a long list of people who would remember seeing us pass through. Have you seen any other groups riding horses? Or even with an open carriage? Much less one with four horses? No. People remember what they don't see often. A group of wagons, though, people here see all the time. Just think of how many we have seen so far. Even in the rain we pass them" was the storyteller's calm reply.

"Why do we have to blend in so much?" Joran asked hesitantly. He didn't want to provoke Elsa.

"We are hiding from the Vibaions. Remember? By now Rick has run off and told his master that we have left. Now everyone will be looking for us. If we traveled the way Elsa wants, it would be easy to find us. We don't want that" was the storyteller's patient response.

Joran mulled on this for a bit. He didn't understand why they would want to hide from merchants. Finally, he risked asking, "What is the point of hiding from them?"

After a breath or two, the old man answered him. "You believe they are just businessmen, no?" Joran nodded. "They aren't just merchants and bankers though. Thysions are what they appear: merchants, mostly. A few are craftsmen, true. Most are merchants though. Now the Vibaions, on the other hand, have no real interest in trade. They simply present themselves as such. It finances their movement around the kingdoms and makes moving around that much easier. They can come and go from cities, towns, even small villages without arousing any suspicions or real interest. The truth is, they are more warriors and spies than bankers or merchantmen."

Joran sat there on the wagon seat. His look transitioned from surprise to understanding to sadness, the last from knowing his simple world that he had grown up in had yet another part of it destroyed.
Seeing this, Elsa thought it best to bring him away from such things.

"Joran," she said, more to get his attention than anything.

"Huh?" he asked, pulled from his thoughts. Looking up, he knew that wasn't the best answer he could have come up with.

"Before you drive that cart off into the ditch and get it stuck or broken, which we know you can do," she added, a not-so-subtle reminder of the one he had gone into the water with years ago, "there are sacks that need tending to." She motioned toward the cargo that had shifted after a cart had slid in the mud going down a hill. Rather than risk getting stuck, the party had kept moving. Now, though, the sacks were straining against the ropes and tarps more each time the cart hit a rough patch.

He looked at the load. *That is a lot of sacks to move. Especially while moving.*

"You want me to restack them while we are moving? Shouldn't we stop first?" he whined, hoping his logic would win out.

No such luck.

"Now," Elsa said, her tone cold.

Muttering to himself, he crawled over the seat into the back of the wagon and started restacking the lumpy sacks. He was smart enough to do it with care, not wanting to bring down more of her anger by damaging the load.

Finally, after days on the road, they crested a steep hill and looked down at the city of Broonard. Past the city, on its far border, the great sea could be seen, its waters a dull slate gray this day. To Joran, the city seemed to go forever. He had never seen walls so high, nor as thick. Even from where he was, he could see entire wagons and horse teams disappear into the gate. Compared to the sea, though, it all paled. The wet salty smell had been teasing his nose for hours; now, though, it was full and strong. He sucked in a deep lungful of the sweet smell. He held it, then slowly let it out. His face had a huge smile on it.

Elsa sniffed, "Took us long enough."

Mouse, who had been driving the lead wagon for the past few miles, drew it to a stop. Pulling the hood of his cloak up a little more, he stepped down into the mud and carefully walked back to the second wagon. He looked up at the storyteller. "Stop here for the night? Or press on to the city?" he asked, wiping a few drops of rain from his face.

Before anyone could say anything, Elsa cut in. "I am *not* sleeping another night in these wagons, in this rain, when there is a city filled with rooming houses within sight."

"Well, she is right. No one who had been on the road long would stay here. They would search out a warm bath, room, and an ale room," the storyteller said.

"Should have known that ale rooms are all you could think of," Elsa quipped.

His question answered, Mouse returned to the lead wagon and carefully drove the team down the slippery hill. Once he was down, and away from the base of the hill, the next wagon came down. Then the third.

To Joran, no stretch of road this far into their journey had seemed to take so long to travel. It seemed at times the Gods were playing with him, stretching out the road and making the city and ocean seem to get no closer.

Finally, they approached the city gates. Several gate guards came out, stopping them just before they reached the bridge to the gates. They seemed reluctant to leave the warm and dry guard shack. Pulling their stained and worn cloaks around them, they kept their rust-spotted helms low on their heads.

"Stop there," the older of the guards said. "Why do you come to Broonard?"

To Joran, this was a stupid question. There were three wagons filled with sacks. What did these guards think? That they had filled their wagons up, tied them down, and drove all this way in the rain for fun? Or that they were there to buy more sacks to add to the already full carts? Dumb question. Idiots.

Joran's thoughts were just about to come to his lips when Mouse spoke up. "Welcome. We are from south of here, a small town of no importance or notable name. We come to sell our potatoes," he said lightly, a smile on his face.

Joran was smart enough to realize his thoughts were best left at that. Instead he played along with Mouse and smiled.

"I see. We will have to search your loads, which will take time," the other guard said.

"In this weather?" Mouse said, turning his face to the heavens and looking at the rain coming down. "Surely the time would be better spent in the company of friends with good food and strong ale in a warm tavern, no?"

"Food and good ale don't come cheap," the older guard mentioned, his tone quiet yet friendly.

"Ah, this is true. You are wise," Mouse said, discreetly reaching into his cloak. "I hope your fortunes turn soon, good man," he said as he brought his hand out and shook the guard's hand.

"I am sure they will, and you are right. In this weather, time is better spent doing more enjoyable things," he said, pocketing the coins Mouse had slipped him.

"Thank you. I hope you and your fellow guardsmen find a good evening," Mouse said as he drove the wagon onto the bridge. The others followed him, nodding or wishing the guards a good day. The guards returned to their guard shack.

Joran's eyes were large as they went through the gate into the city. While Broonard looked splendid and exciting from the hilltop, it was less so up close. He noticed the clustering of the buildings with no real room for moving between them, other than the odd alley here and there. The streets that ran between the high buildings were dirty and littered with refuse. The cobblestones were often covered in mud. Or what he hoped was mud. His nose told him it might be something else. As they drew toward the ocean, the sweet salty smell got stronger, adding dead fish and tar to the smell. Joran's enchantment with the city was beginning to fade. It faded even more when he noticed how unhappy all the people around them looked. He had yet to see anyone really smile. Even the guard at the gate had only smiled with his mouth, and that was only after getting coin from Mouse.

"These people look unhappy. Why?" he asked Mouse.

"Oh, they have a very demanding and unforgiving God" was his reply.

Joran thought for a bit. "Arrah?" he asked.
"Nope," Mouse replied in an amused tone.
"Who then?"
"Not a who, a what. Money," Mouse said.
"Money?" Joran was confused. He had seen
maybe a handful of coin in his whole life, but
he'd never had a need for it. The farm was
almost entirely self-sufficient. They grew, built,
made, or raised almost anything they needed.
"Yes. Arrah himself would be a better God than
money."
"Hush," the storyteller piped up from behind
them.
"Well, it's true, no?" Mouse said lightly.
"Joran, don't listen to everything he says; these
people are just worried about making it through
today and getting everything done that they
planned to get done. That is all."
After looking around a while longer, and not
seeing one smiling face or even a person really
greeting anyone, Joran decided he didn't like the
city much. "This isn't such a great place. Can we
go back to the farm?" he asked earnestly. "I
don't think I'd like to live here. It seems like a
bleak, unfriendly kind of place." He sighed.
"Sometimes I wish we were all back at
VonRich's farm."
"VonRich's is a good place to live; no argument
there," the old man agreed.

They continued in silence until they came to an inn. Mouse stopped the lead cart outside its gate to the stables. The place was close to the water; the smell of the sea was strong here, seeming to have penetrated everything from the clothes people wore to the metal bands on the cart's wheels. The reason Mouse had picked it became clear when they looked through the gate. There were not only sturdy, dry, and clean stables in the back of the rooming house, there were buildings for the wagons.

Mouse hopped down, clearly happy that they weren't sleeping in the rain again. He disappeared into the main building. After a few minutes, he came out and crawled back up into the wagon. Driving it back toward the stables and wagon buildings, he said to the rest, "It is clean and warm. I didn't see any rats in the kitchen or any bugs in the ale either. The price is fair, and the owner keeps guards on the wagons and horses."

"I will decide if it is clean," Elsa said as they climbed down from the wagons. Once she was down from the wagon, she disappeared into the inn, leaving the rest to unhitch and rub down the horses and secure the wagons and their load. It was almost dark when they had finished storing everything and Elsa finally emerged from her inspection of the inn. Her inspection had taken a great deal more time than Mouse's had. *What is she so nitpicky picking about? She spent the week almost sleeping in the rain on the side of a road*, Joran thought. *Now she wants to get all worried about what we are sleeping on?*

"I say it is passable, at best," she said, her tone suggesting that she had found dead crows filling the beds or something.

"Would you rather we go back to the road?" the storyteller asked, his tone sarcastic. "It's not like we are asking you to move in for the next twenty years. Just a couple of days."

Elsa glared at him. "There will be hot water and baths waiting for us in the bathhouse on the other side. We all could use a good washing. They will clean our clothes as well while we bathe." With that, she walked off back into the inn.

Once they were done bathing and in clean, dry clothes, they headed to the main room to eat. While the food was far from what they were used to on VonRich's farm—even the newest kitchen girl could do better—the food was a welcome change to all the potatoes and rabbits they had eaten while traveling there. Joran for one wasn't sure he could stomach another potato. Maybe a rabbit if it was in stew. He ate his fill and then some of the roasted beef, fresh black bread, and honey stewed apples with thick cream for dessert.

Once they were all full and happy, the men stood and eyed the bar across the room. Elsa stuck her nose in the air and sniffed, "Don't get so drunk you can't crawl up the stairs on your own. The boy and I will be going up to turn in." Joran cringed a little when he heard her refer to him as "the boy." *I could be white haired and have a beard to my knees to match, and she would probably still call me that. Here I am, sixteen summers and almost a man. Could she at least call me by my name instead?* he wondered bitterly.

"Can't I stay and have just one stein?" he pleaded.

"No" was her short reply. He didn't argue, just looked wistfully at the smiles on the men's faces as they made their way to the bar. Well, except Sladvick's. He looked a little embarrassed.

Joran awoke the following morning after the first good night's sleep he had had since before they had left the farm. Over breakfast he noticed Mouse and the storyteller were getting ready to leave early, so he made sure to get their cloaks. His hope was to be invited with wherever they were going. No such luck there. Instead he was invited to take care of the horses with Sladvick. So down the back stairs he tromped, feeling a little left out.

Once they had finished feeding and watering the horses, Sladvick picked up a brush and started carefully going over each horse, looking for sores from the harnesses and any other injury the road could have caused.

"Sladvick?" Joran asked. "I have been thinking. This all seems rather strange to me. Especially after the excitement of it has started to wear off. What do you think?"

Without looking up from the leg he was gently probing, he asked, "What is strange? I am not sure what you mean."

Joran hesitated a bit, then answered the blacksmith's question. "Well, you know, all of this," he said, struggling to put his thoughts to words. "Running off from the farm like that. Meeting up with Mouse and his big bear of a friend. Elsa and the storyteller. Especially them. It's like they can't decide if they are running away from something or searching for someone. Maybe searching for something? Then there are the times they talk in hushed tones and think I can't hear them. I don't understand what it is they are talking about; I just know I am not supposed to hear it."

Sladvick took his time standing up, never stopping the brushing of the horse. Much to the horse's pleasure it seemed too. Finally, he looked over his shoulder at Joran. "You are right, Joran, there is a lot about this that doesn't make sense to me. There is a lot that I don't think is as it seems either. It does make me wonder sometimes what is really going on."

"Elsa seems to have changed as well," Joran said. "Have you noticed that? Since we left she has started acting more and more like some highborn woman, and they seem to be OK with it. They almost encourage her to act that way. I don't remember her ever acting like that at the farm."

This time Sladvick didn't hesitate with his response. "You should remember she is a great lady. Always remember that Joran." His tone was almost awestruck. Joran realized that making Sladvick see that Elsa had changed was going to go nowhere. Sladvick still saw her through veiled eyes. To him, she was still Elsa. Beautiful, wonderful, sweet, mild-mannered Elsa.

With that in mind, Joran tried to bring his friend around to how he saw things in a different way. "The storyteller seems different too. Ever since I can remember, he seemed just an old storyteller. Now he seems to have changed into something much different."

"Yes, I see your point there," Sladvick admitted. "I always looked at him as just a world-weary wanderer who had a gift for storytelling. Along with an eclectic wardrobe." He chuckled, then continued. "It seems we have chosen to travel a path of great importance. With some people who are equally important. I think it is best that us not-so-important people let those who are get on with their business without us asking too many questions. Let's just keep our mouths shut and eyes and ears open, no?"

Joran seemed to think that over for a bit while he oiled a harness. Then a thought came to him. "What will you do when this is over? Well, maybe I should ask if this is ever over. Will you go back to VonRich's farm? Back to your forge?" He asked it tentatively, unsure if he was overstepping his bounds with his friend.

Looking at the horse thoughtfully, Sladvick stopped brushing it. That earned him a look from the horse. Standing next to the animal, a faraway look in his eyes, he seemed lost in thought for a long time. Joran waited patiently, his eyes downcast on the harness he was oiling. After a while, Joran didn't think he would get an answer. Then he heard Sladvick's quiet voice. "If Elsa will let me, I think I will stay with her. At least until she sends me away." Joran looked at the strong man for a bit, seeing a side of him he hadn't seen before. Standing to return the harness to its hook, he gently laid his hand on the man's broad shoulder for a moment as he passed. "It's OK, friend. I believe things will go well for you." He then hung the harness, picked up the next one, and started oiling it.

As he was starting on it, he heard his friend sigh softly and say under his breath, "I hope you are right."

In an attempt to bring Sladvick out of his sadness, Joran changed the subject. "Did you ever meet my parents?" he asked.

"Unfortunately, no. You were a baby, barely born, the first time I met you. And boy did you have a pair of lungs on you." He chuckled at the memory. "You were cradled in Elsa's arms and unhappy about something. Or just hungry, like you still are most of the time." He slapped Joran's leg when he said it. There was a smile on his face.

Joran laughed. "What was she like back then?" he asked, glad that Sladvick was in a better mood.

"Honestly? She seemed really mad. Not sure about what. Maybe it was the screaming brat in her arms." He laughed, giving Joran a look. Joran just shook his head while he worked on the harness. Sladvick's tone turned more serious. "VonRich and her spoke for a while in his office, quite a while if memory serves. Then she started in the kitchen. You know how he is, heart bigger than the whole farm. Just can't say no to someone in need who is willing to work hard. Elsa started as just an assistant. You know the job. You have done it yourself. Clean pots, carry food. She also helped cook, though, and no, not the way you 'help' cook."

"Tasting is a good and important part of cooking," Joran shot back with fake and overdramatic indignation.

After a good laugh, Sladvick continued. "She did that for a while. The old head of the kitchen was getting up in years, and her joints were swelling. Shortly after Elsa started, the old cook left. She was having trouble even holding a spoon by then. I think she went south to live with her son and his family. The heat was better for her hands I think. Either way, Elsa stepped into her position and was there ever since."

"Was she much different then? I mean it has been at least fifteen years since she got to the farm."

"Oh, I wouldn't say she has changed a bit since she first walked in the gates," Sladvick said, his voice wistful.

"Oh, come on, Sladvick, everyone ages. Even you," Joran joked.

"No, Elsa is the same as she was the day I first met her."

Joran left it at that for the day.

Later on, Mouse and the storyteller returned. While he was running his fingers through his whiskers, the storyteller curtly said, "Found nothing. After the whole day wandering through the city, we found nothing." Mouse nodded his agreement while nursing a stein of beer.

"Well of course not," Elsa snapped at him.

Both the storyteller and Mouse gave her dirty looks. It was the storyteller who responded first, though, before Mouse could spit something spiteful back at her. "Can't know if you don't look. Best to be sure before assuming anything," he said, shrugging.

About this time the largest member of their little party joined the conversation. Without looking up from the boot he was repairing, he asked, "The two of you found nothing of value at all?" His tone was neutral — curious, if anything. Mouse replied, his tone resigned, "We didn't even get a whiff of anything."

"What did we expect though? They are Vibaions," the storyteller added.

The giant set his boot down, finished with it. Looking out the window, he observed, "The weather is improving. Still, the roads will be a mess tomorrow."

"Can't leave tomorrow anyway," Mouse said.

"Why not?" Elsa asked, somewhat irritated.

"Well," Mouse began, his tone light, "we came in with a bunch of potatoes. I should really sell those before we leave. If we leave with the same load we came in with, someone will notice. Being noticed is bad; that is why we have them in the first place. Remember? So tomorrow I shall go and sell the potatoes. Then we can leave. Maybe with a different cargo this time."

Cutting off Elsa's retort, the storyteller agreed with Mouse. "A day lost isn't good; it's best to be careful though. Besides, the coin will be useful on the road."

"The roads will be dried out some after tomorrow too. I'm willing to bet there will be more people on them; it'll be easier to blend in and disappear," the giant added.

Sladvick had been sitting quietly, something clearly on his mind. "Can you sell that many potatoes in one day?"

Mouse chuckled. "I have no doubt I can sell them. I can probably turn a nice profit on them too."

"I see. Do you think it's wise to pick up another load then? The carts will move faster empty, and we could make up some of the lost time with them moving faster," Sladvick replied.

"Good point. Let us skip the outgoing load. There are plenty of empty carts leaving the city; no one will think twice of them," the storyteller said.

Joran had been fidgeting in the corner. Unable to keep quiet anymore, he blurted out, "May I go with tomorrow? I haven't seen much of the city, just the stables here and the inn."

For some reason, all eyes turned to Elsa. "No harm in letting you go. It would be good for you to see more of the city. Besides, I have errands and things to tend to tomorrow as well," she said.

After a fitful night, Joran was excited about finally seeing the city. He and Mouse set out together to sell the potatoes. Joran was handed a sack full of potatoes out of the back of a cart, and with that, Mouse, who was in high spirits, set off with Joran through the city. "Now Joran," He began as they moved among the people of the city, through the stone streets and alleyways, "When doing business like this, don't walk in looking desperate to sell whatever it is you are selling. That is key. Well, also knowing your market goes a long way too." He chuckled. "Makes sense." Joran panted, not sure why they had to bring a whole sack of the smelly and heavy potatoes. *A half sack, or even just a few, would have been a good enough sample, no?* Mouse continued, seemingly oblivious to Joran's efforts. "I have heard that potatoes are currently selling best either to the distillers or down on the docks. The average price on the docks is higher than at the distillers, so we will start there. Besides, I don't think these are the right kind of potato for spirits. Or are they? Never mind, off to the docks," he said merrily and set off. Joran hurried to keep up with the dirty sack of potatoes on his shoulder.

To slow Mouse down (not just so he didn't have to work so hard; he wanted to see the city as well), Joran asked him the going rate down on the docks.

"Well, per ten weight they were selling for an ice silver."

"Huh?" Joran had never heard of ice silver.

"It is a coin from the northern kingdom. They call it ice silver since the land there is covered in snow and ice most of the year. It is about the same as a silver coin here, slightly heavier, close enough for us though. Usually much better stamped. Pretty coins."

"I see," Joran said, shifting the lumpy sack to a more comfortable position on his shoulder. *Why don't they make these things with a carry strap?* he thought.

"The captain or first mate, depending on the ship, will offer us about a quarter of that. I will ask for three quarters, and the two of us will settle on half an ice silver."

"Why is that? I thought you said they were selling for more." Joran was confused. "And why not just say half an ice silver and be done with it?"

"It is how business is done; the capton must make money on the cargo and still pay his crew, maintain his ship, and such. He won't sell them here; rather he will take them north and sell them."

"Why not just start at half and save the time?" Joran asked again.

"It is customary to haggle; sometimes you get a better deal that way. Besides, it is fun." Mouse smiled, a mischievous look in his eyes.

"How many potatoes do we have?" Joran was trying to do the math in his head as to what they would be paid for the load.

"We have four hundred, ten weight," he said as he watched Joran screw up his face and try to work out what it came to. He decided to help him out. "It comes to two hundred silvers or twenty gold."

"Gold?" Joran's voice was filled with awe. He had only seen gold coins on rare occasions at the farm. Usually just silver or half silver. Copper was the usual coin he saw.

"Yes, gold. I prefer it to silver; it's easier to carry large amounts of money in gold. Silver gets bulky and heavy. On the other hand, gold isn't something that is seen very often, especially in small towns, so silver would be better for blending in."

"How much did we pay for the potatoes?" Joran asked.

"I paid him one hundred even in kingdom silver."

"OK, so the farmer who raised all those potatoes gets one hundred for his work. We get two hundred for hauling them to the city and selling them to whoever buys them, in this case probably a merchant ship, and that ship gets four hundred? That doesn't seem right," Joran said.

"Eh, this is how things work. Now this is important. When we get to the guild house, you keep quiet. Understand? Good. Whomever we meet with will act like we aren't worth their time and will probably ignore us for a while. Once he does acknowledge us, he will probably start complimenting you about something."

"I thought we were going to the docks though. I don't see any docks around here," Joran said, craning his neck around. He could smell the strong sea air; he just couldn't see the docks.

"The docks are busy and crowded, so they come here to do business." Mouse then went back to the subject of the meeting. "The man will assume, wrongly for him, that you are related to me. A son or a younger brother perhaps. The compliments will be meant to soften me up so my price will be lower."

"This just seems like a complicated way to sell and buy things."

"It gets better," Mouse said. The sparkle in his eyes seemed to take on a life of its own. "I will say many things; do not open your mouth, just pay attention to what I say and keep a still face. No surprise or stunned looks. The man will be watching us both very closely in an effort to gain advantage over us."

Joran thought about all of this a moment. "Basically, you are going to lie, and I am to keep quiet and say nothing, like a prop. Correct?"

"Oh, I won't be the only one stretching the truth a little here and there." Mouse chuckled. "The one of us who is better at reading the other will get the upper hand. And the better price."

"This is much too complicated for a load of potatoes."

"It is a game really. I find it very enjoyable, exciting even. This is played all over the world. Pay attention; it is very important you learn to play it well. Those who do become rich; those who don't, don't."

Joran nodded, working to keep his face blank. "Good, let us go find a player...er...buyer," he said as he almost floated up the steps to the door. Joran, on the other hand, climbed the stairs with a steady yet labored step.

Once inside, Joran appreciated the coolness of the building. Once they reached the merchant, Joran was impressed with how well Mouse had predicted what the man in the fine cotton shirt with embossed leather trim would do.

Joran and Mouse stood quietly before the man as he sorted through parchment on his heavy desk with a look of deep concentration on his face. Finally, the man looked up, squinted at them, and motioned them forward.

"What is it you wish to sell?" His voice was hard yet polite.

"Sir, have potatoes to sell," Mouse said humbly. His whole demeanor had changed from what it had been outside. Joran kept a straight face and watched.

"Well now. I would say you are a week late," the man behind the desk said, his face sad. "The ships are overflowing with them as it is. There was a good crop this year. I would lose money if you gave them to me."

"I see. That is fortunate for those captains who sailed early then. I guess I will have to go talk with the Rackians or perhaps the distillers in the city," Mouse said as he shrugged. He turned to Joran. "Come, boy, don't make a mess on the floor with that sack. Let us go and see what we can find elsewhere."

Before Joran could get the sack off the floor, though, the man leaned forward and looked more closely at Mouse. "Just a minute. From your style of dress, you have come from the country, as I did long ago. I remember what it takes to grow crops. As a courtesy for your journey I will take a look at them. Yes?" He was smiling now like they were old friends.

"That would be most gracious of you, fine sir. I know your time is valuable and you are busy; any fool can see that," Mouse said, gesturing to the man's desk. "We should intrude on your time no more. Boy, didn't I tell you to pick that up?" Mouse said as he turned and began to walk away.

"Now, now, let's not be hasty. I have not even seen your load. If it is of fine quality, I may be able to find a willing buyer. Let me see your potatoes."

Joran carried the sack around the table and set it on the floor next to the man, then untied it and stepped back.

For a while, the two men sparred back and forth about what the crop was worth. Joran saw many similarities between the selling of potatoes in the city and the trading of horses or other stock on the farm. Instead of money, though, the farmer would use other goods as trade. He was careful to keep his face blank, though, soaking up everything that was going on.

Suddenly, the man in the fine shirt turned and looked at Joran. His look was thoughtful, as though he had never seen Joran before. "You have a strong and intelligent-looking lad there. He your cousin?"

"No, just a runaway that I took in some time back. I'm trying to educate him in the ways of something other than sleeping and driving a cart. It isn't working as planned though," Mouse replied.

Gee, thanks a lot. I carry that sack all the way here, and you call me mentally slow? Well, the runaway part is sort of right. I did run away from the farm.

"That is kind of you," the man said. His tone made it clear he was disappointed in his attempt at flattery.

Joran caught an odd gesture the man made with his hand, moving his fingers in an odd way. Then Mouse made similar gestures, the man made more, and so on. All the while their hands didn't leave their sides, and no more words were spoken. Joran was lost. Before he had just been confused. Now he was lost and confused. Their dancing fingers made zero sense to him. He knew something important was going on, but he had no idea what. So he just watched. Suddenly Mouse spoke. "Deal?"

"Yes, deal," the man replied. He then wiped the sweat from his brow.

I guess wagging your fingers around for a while is hard labor for him, Joran thought dismissively.

"Enjoyed working with you," Mouse said, extending his hand to the man. "I have been truly educated today. My thanks."

Taking his hand, the man laughed. "I think I should just hand you the keys to my holds rather than go through that again with you."

The men shook hands. Then the man scribbled something on a small piece of parchment, folded it, and sealed it with wax and an impression from his ring. "Tomorrow, please give that to the first mate on my ship. It is in berth six on the docks. He will pay you and have your load transferred to my holds."

Laughing, Mouse took the paper and slipped it into a hidden pouch inside his belt. "You were a good challenge. I thank you."

"You are too modest; rarely have I done business with a man like you. It was a pleasure, if a stressful one."

Smiling, Mouse turned from the man, lightly cuffed Joran on the back of the head, and said, "Come along; you aren't a statue."
Once outside, Joran walked alongside Mouse. "I don't think I totally understand what went on back there," he said.
"Well, the easy response to that is we got the price I wanted," Mouse said happily.
"OK. How did you do that? You two didn't say a word for a while."
"Sure we did. I told you to pay attention."

"All you did was shake your hands at your sides and look at each other. Must have been very difficult for him, since he was sweating so badly at the end."

Mouse chuckled. "We were talking. The hand shaking, as you put it, is really a form of communication. My people created it hundreds of years ago. It allows them to do business in private, even if they are in a busy market. When one gets good at it, they can talk about the horse races from the night before while negotiating prices on silk or spices at the same time, and no one can listen in on them," Mouse said.

"Teach me?" Joran asked, his voice hopeful.

"Oh, I don't know if the slow of mind can learn it. Might take a long time for you to get it," Mouse chided Joran.

"We are heading on a long trip soon, aren't we?" Joran countered.

Faking a mortal defeat, Mouse conceded. "If you insist. It will be difficult, especially with you learning so late in life. For such a long journey, though, it would be nice to have something to make the miles go by faster."

"Thank you. Guess we are going to the rooms now," Joran said.

"No. For us to get into the next city, we will have to pick something up to fill the wagons. Otherwise we will have no reason to enter."

"Huh? The wagons were going to leave empty, I thought."

"They will be."

"Wait. They can't be both full and empty. Unless you mean empty of cargo and full of air."

"Sure they can. We can leave with contracts to pick up items from farms around here. Then we take those loads to the city and sell them. There is someone I know who buys from the farmers around here, usually at the beginning of the planting season. Then, once the crops are harvested, he sends carts to those farms and collects what he bought that spring. He can wait till things are favorable for him and then bring

them in for sale instead of sitting on them and waiting for the markets to turn in his favor."

"If you say so," Joran said, still trying to sort it all out in his head.

Seeing his confusion, Mouse said, "You will get it. This is a lot to take in in such a short time." With Mouse leading, they went to a small building. Inside was an office with a modestly dressed man. He was short and balding, yet he had a look of arrogant disdain for everyone around him. When the two walked in, the balding man was negotiating with a Vibaion. Upon seeing the Vibaion, Mouse tugged gently on the back of Joran's shirt. Stepping in front of Joran, Mouse politely bowed slightly and said, "Pardon me, I did not know you were in a meeting. I can wait outside until you choose to see us."

"We will be negotiating most of this day. Is this business of yours pressing?"

"Not really. I was only looking for a shipment."

"I do not have any," the little man snapped as he turned back to his negotiation with the Vibaion, having barely acknowledged Mouse. Then he stopped and looked back over his shoulder at Mouse. "Wait. You are a dealer of spices and herbs. No? Why would you be looking for common cargo?"

"You are very observant. Sadly, I am a pauper now. The last shipment was destroyed in an avalanche. Probably scattered across the bottom of a gorge now. While this makes for nice-smelling snow, it also makes for an empty coin purse." He shook his head sadly.

With an arrogant tone, the Thysion replied, "Such a sad story."

Mouse toyed with his cloak. "All I have left of my once-great fortune are these carts in sad shape, the horses, and a change of clothes. I am reduced to hauling whatever I can get contracts for."

"Ah, fate slaps us all in the face from time to time," the Thysion said, adding with a chuckle, "although some get slapped harder than others." The Vibaion spoke up, his hard accent softened by his tone of voice. "Never in all my travels did I think I would come across such a famous man. The Gods smile upon me, for I have been enlightened by this meeting." His eyes wandered over Mouse, almost as though he was searching for something in Mouse's clothes. Mouse blushed slightly at the praise, inclining his head slightly. "Your words warm my heart. Thank you, sir."

"I am Ala Maona of Vibaion," the man introduced himself, offering his hand to Mouse in greeting. Turning to the Thysion he continued, "Perhaps our negotiations can wait for a bit, no? It would be good to help this great merchant begin to rebuild his fortunes. I am sure he would do the same for us if fortunes were reversed."

Mouse smiled humbly, lowering his head once more in a small bow. "You are very thoughtful, and I thank you and ask the Gods to smile upon you for many years."

While Mouse was playing humble merchant, Joran was finding it difficult to maintain his slow and dim-witted disguise. His mind was spinning and screaming warnings. Under the Vibaion's scrutiny he couldn't signal Mouse. He was forced to keep a placid face with what he hoped looked like a simpleton's dull look.

"Helping you would be a pleasure," the Thysion said. "The thing is, I have no cargo to ship right now." His voice was sincere. Joran sensed that was the only sincere thing about his response though.

Mouse smiled. "I have contracts for Broonard to Menaminie," he said quickly. "Three full carts of unrefined coal. Elexadra to Tarathon is covered as well, a load of fine silks and felts. Where I am lacking a load is from Menaminie to Elexadra. Those miles worry me; it is a long trip with no load. No load, no gold." His tone was remorseful at the end.

"Menaminie," the Thysion said, his voice thoughtful. He rubbed his chin in concentration. "Perhaps I can help you with that. Pardon me. I will go check my books. I might have something to help you." He quickly left to go to his office.

Ala Maona turned to face Mouse. "It really is such an honor to meet someone such as you. In the east, you are famous. Almost mythical." He chuckled. "Last I heard, there was a bounty worthy of a king on you."

Joran fought hard to keep his face neutral and to keep from stiffening. *Mouse is a fugitive? Great. Just what we need. So much for blending in.*

"Oh, it wasn't worth more than a minor nobleman. It was just some minor miscommunication." Mouse laughed softly. "The kingdom made up some accusations about me. I was simply looking into a spy ring. Took some rather big chances I should not to have. Nothing more."

"Not from what I have heard. If even a small part of the stories are true, you are truly a master of escape. Soldiers of the kingdom searched for you, almost brick by brick of the buildings themselves."

"Ah, true." Mouse laughed good-naturedly. "They were looking under every brick in the buildings. They didn't look under the paving bricks though," he said, winking in a theatrical way at the man.

"Oh, that is rich." He laughed with Mouse. "Does your government still ask for you to help them in such situations?" His tone was casual.

"No, as a simple freight hauler I am not even worth a friendly wave as far as they are concerned. You would think they would at least contract me to haul for them. After all I have done for them, that is the least they can do," Mouse said bitterly. "Unfortunately, since my fortunes have changed, I am no longer useful to them."

"Uh-huh. I understand," Maona said. Everything about him, though, said he didn't buy it. Not one word. What got to Joran was how the Vibaion looked at him. While the look was meant to look uninterested, Joran had a bad feeling that the man recognized him. He didn't know how or why. Yet the feeling of a longtime relationship of some sort was there. Like Joran had been seeing the man all his life, just never speaking to him. Then it hit Joran: the times he had seen the black rider. He had met those eyes probably a dozen times while growing up. A slight twitch crossed the man's face, almost a smile.

At that time, the Thysion came back, a smile on his face. "Do you mind hauling food?"

"Not at all," Mouse replied. "Just hauled some potatoes."

"I have some specially cured beef at a farm near Elexadra. When will you arrive there?"

"Oh, about two weeks."

"That sounds fine. I would be happy to give you the contract to move the meat between the cities. Say eight silvers per wagon load?"

"Whose silver?" Mouse asked quickly.

"Well, Brassel silver, of course," he replied with a wink.

"Now kind sir, you and I are both worldly and experienced. What silver have we always used for our transactions?" Mouse asked, a teasing tone to his voice.

"I should have known better than to try and slip one past you. Very well, we will use the customary Thysion silver." He laughed. "I am truly sorry to hear of your losses; hopefully this will help get you back on the road to recovering those fortunes."

The Vibaion turned to Mouse. "I hope we shall meet again, and perhaps next time your fate will have improved."

"Who knows what the Gods have in store for us?" Mouse said, then left the room quickly with Joran. Once they reached the street and had gone a few blocks away, Mouse muttered, "Cheap son of a donkey." His voice was angry. "If he really meant to help me get back on my feet, he would have given the going rate of ten, not eight."

Ignoring Mouse and his foul mood over the low rate, Joran asked about the Vibaion. "What did you think of the other man?" He was reluctant as usual to talk much about the odd man in black. He felt better now that he had a name and full face to put with the stranger though.

Mouse looked at Joran oddly for a step or two. "He and I are professionals, bumping into each other from time to time. We tend to tell each other little white lies or just fend off inquiries politely, like we did back there. Unless our paths really run against each other, we tend to leave each other alone." He shrugged. "I didn't see anything special about this meeting."

"You, Sir Mouse, are a mysterious man," Joran said.

Mouse put his finger to his lips and let out a quiet "Shhh."

Changing the subject, Joran asked, "What difference does it make where the silver comes from? They are the same size."

"One is from pure silver. The other is from a mix of metals. The pure ones are worth much more. We got the pure ones."

"Makes sense," Joran said, filing the information away along with all the other things he had learned on the trip so far.

The following day, everyone mounted the carts; the horses were harnessed up early that morning. Delivering the potatoes to the agreed-upon destination, they left Broonard and headed south. The empty wagons were bouncing slightly more than they had when they had come into the city.

The weather had cleared up yet was still far from warm and comfortable. The wind carried a dampness that seemed to soak into their bodies, no matter the quality of their cloaks.

Once the city was out of sight, Mouse began Joran's lessons in the sign language of merchants. Moving his agile fingers, repeating the movements several times, he had Joran copy him. "That is 'Hello, how are you?'" Once Joran had it down, Mouse moved on to another one. In this manner, they passed the miles.

Chapter Eight

As the first day ended, the wind finally died off. Having blown the slate-gray clouds out of the sky, a soft fall sun filled the crisp blue sky. The road led the party along the Rhim River, a strong flowing river that started far up the mountains, gaining strength as it splashed its way to the gulf. The country changed as well. Instead of the rather flat lands with slight rolling hills with open fields, the countryside here had a great deal more trees and was much steeper with far fewer fields. Between lessons in the merchant's sign language, Joran took it all in. He also noticed that, despite more hills, they made good time, as the carts were empty. The horses seemed to like the empty carts. Joran wasn't sure he did though. While there wasn't anything for him to carry, the carts did bounce a great deal more over the rocks.

At one point Mouse lightly slapped Joran's fingers. "You shouldn't shout at people."

Joran looked at him, totally confused. He thought he had made the gestures properly. "Shout? I didn't open my mouth." Maybe Mouse was messing with him?

"When you move your hands like that, people take it as shouting or raising your voice. Keep your hands moving in small, fluid gestures," Mouse said, demonstrating with his hands. Joran watched, then said aloud, "I am still trying to get the gestures down, not trying to learn the nuances of speaking softly." His slight frustration came through in his voice.

"True, you are still learning. Now you are mumbling," Mouse said, nodding at Joran's hands. "When you learn new things, it is best to learn them properly from the beginning. If you don't, bad habits become ingrained and difficult to break."
"Now I am mumbling?"
"Think of how you speak. You finish one word before starting in on the next, no? Same with your hands. Finish the first word, then start the next one. Don't start making the next word with one finger while the others are still finishing the first one. Don't worry about how fast you are going; that comes with practice. Practice slowly; become smooth with it. Slow is smooth; smooth is fast. You will get it."
After four days, Joran and Mouse were having about half their conversations in silence, using just their hands. Joran was feeling very proud of himself. He had already started to master a new way of talking in only four days. Or so he thought.
That was until on the evening of the fourth day while they were starting a fire. The storyteller asked Mouse how the lessons in hand talk were going. "Oh, it is going OK. He will learn faster once he is past speaking as a baby." Joran was stunned. So much for mastering it quickly.

Gunnarr let out a deep laugh as he walked over. "It is good to know a special language like that, silent and known to only a few." Holding out a massive paw, he added with a good-natured laugh, "These meat hooks and sword grippers aren't meant for the dainty language of merchants."

Sladvick walked over, an ax over his shoulder. "There will be frost by morning; you can smell it in the air."

Gunnarr sniffed the air. "You're right. We will need more wood than usual tonight." He reached into the cart and retrieved his ax. "I'll help you cut some wood while they get the horses rubbed down and supper started."

"I see some people coming," Elsa said from her perch on a wagon seat.

This brought an end to the conversation about wood and Joran's lessons. After listening for a moment, Gunnarr handed his big ax to Sladvick, who set his smaller wood ax against the cart. Reaching into the back of a cart to get his sword, he said, "Four riders."

"Aye. Sounds like four," the storyteller agreed. "We are far enough from the road though that they shouldn't see us and just keep on going."

Elsa shook her head. "Not necessarily. If they are Jahagi, they won't be using just their eyes." Joran caught the quick movements of the old man's hands and Elsa's quick response. He could only make out a few words. *And Mouse thinks I mumble.*

What he did make out didn't help him much. The storyteller said no to whatever Elsa had signed. "We could...instead." Joran couldn't make out the other movements.

He did understand Elsa's response. He looked at the old man for a moment, clearly thinking over his idea. Then she nodded in agreement.

"All right then, everyone stand still. Don't move," the storyteller ordered them, a look of deep concentration on his face as he faced the road.

To Joran, it seemed like everyone had stopped breathing. He concentrated on the sound of the horse's hooves as they pounded closer and closer to them.

All of a sudden, Joran didn't feel worried or tense. It was as though he had fallen into a half sleep. Or into a dream? He wasn't sure. He just knew he was still standing, yet he wasn't at all worried about the riders coming closer. He seemed to float and yet was still watching the riders thunder past him. Even though he could see they were close, they sounded far off.

He had no idea how long he had been in his dream, only that once he came to his senses, it was silent. The sun had set, leaving them in the dark of the woods. Looking up, he saw wisps of clouds floating across the dark sky.

Elsa drew his attention as she stepped down from the cart, her dress in one hand, the side of the cart in the other. "They weren't just riders. One was a Jahagi. The rest were just Vibaions."

Mouse thought it over a moment, then replied, "In this part of the world there are a lot of Vibaions, all of them on a wide assortment of business."

"True," the storyteller agreed. "It is the Jahagi that worries me. They are rare. Is there a different, more private way to Menaminie?"

"Well of course there is. And I, your well-traveled guide, shall take you there," Mouse said with fake modesty.

"Thank you, oh modest traveler. I think we should move farther into the forest for tonight. Keep people from seeing or smelling our fires," the old storyteller said, tossing things back into the carts.

"Glad we didn't cut any wood yet," Sladvick said, putting the axes in the cart.

Joran was lost in his own thoughts as he went about the evening's chores. While he had been in the dream, as he was thinking of it now, he had gotten a look at the Vibaions. It wasn't a good look, but he still had a feeling one was Ala Maona. He was almost certain of it. He had a feeling that the man on the black horse, dressed in black, would be with him wherever he went in his life. He didn't particularly like that feeling.

In the morning, the party woke to cold noses and a white frost over everything. Sladvick had been right. Joran was glad they had gathered extra wood the night before. Even the horses seemed to be grateful for the warmth from the fire, even with their thick coats. Their breath came out in white plumes of steam as they pulled the carts over little-used cart tracks and frozen dirt back roads. Some tracks were so weed-clogged Joran wondered if they were really tracks at all. All of this made the going slower, yet they felt better being off the main roads.

Six days after the dream experience, as Joran had come to think of it, they reached a little town on the main road about eight miles from Menaminie. The name on the sign said it was Cloudsville. Elsa demanded they stay the night in the old and not very well-maintained inn. She told them, in no uncertain terms, that she was not going to sleep on the ground another night. Joran heard the storyteller mutter under his breath something about how she could sleep standing up like a horse or hanging upside down from a branch instead. Joran kept the laugh to himself.

The food in the poorly lit and rather dirty common room was surprisingly good, much at odds with the surroundings. After their meal, Elsa ordered hot water and a tub to be taken to her room. She was finally going to have a long and hot bath. The men left her to it, instead choosing to enjoy some tankards of beer. Even if it wasn't the best beer.

For his part, Joran made some comment about going to check on the horses and walked outside. While it wasn't really his intention to just check the horses, he did want some time alone. He had come to realize that since leaving the farm, he had not had one moment alone. He had always had one or another adult around. Joran wasn't one to shun company; he had begun to feel somewhat crowded with being around them all the time. He decided to take a break from them tonight. While he did check on the horses, he poked his head in the barn for a second. Yes, they were still there, munching placidly away on their hay and oats. He then started off on a walk through the little town.

He enjoyed his alone time that evening. After wandering the little town from end to end, which took about an hour at a slow walk, he meandered through the streets of tightly fitted stones, enjoying the soft glow of candles in the windows of the buildings he passed. Then it hit him. He was homesick. Very homesick. What were his childhood friends doing back on the farm? He wished he had traded more sweets for kisses. Would he ever get to do that again?

Lost in his thoughts, he was startled when a door opened just down from where he was strolling along. In the light from the open door, he saw a figure who had been hidden in the shadows. At first, he couldn't place the figure, but something vaguely familiar about it pulled at his mind. Then when the figure turned to glare at the unwanted light, he recognized him. Rick.

Joran quietly backed into the shadows, back the way he had just come until he softly bumped into the weathered stones of a wall, keeping an eye on Rick all the while. Rick ducked quickly out of the light; he was clearly trying to hide and not be seen. Once he was mostly in the shadows (the light from the door prevented him from totally hiding), Rick stopped suddenly.

At this point, Joran knew he should quietly slip back to the inn and tell the others what he had seen. That would be the smart thing to do. Joran didn't always do the smart thing though. A certain experience with a stream came to mind reminding him of the not-so-bright things he had done. Pushing it aside, he brought his thoughts back to the present. He was out of sight, concealed in the shadows. This gave him a feeling of being safe. Being curious, he wondered what Rick was up to; he decided to stay and watch instead of going back to the others.

After what Joran thought were hours, although they were only a few minutes, judging by how the stars had moved, Joran saw another figure slinking down the street, trying to keep in the shadows as well. The figure was in a long cloak with a deep hood. With the hood up, there was no use trying to make out a face. Once the figure got closer, Joran noticed it was a man dressed in the usual garb of a man from Brassel. This didn't help his homesickness any. The boots, pants, and tunic really didn't arouse any attention really. The sword under the cloak did though. Joran knew it wasn't illegal for common Brasselians to carry weapons — most, in fact, did carry them — it was just unusual for them to carry anything like a large sword. Shorter ones, sure. This one looked like it would need two hands to wield it though.

The cloaked figure stopped in the shadow with Rick, and they brought their heads close, clearly talking. Joran debated edging closer to try and hear what they were saying. The men didn't talk long enough for him to do anything though. They stopped, and Joran heard some coins being exchanged, and then Rick slipped out of the shadow and headed away from Joran. The other man, though, walked quietly down the street toward Joran.

Maybe I should have gone back to the inn when I had the chance, he thought after realizing there really wasn't anywhere to hide and the man would see him where he was.

Knowing he had limited options, Joran's mind raced through ideas. Hiding was out. Running away would just draw attention to himself and be dangerous. With his luck he would fall on the slippery paving stones. No one familiar with winter snow would run on it. That left the third option. Pulling his cloak around himself, hunching over and bending his knees a little, and keeping his head down to hide his true height, he kicked his foot back against the door, mimicking the sound of it closing, and then purposefully walked down the street toward the cloaked man.

At the sound of the door, the cloaked man stopped and whipped his head up, looking for the source of the noise. As Joran approached, the man reached for his sword and called out, "Who's there?"

Joran kept his head down, pulling the cloak around him more, and answered him, making his voice squeaky and high. "Frosty night, sir. Don't you agree?"

The man relaxed, his hand sliding away from his sword and grunted a reply.

Joran continued past him, keeping his pace steady. He desperately wanted to run at a dead sprint back to the inn.

Suddenly the man called after him, "Hey, you." Joran stopped, turned slightly, keeping his face covered as best as he could. *Lousy time not to have a scarf,* he thought bitterly. "Yes sir?"

"I am looking for an ale house. Is there one near?"

Joran was thankful he had explored the little town before he had run into this man. "Of course. If you keep going down there, the second street on the right has an ale house about halfway down the block. The door is painted bright green. I believe tonight they have fresh bread and stew." Joran had smelled both coming from the ale house as he had walked past.

"Thank you" was the curt reply.

"You're welcome, sir" was Joran's reply, keeping his voice squeaky and high-pitched. The man didn't respond, just kept walking away from Joran.

Joran kept his steady walk until he rounded the next corner, then dropped the act and took off at a run to the inn. Well, more of a fast walk on the hard-packed snow and ice.

By the time he reached the inn, his cheeks were bright red from the cold and his lungs burned from sucking in the crisp night air. He stopped just outside the door, even though he desperately wanted to burst in and spill out what he had seen. He still had enough of his wits about him to know that bursting through the door and then telling everyone in earshot what had happened wouldn't be a good idea.

Instead, he stopped outside the door for a few moments, caught his breath, and then walked inside. His pace showed none of the urgency he felt. He walked over to his friends and leaned over toward them. "Rick is here, in the town," he said, looking at the storyteller.

Mouse looked at the two of them; the question of who Rick was clearly on his face.

The old man replied, quietly and quickly filling the others in on who Rick was, how the farmhand had had way too much gold for an honest farmhand to have, and the confrontation back at the farm.

Gunnarr flexed his great hands and said, "Should have killed him. Buried the body in the fields. No more trouble."

The old man looked at him, somewhat bemused. "This isn't White Bear lands; casual killing here isn't just ignored or accepted." Gunnarr shrugged.

Turning back to Joran, the old man asked if Rick had seen him.

"Rick didn't. I hid when I saw him and watched him meet with another man." Joran filled them in on what had happened. Then he waited for them to think it over.

The storyteller spoke first. Concern was in his voice. "We will be leaving much earlier than we had planned." Then, as an afterthought, he said, "Elsa will be irritated with it." He chuckled.

"She will have to get over it; she is the reason we stopped here in the first place," Mouse said.

Sladvick offered an idea, his voice innocent. "I could gently knock Rick in the head a few times using something soft like a green tree branch. He would lose interest in us quick enough, don't you think?"

Joran grinned. "I like his idea," he said, nodding toward Sladvick.

The storyteller grinned. "I like it too. As much fun as that would be, I think it best we just quietly slip out in the morning. Before people start going about their morning business and see us."

"I am with Joran and Sladvick. Whacking people with sticks is usually more productive when trying to make them lose interest in you than slipping out before breakfast does. Then again, we can't start a fight with everyone we come across who looks suspicious," Gunnarr said.

"That is my point, thank you," the storyteller said.

Mouse got to his feet, stretching his back. "Well, if we aren't going to beat the one we know about the head, I would like to know who the other fellow is. The one with the sword. Easier to know if he is following us."

"Will you please be inconspicuous about it?" the storyteller asked.

"When am I anything but?" Mouse replied with a fake hurt tone. "Where did you send this cloaked man?" Joran gave him directions to the ale house.

With that, Mouse left the common room, pulling his cloak tight about himself.

Gunnarr sat quietly, taking a few thoughtful pulls off his beer stein. Then he looked at the storyteller. "This whole blend-in-and-hide-in-plain-sight plan of yours doesn't seem to be working that well. How about we trade in the slow wagons and draft horses for some fast horses and just gallop off for Elexadra?" he asked.

The storyteller set his empty stein on the table and replied, "For all we know, Rick could be here for something else entirely. He is the sort to get mixed up in almost anything that he thinks would get him easy gold. I doubt that the Vibaions know we are here for certain. If we start just running from any little thing, we will alert them to where we are without a doubt. Personally, I think it best we keep things as they are, quiet. Just slip out of here in the morning and leave Rick to whatever he is up to. Plus, Mouse took contracts on a shipment. One shouldn't go back on what one says he will do. I will go up and let Elsa know that things have changed." With that, he walked off across the smoky room to the stairs up to the rooms. Gunnarr watched him go, muttering something under his breath about not liking it. His face was stormy.

Joran for his part decided to sit quietly with Gunnarr, waiting for Mouse to come back.

In the silence between them, Joran let his mind wander and got lost in his thoughts about how things had changed so much over the short time he had left his home. Back there, things were simple. Happy. Innocent even. Although he had wished things hadn't stayed so innocent between him and Geeta, things in his life had become much more complicated since then. The world outside of the farm had shown him things he had never imagined. Along the way he had lost a lot of his youthful innocence and naïve view of the world. He was now much less trusting. While not going as far as being outright hostile toward some people, he had learned not to just take things as they were presented to him. He had also started listening to his little voice more, coming to trust it more. All of this saddened him. Then the little voice piped in and told him that was childish. He was growing into a man now; it was time he started learning about the world. OK, when did he get to go back to the enjoyable things in the world, like kisses traded for sweets? His little voice was silent on that. Typical.

When the fire in the hearth near them popped, sending sparks up the chimney, Joran was startled and looked up. He saw his friend the storyteller walking down the stairs. Once he had a fresh stein of beer, he joined the two of them, and the three sat quietly waiting for Mouse.

After about a half an hour, and four steins between the two men, Mouse walked back in the common room. Taking off his cloak and standing before the fire to warm his hands, he shared what he had learned. "He is a rather rough man, nothing to speak of really. I think he is just a small-time local hard case."

The storyteller snorted a half laugh. "Good to know Rick is staying with his kind of man. I wonder, though, is he still working for the same people? Hiring lookouts to keep an eye out for us? If so, my guess is they aren't looking for six freighters with wagons. An early start tomorrow should keep them off our trail."

Gunnarr still didn't look happy with this. "I think I will stand guard tonight. Just to be safe." Sladvick agreed and offered to take a shift as well.

"That is a good idea, thank you," the old man said, inclining his head to the two men. "I think if we leave three hours before sunrise we can put a good number of miles between us and anyone looking for us before anyone really wakes up."

Sleep eluded Joran that night. He barely dozed through the rest of the night that he wasn't wide awake. The one time when he did manage to sleep, his dreams wouldn't let him really rest. They brought nightmares of bodiless cloaked men with evil laughs and blazing red swords chasing him through forest and town. He woke in a cold sweat, his chest heaving. When it finally came time to leave, he was sluggish and red-eyed. His head felt like it was filled with wool from lack of sleep.

As Joran tried to clear his tired head, Elsa shuttered the windows and then lit a small candle, keeping it away from the window. Before Joran could get dressed, she brought over a bulky pack Joran had carried up from the carts the night before. Opening it, he saw it was filled with heavier clothes for winter. A tightly knit thick wool sweater with wood buttons down the front. A pair of heavy wool pants followed. Once he had put these on, she handed him a pair of knee-high, oiled leather boots. They had thick soles, and the heavy felt lining went all the way to his knees. In place of laces, which could easily get iced up and have to be thawed out to get open, there were wide cloth straps running all the way from over his toes to the tops of the boots that closed with an odd-looking buckle. Elsa showed him how to work the straps to keep the tops of the boots tight to keep the snow out. Before leaving the room, she handed him a heavy cloak with a fur ruff around the collar and down the front opening. "Don't forget this. It is cold out; put this on."

"Elsa, I am not a child," he said, still half-asleep.

"No, just absent minded today. Or do you suddenly like being cold?" she sniffed.

This brought Joran up short; his sleep-deprived head couldn't think of a way to explain how he felt. He let it go as he listened to the low voices of his friends in the rooms around him. He found it odd that men seemed to talk in low voices, not quiet whispers, whenever they woke before the sun.

There was soft knock at the door, more of a brushing against it really, followed by Mouse's hushed voice. "Elsa. Joran. Everything is ready for us to get on the road."

With that, Elsa and Joran picked up their packs and joined the others, quietly leaving the inn. Outside, the frost reflected the moon's glow, giving anything covered in frost a magical bluish white glow. Joran was too tired to notice though. Sladvick had the horses hitched and waiting behind the inn.

Once they were all together with the wagons, the storyteller quietly asked Mouse to lead them out of the town, using as few main roads as possible. Mouse nodded and walked off, leading them down alleys and through a few back streets as they led the horses to keep things quiet.

Just as they reached the hill outside of town, Gunnarr looked back at the sleepy little place. Expecting to see just dark houses in the moonlight, he was surprised to see the pinprick of candlelight in the window of a house. As quickly as he saw it, it was gone.

"Hey, there is someone awake back there. I just saw a candle in a window," he said.

Mouse looked back but didn't see the light. "Someone just using the outhouse? Or maybe not." They all picked up their pace.

A short time later, once they were out of earshot of the town, the old man helped Elsa onto a cart as the rest followed suit. "We are far enough away now; we can let the horses run some and not worry about anyone hearing us. It will also put some miles between us and the town."

Joran knew running horses on the hard, frozen ground was hard on their legs. He kept quiet, though, the memories of the nightmares coming back to him. He just wanted away from the town.

Mouse took up the reins of the lead cart and lightly slapped them against the horse's rumps. They moved out at a sharp trot. Mouse looked back at Joran, still trying to shake off sleep. "Hang on, sleepyhead." He then turned back forward and slapped the horse's rumps smartly with the reins. This took them to a gallop, hauling the empty cart along behind them over the dirt road. Joran hung on, thinking that this was way too early for all this noise and jostling around. Still, he kept quiet and grabbed the seat. At least he didn't see a stream anywhere near them this time.

Once the sky was turning purple, Mouse let the horses slow back to a walk. Galloping horses with wagons bouncing along behind them would draw plenty of attention. Besides, the horses were steaming from the run and could use a rest, and the town was far behind them now.

Once they had slowed to a steady walk, Mouse handed the reins to Joran and jumped off the still-moving cart. He walked back and checked on the others. After speaking briefly with the others, he jogged back up to the lead cart and hopped in the back, then made his way to the seat beside Joran.

"Up by that big oak tree, turn left," Mouse said, shoving his hands under his cloak. "You drive. I can't feel my hands anymore. Don't work the horses, just let them walk slow now."

Joran did as he was told. The team seemed to share his relief at being able to just walk. Even so, the horses still looked winded and tired. They were draft horses, used to pulling heavy loads for long distances at a steady, slow pace, not running up and down hills for miles at a time.

Nodding toward the road with his scarf-wrapped chin, Mouse said, "There is a small clearing behind a thick stand of pine up ahead about a half mile. Pull off the road there, and we can rest the horses and feed them."

"Don't you think we should keep going? We might be followed."

"Horses are tired and need rest. We could use some food too. This will be a good place to find out if that candle was just someone using the outhouse or if it was something more," Mouse responded, his voice muffled behind the scarf he was doing his best to bury his face in.

As they came up to the trees, Joran drove the cart as far from the road as he could get, making sure the trees concealed them from the road. The others followed. Once the carts were well hidden in the shadows, Mouse hopped off the cart and motioned for Joran to follow him.

"Let's go" was all Mouse said as he set off through the trees.

"Go…where?" Joran asked, more than a little confused. He had already grabbed some straw to rub the horses down with. He was hungry too. He had seen Elsa pulling out some cheese and bread while he climbed off the cart.

"You and I are going to go back and see if anyone is following us."

"Oh."

"We are going to climb up that hill over there and watch the road we just came down, see if anyone else is out at this hour," Mouse said, pointing at a hill a little way away.

Joran followed him, grateful for his new boots and heavy clothes. While Mouse slid among the trees in the dark, making almost no sound, Joran seemed to step on every branch and pile of dry leaves in the forest. After a bit, he figured out the trick to moving quietly. Mouse stopped by a pine tree and watched approvingly as Joran got better at it.

Just before his head would come over the top of the hill, Mouse laid down and slowly crawled up, keeping low to the ground. Once he had reached a place where he could watch the road and not be easily seen, he motioned for Joran to crawl up and join him. Then Mouse settled in and watched the road. He kept his scarf over his nose and mouth, partly for warmth and partly to keep the steam from his breath from being seen. Joran followed his example and pulled the ruff of his cloak over his face, leaving just his eyes uncovered.

They laid side by side for a while, watching the sun come up and saying nothing. Once the sun was up, they saw a cart moving past them, heading toward Cloudsville. After that, nothing. After the sun rose high enough to start warming them through their cloaks, Joran ventured a question. "Can you tell me what is going on?" he asked softly.

"We are watching the road," Mouse replied flatly.

"OK, that we are. I meant what is going on in general. The sneaking around towns, leaving in the middle of the night. Avoiding people. All of it."

"Not sure what you mean; you sort of answered your question yourself," Mouse said, clearly trying to avoid answering it.

"OK, *why* are we doing it?" Joran asked, slightly frustrated. "I have heard some things, pieced others together. Nothing makes sense to me though. Some help here?"

"OK, what have you put together from what you have heard?" Mouse asked, his voice resigned to answering Joran.

"Well, first off, Elsa and the storyteller aren't who they portray themselves as being. Or at least they haven't been entirely honest with who they are."

"No, they haven't."

"Also, someone has something very important that they have either stolen or acquired, and we are trying to get it back because they shouldn't have it."

"Yes."

"Aren't you just a well of flowing knowledge," Joran said, clearly irritated.

"I am answering your questions honestly," Mouse replied.

"OK then. Elsa and the storyteller can…" Joran tried to pick the wording right, then continued. "They can do things most people can't do. Like knowing where this thing is without being able to see it."

"That he can—good for us that he can. Bad for them."

"And Elsa, she put us in that dream, yet we weren't really sleeping. Or I am guessing she was the one who did that? Why did she do that?"

"Well, aren't you the bright boy?" Mouse said, amusement in his voice. He kept his eyes on the road while talking to Joran. Then his voice became serious. "Joran, right now we are dealing with some very dangerous and important times. History has been written over the past thousands of years. Prophecies will come to pass in the coming years. Prophesies that were predicted long ago. History is odd like that. Hundreds or thousands of years will pass with little to nothing really happening. Sure, some dynasties will rise and fall or kings come and go. Yet truly important things will happen only once in a great while. Things that change the world forever." Mouse fell silent and looked at Joran, his face serious and contemplative.

Joran mulled over what he had just heard for a few minutes. He finally looked at Mouse. "After hearing all that, I would like one of those quiet times. Nothing important, just a quiet century or two." His voice showed only a little of the stress he felt.

Mouse stared back at him with a serious face. Then he burst out in a laugh. "Quiet and uneventful? Not me. This is the best time to live. Being able to watch things happen. Important things. Adventurous things. Makes the adrenaline run, which makes the heart race. Makes you feel alive."

Joran looked at the man, not sure what to make of his response. He decided it best not to comment on it and just move on. Instead he asked, "We are chasing something; that much I have figured out. What is it?"

"Oh, we aren't going to pull at that thread yet. I have learned that if you don't know something, you can't spill something. What and whom we are chasing aren't playing nice. Best you know as little as possible." His tone was serious and left no room for argument.

Joran ignored that though. "What, you think I am going to run up to the first Murgo I come across and strike up a conversation centered on what we are chasing?"

"No. I don't think you would purposely tell them. Under…encouragement, though, you might. Or one of the special ones could happen upon you and just pull the information from your mind, no talking involved. You aren't on the farm anymore; this is the real world out here. Remember that," Mouse said.

"No one can just pick things from your mind. That isn't possible," Joran said, his voice skeptical.

"Oh? Why isn't it? What says that things haven't changed or new things have been learned?" This recalled a time not so long ago when Joran had spoken with the storyteller about such things. Maybe Mouse had a point. It was something to think about, if nothing else.

They sat quietly for a while, the sun freshly risen for the new day. Mouse laid there, not taking his eyes off the valley, still hidden in predawn shadows. If one were to look at him, he would look to be a plain man. His clothes were almost boring. From his cloak to his travel-worn leather boots. Nothing bright or ostentatious to draw unwanted attention. An unremarkable man in well-made yet unremarkable clothes. Keeping his eyes on the valley, he said, "Joran, you were brought up as a Brassel. They are a strong, stoic, and very straightforward people. They have little to no patience for foolish thoughts like magic. To a Brassel, if he can't touch it or at least see it, the thing doesn't exist. They won't even begin to entertain that something like a mind reader could exist. In stories, sure. In real life? No. For example, your friend the blacksmith. A solid and loyal man. Well trained in practical things. Even though he wasn't formally trained in leather work, he can probably fix a harness or saddle just as well as he could cure the sick horse they go to. Give him a broken piece of armor, and I bet he can make it better than new. Yet if you asked him about a mage or a fairy in the forest, he would scoff at you and tell you to get back to work."

Joran looked at him. "You are implying I am not a Brassel?"

Mouse turned his head and looked at the boy. "Well, more like I am saying you aren't. No implying about it. I have been around long enough to know a Brassel when I meet one. You lack certain things that a true Brassel would have. Your face alone says you aren't one."

Hearing this pissed Joran off. He wasn't sure why; he just knew it did. "That would imply you know what I am then. If I'm not a Brassel, then what am I?" His voice was cold and challenging.

"Calm down, I meant no insult. Just pointing out some things about you. I don't know what people you come from. Which is odd for me. I have been around long enough to pick out this or that group at a glance. You, though, are a challenge. In time, perhaps it will come to me." He smiled at Joran to reinforce that there was no insult meant.

Joran relaxed and voiced a thought that came to him. "Elsa isn't from Brassel, is she?"

Mouse laughed good-naturedly. "She is most certainly not."

Not sure why he was laughing, probably some inside joke to him, Joran replied, "Well, whatever she is, I am probably the same. After all, she was my mother's sister. Or that is what I have heard anyway. Makes sense then."

"That isn't possible." The reply was dead, no more good humor in it.

"Huh? Why?"

"My cloak is soaked through. We should head back before we get sick lying here in the snow" was his curt reply.

Without a reply, and somewhat confused by Mouse's sudden change in mood, Joran got up and followed Mouse through the woods back to the carts. The rising sun warmed their cloaks as they walked through the crisp fall air.

For the remainder of the day, they stuck to the back roads. At times Mouse led them down roads that didn't look to have been used in months. Not once did he get lost though. The sun was disappearing over the far horizon when they got to the ranch where they were to pick up the load they had contracted for back in the city. Mouse handed the gangly farmer the paper with the seal, and the farmer led them to the goods. Along the way he commented on having to hold them for so long. He could use the space. Mouse sympathized with him, commenting on how some merchants tended to forget that someone else could use the space their goods were taking up.

Changing the subject, Mouse stroked his chin and turned to the farmer. "I know a man that is often through here. His name is Rick. Perhaps you have seen him?" He went on to describe Rick to the farmer.

"Usually in a bad mood at everything from the dirt to the sun?"

"Yes, I would say that describes him well enough. I take it you have seen him?"

"Aye, he has been poking his nose in things around here. The story he gave me and a few others is he is looking for some thieves who took things from the farm he works on. The owner of the farm sent him to find them and return what was stolen. He never said what they supposedly took, just that it was a father, his daughter, and her adopted son. Something like that. Before you ask, it was about a week, maybe ten days ago."

"Shame, I was looking forward to seeing him. It has been a while," Mouse said.

The farmer snorted. "You seem like a reputable man. Why would you want anything to do with someone the likes of Rick?"

"Oh, it isn't that I particularly like him. He made a deal with me a while back, then left without paying. While I am happy enough not to see him again, I do miss the money he owes me sorely." At this, the farmer chuckled and nodded.

"If you wouldn't mind, forget that I mentioned it. I am having enough problems catching him without him knowing I am looking for him around here. I can't imagine how much harder it would be to find him if he knew I was out here looking for him. Would you be so kind as to forget I mentioned him?"

The tall man nodded knowingly. "Why, I don't remember talking about anything distasteful. Just how good your horses look and how pleasurable it has been speaking with a hardworking man such as yourself. As it is late, I would be happy to let you store your carts in the barn and share a meal with my farmhands. They eat in the building over there. Through the door to your left is the bathhouse; to the right is the dining hall. Ask the head man to show you to some spare bunks for the night. Please make yourselves at home."

Smiling humbly, Mouse reached out and shook the man's calloused hand. "Thank you. It has been a while since we have slept on anything besides the soft rocks by the road or eaten anything other than my attempts at cooking."

Landing a friendly slap on Mouse's back, the tall man laughed. "You freight haulers are an adventuring group of men—traveling like the birds and always seeing new lands." His voice sounded slightly jealous yet happy nonetheless.

"Well," Mouse said, shaking his head, "I think it has been glamorized some by storytellers and drunk cart drivers. You forget, birds head to warmer climates in the fall, or they stay and eat poorly in the winter. Much like us."

With that, the farmer laughed and led them to the barn, where they took care of the horses and stored the wagons alongside them. After feeding and watering the horses, they headed to the bathhouse and washed off the dirt of many days on the road, along with the smell of wood fires and horses.

Supper at the farm was simple yet well prepared. Light seasonings lent good flavor to the filling meal. They joined the friendly workers in the dining hall and ate their full of tender beef, grilled vegetables, thick bread, and a dessert of baked peaches in a light flaky crust of honeyed bread in a bowl of rich cream. The meal included a first for Joran. He had never had potatoes mashed with rich cheese before. He found this delicious. Not as delicious as the dessert, though, of which the serving girl insisted he have seconds. Not that she had to insist very hard. Joran's mind wandered to what else he might get from her besides bowls of dessert.

After the meal, the foreman led them to some bunks over the barn. After seeing that they were settled, he smiled and bid them a good night, reminding them to join him for breakfast before leaving in the morning. The bedding was old yet clean, warm, soft, and well maintained. Sleeping inside something other than a cart for the first time in a long time, Joran slept soundly. The familiar feeling of not only being inside at night, but also on a farm deepened his sleep that night.

Waking up well rested, they washed and joined the farm workers for a hearty breakfast that was just as satisfying as the supper the evening before. They stuffed themselves on thick apple pancakes the size of plates and fresh, thick slices of ham. After washing it down with a drink — ice-cold milk in Joran's case or strong black coffee in Mouse's — the two went and loaded the carts with some cheerful help from some farmhands. After a final shake of hands and a warm farewell, they set off with the loaded carts. Shortly after the friendly goodbyes, the day turned cold and windy as they set down the road toward Elexadra. Joran pulled his cloak tighter and flexed his fingers in his gloves as he held the reins. He didn't think either of them was looking forward to the long road to Elexadra. He doubted the horses were either.

Chapter Nine

Over the next three weeks, Joran had lots of time
to think about being uncomfortable. He decided
that those three weeks were the most
uncomfortable three weeks he had ever been
through. The times he was sick with the flu for a
week or two were nice compared to those three
weeks under the dull, overcast, sunless sky. That
wouldn't have been so bad if that were all that
wasn't cooperating. The weather further made
him miserable by adding a cold dampness that
seemed to soak through everything he wore and
chilled him to the bone. While it wasn't exactly
freezing, being cold all the time was far from fun
as they made their way around major towns and
stayed to mostly open and rural country. To add
to his misery, from time to time, just for fun it
seemed, Mother Nature added snow showers,
turning the mountains in the distance into a
black backdrop.

After the first week, Joran decided he was never going to thaw out from this. The cold seemed to have soaked into his bones and had decided to make a home there. No matter how close he got to the small fires his friend Sladvick made each night, the cold just wouldn't leave. There just didn't seem to be enough firewood out here for what Joran considered a proper amount of fires to keep the cold away. Each morning he awoke from the frozen ground, firmly convinced that it was in on the whole scheme to make him permanently cold. The cold from the ground would seep through his blankets, clothes, and into his bones, robbing him of sleep. This did nothing to improve his mood.

One bright star in the whole dull gray trip was his education in the hand language of the merchants. Not only was he learning it, which made him happy, it kept his fingers warmer while he practiced. Not really warm, just not as cold. By the time they reached Elexdra, he could hold simple conversations at a decent pace. Mouse had noticed that while he couldn't always sign a word, Joran could follow a conversation easy enough. He was getting it.

Elexadra was one of those cities that seemed to have been on earth since the earth was created — sort of a first run at making a city and not a good attempt at that. Elexedra was a poorly laid out, almost downright ugly city that didn't seem to have any reason for its haphazard streets and buildings. Looking at a map of the streets, one would wonder if a two-year-old with a pencil had just scribbled something down, and the city planners had followed it for the street layout. While it was an old and ugly city, those things did nothing to stop it from hosting the annual market. What had started as a small local fall market had become a great bazaar, drawing people from all over the lands. Everything from great herds of horses to skilled tradesmen ranging from goldsmiths to cloth makers made the journey every year to attend the bazaar. The fields outside of the city were usually empty most of the year. When the bazaar was going, they were filled with multicolored tents and large pens filled with cattle and horses for sale. The overflow from those pens filled the year-round pens inside the city. Some tribes made an entire year's worth of purchases at the bazaar, filling carts to take back to their homelands. Joran and the group didn't get to see the bazaar at its height though. They arrived at the city just before the end. Only the leftover cattle and horses were in the pens — often little more than nags and tough old beef cattle. The goods the merchants left with were about the same. Poor quality goods. In some cases, poor quality merchants as well. Mouse drove the lead cart through the remains of the bazaar. To Joran, however, it was still a huge event. For a little bit, he forgot his cold and misery and just looked around wide-eyed.

Once they reached the drop-off point for the load, things went smoothly. They had help from some local workers, which Joran appreciated — anything to make getting someplace warm faster. That warm place turned out to be an inn on the outskirts of town. Mouse drove the lead wagon into the forecourt of the inn.

"I have stayed here several times before. It is a well-kept inn — fresh linen and good food," Mouse said. Then he added with a wink, "And better beer." Sladvick chuckled along with Gunnarr.

Elsa, for her part, sniffed, "I hope you aren't overstating this inn. In this city, they tend to have a poor reputation. A well-earned one from what I have heard."

"True, there are poor inns here. As there are in every city. In this city, those taprooms with rooms to let, as they aren't true inns, are on the far side of town. I have…been to them before," Mouse said somewhat tentatively.

"As long as this isn't one of those, we shall be fine."

"Sometimes my other work requires me to stay in less-than-fancy places" was his dead-faced reply.

Joran, for his part, didn't care if it was spotless or even a dirty common room with flat, stale beer as long as it was warm and dry. Once they were inside, he noticed that Mouse had been right. The inn was well kept. Even the other travelers at the inn were of the upper merchant class. The kind of people who knew what soap and water were for. Not just from stories either. After looking around a bit, he noticed something.

"Mouse, I was under the impression that there would be lots of different travelers at the bazaar. I only saw people from Brassel downstairs," he said as he and Mouse hauled their belonging upstairs to their rooms.

"You are right; there are many different people here. They just tend to stay with their own. Travelers from each kingdom take to different parts of this city."

"Why is that? Wouldn't they want to be around one another to help strengthen trade ties?" Joran asked, puzzled.

"Good logic — it just doesn't work out that way in real life here. After doing business all day, sometimes with tempers getting out of hand, they like to keep away from what are often natural enemies. At the end of the business day, they each retire to relax among their own group. It's better for business — dead merchants don't make much money."

"Good point," Joran said, then changed the subject as they started unpacking in the room. "In all of our travels so far, I haven't run into an Efrican."

Mouse made a face as though he had just chewed on a bad lemon. "They are an uncivilized and in my opinion vile group of people. I use that term loosely too. People, not uncivilized. Even dogs and horses can be civilized."

"I thought they were much like the Vibaions," Joran replied, somewhat confused.
"Not sure where you got that idea. They really aren't anything like them," Mouse said, then continued, "The Efricans follow the Serpent God Gaha. For some reason, they got this idea in their heads that it is a good thing to be as serpentlike as possible. They try to take on the characteristics of the serpent. I for one find it rather repulsive myself." Mouse shuddered a little at the thought. "To make things worse, they slayed their neighbors king. The King of Sykavik. Since then, things haven't been all that warm between the two kingdoms," Mouse said. His joke fell flat though.

"Um, I thought they didn't have a king," Joran countered, remembering some of his lessons he had had to sit through back on the farm.
"Well, after the serpent lovers killed the one they had, they haven't had one since," Mouse explained. "A queen named Tunia wanted him dead. It's just the Efricans did it and not her."
"When was that?"
"Oh, I'd say it has been about fourteen hundred years now," Mouse said as though he were commenting on dessert.
"They are still mad about it after that long?" Joran asked.

"To some people, some things are unforgettable. This is one of those things, and it is something the Ice Men will probably never forget," Mouse said, his tone serious.

Joran let it go at that.

Rather than waste the rest of the day, Mouse and the storyteller decided to explore the city for the signs that only the old man could sense that would tell him if the thing they searched for had been here or was still here. Joran opted for thawing himself out. After stripping off his clothes down to his pants and a light shirt, he parked himself in front of the hearth in the room he and Elsa had. Extending his bare feet toward the fire, he let out a small, quiet sigh of relief as he wiggled his toes in front of the flames. He was warming up finally. Elsa seemed to have the same idea. She was sitting off to one side, mending the travel-worn clothes they all had while warming herself. The sharp needle looked orange or yellow in the firelight, depending on how the light caught it when the needle slid out of the material.

After watching her sew for a bit, Joran asked, "Do you know the name of the man who was King of Sykavik?"

Elsa's needle stopped halfway through the shirt she was mending. "What brought that on?" she asked, trying to keep her voice light.

"Well, earlier today Mouse and I were talking about the Efricans. For some reason, a queen had the Sykavik's king murdered," Joran replied.

"That just doesn't seem right. What reason would there be to go that far with something?" Even Joran knew that killing a king wasn't to be taken lightly.

"Well now, thaw you out, and suddenly you have lots of questions about things you and Mouse talk about. Maybe he has the wrong name, since mice are quiet and he doesn't seem to be so quiet," she said, returning to her sewing. Joran held his hands out to the fire for a bit; for some reason his fingers just didn't want to warm up. He wished they would stop tingling at least. "We talk about many things while we travel."
"You'll burn your fingers if they get any closer," she said absently.
Keeping his fingers where they were, Joran continued. "We talked about my heritage. He told me he couldn't figure out precisely what I was. He said I wasn't a Brasselian though."

"Yes, he has the wrong name. He makes too much noise," Elsa replied primly.

This irritated Joran. "At least he talks to me and tells me things. You don't tell me anything except to bundle up; it's cold out. Or don't put your hands in the fire; they will get burned. Or don't eat cookies before supper; you won't want to eat your vegetables," he said, his tone rising.

Elsa looked up for a moment from her sewing, then replied soothingly, "Joran, I tell you things I think you should know, when you should know them. I don't see long-ago history as something you need to know right now."

"No, all you want is for me to stay a little boy. One who does what you say when you say it and does it with a smile. I am not a little boy anymore, in case you didn't notice. Manhood isn't that far away for me, and I don't even know where I come from, who I am, or even what I am," he retorted testily.

Tying off her sewing on the shirt, she quietly replied, "Joran, I know who you are."

"Care to share it with me?"

"You are the young man who is about to fall into the fire if he doesn't stop leaning forward on the front two legs of his stool."

He let the stool drop back onto all its legs. "That isn't an answer. You told me you knew who I was, not what I was doing." His tone was resentful.

"How very observant," she said as she started fixing a cloak. Her tone was pleasant and calm.

"You won't tell me, will you," he sulked.

"When the time is right for you to know, you will be told. Not before."

"Don't you think I deserve to at least know what I am?"

"In case you haven't noticed yet, life isn't fair. It will probably never be fair. That is how things go. Now, since you are almost a man, go down to the barn and check on the horses. When you come back, stop and get some more fuel for the fire."

He stood and jerked his boots on, barely noticing that they were dry for the first time in a long time. Standing, he pulled on a heavier shirt and stomped out of the room. Just before he got to the door, Elsa called to him, "Slamming the door would be poor manners."

After doing as Joran had been told, he saw the storyteller and Mouse return. Joran noticed that his old friend's mood was sour, much in contrast to his normal light-hearted personality. Sitting in a high-backed chair in the ale room, he just stared at the dancing flames, his face a mask of frustration. After nursing a stein of beer, he leaned forward. "I can't feel it here. We have been all over the city, and nothing. With so few places left to try, I am convinced it isn't here and never was."

Gunnarr ran his hands through his thick hair. "I take it you are thinking we go to Tarathon then?"
"Tarathon probably should have been our first attempt. Hindsight, though, is usually clearer than foresight, even though foresight is more useful," the old man said, the frustration clear in his voice.
"I understand your frustration; we had to start somewhere though. It wasn't a bad decision. After all, we now know where it is not," Elsa said. "What I don't understand is, why would he go there if he was going to the Kingdom of the Arrahs?"

"There is no reliable reason to know he is even going there," he muttered, the frustration clear nonetheless. "There is always the option that he had no intention of giving it to anyone in the first place. He has always envied it." With that, the storyteller fell into his own thoughts and watched the flames dance, perhaps looking for the answer in their beauty.

Mouse cleared his throat quietly. "If we wish to go there, I should find something to be hauling there. That is, if you wish to keep traveling unnoticed."

This seemed to bring the old man back from wherever his mind was. "No. The heavy carts don't move fast enough. Especially with the winter coming on. Any good blizzard, or even a ground blizzard, could stop the carts for days or weeks. If not for the whole winter. Our little masquerade might have to be traded off for speed." He then added as an afterthought, "Besides, it isn't unusual for a merchant to return after the bazaar with empty carts, having had a good year there and selling everything."

Suddenly, Sladvick bolted to his feet and started toward the door, knocking over the chair he was sitting on and spilling the meal he was enjoying. Gunnarr was on his feet in an instant, looking for trouble. "What is it?"

"Rick is here. The doorway," he answered, never stopping.

"Nonsense," the storyteller said, clearly still irritated about not finding whatever it was they were looking for.

"It was him," Sladvick replied, coming back to the group, having lost sight of the man.

Mouse uttered some words Joran seldom heard, and some he didn't know, although he was sure they all belonged in the category of don't-speak-them-in-front-of-a-lady. Elsa didn't seem to mind though. Following up on the little stream of profanity, he said in a calmer tone, "He proved better at tracking us than I thought he would."

"Aye, he did. I don't see how it will matter now though." He almost sounded happy that they had lost their ability to hide in plain sight. "Now we must make great haste."

Sladvick started to the door again. "I'll go harness the horses. Joran, come with and help."

"No carts." The old man's voice brought him up short. "The carts and draft horses are too slow," he said, almost jumping to his feet. "We will go and purchase fast horses and leave the carts here. From now on, we travel only with what we can carry easily."

"What shall we do with the wagons?" Sladvick seemed distressed about leaving them behind, for whatever reason.

"Leave the wagons." The old man's voice was final in that. "Hurry to your rooms and pack only what you need and can carry yourself. We will meet in the yard out front in a few minutes." With that, he hurried up the stairs and was gone.

For a moment, the rest stood and looked at one another, then hurried after him. A little while later, no more than ten minutes, the small traveling party was out in the yard. The crisp air left no mistake that it was getting toward winter. A few light flakes of snow hung in the air, reluctant to fall to the ground. Each person in the small party carried a hurriedly packed bag with them. The big fella, Gunnarr, sounded like a leather pouch full of coin when he walked. Joran could smell the oiled metal of his armor under his cloak though. No coins were there, unless you wanted to try and take the metal off his armor. Joran was pretty sure the big man would have some issues with that though. Sladvick had been the last to come out. In his hand, he had a leather purse, maybe half-full. This he gave to the storyteller. "I didn't want to leave anything behind of any worth. Doing so tends to pester a man's mind and distract him from the task at hand. Sadly, the owner of this place seemed to know I couldn't sit around and haggle, so he took advantage of things. I believe this has about half the real worth of the carts. Better than nothing though."

Letting out a short laugh, Mouse said, "Sladvick, you truly have the mindset of a Brasselian." Giving a slight nod of his head, Sladvick thanked Mouse for the compliment and smiled.

Weighing the coin purse in his hand, the storyteller somberly replied to Sladvick, "I think you did well given I didn't even think to try and sell the carts." Slipping the purse into a hidden pocket of his cloak, he took up the reins and started walking away from the inn. "It would be foolish to try and ride through these alleys and street, much less run the horses through them. We will lead the horses until things are better for hard riding." Joran didn't understand why they were taking the horses though. He decided it best to remain quiet and see what unfolded. Joran expected Mouse to take the lead and guide them through the city, which led to his mild surprise when the big man with the oiled shirt stepped to the front. "Trouble may come. I would say I am the best one here to deal with it," he said, his sword already in his hand. "Trouble is best dealt with when an armed friend is near," Sladvick said, picking up a stout piece of wood lying by a pile. While he would have preferred the battle ax hanging off one of the horses, he knew it would draw too much attention and be difficult to handle in the cramped alleys. On the other hand, a walking stick drew no attention and could be used more effectively in cramped quarters. "I shall lead with you, my well-fed giant of a friend." Gunnarr laughed lightly at his friend, eyes bright. Then, taking the reins, he led the small band of travelers out of the inn's yard.

Having watched his friend, Joran decided to follow suit and picked a solid piece of hickory from the pile as he walked past. The wood felt familiar and almost comforting, not just as a possible weapon, but because it was what they used for most tool handles back on the farm. Tree-felling axes, pickaxes, hoes, and rakes were all fitted with hickory. Joran remembered using all of them many times. The memories made him stop for a moment, then seeing Elsa walking past, he put them aside and hurried to catch up with the others. There would be time enough later for reminiscing.

As though to prove the old storyteller right about getting caught in a blizzard, fluffy white flakes of snow began to come done heavier. Hurrying through the shadowy streets and alleys, the lazy flakes of snow seemed to spook the horses, making them keep close to those on the other end of their reins.

The surprise of the attack was aided by its quickness. It appears the shadows themselves were attacking the small band of travelers. For all the surprise and choice of location, it almost seemed to lack the level of violence one would expect from an ambush. The first Joran knew that they were even being attacked was the crash of steel on steel from Gunnarr's sword expertly fending off a blow.

From where he was standing, with his horse in one hand and his improvised club in the other, Joran barely distinguished attackers from shadows in the crisp night air. It was about then that another memory came flooding back to him. One from his not long-ago boyhood. Of playing knights and his friend taking more of a beating than either boy had intended or expected him to ever take while playing. Joran's heart started pumping fast and hard; his vision actually cleared even though it became narrowed. The attackers no longer looked like shadows; he could make them out clearly. Now that he could see them, it was time to attack them. He vaguely heard Elsa scream something as he launched himself at one of the enemies.

A hard blow from a crudely carved club to Joran's thigh told him who his first opponent would be. Seemingly without thinking, he lunged at the man, swinging his chunk of hickory in a controlled yet vicious attack. Feeling the first blow of the solid hickory make a solid connection with his opponent's shoulder, he followed it up with blow after blow, aiming at the most sensitive or most vital parts of the body. He seemed to know where these were by reflex. He didn't think so much as just know where to bring the club down. And bring it down he did. Hard and fast. As a hard-earned reward, he heard grunts of pain and a few times felt sharp cracks through his club. Usually these were from his opponent managing to block the strikes with his own weapon. A few times the sharp cracks were followed with sharp high-pitched cries of pain though. Oddly enough, Joran felt satisfied with those cries. They had attacked him and his friends. They should pay for it dearly.

As aggressive as the fight around Joran was, the one surrounding Sladvick and Gunnarr was in truth the major attack. The melody of swords ringing against Gunnarr's sword were accompanied by the dull thumps of Sladvick's club as the two stood back to back and fought the attackers, who realized a little late that they should have been more violent in their initial attack. Danger really was best met with armed friends.

From behind Joran, someone yelled, "He's there!" Turning, Joran saw a man pointing at him as he ran toward him. A second man followed. Both carried crude yet deadly-looking weapons. One had what looked like an old ax handle with spikes sticking out of one end at all angles. The other end was wrapped in leather. His companion had what looked like it had once been a butcher's meat cleaver. Now it resembled more of a crudely made, curved knife with a wood handle held on with badly wrapped copper wire. Even in his current state, Joran seemed to know fighting the two men alone was a losing proposition — with him being the loser. Nonetheless, he raised his club. *I can lose fighting, or I can lose begging. Fighting, I can at least make them pay for their victory.* Suddenly a slight figure was flying at the two attackers. It landed feet first, sliding across the slick ground and striking the legs of both attackers and felling them. The pile on the ground of the three looked like a mishmash of legs, arms, and weapons. This only lasted a few seconds. The slight attacker turned out to be Mouse, who rolled out of the pile and proceeded to stand, turn, and plant his foot upside the head of one of the two. The man promptly decided to sleep. The second man made a stumbling run for it while trying to stand and look back at Mouse. He ran straight into Joran's club. Well, maybe the club ran into the man's head, with some help from Joran putting all his weight into swinging it. That was up for debate at another time. Either way, the man promptly crumpled onto the ground and lay still.

Joran looked down at the pile of man at his feet, then at Mouse, who was almost happily walking over to him when he asked, "You look OK, anything I missed? Broken bones? Cuts? Bruises? Hurt feelings?"

"No. Thank you though," Joran replied a little shakily. His pulse was returning to normal, and the adrenaline was beginning to leave his system. He looked at Mouse for a moment, thinking something over.

"What are you thinking?" Mouse asked, noticing Joran's look.

"For a merchant, you seem well trained in fighting."

Mouse grinned. "I am also a tumbler, like a court jester. Once you learn to tumble, fighting isn't much different."

Joran looked past Mouse, down the alley. "Those two are going to get away," he pointed out to Mouse.

Mouse looked back over his shoulder and saw the one he had kicked was up. He was a little shaky on his feet, but he was up and dragging the one Joran had knocked in the head into a dark alley.

At about the same time, they heard Gunnarr bellow with victorious pride. Turning back to the front of the little procession, they saw the remaining assailants beating feet to get away from them. The rest just napped on the ground around the head of the procession.

Looking up from the thugs fleeing Gunnarr and Sladvick, they saw Rick. He was looking out a second-story window, practically bouncing with fury as he screamed at the hired toughs, "You fools! Idiots!" Seeing that they had noticed him, he abruptly stopped screaming and bouncing around in the window, turned, and ran before they could find a way up to him.

Turning back to Mouse, Joran noticed Elsa coming toward him. An angry Elsa, judging from the look on her face. Joran had lots of experience judging her looks and learning what they meant. From his extensive experience, the look on her face now told him he was in deep trouble. Not the smile and say sorry kind. The kind he was going to really get chewed out for. If he was lucky, that is all he would get.

"Elsa, are you hurt?" he asked, his tone concerned and a little innocent. *I can always try and get out of this before I get into it…*

"Don't you Elsa me young man! Of course I am OK, aside from the heart attack you gave me with that foolish stunt with the stick!"

So much for getting out of it. I'm already in it. And it isn't a stick. It's a club.

She continued, "You should never have gotten into that fight! You are neither trained nor big enough to be doing such things!"

Maybe we should go ask the ones I beat on with the stick here how they feel about me being suited for it. Wisely, he didn't voice that idea to her. "I did OK. I got some good blows in and didn't get hurt," he said a little defensively.

Before Elsa could lay into him again, Sladvick came jogging up to them. "Did anyone get hurt? Elsa? Joran? Mouse? No wounds or anything?" he asked apprehensively as he looked at them each in turn.

While Joran appreciated Sladvick's concern, he felt bad that his friend was catching Elsa in a foul mood. "How do we look? We aren't dead in the gutter, are we?" The last was aimed at Joran. Her tone was far from friendly.

"Not that I can see. Glad you are all safe," Sladvick replied, ignoring her angry tone. "I will go help the storyteller with the horses," he said before she could let out another lungful of tongue-lashing at him. He had to admit she had a pair of lungs.

For his part, Gunnarr seemed happy about the whole thing. While alternating between wiping sweat from his brow and cleaning off his sword, he said; "Now that was a marvelous little spat, just enough to get the blood going and keep you warm. Too bad that things were so cramped — couldn't really get any good hard-swinging blows, and the snow made staying on your feet something of an interesting challenge. Not much blood to slip and slide around on at least." His eyes were still dancing merrily.

Elsa had other thoughts on the little incident. "I am overjoyed you find these things good for getting the blood pumping. Personally, I prefer a brisk walk in the fields. I don't see any of the street toughs here yet. Didn't anyone get left behind?"

The big man returned his sword to its sheath and shook his head. "No, we didn't leave anyone behind. I know that several of them were damaged pretty well though. At least one or two have bad cuts, and one at least has a newly shaped skull. Otherwise, they were more like little messenger boys, good at running. Even those we knocked out woke up and ran away."

Just then, Mouse came strolling up from the alley where he had chased the two he and Joran had played with. He looked very pleased with himself; his smile was devious and reaching all the way to his eyes, which were all shiny and alive. "Oh, that was great fun," he said, then looked around and suddenly burst into laughter for no reason. Well, none that any of the others could find.

His laughter quieted when he heard the horses clopping on the stones. The storyteller and Sladvick joined the group, the now-quieted horses with them. The horses' shaggy coats had turned wet from the snow.

Joran, still coming off the rush of battle, couldn't help himself and kept talking. His mind clearly hadn't managed to keep up with his mouth. Things came pouring out that his mind should have warned him about saying out loud before thinking about them thoroughly. "Rick knew we were here. How did he know that? How did he know we would be here?" he blurted out in a rush, barely taking a breath.

This surprised the group, bringing them up short. Mouse looked at Joran, his eyes calculating and questioning. "These are good questions. He knew the last place we were; it isn't difficult to follow a group on the open road. Did he follow us here?"

"How could he? When we left, no one was following us. We stopped and watched the road behind us every day, changing the times and who watched," Joran said, shaking his head. The adrenaline was finally wearing off somewhat, and his speech was finally returning to a normal tone and speed.

Joran looked around, and when no one said anything, he continued. "When the game master on the farm was teaching us to hunt, he said the easiest way to track an animal is to know where it was intending to go. Just go there, instead of spending all day wandering around looking for tracks. I think Rick knew where we were going and met us here." Joran stopped abruptly. He was fighting an odd feeling, one telling him to stop talking. Not to share what he had pieced together in his head and now saw fully.

After a few second, the storyteller gently prodded Joran, "You put something together in your head. What is it?"

Slowly, fighting the odd and unpleasant feeling not to speak, which had grown so strong that his tongue felt strange to him, he continued. "Someone sent him here; someone knew."

Gunnarr looked worried and angry: two things you didn't want a man that size, with a sword in hand, to look. "Who?" he asked, a little confused too.

Mouse spoke up, working through Joran's line of thinking himself. "Well, the merchant who hired us knew. He wouldn't talk to someone like Rick, though; they are of two totally different classes."

"There was another man in the room, though, when we were hired," Joran said, his tongue feeling numb now, making speaking even more difficult. *What is wrong with me?*

"He not only didn't know who we were, he wouldn't know Rick. Again, two different classes that don't associate with each other. Even if they did run into each other, what concern of theirs would one small business transaction be?" Mouse asked, trying to get to where Joran was in his thinking.

Though he was trying to keep his mouth working, whatever was affecting his tongue seemed to be interested in his entire mouth now. This didn't make Joran's speech any better. Still he fought on to share his thoughts. "Remember that group that passed us on the road a while back, when we had to hide and you said one of them wasn't a normal Vibaion? What if the man in the room was one of those? Couldn't he have known who we really were?"

Mouse's eyes shot open. "If he was, he would know who we were and what we were about."

By now Joran's mouth was really fighting him when it came to speaking. He still managed to get out some words. "If it was the same one, could he have been going to find Rick and not looking for us on the road? That could have just been a coincidence; there are only so many roads to one place. He could have already known where we were going and was on his way to tell Rick."

The storyteller spoke up, his voice quiet yet insistent. "Can you describe this man you saw there?"

"Nothing more than a Vibaion. He appeared normal, possibly a spy on some other mission with nothing to do with our little adventure here," Mouse said. "Seems I was dozing during that part of the day."

Sladvick changed the topic quietly yet quickly. "We are being watched from that balcony," he said, nodding slightly toward the one he was watching.

Joran spun around, glad that whatever was affecting his mouth and tongue hadn't asked the rest of his body to join in on the game of not doing what he asked of it. The observer, who was nothing more than a dark shadow in lighter shadows, had an unpleasantly familiar look.

In contrast to Joran's quick turn, the old man stood quietly, his face becoming almost serene as he stood in the falling snow. Then he seemed to come out of whatever trip his mind had been on, and his face turned hard, angry. "A Jahagi."

Without warning, Mouse moved, his arm becoming a blur as it drew a flat throwing blade from under his cloak and spun, throwing it in a smooth underhand throw. The blade caught what little light there was and glinted as it flew at the balcony. The shadow moved quickly backward, crashing through the door with a sharp, almost surprised cry of pain. Then it was gone. Joran jerked his arm, looking down at the sudden prick of pain. Yet nothing seemed to be wrong with his arm.

Gunnarr smiled at his little friend. "Nicely done. Too bad you won't get the knife back."

"True. And I liked that knife," Mouse said with an exaggerated sadness.

"If nothing else, he will have something to keep his mind busy now," the storyteller said. "Well, now that everyone in this part of town knows we are here, there's no point in being quiet." He mounted his horse, and the others followed suit. The group moved at a quick walk, not quite a trot, through the snow-slicked streets.

Even though Joran's mouth and tongue were now back to normal, he didn't have an opportunity to tell them the rest of what he wanted to share.

The edge of town wasn't paved like the streets inside were, and the softer ground gave the horses better footing, and the riders let them canter along through the heavily snowing night.

"Tonight, it will be cold," Mouse huffed as he pulled his cloak tighter around himself.

"Ah, little friend, we could always go back and find someone else to play with in an alley; that should warm your blood plenty." Gunnarr laughed merrily as he cantered alongside Mouse.

Mouse's eyes danced in the night, and he nudged his mount on.

They came to the tent village of the Bedans, some five leagues outside of the town. The sprawling area had a fuzzy look about it in the dense snowfall. Through the snow, the fence of logs was barely visible around the tents. One site that wasn't blurred was the main gate—what looked like the only gate to the tent village. Here there were bright torches sputtering in the snow and wind. They put off enough light to show the tips of the spears and the powerful guards holding them. Their heavy leather pants and matching coats were dusted with snow. Their metal helmets were dully reflected in the torchlight.

Stepping forward, one burly guard lowered his spear to about chest height of the storyteller's horse. "Stop!" he shouted above the wind. "Why are you here at this hour?"

Smiling, the storyteller leaned forward to he heard better. "We would greatly like to trade horses. May we speak with the master horseman?" he said formally. "May I dismount?"

Rather than answer him right away, the guard stepped back, never raising his spear. He spoke quietly with the other guard, never taking his eyes off the group, and then returned.

"Only you may leave your horse; the others are to wait just inside the torchlight."

The storyteller carefully dismounted, then making no sudden moves, slid his hood off his head and walked to the guards.

Suddenly the two guards dropped to their knees, bowing to the old man. They laid their spears on the snowy ground beside them. Neither would look at the storyteller. They kept their heads bowed and eyes on the ground in front of their knees.

With some irritation, the old man motioned to them to stand and said, "Thank you. I am in something of a hurry though. Please hurry and go let your master horseman know I am here."

Without a second glance at the storyteller, the older of the two guards grabbed his spear, bound to his feet, and raced through the gate.

Totally confused, Joran looked at Elsa and began to ask what was going on. Before he could say anything, she quietly snapped at him, "It is best not to ask questions here."

About thirty minutes passed. The small bunch waited in the night snow, their horses' coats wet from the snow melting on them. Suddenly the gate was shoved open, and out rushed six horses complete with tack. Herding them were about two dozen warriors, all dressed as the guards had been; the only differences were the weapons they carried. Some carried bows with quivers of arrows, while others carried swords or spears. They herded the horses into a neat line and waited as a skinny little man walked out of the gate. The man wore his hair shaved at the sides and back, leaving a long braid that ran from the middle of his head down the back of his cloak. Walking up to the storyteller, the man spoke. His voice was reserved. "We thank you for the honor you have shown us by coming to us in your time of need. I wish you safe and quick travels."

"I am sure we will have no trouble moving fast with these fine horses. My thanks," the old man replied.

"Also, I will send these warriors with; they know this area well and can get you where you wish to go much quicker than the main roads. Once you are on your way, they will camp and watch to be sure no one decides to join you on your journey. Unwanted guests can be so rude. No?" His smile was mischievous and made his eyes twinkle in the torchlight.

Extending his hand, the old man thanked the man. "You have honored me greatly with your help and kindness."

Clasping the old man's hand firmly, the Bedan looked at the old man and replied, "It is my tribe that is grateful to you for trusting us in your time of need. I can only hope we have done enough to aid you."

Changing to their new mounts only took a few moments. Two of the warriors rode abreast in front, leading the group. Two more rode a little behind the group, keeping watch in case they were followed. The rest rode to the sides, forming a protective box around the six travelers. Then they were cantering off into the dark night, the snow stinging their faces and the horses pulling at the reins.

Chapter Ten

Joran noticed the darkness was starting to give way to a hazy dawn. For the entire night, their new mounts had cantered steadily through the snow and darkness, never seeming to tire as a steady stream of vapor pulsed from their noses with their steady breathing. Chancing a look behind him, Joran saw their tracks in the now ankle-deep snow filling in quickly. They had left their guard behind about three hours earlier. The warriors had promised to keep watch and stop anyone whom they found following the group.

Once the sun was fully risen, or seemed to be through the clouds, the storyteller brought his horse to a walk, letting it shake its head with a free rein. Its wet mane threw drops of water into the falling snow. "Mouse, where are we?"

The little man unwrapped the scarf from his face and shook the snow from the folds of his cloak, much the same way his horses was shaking water from its mane. Looking around, he said, "About twelve leagues from where we started. Maybe more. It's tough to tell in this weather."

Moaning slightly as he tried to find a more comfortable position, Gunnarr muttered something about better ways to travel.

"Oh, come now, my big friend. Just think of how your horse feels, running all night with your big self on his back," Mouse said, amusement in his voice.

"Enough, you two. How far do we have to travel yet?" Elsa asked.

"We have covered about a fourth of the distance," Mouse replied.

"I don't care what horses we are riding; they can't go that far without rest. Neither can we, especially in this weather. We all need rest, no matter if we are being followed or not."

"Being chased isn't something I think we need to worry about just now. The Bedans will want to talk to Rick and his little friends, who like to run rather than fight," the old man said. "There is a boarding house not far from here, perhaps three leagues, if my memory serves correctly. We should be able to reach it in a few hours. Then we can rest the horses and ourselves."

Sladvick looked doubtful at this. "I don't remember hearing that the Thysions are all that friendly. Will we be allowed to stay there?" he asked.

"All they know is selling anything to anyone who has the coin being asked," Mouse replied. "It will be a secure and quiet place to rest. Rick and his associates won't be allowed to cause mischief there."

Noticing the spirited horses were getting restless, the storyteller suggested they get going. Once they arrived at the boarding house, the day had reached a cloudy noon. Dull light shone down on the short and blocky buildings. Surrounding these was an even blockier and shorter wall made of tightly fitted gray stones cut into blocks. Once inside the compound — it was difficult to think of it as anything else — Joran noticed the weathered and lean men in their well-maintained armor and brightly feathered helmets were all Thysion. He was surprised: not only was this not their country, the men weren't primped and oiled like the merchants of their race were.

Noticing his surprise, Mouse leaned over and whispered, "Where the roads are, the guard will be. Seems you can't have one without the other." Once they were seated in the mess hall, they found the food filling and substantial, if plain. This did nothing to cover up the ridiculous prices they were charged for everything from a pint of mead to a loaf of bread. Like the mess hall and the food, their quarters were simple yet functional. The linen was spotlessly clean. There were even creases in the towels where they appeared to have been hot-iron pressed. The bed frames were sturdy. The blankets were very thick, made from the wool sheared from local sheep, a breed that was known for giving a special kind of wool. It was softer than any other sheep's wool, almost buttery soft to the touch. These blankets made up for the lack of softness from the sleeping mats laid out on the beds. While clean, the mats were far from soft and comfortable. Joran thought of them as adequate, at best. It was a repeat of the mess hall, though; everything was expensive. After seeing to the horses, again in meticulously maintained buildings, Joran began to wonder just where all the money was coming from for this. The old man's money pouch was only so big, and these people seemed determined to take as much of it as possible. Joran thought they would take the pouch itself if they could figure a way to do it. While relaxing over a mug in the mess, the storyteller suggested they wait in the boarding house until the weather cleared. They all agreed that it should blow itself out by morning and that thrashing blindly through the snow was just asking for something to go wrong or for the wrong people to cross their path.

At Elsa's suggestion, an exhausted Joran happily agreed to go up to his bunk and sleep. When he stood to leave, though, he found his legs didn't entirely agree with what the rest of him wanted so badly. Almost tripping on his now-shaking legs, he caught himself and started to leave again.

Elsa noticed the issue he was having with his legs. She stood and reached to help him. "Let me help you," she said quietly.

"It's OK. I can get there myself," Joran mumbled as he stumbled off toward his bunk.

"I am sure you can; your legs just don't seem to agree with your mouth." And she helped him to his bunk and to get in it.

After he was under the thick wool blankets, she reached over and felt his cheeks. "Stay tucked in tight; the winter night will be very cold."

Seeming to ignore her advice about the blankets, he said groggily, "I'm curious. Would you please tell me my parent's names?"

Elsa sat up, surprise crossing her face briefly before it returned to a mask of calm. "You and I can talk about that another time," she said gently. "Now sleep." Joran's stubborn streak decided it wasn't tired though. "You can at least tell me their names now. We can talk about them more another time." His voice wasn't as groggy this time.

She sighed softly, realizing the best way to get him to sleep would be to simply answer his question. "Your father was named Amal. His wife, your mother, was named Agatha."

After a brief time, Joran opened his eyes. Elsa could see him questioning her as he looked at her. "Their names don't sound Brasselian."

"You said we would talk about them later," Elsa chided him gently, hoping he would just doze off.

Joran persisted though. "They weren't Brasselian, were they?"

"Joran, that is a very long story, and not a good bedtime one. We will talk about it at another time." Her voice was a little more forceful this time.

Without warning, Joran slipped his hand out and touched the lock of white that ran through her hair. The odd sensation was there, as it always was when he touched her hair like that. The thoughts that the touch usually brought were very different this time though. Instead of lighter feelings, these were filled with anger and rage. This was directed at a face that floated in his mind. One that looked very much like someone he already knew. Not just from a memory either, the face resembled the storyteller's. It wasn't exactly his though. Similar.

Elsa quickly moved her head away and gently yet firmly moved his hand. "Now Joran, I have asked and told you not to do that," she scolded him. "When you are ready we will explore that part of life."

"Someday you won't be able to avoid telling me," he said, his eyes closed and his voice fading off toward sleep.

"Maybe. Who knows?" she said quietly as she watched him finally find a deep sleep.

The group awoke to an eerie silence. The snow and wind had stopped sometime during the

night, leaving behind a deep white blanket that seemed to soak up sound. The morning fog that had replaced the wind and snowfall seemed to amplify the effect of the snow.

Mouse was picking at his breakfast, overpriced for what it was. At least it was in his view. "Based on the weather here, I am surprised they aren't stuck in the stone ages. All this soggy weather should have rusted away any metal." His tone seemed to be the only dry thing that morning.

After breakfast, they packed, settled their bill, saddled their well-rested horses, and left the hostel, letting the horses lope along happily at a league-eating pace. After a brisk day of traveling through the snow — again their horses were happy to canter along all day, seemingly oblivious to all the miles passing under their hooves — they arrived at another boarding house. This one looked almost identical to the one they had just left that morning.

While rubbing the horses down, Joran commented on it to Mouse.

Mouse just laughed. "Joran, the one thing these Thysions are, if nothing else, is methodical. You can travel any royal road, and the waypoints will all be the same: laid out the same, same design, same number of stairs to the hay barns, everything. They come up short in the creativity side of things I would say."

"Seems boring. Don't they get tired of the sameness of it all?"

"I would say they feel comfortable with it, knowing it looks the same from place to place. Enough questions—time for more bland and overpriced food," Mouse said, rubbing his belly. Even the weather here seemed to like the comfort of sameness. It snowed again that night, and the morning was a repeat from the previous morning. Around lunch time, while eating a cold meal in the saddle, something did change finally. The smell of the snow became mixed with the smell of the ocean. Joran inhaled deeply and realized that the days of cantering across the snowy fields were finally over. They had reached the largest city in the kingdom: Tarathon.

Tarathon was a rambling city that had been around since before anyone could remember it not being there. There was a mighty river that ran to the sea through the great city. Several major roads also ended at the city. Someone once had said that you could get to Tarathon just by floating down any river or walking far enough on any road, as both would bring you to the city sooner or later. As Joran saw it, this wasn't far from the truth.

It was late in the day. The brittle air made a thin crunchy coating over the soft fluffy snow under it. As the traveling bunch crunched their way to the city, Elsa reined her horse up short. "I have noticed we aren't pretending to just be poor cart drivers. That means there shouldn't be any reason we can't stay someplace nice this time. I have earned a true hot bath with good soap. I feel a real meal, not just a filling one, for me is in order as well. A soft mattress and not some half-filled sleeping mat would be nice too."

The old man looked a little surprised. "Never gave it a second thought," he said.

"Well then, I think this time I will pick where we stay," she said primly and heeled her horse back to a canter and made off toward the city.

Following suit, the old man muttered something about fancy lodgings.

After a few more leagues, they came to the gates. A guard wearing a heavy fur coat and matching leggings over his armor stopped them with an upraised hand. "Halt. Why are you wishing to enter the city?" His bored tone was in sharp contrast to his alert eyes and well-cared-for equipment.

To Joran's surprise and horror, Elsa pranced her horse up to the guard. "As a member of the governing family of Menaminie, my business and that of my companions will remain our own." Her voice was arrogant and short; she was clearly irritated with being stopped and questioned.

The guard retreated a step and bowed to her. "I did not know who you were; no disrespect was meant." Looking up and seeing her face was still angry, he continued. "Is there anything I can do to help you today, m'lady?"

The look Elsa wore was one that said she doubted the man could even tie on his own boots in the morning. Nonetheless, she proceeded to ask, "What is the best inn here in the city?"

"That would be the Singing Dove," he answered quickly.

Elsa just stared at him, her face impatient. Catching on, the guard answered her silent question. "It is down past the banking district. Just keep on the main road here until you reach the large fountain in the center of the square. Anyone around can point you directly to the Singing Dove from there."

Elsa made a sharp motion toward the guard, clearly done with him, and let her horse walk into the city.

The old man leaned down as he passed the guard and handed him some coin. "Thank you, sir," the guard said, slipping the coin into a pocket inside his furs. He continued, "She has a temper on her; one to match her fine looks."

"Oh, we noticed you noticing that," Mouse said with a conspiring grin as his horse walked past. The guard returned the smile and went back to his guard shack.

Once they reached the fountain—Joran had to admit it was a large one—Gunnarr randomly picked a passerby and pulled his horse up in front of him. "Pardon me, sir, would you be so kind as to direct us to the Singing Dove?" Startled, the passerby simply looked up at the giant man on the horse, then pointed down the street to their right. "There is a sign of a dove with musical notes hanging over the door." Backing his horse off the sidewalk, Gunnarr thanked the man and underhanded a coin toward him. More out of reflex than anything, the man caught it as he watched them leave.

Looking sideways at Gunnarr, the old man grumbled, "Really? Couldn't have just ridden next to him and asked? Had to ride up on the sidewalk and terrify the poor man? People remember things like that. We don't want to be remembered."

Elsa cut in, "What they will remember is an arrogant woman from the ruling class and her attendants and guards coming past. Nothing more. It is about as good as trying to hide as cart drivers. Just with better lodging."

Once they arrived at the Singing Dove — the sign over the door was very well carved, in Sladvick's opinion — Elsa kept up her arrogant upper-class act. Instead of just asking for a few rooms, as Joran thought she would, Elsa practically pranced into the inn and told the poor man behind the front desk that she would be taking two full suites. With hot baths ready in both. Pointing at the storyteller she said, "My attendant here will take care of the payment. As the rest of my party is a few days away, and my clothes with them, send up a skilled dress maker and cobbler." Without looking back, she took the keys offered to her and sauntered up the stairs.

"Such a pretty woman to have such a demanding personality," the desk man ventured timidly.

"Oh, you don't know the half of her personality." The storyteller chuckled as he set coins on the polished stone countertop. "You don't want to be the one to tell her no. Ever," he continued.

Nodding his head, the man agreed. "I will take your wise counsel on that. As for a seamstress, my daughter is known for making dresses for many of the high ladies here. She will be happy to help the lady. I will send a runner for the cobbler. There is a very skilled journeyman cobbler down the road."

"We thank you greatly," Mouse said. "She can get rather…" Mouse seemed to search for a word, then continued, "Cantankerous. Yes, that is a good word for her. At least when she is made to wait for things she wants."

With that, they went up the stairs in search of Elsa and their suits. Finding both was easy enough. The suites took up the entire two corners of the floor. Upon walking into the room, Joran was amazed by what he saw. Never had he seen so many fine rugs in one place. Not only were they laid neatly on the floors, they were hung from every wall. Each rug was lavishly decorated with fine detail. Following the walls up, he came to the chandeliers hanging from exposed beams. The polished pewter softly reflected the light of the real beeswax candles. This was the first time Joran had be seen pure beeswax candles. He had seen many paraffin and soy wax candles. Also, a few candles of mixed paraffin and bees' wax. Never pure beeswax. The smell was sweet, almost like someone was boiling honey in the room.

The great hearth Elsa was sitting near, removing her travel-stained shoes, was huge and framed in dark stone, highly polished. It almost looked like pewter to Joran as it reflected the candles' light. She wore a content smile on her face after dropping the second shoe on the floor. "Ah. So much better than some stinking dockside tavern," she said, her voice content.

"At least the stinky dockside tavern was something we could afford. This place has a rate that would buy enough corn seed to plant VonRich's farm for two years," the storyteller chimed in. "Those taverns were also much less conspicuous as well."

"Well, this ruse gives us more mobility and much more comfort. Who takes a bunch of highborn travelers to mind anyway? And those wagons did nothing to keep Rick from finding us — slow, uncomfortable, noisy," she sniffed.

"This could all come back to bite us in the backside," Mouse muttered.

"Oh, quit your worrying," Elsa said.

"Yes, Your Highness. As you command," Mouse mocked her, his bow dramatic with his head almost touching the floor.

"Good, you are learning."

Sladvick quietly cut in, his voice somewhat confused. "Um, Elsa? I am not entirely sure how to act in this new role you have chosen for all of us. At least as wagon drivers, we all knew how to act. For some of us, it wasn't acting. It was just being who we really are."

"Oh, it is very easy." She eyed him appraisingly: his solid build, honest and sun-worn face, and work-hardened hands. "You would make a fine master of the horses and overseer of the barns." Shifting his weight uncomfortably, he replied with a nervous laugh, "I have done all those things most of my life in some form or another. Adding regal titles to them makes me uncomfortable even though I am comfortable with the work itself."

Mouse slapped the man on his broad back. "Master of the stables and horses fits you like a finely made boot. With your sincere attitude and strong bearing, no one will think twice about it."

"And you, Sir Mouse, I think you will make a fine jester. You are accomplished in aerobatics and can tell a fine joke when you choose," Elsa said. She seemed to be enjoying assigning roles to them.

With an ear-to-ear smile, Gunnarr asked what he would be.

"Oh, you will be my personal master of clothes," she said, her face serious, before she broke out in a smile and laughed. "The look on your face was priceless. Couldn't help myself there." She giggled, then continued. "OK, you can be my master of the guard. I can't see any other role you could be. Simply stand by me all the time and look like you are begging for an excuse to twist someone's head off." Gunnarr just smiled. Joran, his tone a little nervous, asked what his role was to be.

"You will make a fine attendant," Elsa said.

"Um, what do they do?"

"Hold things for me. Go get things. Tell me how beautiful I look all the time." She giggled.

Mouse whispered in Joran's ear, "That last part, that is the most important." Joran held his laugh and just smiled.

"I already do get things and carry stuff. Is that all?" Joran asked.

"Joran, don't be disrespectful of the lady. In addition to those things, you are supposed to attend to the visitors—answer the door and announce them, that sort of thing. When she is feeling glum, you are supposed to cheer her up by reciting a cheery poem or dancing for her," the storyteller informed Joran.

Looking somewhat unsure of himself, Joran croaked out, "Poems? Dance? I thought Mouse was the jester; isn't he supposed to cheer her up?"

"Well, it is the traditional role of the attendant," Elsa said airily.

"I doubt my poems or dancing will cheer her up," Joran muttered, thankful no one heard him.

The old man, clearing his throat, said, "Seems I have already been given my role to play in this little charade. I am the chief administrator to my lady."

"Oh, more like accountant and master of lands," Elsa corrected him.

"How did I miss the master of coin for you as well? I must be slipping."

They were interrupted by a quiet knock at the door.

"Attendant, stop lazing about and get the door," Elsa said, motioning to Joran to get the door.

"Oh. Yes," he said as he hurried to the door. Opening it, he was greeted by a slightly built lady, maybe all of sixteen summers. Her long dark-red hair was held in place by a neatly pressed light-gray bonnet, which matched her apron. Her plain yet well-made dress reached her ankles. Joran didn't really notice any of this though. He was taken by her large bright-green eyes, which, had they been brown, would have looked just like a doe's eyes. For a moment, he forgot himself and just stared at her eyes.

The spell was broken when she spoke. "This is the royal lady's suite, correct?" Her voice was soft and a little hesitant.

"Yes, it is," Joran blurted, suddenly remembering how to speak. "M'lady, the serving girl is here." He turned and let the girl in, all the while trying not to stare.

"Welcome. Please ignore my attendant; he is still learning his job. What is your name?" Elsa asked.

"My parents named me Greta, m'lady," she said, giving a slight curtsy.

"My, what a well-mannered young lady—and a lovely one as well," Elsa said.

Greta turned slightly red-faced and curtseyed again, keeping her head down, partly to hide her blushing and partly to hide her smile at the praise. "Thank you, m'lady."

"Well now, enough of formality. A tub filled with hot water and plenty of soap would do as a good start to our stay here," Elsa said.

"If you follow me, I will take you to the bathhouse," Greta said, gesturing toward the door. Elsa beamed and followed the sweet girl out of the suite.

The following morning greeted them with lots and lots of white stuff. Snow had fallen through the night, and roofs were now buried thick under it. The narrow streets below were made much narrower by the heavy snow.

Sitting by the window, looking at the morning snow through the thick bubble-filled glass panes, the old man addressed the group with him. "If I am correct, our travels will soon be over." His breath fogged briefly on the window glass.

"Perhaps you are right. I don't think the one we are searching for would remain in Tarathon long," Mouse said.

"I agree," the storyteller said, nodding slightly. "When we find his trail, though, we can travel much faster. What do you say we go into the city and see if we were correct in coming here?" Mouse answered by getting their cloaks and leading the way out the door. For Joran, this was a pleasant change of events. It left him alone with Greta for a while. Joran found her not as physically attractive as Geeta. Greta's voice was much more appealing though. And her eyes. Joran had to force himself to look away from them. Things were going well with her until the seamstress showed up and Greta was called to help with fitting Elsa for her new clothes. Sladvick had gone out to the stables to tend the horses after his morning meal. He wasn't comfortable in the lavish suites and felt more at ease in the barns. This left only Gunnarr to keep Joran company. Not very comfortable company though. While Joran felt no ill will toward the huge man, he never felt totally at ease around him either. Gunnarr seldom said anything, and he seemed to carry a cloud of violence with him. Even when he was gently tending to the horses, it felt as if he could go from rubbing a horse down to ripping a man's head off, then back to rubbing the horse down and not miss a beat. Joran decided to look at the intricate rugs hanging in the room while Gunnarr tended to his armor.

The rugs were woven much like a tapestry, showing scenes of battle with the knights in silver armor on great horses. Or they showed scantily clad women sitting around pools of water eating fruit. Joran was admiring the swords in one scene of battle when a deep voice made him jump. "Gurnish." The mountain of muscle had silently joined Joran in looking at the scene.

Getting his heart out of his throat, Joran asked, "What makes you say that?" *How does a man so big move so quietly?* Joran thought.

"Since the men like going out and putting nicks and dents in rival households' armor, the women stay back and weave rugs or do embroidery," Gunnarr answered.

Looking back at the picture of battle, Joran asked a little skeptically, "That is a real scene? With all that armor? How do they even move?" Chuckling, Gunnarr answered him. "Move? They clumsily totter around. They even put armor on their mounts. Really very dim-witted if you ask me."

Looking down, Joran ran his foot over the rug they were standing on. "This looks different; is this Gurnish as well?"
"No, this is from Khanikstran."
"Someone brought this from there to here? I thought Khanikstran was on the opposite side of the world."

"I'm not sure it is that far away, but it is a very long trip," Gunnarr said. "If you are a trader, though, you would go even farther to make a profit. Trade items such as this move along the major roads through kingdoms. Rugs such as these are highly sought after by those in high society. Nobles and such. Personally, I am not one to look for these. Don't much like anything to do with the Mulsins."

"I have heard there are several breeds of Mulsins," Joran said. "I have heard stories about ancient battles as well. Past that, I don't know much about them."

"You are fortunate," Gunnarr said, returning to his armor, working the leather straps with an oiled rag. "There are five tribes, not breeds, of them. The Vibaion, the Rackians, the Cosllaans, and the Khanikstranns. Well, the Jahagi too. Even though they don't live in any one kingdom or area really."

"How can they not have a kingdom or even a city?" Joran asked, confused. Not only by the lesson, but by the fact Gunnarr was saying more than three words at once.

"Jahagi have no need for a kingdom or city. They are the holy men of Arrah. If you use that term loosely. They roam freely through the lands of the Arrah. They are the ones who kill people in the name of Arrah. Those curved blades of theirs have sent more Mulsins to their graves than any three great battles fought between kingdoms combined. Men of peace. Bah!"

Joran stood in surprise for a moment, trying to make sense of it. Failing, he asked, "A God would demand his own people as sacrifices and enjoy it?"

"If he is a truly messed up and bad God, yes," Gunnarr replied. He continued without looking up, "Legend has it that when he forced the jewel to break the earth, the jewel made him regret it by twisting his mind and maiming him physically."

"He broke the earth? That just never made sense to me in the stories," Joran said.

"It doesn't mean break the earth like you have seen a plow do during planting time. The jewel possesses such power that it can break mountains. When Arrah took the jewel and forced it to do his bidding, the mountains gave way to the oceans. The water came in and flooded what was once dry land. It is an ancient story; I think that part of it is accurate though."

Joran was silent for a bit, then blurted out, "Where is the jewel?"

Gunnarr kept working the oil cloth over his leather, barely raising his head to look at Joran. His eyes, though, didn't seem to be looking at Joran at the moment. They were absorbed in some other thought. He said nothing.

"The jewel was stolen, wasn't it? You don't know where it is or who has it. Do you?" Joran asked, words spilling from him faster than his mind could process the thoughts. "The storyteller is following the jewel, trying to, at least. He is looking for it. Just like the rest of you. Is that it?"

"Boys such as you shouldn't be thinking so much or asking after things like that," Gunnarr said. His tone carried a soft warning.

"You all treat me like a stupid kid," Joran protested. He had heard the warning in the big man's voice and had ignored it. If you looked at it, why should now be any different? Joran plunged ahead. His wonder was pushing him past caution. "Shouldn't I know what we are doing? Besides running all over the world. Half the time we are hiding and trying not to be found; the other half we are running away from people who want to kill us. The old man is clearly not what he makes himself out to be. Who, or maybe what is a better question, is he? The Bedans don't act the way they did with him just because he is just any old storyteller. Even if he is some great storyteller, how can he just walk through a city and tell us that whatever or whoever it is we are trying to find isn't there?" Joran stopped for a second to get another lungful of air, then continued. "Come on, Gunnarr, you aren't as dumb as you try to make out either. That me-all-muscle-no-brain-me-smash act doesn't fool me. You know tapestries and rugs, of all things. Tell me what is going on. Please?"

Without looking up, the big man chuckled—a good deep belly one—and replied, "Oh, I am not that brave or stupid as to do something like that. Elsa would tie me naked to a fence and let a hungry calf out at me. And she would smile the whole time."

Joran eyed the big man. He couldn't decide if he was being made fun of.

Seeing that Joran wasn't totally buying it, Gunnarr continued. "Before you ask, yes, I have a healthy respect for her. You should as well, as would any man who knows her well." With that, he put away his cleaning supplies and placed his armor out of the way.

Joran still wasn't sure. "You think I should be afraid of her too?"

"Well, aren't you?"

"No" was Joran's reflex answer. Then he thought about it. "It isn't really fear of her. I would say it is—" He stopped and tried to find the words to explain what he felt.

"I know what you are trying to say," Gunnarr said, his tone understanding. "Even with years of battle and training behind me, it would be reckless of me to start going places I shouldn't be when it comes to her and what she wishes you to know. If you want answers, you will have to take it up with her. I would be a little more...tactful and careful in asking her though." He winked at Joran to let him know there weren't any hard feelings.

Joran sullenly shuffled his feet. "Well, she won't tell me anything. Even when I ask after my father and mother, she is vague and reluctant to tell me anything. It took me years to get what my father did for a living out of her. Even then it was vague." Gunnarr looked at Joran closely, his expression sad. "Odd" was all he said.

"About all I know, well think I know, is that my parents weren't Brasselian," Joran mumbled. "Mouse said I am not Brasselian, at least I don't have their features physically. Even my parents' names don't sound like Brasselian names." Gunnarr sat there quiet for a bit, just looking at Joran with an unreadable look on his face. Finally, he nodded. "There is very little, if any Brasselian blood in you," he said, almost to himself. "Not quite Sykavik either. You're too small, although you might grow into one yet. Perhaps a small one." His tone was thoughtful.

Joran, trying to make some connection to his past, asked, "Is Elsa Sykavik? I don't think I ever met one."

Gunnarr sat back. "And we just wandered back into questions you should be asking her," he said. His face was friendly though. Joran knew the big man would tell him if he thought it was his place to tell Joran. He harbored no ill will toward the big warrior, just frustration at not knowing where he came from and not knowing where to direct it.

Seeing that Joran was feeling down, Gunnarr wanted to cheer him up. "I have been cooped up long enough in these all-too-fancy rooms," he said as he stood. "Let us go out and get some stink blown off us. I will start your education on fighting," he said, ruffling Joran's hair as he walked past. "Come on, time for you to learn more than being a sissy little primped-up page," he teased gently.

Taken off guard, Joran blurted out, "Me?" His glum mood blew away like smoke in a storm. "You are plenty old to learn. Kind of surprised no one has started teaching you before now. You have more than enough years on you to have been taught at least the basics of unarmed ground and pound, if not sword fighting," Gunnarr said as they walked out back to find a place to train.

It was just before full sunset when a bruised, sore, dirty and somewhat more experienced Joran made his way up the stairs. Gunnarr on the other hand was clean, unbruised, and in fine spirits as he followed Joran slowly up the stairs. Much of the glamour of becoming a warrior of legends had been knocked off Joran's original impressions of what it took to become one. This side of being a warrior was never mentioned in the stories or songs. His right arm was sore from using the big man's sword. Lifting his arm to open the door, he thought better of it and used his slightly-less-abused left arm to open the latch. Gunnarr had insisted on teaching Joran unarmed fighting as well. Joran had learned why Gunnarr called it ground and pound quickly enough. Gunnarr would ground him and then pound him. Joran hadn't figured out how to turn the tables yet. He had the bruises to prove it. He also had learned just how far his legs would really bend in odd directions. Even so, he was proud of himself for never giving up and glad he was learning something a man should know.

Upon entering the room with the tapestries, Joran and Gunnarr were greeted by a wet yet clearly triumphant storyteller. His eyes shone, standing out even more against the bright-red cheeks from the cold. Or was it ale that gave them that rosy red color? "Joran, run along and get Elsa," he said before Joran even had a chance to take off his muddy shirt.

Too sore to ask questions, he hurried off as best he could to get Elsa. He wasn't sure he would ever walk straight again. He rapped on her door, where she had been most of the day with her seamstress. "Yes?" was the answer from inside.

"The sto — um — your master of coin has come back," Joran stuttered through the door, then quickly added a m'lady.

"I see. Just a minute." A moment later, Elsa strode out the door. She made a point of closing the door behind her, making sure the latch was closed.

Joran just stared at her, his mouth falling open. The deep-green silk gown she now wore was unlike anything he had ever seen her wear. From the plunging neckline above the tightly laced corset to the fine lighter-green trim along the bottom of the dress, she looked every bit the lady she was playing at being.

"Joran, a page doesn't stare at his lady like that. Or at anyone like that. It is rude."

Joran managed to close his mouth, his teeth making a click. Then he promptly opened it again. "Elsa...you are gorgeous," he breathed, his eyes wide.

"You're sweet, little puppy," she said, taking him by his shoulders and turning him back in the direction he had just come from. "Now where did the old man get to?"

"This way, m'lady," he said, leading her across the hall to the room with the others waiting for her.

After opening the door for her, he stood aside and let her sweep into the room.

"Well, aren't you the fine-looking lady. That is a very good color on you," the storyteller said, looking up and seeing her choice of clothes.

She spun around in a circle, almost girlish in her actions. "I am glad you think it is pretty, as it is costing you a pretty coin." She giggled.

"Of that, I have no doubt." He laughed at her joke.

Joran closed the door behind him and caught the look on his old friend's face and was saddened by what he saw. Sladvick was standing off to the side of everyone, still clearly uncomfortable with the opulent surroundings. When he saw Elsa, though, his eyes bulged and his face went from pale and surprised to deep red and sheepish. His face then became a mask of such longing that Joran felt sick for the man. It was clear though that Sladvick hadn't meant for anyone to see his reaction, and Joran looked away before Sladvick would see that someone had seen his face.

Joran was equally surprised by the courtly reaction from Gunnarr and Mouse. Almost on cue, the two bent a leg to her, their heads almost touching their knees. (Which Joran knew from recent experience was totally possible.)

Breaking the spell, the old man turned serious. "We are on the right track; it was through here."

Whipping around, Elsa snapped at him, "Why didn't you say so before now?"

"Well, you were enjoying us menfolk fawning over your new dress," he said, a little gleam in his eye. Then, turning serious again, he said, "The aura of it practically oozed from the boards of the buildings it had been in or carried past."

"He better not have come by ship," she snapped. "We could have avoided a great deal of rough travel if we had come by sea."

"Elsa, it didn't come by ship. I think he took a small boat partway up the coast and then came ashore in some smuggler's landing somewhere and then made his way to the city."

"Did he take a ship out then?" she asked pointedly.

"The man isn't a seaman; he is uneasy on large bodies of water out of sight of land," the old man said, shaking his head. "He wouldn't take a ship unless he had to."

Gunnarr spoke up, his tone thoughtful. "Besides, a smart man doesn't try and hide out in the ocean from the Chanese. They could find him in little time."

"I agree. The sea isn't the way he would go," Mouse agreed.

"Well, where would he go then?" Elsa snapped again, clearly frustrated at how the conversation was progressing. Or wasn't, as she saw it.

As though she hadn't said anything, the men continued working through the options. "I can't see him wanting to risk running into the Vangarth. That rules out the North Road," the old man said.

"Well, that pretty much leaves the Oslugs." Mouse shrugged.

"Well, he could go with the other option," the old man said. "The Gurns. I think that will be his safest bet."

"I don't mean to sound thick," Sladvick said from where he was still trying to pull his eyes off Elsa. *He better not let Elsa catch him staring; she will tell him it is rude,* Joran thought with a well-hidden chuckle. "I am really confused though. While I don't mind coming along and helping, I don't know who we are running after."

Elsa, the storyteller, Mouse, and Gunnarr all exchanged a quick look before Mouse quietly answered Sladvick, "Brave Sladvick. The person we are after has certain…powers. If we were to say his name out loud, he could then know where we were, even from thousands of leagues away. All it takes is one utterance of his name."

"We are chasing a wizard?" Sladvick said. The surprise finally made him draw his eyes from Elsa and look squarely at Mouse.

"Well, I would use a different name," the old man said. "Wizards are skilled in other things. The thief we are after is skilled in different areas. While there are several other things I would call him, 'talented thief' would fit him the best."

"Can we get back to where the person in question is going?" Elsa said. "If he is truly heading to the land of the Mulsins, can't we take a ship and catch up to him?"

"No. Now that I have found where he has been, I don't want to leave the path he has chosen," the storyteller said. "Not only don't we know where he is heading, we don't know his intentions. Will he keep it? Was he hired to steal it and taking it to his client? If he chooses to keep it and break a contract, where will he go to hide?"

"Do you think he would really do something like that without first asking permission of Queen Tunia?"

"Good point. She has an annoying habit of sticking her fingers in things that aren't any of her concern," the old man said.

"Maybe it is time her and I met to discuss things once and for all," Elsa said. The tone she used told Joran that she had no intention of sitting down to cookies and tea and quietly discussing things though like proper ladies. More of what Gunnarr would call ground and pound. Or if she had one of her kitchen knives, stab and slab: stab them or cut slabs of meat off them. Did ladies do that though? Joran decided he didn't want to know.

"For now, let us get some sleep tonight, and tomorrow we can get the supplies we will need for the road and then take up the trail again," the old man said. "After we have a better grasp of what he is thinking or where he is going, then we can revisit options."

Their discussion was abruptly interrupted by shod horse hooves on the stones in the courtyard.

Turning and looking out the window, Sladvick said, "Mounted cavalry."

Gunnarr walked over to the window.

"Apparently they are royal guard," he said.

"Nothing to worry about; they can't possibly be interested in us," Elsa said.

"We can't be sure—could be a ruse to lure us into a trap," Mouse said. "Any seamstress can copy a king's guard uniform, and most men can ride a horse."

"Perhaps we can learn what they want," Mouse said, opening the window a bit and letting the brisk night air in.

Pulling the curtain closed behind him to keep from being silhouetted against the candles, Mouse stood at the open window and listened intently to the conversation in the night below them. "We have been sent about an older man, average height with white hair. I understand you have a man matching this description taking a room here," the captain of the detachment said to the flustered innkeeper.

"M'lord, I have a man matching that description here. He is with a lady of high blood though. I can't imagine he is the one you are looking for. A lady of high birth would never employ a criminal in her open court," he stammered.

"A lady from where?" the officer asked.

"I don't remember, m'lord. She is a fine-looking lady. She possesses a great grace and noble bearing."

Dismounting, the officer walked over to the poor innkeeper. "Would you please let the lady know the royal guard would like to speak with her?" His voice was polite, not an even a hint of a threat in it. To further show there was no threat, he smiled at the man and put his hand out in greeting.

Nervously shaking the knight's hand, the innkeeper replied, "Of course I will ask her, m'lord." Then he quickly headed into the building.

Mouse carefully left the window and relayed all he had heard.

Sladvick moved to the door, his pace purposeful. The old man seemed to know what the blacksmith was thinking. "Sladvick, while noble in your intentions, there are too many with him for you knocking him on the head to end well. Besides, these men have done nothing to us. They are simply here following orders."

Sladvick simply nodded and went back to where he had been leaning against the wall.

"We could always slip out the service entrance," Mouse suggested. "Although Elsa would have to change into something less…attention-getting."

"This captain seems to be pretty squared away. I would be willing to bet he has some of his men out back too," the old man said.

"He is here to talk to a lady. Why not just let him in to talk to one and get it over with?" Elsa asked.

They all turned and looked at her. "What are you thinking?" the old man asked.

"You all go to the other room, except you, Joran. You stay. And change your clothes quickly. He can come and speak with me, and then he will leave, his curiosity sated."

"All right, we will give your idea a chance," the old man said, opening the door and leading the way to the other suite. Joran for his part pulled a clean — well, cleaner — shirt and did the same with his pants. His boots he would hide by standing behind Elsa.

"Joran, remember you are my attendant. Just stand and look attentive," Elsa said as she sat down, taking the most comfortable chair in the room and settling her new dress about her. Before Joran could answer, there was a polite knock at the door.

Joran rushed to answer it, greeting the innkeeper and the lanky man behind him while holding the door wide open. "Yes, how may I help you?" Joran asked in his best and most polite tone.

"I am very sorry to bother you," The innkeeper said, keeping his head down. "This is a captain of the royal guard, and he very much would like to speak with your lady." His voice was strained toward the end, whether from fear or just stress of the royal guard being there. Joran figured it was the latter, as the knight hadn't done or said anything to threaten anyone.

For her part, Elsa looked at the innkeeper calmly, almost with indifference. Then after a moment she airily said she would see whoever it was that wished to speak with her.

The relief was apparent on the innkeeper's face as he turned and practically scurried from the room and the captain.

Once the nervous little man was gone, the captain bowed smoothly to Elsa. "M'lady."

"Captain," Elsa said, her tone arrogant yet respectful. *No point in making him mad for no reason,* she thought.

"M'lady, I only bother you this evening due to a request from the king. I am sure you can be sympathetic to my delicate situation," he said politely and, with a slight smile, continued, "and we both know it is usually unwise to ignore such requests. In my position, I would probably wind up as a lowly private guarding some long-forgotten hostel on the northern border."

Elsa laughed lightly. "Well, we can't have that now, can we?"

"Thank you for your understanding. If we could keep the part about my possible demotion between us." He smiled again. "Now to get to the reason of my rather rude intrusion on you this evening. His majesty would like to have a certain old man brought before him." His tone now turned slightly stern. "I have been told you have such a man with you."

Elsa looked shocked. "Is this man a dangerous bandit?"

Bowing his head slightly, the captain replied smoothly, "M'lady, you know kings don't give reasons for their requests to knuckle-dragging, sword-swinging soldiers. Kings simply tell us were to go and what to do when we get there. In this case, he told me to find an old man who matches the description I was given of one such man with you." The captain made to continue; Elsa politely cut him off. "I don't see what a servant of mine would have to do with the king or his court. Unless he was having an affair with one of the ladies of the court?"

Picking up where he had been cut off as though Elsa had said nothing, the captain continued, "I am also to bring all those with him before the king."

Elsa took a slight pause at this. "I see nothing that anyone in my party would have to contribute or have that would be of interest in court. I myself seldom go—such dull boredom all day."

The captain looked her in the eyes and held them. "M'lady, I am not only a captain of the royal guard; I have the honor of holding noble title as well. My father is a duke. Through him I have lands and, with those lands, hold the title of baron until the day my father dies and I assume his title."

"Ah, I see. That would explain the excellent manners and well-educated speech," Elsa said, a slight smile on her face.

"Thank you. My parents would be proud to hear all those years with private tutors and hours of teaching me how to bow have paid off. My point is, I have grown up attending court many times, and since joining the royal guard, I have spent a great deal of time there. In all that time, I have never seen or heard of one such as you attending court. Ever." He then inclined his head slightly and continued. "A woman such as you would certainly have been noticed and spoken about for a long time after she has left. I have never heard of such a woman."

"Thank you for the great praise," she said, smiling at the compliment.

"You are welcome. My upbringing, however, has also taught me who holds what lands and titles in the kingdom and those around this

kingdom," he said, watching her closely. "It has also taught me who my relatives are. Unfortunately, I am not related to you. I would be if you were from the lands you say you are from. While I do have several aunts or second aunts from where you claim to be from, not one looks as you do. Most are short, fat, or both. None have your fine voice."

Elsa looked at the captain with pure daggers. Joran had seen that look only once before, and it still scared him. *Either the captain has ice in his veins and tempered steel for his manhood, or he is totally stupid to know that a look like that isn't good*, Joran thought as he stood silently by.

The man continued calmly, almost embarrassed by having to educate her. "M'lady, not only do I not have an aunt like you, the family name you are using was lost many generations ago and is only a name in some old dusty books in the castle records."

Hope he has his affairs in order, Joran thought.

"I appreciate the ancestry lesson," Elsa said, her tone dead.

"While it has been entertaining, it has drawn us away from the point of all of this, hasn't it?" the captain said. "Now I must ask, do you or do you not have a man such as I have been sent to find with you? On your honor, do you?"

Well, that didn't well, Joran thought in a sudden frenzy of thoughts. He almost ran from the room to alert the others. He hadn't thought much past that. Sort of like his brief run through the night woods so long ago that ended abruptly. He didn't think of what would happen after alerting them. Like when the guards came to get them. Luckily, the old man saved him from finding what holes there were in his plans. The door leading to the adjoining room opened slowly, and the storyteller calmly walked into the suite. "Enough. This is getting tiresome," he said. "Captain, I believe I fit the description of the man you are looking for. Yes?" The captain nodded. The old man took this as a sign to continue. "Now that that is out of the way, could you tell me why the king wants to interrupt my journey?"

The captain politely replied, "As I told the lady, the kings are seldom wont to tell lowly guards their motives for things. If you will join me, I am sure the king will explain it to you himself once we arrive at his court."

"You are right; kings seldom tell anyone their motive," the old man agreed. "We would like to continue on our journey with as little time lost as possible. When would you like us to leave for the castle?"

"First thing in the morning. I would also ask a small favor from you, for all parties concerned." Seeing the old man nod, the captain continued. "As the cells at the local garrison are on the uncomfortable side, I would like your vow that none of your party will leave during the night. If you give it, I will be happy to allow you and your party to remain here in comfort and have a good meal before we leave in the morning."

"That is more than gracious of you, thank you. I give you my word we will stay and be ready to leave after first light tomorrow," the old man said, then offered his hand, and the captain took it.

"Thank you. You have also saved me a goodly amount of paperwork." The captain smiled. He continued. "I mean no offense; however, I will be posting guards around the inn. Just to be safe. After all, the lady here was passing herself off as someone she isn't." His smile took the sting of the insult away. Mostly.

"None is taken. I would do the same in your position," the old man replied.

With that, the captain turned and left to join his men and post guards.

While the beautifully carved door was only made from dark walnut, to Joran it lost most of its beauty when it closed behind the man. To him it had turned into an iron cell door.

Chapter Eleven

After eleven days on the road to the capital city,
where the king was awaiting them, Joran
wondered if they would ever get there. The road
was rough going in drifts left from the snow.
The wind, which made the drifts in the first
place, made travel even more miserable by
biting any exposed skin and whipping their
cloaks and scarves around at will. Joran was sure
he wasn't the only one in the party who wished
the captain would stop messing around with
making sure the guards were arranged so that
no one would even think of trying to sprint off
into the white wonderland of cold and snow
drifts. Not that anyone would get far in the
snow. If they did manage to somehow fly over
the deep snow, the cold at night would make
sure they didn't run far. Not only did the ever-
vigilant captain keep his men arranged carefully,
he also measured their pace to make it from one
rooming inn to the next in one day, leaving just
after dawn and arriving just before dark. Joran
concluded that soldiers were promoted based on
their vigilance. And how slow they could march.
His conclusions came not just from the way they
moved during the day, slow and methodical. At
night they were also posted outside their rooms.
Joran did appreciate the inns. While nowhere as
nice as the fine suites they had in the city before
they were found, the rooms were warm and dry,
and the sleeping cushions were soft.
On the third night of their journey, Joran found
himself feeling very alone and sought out his old
friend, whom he had known since he was a
child.

He found Sladvick sitting in the common room. He had pulled a chair up near the fire and was staring at the dancing flames with a distant yet glum look. Clearly his mind was not here in the common room. Nor was it on the still-full, if now flat, mug of ale in his hands. Still, Joran felt an overwhelming need to spend time with him. Quietly Joran sat on a stool near him.

"Sladvick?"

Without taking his eyes from the fire, he answered in a sad voice, "Joran."

"I've never been in a cell before." His voice was quiet and heavy with worry.

"Neither have I. Why would I have been?"

"I didn't mean you had been in one as a prisoner. I thought you might have seen one—been in a dungeon to work on the doors or something. Blacksmiths do that kind of work, don't they?"

"Aye. They do work such as that. Good people don't go near places such as dungeons though," Sladvick said.

"Are they really full of mice and damp and dark and dreary?" Joran gushed.

"Why all the talk of such places?" Sladvick asked.

"Won't be going to the dungeons soon?" Joran asked, somehow managing to keep his voice from cracking.

"I see. Why would we go to the dungeons? None of us have done anything illegal."

While Joran had a hard time not seeing his old friend's side and the logic behind comment, he still had fears. "Do kings usually go around sending their royal guards to get people? I would think they would have something better to worry about than some folks from a farm and a businessman and his friend."

"We still haven't done anything wrong," Sladvick said doggedly.

"It seems that the storyteller has done something, though, or at least the king thinks so. All these soldiers from the king and the caution they are taking? We might be in the cells with the old man just for traveling with him. I don't want to find out what a dungeon is like."

"We still haven't done anything illegal. Just traveling with someone isn't illegal. Besides, I don't believe things like that happen here." Sladvick's tone was determined.

Even though he let it drop at that point, Joran still had doubts.

The next morning, the weather seemed to share Joran's mood. While windy, it was warm by the time they were having their midday lunch. The snow that had melted mixed with the dirt and made the road a mix of snow and mud. This kept most of the party in their saddles. No one seemed to want to get their feet wet. Shortly after they finished their cold meal, the rain decided to join them. The group rode on; the general mood was gloomy. Listening to the wet sucking sound of the horses' hooves in the mud did nothing to help anyone cheer up.

Over supper at the next rooming house they came to, the captain of the royal guard announced they would be staying there until the road improved. "By tomorrow the road will be one big mud pit. No point in even trying to continue until things improve."

What they had thought would be a day delay turned into a three-day rest at the boarding house. While it was a much-appreciated and needed rest, unfortunately, it was under the alert eyes of the royal guard. Joran was glad whoever had built the rooming house had known what he was doing. He was also grateful that the owners had maintained it well, especially while sitting in the meal hall and listening to the wind and rain assault the walls and little windows. The third day had Mouse laid out on a bench near the roaring fire, his eyes closed and head pillowed on his cloak. His boots rested on the floor under the bench, and his stocking feet were crossed. Joran knew he wasn't sleeping though. Joran quietly went over and sat on the bench across from Mouse. "Mouse?"

"Joran?" was the sleepy response from Mouse.

"Is the king a good man?"

"Which one?"

"Don't be smart," Joran said, a little irritated. How could he ask? "What king is taking us to his castle under guard? That one."

"Oh. Brassel. Why didn't you say so in the first place?" His tone was light; he still hadn't opened his eyes yet. "Like most rulers, he is usually pretty idiotic. He is like most kings in that aspect. Perhaps a little more stupid at times. Why?"

"Um." Joran knew what he wanted to know, just not how to proceed. He decided to just dive in and hope for a better result than when he had been pitched in the water off the cart so many years ago. "What would he do if someone angered him and, when he found that man, he was in a group with others? Would he hold those with the man accountable as well? Or

would he just take the man he wanted and let the others go?"

Mouse opened his eyes and looked at Joran and saw the worry written on his face. Yet Mouse felt Joran was out of line on this. "Joran." His tone was hard. "That is a very poor way to think of kings. Such thoughts are beneath you."

Somewhat chastised, Joran felt his face flush. "Mouse, I am scared. I've never been in trouble so bad the king took notice. I don't even know what happened that would make a king send his guard to get us. I don't want to spend years in a hole without knowing what it was for."

Mouse looked at him and relented a little. "Joran, the kings of Brassel might be lacking on the intelligence side of the stick, but they are fair and honorable men. I have never heard of one not being fair with his subjects. I can't say that about all men. Common or royal."

Joran looked at Mouse for a moment with confusion on his face. "That makes no sense. How can a man be fair if he is stupid?"

"A high intelligence level is certainly helpful with a king; it isn't a requirement though. If it were, the current kings would be replaced with men like Sladvick."

"Then how did these not-so-intelligent men become kings?"

"Usually it is a birthright." Seeing Joran's look, Mouse continued. "Their parents were kings and queens. Therefore, they followed in their parents' footsteps. Brasselian kings are somewhat different."

"How so?"

"They are voted in. By the commoners."

"Voted in? How is the done?"

"Well, usually very poorly." Mouse chuckled. "It is a very badly thought-out way to select a ruler. While the other ways are sometimes just as stupid, having a vote for one is far from the best way to do it."

"That didn't really tell me how you vote for one," Joran said.

Sitting up and looking at the poor weather outside, Mouse decided it wouldn't be a bad way to pass the time. He then leaned back against the table next to the bench he had been laying on and stretched out, enjoying the warmth from the hearth on his stocking feet.

"Well, the best place to start is usually at the beginning." Then, raising his voice to be sure the guards and the captain could hear him, Mouse continued. "About a thousand years ago, maybe a little more, Brassel was little more than a piece of land that no one really seemed to want all that bad. It was ruled at one time or another by one or another of its neighbors. This continued for many years until finally the wars, some little more than squabbles among kings, came to an end. Then a king got the idea of making a separate kingdom here."

Joran was confused. "An emperor?"

"A king," Mouse corrected him.

"Make a rule like that for a land he didn't have any rule over in the first place?" Joran asked.

Chuckling a little, Mouse answered him. "If your kingdom is very large and influential, you can do things like that. Keep in mind that the main road in the north was constructed during the fourth generation of the Haggas. I forget what one it was that came up with the idea and started it though. Third or fourth something or another."

Without looking up from what he was reading, the captain helped Mouse along. "It was the fourth of his name that started things on that particular project." His tone implied he was less that happy with the conversation.

"I appreciate the help, thank you," Mouse said brightly before continuing. "Well, since the Brasselians already had their soldiers in the area, it led to them already having some authority over this decision. Wouldn't you agree there, my fine captain?"

Without looking up, Paulski muttered, "You're the one telling the story."

"Very true, I am" was Mouse's happy reply. "Keep in mind that this wasn't just some act of kindness or charity on the king's part. It was more self-preservation on the part of the Thysions. When the king created a separate kingdom, it prevented the Stutgath from not only expanding north, it also prevented them from having easy use of the trade routes."

"This is awfully complicated," Joran said.

"Joran, it is just politics, and that isn't a very difficult game to play at all. Is it, Paulski?

"I would not know," Paulski said without looking up.

Mouse seemed genuinely surprised. "No. You have been with the court for what sounds like your entire adult life, and you don't play at politics? That is a strange thing. Well, back to the story. Once they had a kingdom, the Brasselians were then presented with the problem of having a land of their own to rule, yet not one bit of royalty with an honest claim to being king. There were, of course, retired politicians from other countries or noble families living in the newly formed land, along with some nobles with land holdings. One or two warlords were tossed in for flavor as well. None of this, though, really helped settle the issue of no king. This brought the notion of the commoners electing their first ruler. The general feeling was, once he is elected, then he can start creating the noble families for the newly formed kingdom. To them, this was a simple and practical solution for the issue."

"It was that simple? They just elected a king?" Joran asked. His fear of being imprisoned was being forgotten in the face of the history lesson he was receiving.

"Well, it's not quite as easy as it sounds. If memory serves me correctly, it took them over ten years to get a ballot from everyone. Even with all those years used for it, only four attempts at cheating were recorded in the books. Since this was something new, the other nobles in the world looked at it as something that was funny and none too bright and simply chuckled at the new nation's way of solving the problem."

"It was actually only five years for them to get all the votes cast and counted. One for each person in the new lands. Parents probably told their children who to vote for. Still, there were over nine hundred options."

"The number was more like six hundred eighteen," Paulski corrected, still without looking up.

"And the educated and regal captain of the royal guard has educated this poor cart driver." Mouse smiled broadly and continued, "I have little schooling in the history of the world and its many kingdoms. Both current and deceased. Now getting back to the voting history, as it were, on the nineteenth ballot, a king was finally elected. One from humble beginnings. He was a wheat farmer. His name was…" Mouse stopped for dramatic effect and was about to say the name when Paulski rather rudely and without flair gave the name.

"Schmidt," he said in a flat tone. "He didn't just raise wheat either."

Slapping his own left hand with his right, he said, "Shame on me. Oh, how could I ever forget? The beans. He raised beans too." He turned to Joran. "One must never forget the beans. Beans are very important too." Joran tried not to laugh at Mouse, and he succeeded for the most part. Mouse continued, "Once it was announced he had won, all those people in the land who thought they were so special and important set off to the farm where Schmidt worked and lived. Once they had arrived they would run from their magnificent carriages and fall before him as he worked his farm. Many yelled, 'Long live the king!' or some such thing."

It was here that Paulski cut in again, his voice more pleading than anything. "Is this really something we have to drag up and discuss?"

"Captain. I am surprised at you. Here we have a young man who is showing an interest in the history of the world. As adults, I would think it is our duty to teach him what we know. Especially you, as you seem very schooled on the topic," Mouse said.

"Go on then. Do as you wish," he said crisply.

"Why thank you," Mouse said formally, bowing theatrically. Then he continued. "What do you think the new king said to those who fell before him on the ground?"

"I don't know," Joran said.

"You're no fun; you didn't even try and guess," Mouse sniffed, then continued. "He said to them, 'My good man, please rise and go wash your clothes and bathe yourself, as I have just fertilized that ground you are kneeling on.'"

Gunnarr, who until now had been sitting quietly and listening to the performance of his little friend, started to laugh a deep belly laugh and slap the table at which he was sitting with one of his massive hands.

For his part, the captain of the royal guard stood up and looked at Mouse with much less humor than Gunnarr was showing. "Dear sir, I find this lacking in tastefulness. Have I made so much as one joke about the king of any other kingdom?"

"No, of course not. As is expected of a man of your upbringing, you are a polite and tactical gentleman warrior. Me, on the other hand, I am simply a little merchant, making my way in this big world."

The royal captain looked at Mouse for a second, then turned and stomped out of the great room. This ended Joran's amusing history lesson. At least he could tell Elsa he had received some book learning today.

The next day dawned to much better weather. The wind had left and took the rain with it. Unfortunately, the wind and rain forgot to take the mud with them. The road they had to take was nearly unpassable; the soft sticky mud was over the fetlocks of the horses. Still, Paulski insisted they had to move on. They had wasted too much time where they were. Even riding, the journey to the next rooming house was a challenge. The horses seemed to think it was foolish to travel with the roads in such condition. Who could blame them? They were the ones doing all the work. Fortunately, the following days saw steady improvement to the road's condition as the mud dried.

For her part, Elsa showed no interest in having been summoned to the king's castle. Even the fact that she was being escorted there by royal guard seemed to have no effect on her. Rather, she insisted on maintaining the role of being of royal descent. Joran for his part thought this was a waste of time and prayed she would stop playing at being a lady of the court. He missed the former Elsa, who had a simple and straightforward way of living. From overseeing the kitchen back on VonRich's farm to taking care of injuries, she had always been practical and willing to work hard. Now she was little more than an insistent and difficult woman. Almost whiny at times. None of it Joran liked or really understood. It took him a while to work out what it was that was bothering him; it was more than just Elsa acting like a spoiled and headstrong woman of high birth. It was the change in their relationship. Never before had he felt a gap between her and himself. They had always been close. To make the empty feeling worse, if it could be worse, something that Mouse had said had slowly yet steadily been gnawing away at his mind. When Mouse had pointed out that she couldn't really be his relative, and with such conviction, Joran hadn't paid much attention to it. Over time, though, it had grown into something that made him ask himself two things more and more. "Who were my parents, and who am I really?"

Now that might not have been so bad, except his old friend the storyteller had changed a great deal as well on the trip. Where he had been talkative both on the road and at the inns or campsites at night, the old man had withdrawn into himself and rarely spoke to anyone. Even his once-happy eyes had become dull and crabby most of the time.

After eight days on the road, the scenery started to change. Instead of mostly flat and wide-open swampy land, they began to see flowing hills. As they crested one such hill, they looked out and saw the great city of Brassel. Its great walls surrounded it and protected it as it looked upon the ocean beyond.

As they entered the city through a great gate, the sentries snapped to attention when they saw the royal guard and the captain. Only once they had all passed did the gate guards relax. The wide boulevards, all carefully paved in stone, were filled with important-looking people. Each of them bore a serious look that made you wonder if their faces would break if they happened to smile. They all appeared to be on important missions from the king, even if that was just getting bread for supper.

Looking around with a disdainful look, Gunnarr muttered, "Toadies."

"What was that?" Joran asked as he rode beside the big man.

"Toadies. These are just people of the court. None of them real men."

"Come now, my big friend," Mouse said over his shoulder as he rode ahead of the two. "They are necessary for the kingdom to function. Small little jobs are good for small little people. Without those little jobs, and by extension these toadies, the kingdom would fall flat on its face."

Joran took it all in. After a short ride, which took them past a beautifully sculpted fountain that had four rearing horses facing all four points of the compass, they entered a wide road. This gave them an unobscured view of the entire castle that towered over the city. It had many wings that seemed to grow from the central structure. Sitting high above even the highest story of the central structure was a tower with a pointed roof. This was easily the highest point in the city, if not the surrounding countryside.

Joran had concerns much closer to the ground. Or under the ground as it might be. "Do you think the dungeons are under the central part of the castle?" he asked Sladvick in a hushed voice.

This brought a worried look to his friend's face. "Perhaps we could keep to subjects other than dungeons. Please?"

Joran just nodded in response and kept quiet.

The procession stopped before a prissy-looking sort of man. He wasn't so much dressed as decorated by his clothes. Everything from his silk-and-fur hat to his overly tooled leather-and-feather boots — *Who puts feathers on boots?* Joran thought — seemed to be there for decoration. His robes were embroidered to the point of looking like rugs had been cut up and used to make the clothing. Even the hat he wore was decorated to the point of ridiculousness as far as Joran was concerned. The man looked more like he had been gift-wrapped than dressed.

The prissy little man and the captain spoke briefly, then changed quickly to what appeared to be arguing.

"The king ordered me to bring these people to him as soon as possible. He wants to see them as soon as we are to the castle, not after you have primped and powdered them to your heart's content. Bring them before him." Paulski's voice was strong and sure. It was easily heard by all in the party.

In contrast, the silly-looking little man's voice was high and somewhat difficult to hear where Joran was sitting on his horse. Yet he could make out what the man was saying. "You have your orders, and I have mine. Also from the king. I am to clean them up and dress them in a tolerable fashion for court." He passed an arrogant and somewhat disapproving look over those not part of the royal guard.

"Fine. I will keep them under guard while you do your primping, Sir Millan," Paulski said. His tone left little room for argument.

Still, the little man found some room to argue. "You will not have your filthy soldiers tromping through the king's home."

Crossing his arms and looking down at the little man, the big captain calmly responded, "We protect that home and by extension you, you ungrateful peacock. To get things going, though, I will stay here, and you can run along and lead the king here. While you are at it, you can explain to him why you are inconveniencing him and his royal guardsmen."

The little man's face turned beet red, and he sputtered. Finally, he managed to make sounds that were words. "I will do no such thing! I am a duke and hold the position of head manservant to the king. I do not run along and get anything or anyone! Much less the king himself!"

Shrugging, Paulski made to turn his horse and leave. Before he could gather his reins, though, the little walking carpet conceded. "Can your soldiers at least mop off their filthy boots before entering the castle?

With that, they all dismounted their horses.

The little fellow leaned over toward the captain and in a low voice said, "This won't be overlooked and forgotten."

"I didn't think it would, manservant," Paulski said just as quietly.

Once they were all dismounted, the royal guards formed up around them, and they escorted them into the castle.

Once inside, Millan politely inclined his head toward the insides of the castle and said, "If you would all be so kind, please follow me." Giving the road-worn soldiers a dirty look, he led the procession inside.

Joran paid the little man no mind at this point. His mind was occupied with an internal tug of war over theories. On one side was the thought of being tossed into the dungeon. On the other side was the comment that he was to be cleaned up and taken to court. The implication to him was that he wasn't about to be tossed into the poorly lit and dank, lice- and flea-infested stoned-walled cells below the castle where they kept such things as flogging crosses and suspension harnesses for overly creative, if somewhat depraved guards to use on him and his friends. These rather unpleasant thoughts were being run over though by the fact he had never been inside a castle. He tried to take it all in at once. His eyes were wide and filled with the architecture of the palace. About this point in time, the quiet little voice in the back of his head decided to point out that his gawking at everything just made him look like a county hick and that his fears of fighting mice for his bread were probably pointless.

The head manservant walked down the corridor and stopped before several polished copper doors. Turning to face the group, he announced, "This one is for the young man." He pointed at a door. The soldier standing closest to the door opened it and politely motioned to Joran to enter. Hesitantly he stepped over the threshold and then glanced back at Sladvick.

"Didn't anyone ever tell you it is best to look where you are going, not where you have been? Now come get in here and close the door behind you." The hurried voice almost made Joran jump out of his boots. He spun around and was met by a spotlessly dressed man. Beside the man was a tile tub, steam softly drifting off the soapy water it held.

"The king shouldn't be kept waiting now. Get out of those road-worn and filthy clothes and step into the tub."

Caught off guard, Joran stiffly undressed and did as the man had told him to. He wasn't sure why he needed someone there to help him take a bath. He wasn't sure he liked it either. He did as he was told, seeing as how it was better than being tossed in a cell.

After a luxurious hot bath that loosened tight muscles from riding and removed all the dirt from his hair and body, he stepped out and dried himself before the man sprayed him with scented oil, which Joran wished he hadn't done. The man then combed his hair out. Finally, he pointed to the clothes neatly hanging by the bath and had Joran dress. The sturdy farmer's clothes were replaced with much finer, if less sturdy, clothes. His shirt was no longer heavy, thick woven cotton. Instead he wore a soft silk one that had been dyed a deep green. Even the eyelets for the silk threads to lace it were embroidered in deep-blue silk thread. His pants, also a heavy cotton, were replaced with much tighter pants made from unborn calfskin in a deep brown. Joran wasn't a fan of the tight pants. He did like the wide leather belt that was clasped at the front with a tooled silver buckle. When he reached for his sturdy and worn-in boots, the man tsked him and handed him a pair of soft doe-skin shoes that stopped at his ankles. Joran thought they felt more like thick socks than actual shoes. Finally, he was handed a cloak made from satin trimmed in mink fur. After putting the cloak on, the man busied himself picking up the old clothes. Joran took advantage of the man's inattention and slipped the knife VonRich had given him into the small of his back inside the belt. While he was unhappy to give up his boots—they were the best he had ever owned, and they were broken in as well—he was simply not going to give up the fine knife Sladvick had made and VonRich had given him. After all, he wasn't sure if he was ever going to see the things the man was picking up.

Once he was finished picking up the clothes, the man looked Joran over with a serious expression on his face. "Well, that is the best that can be done with you in such a short time. You won't be a total wreck when the king meets you." Joran wasn't so sure about that with the leather pants he was wearing. Who would want them so tight? Gunnarr was right. Silly soft men worked in the castle.

Remembering his manners, Joran said thank you to the man who had helped him, then stood and waited for directions on what to do next.

"Do you like my company so much that you would rather sit here than meet the king? Go," the man said, waving his hands at Joran to leave.

Joran walked out into the hall and found Mouse and Gunnarr standing off to one side softly talking to each other. Both had been through much the same treatment Joran had been through. Gunnarr, however, looked oddly undressed without his weapons.

"Mouse. Gunnarr," Joran greeted them. "Why were we given this treatment?"

"Royalty isn't used to common, hardworking folk. As we are to be introduced to the king, our working-class clothes had to go," Gunnarr said sarcastically.

Just then, one of the doors burst open, and Sladvick rushed out. He was dressed in finery as well. "That little womanly man tried to bathe me!" he said in indignation.

Chuckling softly, Mouse informed him that that was the custom here. Nobles were given baths before being shown to the king.

Gunnarr grunted as he smiled. "I do hope you didn't harm the little fella. Did you?"

Not seeming to have heard them, Sladvick barreled on, "Told that little fool I was a grown man and could bathe myself just fine. When he insisted on washing me, I told him if he touched me again I would hold him under the water until his face was the color of blueberries in the fall. He understood that. Too bad I didn't tell him to leave my clothes. He stole them and left this for me to wear." He motioned toward the court's clothes he was wearing, much like the other three wore. On his face was a look of utter dismay. "Then he came back and started spraying me down with some oil that smelled like roses. No man should wear perfume. It is a good thing we are so far from the farm; I don't want someone I know to see me dressed in this foolishness. Where do they get the not-so-bright idea that pants should be so tight?"

Joran smiled a little at that, glad he wasn't the only one who didn't like the pants. "Gunnarr said the king doesn't like to see working-folk clothes in his court."

"Oh? Well, if it gets me back my normal clothes, I will go shoe horses in the stable for his majesty. Besides, I didn't ask to come to court; that would be different. He made us come."

"Come now, big fella," Mouse said. "It won't take long to get things all worked out with the king here, and then we can get back to wearing what we want. Although those pants do show off your legs nicely. The ladies at court will be all over you." Sladvick just turned beet red.

Comparing Sladvick's mood to the storyteller's, though, was like comparing a candle to a hay-barn fire in its full glory. The old man didn't walk out of his room as much as he stormed out. Where the rest of the men were dressed much alike, he was wearing a long flowing robe of brilliant white satin with a deep opening at the neck and no laces to close it. On his feet were matching satin shoes that looked more like slippers. "This is an insult and an outrage!" he roared. "Who is responsible for this?"

"Oh, I don't know. I think you look regal," Mouse said. "Almost pretty."

"Yes, the slippers really make the whole thing come together," Gunnarr said while trying very hard not to giggle.

Both earned an arctic-winter-cold glare from the old man.

Sensing a change of topic was in order, Joran asked where Elsa was.

"She hasn't come out yet," Mouse said.

"Doesn't surprise me," the storyteller said as he sank into a chair by the copper doors. "Women always take the longest to get dressed. She will probably be in there till supper. Might as well get comfortable." They all agreed and made themselves as comfortable as possible.

Captain Paulski returned, having changed out of his travel-soiled uniform and into something more fitting for court. Rather than sit, though, he paced the hallway as they waited for Elsa to finally get herself together. Joran took the time to think through their greeting at the castle. While they seemed to be honored guests and were being treated as such, he couldn't get the thoughts of dungeons out of his mind. Those thoughts were more than enough to keep him tense and fidgety.

Finally, Elsa came out of her room. The gown that she had had made at the inn before they were taken by the royal guard looked wonderful on her. Her hair was done in small intricate braids and had silver strands worked into it around her head like a crown. Much to Joran's dismay, instead of losing the royal attitude she had acquired, it had become worse.

Sitting slouched in a chair, the storyteller glanced up at her. "My dear, I hope we didn't cut your bath short."

With an arrogant air, she ignored the comment and turned to the others and looked them over. "I guess this will have to do." Then turning to the old man, she said, "Come now, stand up and escort me to the royal court. I would like to know what the king wants with us."

As commanded, the storyteller stood and put his arm out for Elsa to take. They then started down the corridor with the royal guards forming up at a slight nod from their captain.

"Please, let me show you to the king's court," Captain Paulski said politely.

Without so much as a turn of her head, Elsa replied, "My friend and I know where we are going. Thank you."

After walking down a few halls, they came upon two huge and highly polished wood doors, where stood Sir Millan. As he inclined his head toward Elsa, he made slight gesture to the guards standing by the doors. On silent, heavily greased hinges, the doors swung smoothly open.

Standing on a raised portion of the floor opposite the doors was a frumpy, blond-haired, short, and rather chubby little man. Behind him was an ornately carved throne made from what appeared to be pure-white marble with gold inlay and a satin pillow to sit on. While the throne was very large, it looked almost like a stool for a child when you took in the entire room it was placed in. The throne room's vaulted ceilings rose high above the highly polished black-and-white marble floors. Chandeliers the size of beds were hung from the ceiling, every one of the many candles in them lit and reflecting soft light from the brilliant white ceiling. The tall windows were framed in what looked to be miles of thick velvet and silk drapes. Interspaced among the windows were dozens of candles mounted in man-high candelabras. Around the room strolled men dressed in tailor-made clothes, all but ignoring the man standing in front of the throne.

Leaning over toward the old man's ear, Sir Millan politely asked in a whisper if he should announce them.

Shaking his head slightly, the old man replied quietly, "No thank you, sir. The king knows who I am." With that, he all but marched down the suddenly silent throne room with Elsa on his arm. Joran and the rest followed with soldiers close behind in a tight formation. All eyes followed the procession silently.

Stopping at the first step to the raised throne platform, Elsa curtsied, and the storyteller bowed. Neither showed any warmth in their greeting. The rest followed suit, although Joran and Sladvick both showed their lack of practice. They all then stood and faced the king, wearing blank looks. Some of them bordered on disdainfulness.

From the head of the guards' formation, Paulski's strong voice sounded forth. "Your Highness, as you commanded, here are the ones you sent me to find." His voice rang off the ceiling and then fell silent.

"Yes, yes. I knew you would complete the mission I sent you on," the king replied. Surprisingly his voice had very little of the captain's strength to it. "I owe you many thanks and am glad your reputation is well earned. Thank you." He then directed his attention toward the group in front of him. His expression gave nothing away.

Feeling his knees start to grow weak, Joran concentrated on locking his knees in place and not letting his legs tremble. He also concentrated on not thinking about dungeons.

Finally, the king looked at the old storyteller. "Ah, my dear longtime friend. I have missed you; it has been too many years since we last saw each other." His tone was warm and friendly. This totally caught Joran off guard. Maybe they weren't going to wind up in the dungeons after all?

"Has your brain taken leave of your head?" retorted the old man.

And with that, we are all going to the dungeons for life, Joran thought miserably. *Thank you very much.*

Anything after that, Joran couldn't hear, even though he could see the old man's lips moving. For his part, the king could hear the words just fine and clear. "You daft, cabbage-headed fool. You have decided now is a good time for a reunion? Now? I hope the trees get an apology from you for you wasting their hard work making the air you just used to say that. As for this" — he pulled at the robe he was wearing — "What on earth made you think this was something I would ever want to be seen in? Dead or alive? Are you trying to tell every Vibaion in the kingdom where I am?" While no one else in the great hall could hear the words, Joran was pretty sure they weren't friendly. Joran started making a list of things to occupy his time while locked in the cells. First on the list was beating the storyteller with whatever hard object he could find.

When the storyteller stopped to take a breath, the king responded in a just-as-quiet tone, his words only meant for the old man and Elsa, even though all could see the stress and sadness on his face. "I figured you would be less than happy with me about this. Let me explain when we are alone." Without waiting for a response, he quickly turned to Elsa, and the look of politeness and formality returned to his face as he addressed her. "My dear lady. It has been even longer since I have spent time with you. I have greatly missed our time together, as have the children. They often ask when you will be returning."

"The king is sweet in saying such things," Elsa replied, her tone cold enough to frost a full beer stein.

Slightly flinching, then recovering a neutral expression, he replied, "M'lady, I had hoped you would at least hear me out before coming to a conclusion on my actions. I will say my reasons are dire. I take it Sir Paulski was nothing short of polite and professional."

"He was a man of virtue," she said, frosting another stein and looking at Paulski. He looked a few shades lighter than he had a few minutes before though.

The king continued to try and make a bad situation better and turned to Gunnarr. "M'lord, how is your cousin? King Chang is doing well?"

Stiffly Gunnarr replied, "When I last had supper with him, he was in good health and deep in his barrels. Although that is normal for him."

The king laughed a little hollowly, then recovered and looked at Mouse. "It is a pleasure to see you as well, Prince LaRooch. It is a fine day to find such royal travelers in my lands. It is a little hurtful that they choose not to stop and offer us the chance to show them our hospitality."

Bowing slightly, Mouse replied, "Your Highness, we are in such a hurry that we were unable to allow ourselves the pleasure of your hospitality."

Joran was surprised to see the king's hands expertly spell out a warning in the secret sign language Mouse had been teaching him. The king's hands moved so subtly that he barely could make out what he was saying to Mouse. "We will talk later. In private." He then turned and looked at the last two. Sladvick and Joran.

Joran was glad that Elsa picked Sladvick to introduce first. "This is Sladvick, master journeyman of metal working. He is a courageous and truthful man. One I am proud to call a friend."

"Well, I would like to welcome you to my kingdom, Master Sladvick. Perhaps someday pretty ladies will say such nice things about me as well," the king said, a warm, honest, and open smile on his face.

Sladvick was red with embarrassment, yet he managed to pull off a passable bow for the king. "She is kind to say such things. I am just a humble tradesman though. Nothing more than a loyal man of the king. Although I will agree: she is very pretty."

Laughing lightly, the king turned to look at Joran. Elsa spoke up before the king could ask. "Your Highness, he is just a young man whom I was put in charge of many years ago. I watch over him because I gave my word to take care of him. Nothing more."

At first Joran was expecting something nice like Sladvick had received as an introduction. His first thought at hearing what he got instead was, "Wait, what? Sladvick got a highly praised introduction, and I get this?" Almost instantly his mind went to an empty, hollow, despairing place. One that sank to the bottom of this stomach and sat there like a cold rock. She hadn't even bothered to try and make it sound nice. Just tossed it out there like he was a trivial tagalong in life. In that one introduction, she had, in essence, crushed him and hurt him deeply all in one hard blow.

Not noticing Joran's pain, the king turned his open smile on Joran. "For a young man, you have done well for yourself, traveling with such royals. I would like to welcome you to my kingdom as well. Let your visit be an enjoyable one."

Enjoyable my foot. I was just told I am an inconvenient tagalong. Keeping his thoughts to himself, Joran replied somewhat woodenly, "Your Highness, I had no idea. They rarely tell me anything aside from I need a bath."

With an understanding smile, the king replied, "In time you will appreciate these days. Being innocent has many advantages. Years from now you will look back and decide it was better not knowing many things. I, for one, have heard many things I wish I had never been told."

"OK, introductions and greetings are over. What do you say we go talk in private now?" the storyteller piped up. His tone was still on the irritated side of friendly.

Completely ignoring the tone, the king smiled as he replied, "We will get to business in time. For now, I have planned a feast to be set out in your honor. Let us drink and eat tonight. The children and Lady Elizabeth look forward to seeing you, Elsa. Afterward we can spend time on less enjoyable things." With that, he regally walked down the steps and left the room.

As they were leaving, Joran found himself walking beside Mouse. Only now he thought of him as Prince Mouse. Still, Joran was looking for something to distract his thoughts from what had just happened. "You're really royalty?" he asked Mouse.

Mouse sighed softly, then answered. "Joran, we have no control over whom we are born to. I will point out I got lucky in being only a minor relative of the king. This raises my chances of never having to wear that crown."

"Gunnarr is royal blood as well?"

"I don't remember his exact title or relation. Where exactly do you fall in the whole royal family tree?" Mouse asked, looking back over his shoulder.

"I am a cousin of the king of my homelands. My official title at court is High Regent of Mountfurt. Or some such nonsense. Why the interest now, little friend?" He chuckled at the last part.

"Oh, Joran here was trying to get his mind around all of the new titles, and I didn't know the total answer," Mouse said.

"Ah, I see," Gunnarr said. "Don't worry over it much; it is all foolishness anyway. When the current king of Chanese rose to his position, someone had to take the position he vacated. In this case, regent. Someone can't have two titles in my lands. Other royalty finds it poor fortune."

Mouse chuckled lightly. "Bet they do."

Gunnarr smiled. "It is just a hollow position anyway. The last tribe wars were over thousands of years ago. I see no point in staying around when there isn't anything really for me to do. In light of this, I let my little brother take the position in my absence. It keeps him busy. Then again, he is easily entertained. Paint a face on a stick, and he would probably talk to it all morning. Sweet lad, just a little slow upstairs. Has a way with animals though." He laughed, then continued. "Another benefit is it irritates my wife constantly."

Joran's head snapped around to look at the huge man. "I didn't know you had a wife."

"Well, that is the official way to label it anyway."

Joran got a sharp elbow in the ribs from Mouse. He took the hint that he had just wandered into a bad patch of conversation.

"You never said anything about your real names and family," Joran said. His tone was accusing.

"You see us any differently now than you did yesterday?" Mouse asked lightly.

"Um. Not really. No. Well, aside from the clothes, no," Joran said with a wink. "You — " he stopped there, trying to put his thoughts into words. Never being that good at it in the first place, he finally stopped trying. "None of this makes sense to me," he muttered as he hung his head.

"It's OK," Mouse said, lightly slapping Joran on the back. "In time things will work themselves out. For now, let us just eat and enjoy life for a while," he said as he pushed the door open to the meal hall, where the feast was laid out in royal fashion.

Joran forgot his frustration for a while as he tried to take in the massive hall. While not as big as the throne room, it was still a massive hall. The long heavy tables bore white tablecloths on which sat fine silver plates, silverware, and heavy steins. Platters that matched the plates were piled high with food. As with the throne room, there were candles everywhere he looked. Behind those seated at the table stood liveried servants. Bustling around the hall was a short, round woman with an open smile on her face. What set her apart was the crown that looked like it would fall off her elaborately braided hair at any moment. As soon as she saw the group enter, she hurried over, a happy twinkle in her eyes.

"My lovely Elsa," she said cheerfully. "It has been so long, and you look as young as ever." Joran was stunned to see the queen wrap Elsa in a warm hug, which was returned wholeheartedly. When they broke the embrace, the two women started chattering away as they walked over to a quiet corner.

Noticing Joran's wide eyes, Mouse filled him in. "That is the queen of Brassel. They call her Grandmother of Brassel. If you look over there" — Mouse gestured to four nobles sitting together at the head table — "you will see some of her actual children. She has more; they are more than likely off on court missions. The king has made it clear he expects his children to do more than just lay about acting like spoiled kings. They are to learn what it means to members of a royal family: how to act, manners, politics, war, and so on. There is a standing joke among the neighboring kingdoms that she has been with child since she was married. Personally, I think it is from the neighbors being expected to send gifts for each birth. With royalty, that can get expensive. The queen has a kind heart, though, and manages to keep the king from falling over his feet too often."

Joran was still a little shocked — maybe uncomfortable was a better description of his feelings over Elsa knowing the queen so well. "A queen is that close with Elsa?"

"Oh, don't worry over that. Elsa either knows or is known to everyone," Mouse reassured Joran.

Looking around, Joran realized he really had no idea what to do. Moving his hands subtly, he signed to Mouse, "Please help me get through this without looking totally stupid."

Mouse smiled and nodded. He knew this could be fun.

They found their seats and were quickly served. Watching Mouse, Joran realized it wasn't that difficult to figure out all the finer points of royal dining. He calmed down and began to enjoy the meal. It really was very good food. Discreetly looking around, he found that while he really had no idea what most of those around him were discussing, he figured he would be OK if he kept his head down and mouth still. Who in the royal court would want to talk to a nobody? Especially at a royal feast? Sadly, for Joran, his plan only lasted a short while. As usual, there was that one little unforeseen problem that liked to pop its head up after the plan had been formed. In this case it was an older gentleman sitting next to Joran.

With a somewhat arrogant tone that was somehow at the same time polite, the man addressed Joran, "I have been told you are a traveler of the kingdom. What have you seen? Are things going well?"

Horrified he was being asked a question that he really had no answer for, he slipped a piece of meat in his mouth to buy time, caught Mouse's eye, and signed a hurried question. More like a yell for help than a question.

Mouse replied with a quick motion of his fingers, telling Joran to simply tell the man that the lands are getting along as well as one would expect for how things were today.

To Joran that sounded like a bunch of words that said nothing. Still, he followed Mouse's directions. After swallowing, he looked at the man and politely repeated what he was told to say.

With a knowing nod, the man replied, "I expected that. For one so young you are very perceptive of the world. It is one of the reasons I enjoy talking with the young of the kingdom; they have different views and understandings of the world."

Damn. So much for keeping my fool head down and making it through this unnoticed, Joran thought as he signed Mouse again. "Should I know who this is?" was his hurried question this time.

Mouse replied simply with, "He is a boring old man; just call him m'lord and be respectful. He should become bored with the conversation soon enough."

"I heard you came in on horseback and not in a carriage. Are the roads in such disrepair that one can't travel by carriage?"

Mouse again prompted Joran. "At this time of year, a horse makes faster time and is more comfortable."

"That is true. How perceptive you are."

Things continued this way for some time. *So much for him losing interest quickly*, Joran thought. After a little while, though, what had started out as a terrifying situation for Joran turned into an odd three-way conversation that he started to like. Occasionally, Mouse would throw an intriguing thought into things, just to keep things fun. These seemed to astonish the old man even more.

Finally, things at the feast started to wind down, everyone having eaten their fill. The king slowly stood from his seat at the head table. "Seems even a king can have eyes bigger than his stomach, especially with such cooks as have prepared this meal," he said, his voice only slightly slurred from wine. This was greeted with polite chuckles. "After such a meal, the queen and I would like to spend some time in private with our guests. Please, continue to enjoy yourselves while we retire to more private settings." With that, he turned to Elsa, offered his arm, and proceeded to lead the small group out of the large hall. The storyteller turned to the queen and offered his arm. She happily took it, and they followed the others out.

Before Joran and Mouse could slip from the room as well, the man who had been talking with Joran straightened up and looked right at Mouse. "Your conversation has been much enjoyed, Prince; however, your friend's accent here is odd. Even an old boring man like me can see that." He chuckled, referring to Joran's signing.

Joran was horrified. Mouse, though, just laughed. "It was foolish of me not to think you knew the silent language as well, m'lord. You are correct; he does have an accent of sorts. It is born of learning while the weather is making your fingers stiff. It is something we will work on when things warm up. Once I can move my fingers in the proper way. He will learn in time."

Rising, the lord heartily slapped Joran on the back and walked off while laughing softly to himself.

Somewhat angry, Joran looked right at Mouse. "He understood all the time?"

"Yes. You and I aren't the only ones to know the language. Spy services learn all they can about other countries, and the silent language is something they know all about. Sometimes we find it best to let the enemy overhear something," Mouse said, then continued, "While that man might be as ingenious as I am, he also might very well be more so. Do not underestimate those around you. Ever. Besides, look how happy he is that he caught us. It was all in fun tonight."

Joran moped though. "You are incapable of doing anything straightforward, aren't you?" While he couldn't really put his finger on it, he knew he was on the short end of a joke.

Chuckling, Mouse replied, "Oh, if there is no other choice, I can be. It isn't anything personal against you. With my life, staying one step ahead of the opponent means I stay alive. This means I use any opportunity I have to practice. It helps keep my mind from getting dull."

"Rather difficult way to go through life," Joran said. Then, listening to the little voice in the back of his head, he added, "I doubt you have ever totally believed anyone."

"Joran, in this life, if you want to play this game, you will learn to be very cunning. At least if you want to play the game for any length of time. We all know the players who are on the board, so to speak. It is a small one. While the winner can take great prizes, you can't keep playing just for those. In time, you become addicted to the joy of winning at it. If not, you stop playing. Sometimes not by choice. Either way, you stop playing. You are correct, though, I don't remember the last time I trusted someone fully, and it has taken me down a lonely path in life." Mouse's eyes twinkled, and he continued. "Lonely, yet full of adventure, excitement, and the thrill of living."

Politely Sir Millan inclined his head and interrupted their conversation. "Sirs, the king would like me to escort you two to his personal quarters. The rest of your party are waiting there now with the king and queen. If you will please follow me." He turned and led the way to the king's quarters.

"Well Joran, hurry along. Mustn't keep the king waiting," Mouse said happily and set off after Sir Millan. Joran scurried along, catching up with the pair, and then walked behind Mouse to speak with the king.

Joran was somewhat surprised by the king's personal chambers. In stark contrast to the rooms he had seen, with all their opulence, the personal rooms were almost bland and boring. The woodwork lacked the carvings of the other rooms, and the chandeliers were well made, yet simple. Even the furniture was almost plain. Comfort was the main focus. In that aspect, the craftsmen had done a good job. The king was standing in one corner, softly talking with Gunnarr. Joran almost didn't recognize the king. He'd removed his royal robes, and the crown was on a velvet pillow off to one side of the room. The king instead wore simple clothes, like any business man would wear in the city. In the opposite corner, the queen and Elsa were absorbed in their own conversation. Catching sight of the old storyteller staring out the window alone, Joran knew at one look why no one was talking to him; his face was a mask of frustration and anger. Sladvick for his part was standing over by the fireplace and doing his best not to look completely uncomfortable.

On seeing them entering the room, the king politely broke off his conversation and walked over to them. "Prince LaRooch. I was beginning to think you and Joran had found a few lonely ladies of the court to occupy your time," he said with a friendly voice and a wink at Joran. Joran reddened slightly, partly from the king's joke and partly from not knowing what to say in the presence of royalty like this.

Mouse saved him from saying anything foolish. "We were having some fun with the gentleman with us at the table. Made for an enjoyable meal."

"I saw that the young lad was making friends with the nobleman. With your help, I noticed." The king grinned at Mouse, then continued. "I would be cautious around him. He is a very crafty old man. Perhaps more so than you, prince. He has age on his side, and that counts for something."

Mouse feigned a very serious face. "I shall take your advice with that sliver fox. Thank you, Your Highness." The king laughed.

Looking around, the king caught sight of the old storyteller. Taking in the expression on the man's face, the king took a deep breath and then said, "No point in continuing with the diplomatic protocols. Time to address the unpleasant side of this reunion. My queen, would you please take our other visitors and show them the library? Or take them on a tour of

the castle? Thank you. Seems the time has come for me to take the harshly worded reprimand I am sure to have coming from the old man and Miss Elsa."

Smiling her radiant smile, the queen stood smoothly. "I would be happy to. Please keep things down, though; there's no point in waking the children." She crossed to the king, and he kissed her softly on the forehead and gave her a quick hug. She then ushered them out of the room and into the adjoining room and closed the door. This room was filled with soft couches and chairs. The walls were covered floor to ceiling with books with the odd tapestry here and there. "After such a long trip, I thought you would all prefer some time off your feet. Besides, I think these are the most comfortable chairs and couches in the castle." She winked at them as they walked into the room. Joran was wide-eyed at all the books.

Mouse smiled broadly at the queen. "Thank you for your consideration, Your Highness." He then became very formal and bowed stiffly. "On a more formal note, my queen has requested I deliver you a greeting from her. She apologizes for her lack of writing. She would like me to deliver a message of some sensitivity to you in person."

Smiling, the queen nodded, saying, "There is no need for forgiveness. She is a wonderful young lady. Her beauty and sunny disposition are far too great for her to be married to that mean-spirited stick of an old man she was married off to. I do hope he at least tries to keep her happy."

"Your majesty will be surprised to learn that she is very happy in her marriage. Her husband is also thrilled with his young and beautiful wife. I believe he thinks the sun rises and sets on her. Watching how the two of them love each other is often amusing—or nauseating, depending on how you look at it," Mouse said.

"Now, now, someday a fair maiden will come along and make you fall head over heels in love with her and forget yourself as well." She laughed. "Then all the royalty will have something new to joke about, how the infamous prince LaRooch has been taken off the eligible bachelor list. Now get on with it. What is the message she wants you to share with me?"

For the first time since he had known Mouse, Joran saw him somewhat uncomfortable. For some reason, he found this amusing. With no small level of self-control, he didn't laugh at Mouse's clear discomfort.

Coughing softly, Mouse leaned close to the queen and quietly spoke to her. "Well, she would like to present her husband with a son." At this point it almost looked like Mouse was squirming to get out of this. "Knowing you are revered the kingdoms over in this, um, area, she would like your, ah, guidance in this."

The queen's face reddened slightly, and she giggled. "I will send her a letter tomorrow. Thank you."

Joran for his part had only been acting like he was paying any attention to the goings on between the queen and Mouse. Instead, he was trying to make his way unnoticed to the door they had just come through in the hopes of doing something he had been taught was not on the list of polite things to do: eavesdrop on the conversation in the other room. Once he had reached the bookshelf next to the door, he began to closely read all the titles and authors on the leather bindings. After a few seconds, he could make out what was being said in the other room, even though he wasn't supposed to be hearing it in the first place.

The first voice he could make out was the storyteller's. "Why the idiotic façade?" the old man snapped at the king.

Great, we are now going to the dungeons after he speaks to the king that way, Joran thought.

Joran was even more surprised when he heard the king's voice after the old storyteller had spoken so harshly to him. The king almost sounded contrite. "Old man, before you jump to conclusions, there have been things happening that you might have overlooked."

"Horse apples," the old man snapped. "I know all that happens; you are well aware of that."

"Then you already know that the Evil One stirs. What kept him asleep has been taken."

"Yes. What do you think I was doing running all over the world when your royal guard caught up to us? Taking in the foods of the kingdoms so I could write a cookbook?"

Shaking his head sadly, the king continued. "I don't like being the messenger of bad news; therefore I usually send a messenger. Your search was about to be at an end anyway. The kings of the north have sent their spies to find you. That was over four months ago. It is a wonder they haven't caught you by now. They have gone so far as to have a detailed description of you and even a drawing of your face from the royal painters sent to every ambassador, spy, informant, and royal at court in this part of the world."

With an impatient wave of his hand, the storyteller replied, "Just tell them to find someone else to hunt down. That brings up a good question though. Why am I so interesting to them now. After all the years I have been wandering around, why now?"

"They seek your advice," the king replied simply. "The kingdoms are mobilizing their armies. Even I have placed my military on alert. Quietly though. We all know what will happen if the Evil One is set free. Death. Destruction. Basically, nothing good and everything bad will come of his awakening. Orrlick, you know full well that the first thing on his list of things to destroy will be these kingdoms. I don't need to remind you either that without the King of Sykavik coming back to us, there is basically nothing we can do to fight the Evil One."

Joran almost fell into the shelf of books he was supposedly reading the titles of. He must have heard wrong. Orrlick was simply a name in stories of old. The old storyteller couldn't possibly be the Orrlick. No one can live that long.

"Simply tell the nervous rulers that if they just leave me alone, I will catch the little sneak thief and return the item he stole before anything else bad happens."

Elsa, having been quiet yet attentive to the conversation, spoke up. "I am starting to become displeased with you. Not only are you costing us time and distance, you are tempting destiny. Not in a good way."

The king turned and looked at her. Neither his face nor his voice gave any sign of fear as he answered her, "Lady Elsalia." Hearing her full name, Joran forgot he had begun to lean in toward the books to hear even better. This forgetfulness was promptly remembered when he slammed the back of his head into the shelf over his head, bringing tears to his eyes and some muffled words that would have gotten his mouth washed out with soap if Elsa had heard them. "I know full well what you are capable of. You also know that a man who gives his word is bound by it. This is many times strengthened when the man is a king and the man whom he has given his word to is another king. I am bound by my word. I said I would provide the king of the north an audience with you, and I shall deliver you for that audience."

Joran thought that they had left the room at first. The silence on the other side of the door stretched on while Joran rubbed the back of his head and tried to hear if they were still in the other room.

Finally, Joran heard the old storyteller sigh, then he answered the king. His tone was resigned. "Anderson, while I can't say you are as bright as I would like you to be, you are a good man. I respect that. It took courage to say what you did to us. We will not fight you on this. Will we, my loving daughter?"

"I never said I would go along with this" was Elsa's icy response.

"Always were the stubborn girl. I said we wouldn't fight him. And *we* won't. Let's go and reassure the north men. We can travel light and fast, get there with little wasted time, and explain things to them. Then they will stop being meddlesome, and we can make up lost time."

"You are getting soft in your advanced age, Father," Elsa replied. "Just send this king. He can keep his word by taking a message from us to them, and then we can stop wasting time with this foolishness. They have no right to demand we explain what we are doing."

Shaking his head sadly, Anderson answered her, "As your wise father mentioned earlier, I am not all that smart. He isn't the only one who feels that way. Those whom I gave my word to feel the same way about me and won't pay me any attention. They would just send others to escort you. Paulski was nice about it, I am sure. The next person may not be so nice."

"You do know what I can do to a man, don't you? That ill-fated man would have an unpleasant rest of his life then. Maybe I would make him into a grape. A grape in a vineyard. See if he likes being squeezed for wine. Live his life out in a bottle," she said lightly while examining her nails.

"Elsa," the storyteller snapped at her. "I said we will not fight them. We will go and play nice with them. Do you understand?" His tone left no room for questions, not that he waited for one anyway. He continued, "Anderson, I think taking to the sea would be the fastest way to travel now. Do you have a boat we could please use?"

"I have a ship; I think that would be more to your liking than a boat." The king smiled. "It is currently tied at the docks. It is a fine and solid craft, sent by the King of Cherek himself for your travel. It seems they don't find me bright, just trustworthy." He chuckled a little at that.

"That settles that then. In the morning, we shall board and begin a nice sea trip," the storyteller said. "I should think you would approve — no more sleeping on the hard ground, Elsa." Turning back to Anderson, he asked, "I would like to thank you, from all of us, for your excellent hospitality. Or will you be sailing with us?"

"I will be joining you. The meeting is an open one. I am involved, so I have to come."

Elsa, who had been glaring at Anderson, piped in, "This isn't the end of this."

"Elsa, I said enough. Do I have to punish you like I used to when you were a child? Don't think I can't still put you over my knee, daughter. A red bottom will just make the voyage that much more unpleasant. The king is doing what he thinks is right. There is nothing wrong with a man doing that. He has done nothing to earn threats from you. Now leave him alone; this will be cleared up at the assembly when we get there."

Joran just stood there, which at this point was all he could do. His legs felt weak, and he was light-headed. He had forgotten about the knot growing on the back of his head. Joran had been brought up to question things like this. He was having trouble even beginning to wrap his mind around something as bizarre as what he had just heard. After a bit, he finally made himself look at things head on.

Could the old man really be over five thousand years old? *I have to admit he looks pretty good for being so old,* Joran joked to himself. Then he turned serious again. Elsa was his daughter? A true enchantress? *That would explain her great cooking.* Even in his head that attempt at humor fell flat. She would be only a little bit younger than her father, the storyteller. Then it all fell into line for Joran. Everything that hadn't added up in the past now made sense to him. Mouse was right. Joran was an orphan. Alone. No blood family in the world. Nothing to hold on to from his past. A deep sadness sank into his bones, along with a longing for his former life, the one he knew before that hurried departure from the farm he had grown up on. It was the one place he remembered being happy. There were no mysteries that no one wanted him to figure out. No lies. Nothing except honest people who worked hard and treated him kindly. No enchantresses, old Gods, or mysterious quests to find something when no one would tell him what they were looking for in the first place — and most importantly to him at that moment, no heartless jokes being made of his life. Like Elsa had done.

Chapter Twelve

The next morning, they made their way to the docks. The sound of their horses' hooves echoed off the buildings around them in the half light of early dawn, giving the sparsely populated streets an almost haunted feel. They had returned to wearing their sturdy traveling clothes, leaving behind the court jester costumes, as Gunnarr referred to them. The old man tended to agree, having disliked what he called his formal bath robe from the night before. Their clothes had been thoroughly cleaned and mended where needed. Even Elsa had to approve of the stitching.

Joran was somewhat surprised that even the king and lord who were accompanying them were wearing clothes of commoners. Granted they were made to measure with silk and satin linings. The outer clothes were heavy wool and leather though. No fancy embroidery in the cloth or tooling in the leather. Even the fur was common wolf or fox. No ermine or mink. Just sturdy and warm traveling clothes. Instead of royalty, they looked like some moderately well-off businessmen or traders going on a voyage. The only one in the party not going on the ship who was still dressed plainly was the queen. She looked like she was about to burst out into tears at any moment, yet she controlled herself with royal dignity as she rode alongside her husband and spoke with him in hushed tones. Spread around them were the royal guards; their armor and fine weapons were covered in plain cloaks. Their finely made saddles replaced with common saddles. The soldiers also had their faces covered in thick wool scarves to protect them from the bitter wind from the sea. They also served to hide their ever-alert eyes and hardened faces and, in more than a few cases, to hide battle scars as well.

Once they reached the docks, they could see their vessel tied to the stone docks of the bay. It rocked on the rough sea, fighting its moorings with each new wave. The ropes creaked in protest of the assault. The ship wasn't quite what Joran had expected to see. Examining it took his mind off the pain of the previous night. What caught his attention first was how thin she looked, like a underfed cow. Even the front end—Joran had no knowledge of ship terminology—looked like a cow's head raised high to look around. Only instead of a mild and meek cow, a dragon's head was intricately carved on its front. None of this made his nerves at his first trip on the seas settle down. The boat (he couldn't really call it a ship), looked like it would tip over as soon as it was cut free of the docks. *Well, at least the water is deeper than the creek was. I won't bump my head on the rocks at the bottom this time*, he thought.

The sailors—Joran assumed they were the sailors for this boat—did little to make him feel better. They lay about the docks smoking pipes or working ends of rope with cord. He recognized what they were doing: backlashing the ends so they wouldn't fray yet not using big clumsy knots to tie the rope off. The sailors looked more like sell swords or bandits than sailors. They were all dressed in furs or sheepskins with the wool still on them. Granted, they were very large-looking sell swords or bandits. They looked much like Gunnarr, which made sense, seeing as they were all from the same kingdom.

A bear of a man up in the sails startled Joran from his musings when he called out to Gunnarr. Looking up, Joran watched the man nimbly come down a rope that was tied to the top of the mast on one end and the side of the boat at the other. Once the man was close to the bottom of the rope, he dropped gracefully down, leaped over the side of the ship, and landed on the dock.

"Lothur!" Gunnarr bellowed in response. He then hopped from his horse (much to the horse's happiness), ran at the sailor, and hoisted the big man from the ground in a big hug. Then he set him down solidly.

"I see you two know each other," the king said dryly.

Watching the greeting between the two men, Mouse dryly said, "This is quite disturbing. While I had the impression we were expected to actually arrive at our destination, I see I was mistaken. A clear and level-headed captain who has years of experience and an unadventurous personality would be what a king who actually wanted to see us would have sent."

With a somewhat confused tone, the Lord of Valmore looked at Mouse and said, "I was informed that Captain Lothur was of the highest quality. I believe they described him as, and I quote, 'A fine example of a captain from the north.'"

"Um, well, that does sound like a wonderful endorsement," Mouse said, his tone a little distressed. "I think you will find that the Northmen sometimes base their evaluations on things a little different than those from the south." His face showed his disapproval as he watched another sailor hand down two steins of beer to Gunnarr and Lothur. They merrily grabbed them and proceeded to slam the steins together, spilling much of the beer. They then downed what was left in deep gulps to celebrate their reunion. Pure happiness was written on their faces.

The two ladies of the group, the queen and Elsa, dismounted and hugged each other. With a nervous laugh, the queen said to Elsa, "You will watch out for him, won't you? Keep him from getting pushed into doing something stupid by those overgrown Northmen? Please?"

"You needn't worry," Elsa said, squeezing the queen's hand reassuringly.

"My wife, I will be fine. After all, I am a mature ruler of a kingdom." The king's voice sounded slightly hurt by his wife's words.

Looking at her husband, her love for him written on her face, Sabrina whispered to Elsa, "Best you watch over him." Elsa fought to keep a straight face. To her husband, Sabrina continued, "No running through the snow naked or staying up all night playing drinking games with the Northmen. Remember what happened last time."

"It was only a slight cut," the king grumped.

"You almost lost your hand in that game of theirs with the axes and beer steins," she sniffed. Then she turned and raised herself up on her tiptoes and gave the old storyteller a peck of a kiss on his cheek. "I look forward to you coming to visit us when you can stay longer. Please bring Elsa with you."

Reddening a little, the old storyteller replied he would be sure to do that.

"Aye, we should be getting aboard and ready to set sail. Don't want to miss this tide," Lothur said.

"Take care, my love," the queen said as she embraced the king and hid her face in the fur of his cloak.

"I will, my dear wife," he said as he clumsily hugged her, somewhat embarrassed by her show of affection in public.

"Now get along before I break down and cry right here," Queen Sabrina said.

Joran's stomach clenched at the realization that he now had to get on board the boat. Looking at the slippery rocks of the dock and the little plank bridge of sorts that led to the heaving boat, minus any rails, he doubted they would all make it aboard without either getting soaked or — worst case — being crushed between the dock and the boat after falling into the ocean. Much to his pleasant surprise, they made it onto the boat without any mishaps. Once they were all aboard, the sailors tossed off the ropes, picked up their oars, and took their positions at the oarlocks. Captain Lothur stood by the tiller with Gunnarr beside him and nodded to a sailor sitting near him. The sailor picked up a wide drum made from lacquered sail canvas and an old barrel. Placing it on a stand, he then proceeded to beat it with two sticks, their ends wrapped in cotton-stuffed leather. The sailors pulled their oars in time to the deep, rhythmic beat of drum. Joran was surprised at the speed the sailors coaxed from the big boat — OK, ship — as they rowed past the bigger and clumsier trading vessels. The king for his part didn't seem to notice any of this as he stood at the rear of the ship and watched his wife fade from sight.

After leaving the safety of the docks and the anchorage for ships, the water seemed to become something else entirely, going from a rough rocking motion to waves so big they reminded Joran of closely spaced rolling hills. The ship—Joran still thought of it as a big boat—slid down the back of one wave and up the front of the next in its path. Between the dull cloud-filled sky and the deep, gray, and frothy ocean, Joran thought he was being taking to his doom. The dull thud…thud…thud of the drum that kept the men working the oars in time wasn't helping anything either. Maybe if he could still see shore, things would be better. Even the land seemed to be bidding him farewell, having moved out of sight.

Shortly after losing sight of land, Joran found a reasonably comfortable place at the bow of ship. Granted, comfortable was all in what two things you compared. While he was still on the ship, he was drowning in the dark hole his life had seemed to become. He wasn't sure if the shaking of his body was from the cold, his silent crying, fear of the boat sinking, or a combination of them all. He just huddled under his cloak and shook. The truth that Elsa wasn't even really related to him made him feel alone and lost in the world. He couldn't bring himself to believe she was Elsalia and the storyteller was really her father, Orrlick the Sorcerer. His mind could only go so far. It was bad enough she wasn't even remotely related to him in any real way. Throughout the day he avoided her and spoke to no one.

Shortly after nightfall, Joran stirred from his spot at the bow and moved to the stern, where he ventured under the deck to a crowded cabin where they would all sleep. The storyteller was seated at a small table that was bolted to the floor, speaking with the king and Lord Valmore. After finding his sleeping pallet, Joran stole glimpses at the old man. He seemed to see him in a different light now than he had before. The three wicks of the whale-oil lamp swinging from the beam overhead gave his thick hair an almost snow-white glow. It carried down to his trimmed beard as well, seeming to light it from within. Otherwise Joran could see no change to him. He still looked like his old friend, the storyteller. Well, maybe not truly his friend — a friend wouldn't have kept so much from him over the years. With that thought, Joran rolled over and gave in to sleep.

In the morning, Joran heard they had rounded a peninsula. He didn't catch the name; he had just heard some of the sailors cheering their good time. With the sails raised and full of the wind, the oars had been shipped and the men were taking a break from the hard work. Joran was just glad the drum was quiet now. It let him muddle over the problems he now had with Elsa and the storyteller.

The third day out seemed to mirror Joran's mind. Thick ice mixed with rain was driven into the sails and mast of the ship. Everything from the ropes to the sails were caked thick with ice. The ice-mixed rain pelted the sea and looked like thousands of arrows hitting the water.

Gunnarr was standing at the stern of the ship, eyeing the weather warily. "This could make passage through the channel interesting. Hopefully the weather decides to calm down soon."

Sladvick was half standing, half hanging on to a rope near Gunnarr. Between having just gotten over being sick, his first time at sea, and the rough water, standing was something of a challenge for him that day. Hearing Gunnarr's comment, he asked, "Channel? I thought they were only near land. I don't see any land anywhere." His voice was a little shaky with nervousness.

"The Straights of Chanese. We call them the Channel for short," Gunnarr replied. "It is only about a league wide. It is full of undercurrents, swirl pools, crosswinds—all those fun things that one finds at sea. It is nothing to worry about. Lothur knows it well, and while it might be a little rough, he will get us through with no worry." Gunnarr paused, then smiled and continued. "That is, if we aren't luckless. In that case, we swim."

"Oh, that is so helpful. Thank you for lightening our spirits with those words of happiness and cheer," Mouse piped up from nearby. The only thing dry about him was his tone. "I have been trying to forget we have to go there since we got on this ship."

Sladvick looked green again. "Is the Channel really that bad?"

"Oh, it isn't that bad. I just make sure I am good and lost in a stein of beer or ten before going through it," Mouse said. Laughing, Gunnarr said, "The Channel is a mixed blessing from the Gods. On one hand, it is a difficult and dangerous passage. On the other, those dangers are what keep the neighboring kingdoms from invading and annexing Chanese."

"Yes, it is a powerful political ally. Thank the Gods for that," Mouse said. "Personally, I would rather never sail through it again if I could."

The next morning found them near a rocky and desolate coastline. The captain had dropped the sails and let the ship drift, waiting for the tides to go in his favor. After a peaceful wait, the water began flooding back into the Channel. The strong wind now filled the sails, taking the ship with it.

"Joran! Grab hold of something anchored to the ship!" Gunnarr bellowed as the bear of a man strode toward the bow, a huge smile on his face and a gleam of happiness in his eyes.

Seeing his friend stride fearlessly forward, Joran came out his brooding and followed him. Joran's little voice of reason said this was stupid; go find someplace else to stand. After days of being along with the issue of Elsa and the storyteller and not getting anywhere with it, the little voice was beat back into a corner and ignored. Instead, Joran grabbed hold of a thick rope that was tied to the bow and stood resolutely next to Gunnarr, facing into the Channel.

Looking over and seeing his little friend taking his place, Gunnarr let out a roar of a laugh and slapped Joran happily on the back. The blow, while not meant in anger, was still filled with power and shook Joran to his feet. He stood tall, though, and faced forward. "That is a true man, standing to face the Channel in the eye." He laughed again and continued, "Together we will ride the devil's waves to their outcome."

Not sure where to go with that, Joran decided to just let it go.

Between the wind pushing from behind and the tide rushing in, the ship shot through the Channel like a cart racing down a mountainside without a brake. Or in Joran's case, it was a flashback to the one he and his friend had made on the farm. Joran just hoped this ride would end better. The bitter, cold saltwater soaked their clothes and half blinded them, forcing Joran to let go of the rope with one hand and keep wiping his eyes clear, trying to ignore the stinging. Suddenly, his ears were filled with a brain-shaking thunder. Peering ahead, he saw the water spinning in a huge pool. Pulling on Gunnarr's cloak, Joran shouted, "Can we make it through that?"

Gunnarr put Joran's hand back on the rope and bellowed, "Hang on!" Joran took that as an answer to his question and did as the big man said. His knuckles turned white as the captain turned the ship not away from the giant whirlpool, but directly at it. Joran could barely see the other side, and panic ripped through him as he realized that the captain fully intended to enter the gates leading to a watery hell, as Joran saw it.

"What is he doing?" Joran yelled at Gunnarr, who for his part looked happy as could be.

"It is the only way through the Channel," Gunnarr roared in reply. "The captain guides his ship into the pool, letting it take two turns around in it, then letting that energy carry it out of the pool safely to the other side."

"What other side?" Joran yelled back.

"There is another side; you will see. If the ship doesn't come apart that is," Gunnarr said happily in reply.

"*What?*" Joran yelled, horror written on his face. He had never thought about the boat — ship — coming apart.

"Once in a while, a ship gets pulled apart in there. Then the sailors swim to the bottom," Gunnarr yelled back. Then he looked around the ship dramatically and continued, "This one looks strong enough. We shouldn't have to swim today." He beamed.

Any further discussion of swimming or ships coming apart was cut off when the bow dropped out from under their feet and they were hurled into the abyss. Gunnarr roared with delight, looking down into the mouth of the whirlpool. Joran, after taking a quick look at it, kept his head turned away from the middle of the pool as he listened to the fast drumbeat and watched the oars bend under the strain of the strong men manning them as they took their ride around and out of the whirlpool.

Then it was over, as suddenly as it had started. They punched through the waves at the top and were propelled to smooth water. The wind, tides, and energy of the whirlpool quickly brought them to the sheltered water on the other side.

Trying to pry his hands from the thick rope, it seemed all feeling had left them somewhere along the wild ride. Joran listened to Gunnarr laughing. "You are a strong one. You didn't even piss yourself on your first trip through," Gunnarr congratulated Joran as he rung the icy saltwater from his beard.

As Joran got his hands to work, and the feeling came back to them, he heard a shrill voice behind him. *Ah damn, now I am in trouble. Again. Thanks, Gunnarr*, Joran thought as Elsa descended on him with the fury of the Gods of every religion all combined into one. Joran seemed to forget that standing at the bow had been his own idea.

Gunnarr stopped laughing as Elsa lit into Joran with a tongue-lashing that Joran hadn't seen in years. For his part, Joran just stood and watched. He seemed to know that slinking away would do no good. *Maybe we can go back through the whirlpool again instead of facing Elsa*, he thought.

"I would like to know who's responsible for such stupid behavior," she said, fixing Joran with a furious look.

"I wanted to see the passage, so I came up front," he mumbled. "Gunnarr had nothing to do with it. It was my idea." He didn't see any point in them both being in trouble, especially since he had to admit it was his idea to stand up there. Out of the corner of his eye, Joran caught a friendly wink from Gunnarr.

"It was now, was it?" She put her hands on her hips and stared at him. "What possessed you to do such a foolish thing?" she demanded.

At this point, the previous feelings of frustration, hurt, and betrayal, to name a few, came to the surface. Not in the best of ways either. "I wanted to," he said, his tone firm and defiant. For the first time in his life, Joran was feeling rebellious.

"Excuse me?"

"I. Wanted. To," he spat back at her, exaggerating each word. "Like the reason matters? All you are going to do is give me some punishment, whatever you feel like, regardless of the reason why I did it," he shot at her. He was beyond any care now.

Elsa stood. Her hands dropped to her sides and began clenching and unclenching. Her eyes were lit with fury.

Then came chuckling. Not from Gunnarr or Joran. The old man was standing off to one side and had begun chuckling softly at the goings on.

Elsa reared on him, directing her anger at him now, for which Joran was somewhat thankful. "You find this kind of reckless and just stupid behavior amusing?" she snapped at him.

"Oh, a little. How about you let me talk to the boy and take care of this?" he suggested.

"No. I will take care of this," Elsa snapped back.

"Well, you are right; you can deal with it. The issue is, will you deal with it properly? The answer to that is, no. You're too emotional and worked up. Plus, you have a mouth that is like a leather lash. You forget he isn't five and sneaking cookies anymore. Well, maybe he is." The old man winked, then continued. "That isn't the point though. This is a special problem — and one that will be dealt with in a special manner." He took a step toward Joran before Elsa quietly responded, "I will take care of it."

The old man stopped and turned to her. The smile had left his eyes. "No. You will not." His tone was rock-hard.

Elsa stood there for a second. "Fine." Then she turned and stomped off, her hands clenched at her sides.

"Come, Joran. Sit," the old man said, gesturing to a neatly coiled rope by him.

"She is so cruel these days." Joran spit it out without thinking.

"No, Joran, she isn't," the only man said softly. "She is that way from fear. What you did scared her."

"Oh," Joran said. Some of the defiance and anger left him.

Looking at Joran with soft yet searching eyes, the old man studied his face for a moment. "Joran, what is eating you?" he asked kindly.

Joran's mind raced through everything that had happened and came up with one response. "People call you Orrlick," he said. "And Elsa they call Elsalia." In Joran's view, this explained it all in two short sentences.

"And?"

"It can't be true."

"I think we talked this over a long time ago."

"Are you him?" Joran asked bluntly. Might as well cut right to it was his thought.

"Well, I have been called that before. Yes."

"I can't work my mind around how that can be."

"I understand that. If you can't get there, you can't get there. There's no way to force you to believe it or understand it. That will come on your terms."

"Thank you," Joran mumbled.

"That brings up the situation of you being defiant with Elsa," the old man said gently. "What brought that up?"

Joran stuttered, trying several times to put his thoughts into words. His thoughts became a jumble of ideas that wouldn't separate into separate thoughts. His biggest fear was asking the question that had been eating at him for so long and having it finally and forever answered. Did he have any family at all in the world?

"Your mind won't organize things the way you want?" the old man asked kindly, seeing Joran struggling. "Life has changed so much in such a short time that everything you believed to be right in the world is suddenly being questioned. This makes you scared and angry. No?"

Joran nodded slightly.

"I understand; you want to put the blame of things on someone, and she is the easiest to assign it to."

"You make this sound simple. Almost stupid," Joran replied quietly.

"Wouldn't you agree that it is? When you break it down and look at it, isn't it?"

Joran didn't reply; he just studied his boots closely.

"This is something that you have to work through. Making others miserable or scared or angry because you are isn't right, is it?" he asked kindly.

"You are right," Joran said softly.

"Joran, Elsa and I are what we are. Nothing more, nothing less. Yes, there have been stories about us, and lots gobbledygook" — Joran smiled at that word — "has been said and even written about us. None of that has any real effect on what we have to do. What can and does affect us is how those we care about treat us. Acting like the world owes you everything that you want is just foolish and selfish. I know you are better than that. Take what you are handed in life and work with it, deal with it. That being said, maybe you should hurry along and make peace with Elsa," he said. "You and I both know that the longer a woman is angry, the harder it is to make peace." He winked at Joran. Somehow that one wink made things all the better in Joran's mind.

"All right. I will go make peace with her," Joran said resignedly. He would still rather face the whirlpool again than go find Elsa.

The old man gently patted Joran on the shoulder. "It was good we could talk like this. Hope it helped you some, no?" Joran nodded. "Best you hurry and find her; she can stay in a bad mood for many years. I should know; she has been cross with me for as long as I can remember. No idea why — I've long since forgotten what I did wrong in her mind."

Joran sighed and stood. His old friend gave him a reassuring smile, and Joran straightened his shoulders. Like Sladvick once said, there was no point in putting off the hard things; they just got harder the longer you avoided them. With that thought, Joran set off to find Elsa. Not that it was that hard to find her; it was a small ship after all.

Joran found Elsa standing at the back of the ship, where she was leaning against the side, seeming to stare out into nothing, yet she wore a sad look. "Um, Elsa."

"Yes?" She turned and looked at him.

"I would like to apologize for standing at the front of the ship like that. It was foolish and childish." He was surprised that his voice wasn't faltering, even under her steady gaze.

"Joran, you are right. It was wrong and childish," she agreed. Her tone wasn't angry though. Almost sad. That hurt Joran more than if she were mad and yelling at him. He almost wished she would yell.

"I won't do anything foolish again. I promise."

Her laugh surprised him. The hug that followed was warm and motherly and even more of a surprise. He had expected at the least a tongue-lashing, if not an actual lashing for what he had done. Instead she hugged him. *The old man is right; women are a fickle bunch*, Joran thought. He was smart enough not to say that out loud though. "Joran, we both know you can't keep that promise. I seem to remember something about that after a dip in the creek a while ago." *She has to remember that?* Joran thought. He didn't mind this time, though; her anger with him seemed to have left.

Compared to the wild ride of the whirlpool, the remaining days were quiet. The snow-covered coast was a welcome sight to Mouse, who seemed to relax at the sight of land again. Gunnarr, in his true helpful self, just had to remind Mouse that if they went into the water here, they would be blue ice cubes before they could swim to shore. Mouse looked a little sick at this reminder. Still, the weather seemed to want the rest of the voyage to be smooth, if bitter cold and windy. They slid into the cove and tied at the pier after four more days.

Unlike any city in the kingdoms of the south, the houses, stores, and warehouses were all so old that they seemed to have been there from the beginning of time—more like shaped stone from the beginning of the world that people had just moved into. The twisting and narrow streets and alleys added to this feeling. They had the feel of streams moving between stones, not something planned and laid out by man. On top of all of that was piled snow. Lots of snow. The roofs looked like something from a tale of long ago; the snow gave them an otherwordly look. Even the mountains that flanked the city were covered in the white stuff.

Awaiting them at the wharf were sturdy and solidly built sleighs. The horses harnessed to them were huge, with the longest and thickest coats Joran had ever seen on horses. With each impatient stamp of their huge hooves, snow billowed up in little clouds around their fetlocks. The drivers of the sleighs matched their horses, big solid men with long hair and thick beards. Some had decorated either their beards or hair with beads or intricate braids. In their thick cloaks and furs, they were fierce-looking warriors. Even though they looked like something from a story about giants, they were quick to smile at the light clothes Joran and his friends wore and hand the travelers heavy quilted cloaks or thick, soft, rich furs. "Aye, can't have you freezing to the sleigh—wouldn't get you off it till spring," one driver joked as he handed Joran a thick quilted cloak that was surprisingly light yet warm. Its fur-lined hood did wonders keeping the wind off his face.

In the last sleigh, Gunnarr climbed in and clapped the driver on the shoulder. "Think we can catch up to the rest?"

"Aye, you talk too much." The driver laughed back at him.

"Well, you might be right about that sometimes." Gunnarr laughed as the driver chuckled and lightly slapped the reins against the horses' backs. They all but jumped forward in response, eager to run. The driver held them back to a steady trot though.

All through the city, huge men strode up and down the streets, all wearing heavy cloaks or coats. Gunnarr returned yelled greetings and good-natured insults, his smile wide at being home. Their efforts to catch up with the others came to an abrupt halt when two men, both naked to the waist and barefoot, rolled out of a tavern into the snow-covered street. They kept at each other as though it were a summer day. The bitter cold didn't seem to affect them at all as they tossed each other across the street. Gunnarr for his part laughed. Joran just stared, expecting to see the two wrestlers turn to ice sculptures any moment.

Once it had cleared the street, the sleigh continued its way through the ancient city. A huge building appeared ahead. "Gunnarr, is that the king's castle?" Joran asked as he gestured at the solid-looking building.

"No, that is a temple—common enough mistake of those who are new here," he said kindly. "I have heard it said that the Snow Bear God's spirit lives in there." Gunnarr shrugged. "Personally, never saw him in there. I don't think he would want to live in there anyway. I think he lives out on the tundra or in the mountains. Why would a bear want to live in there?"

Joran had to agree that Gunnarr had a good point.

As they passed the temple, an old crone stood at the foot of the steps. She wore a threadbare dress of heavy wool. Her fur cloak was so old the hair was falling out in patches here and there—either that or someone had killed a mangy reindeer and given her the badly tanned hide for a cloak. In her claw of a hand she gripped an oddly carved staff. She waved her other hand at them, and her old voice carried to them through the crisp cold air. "Gunnarr, the lord of the land. Your dark fate is still coming."

Gunnarr snorted and snapped at the driver, "Hold here." He lightly leaped from the sleigh, leaving his heavy coat inside. As soon as his feet hit the ground, he roared at the old woman, "You have been told many times to stay away from here. The monks will take you and light you on fire for being an enchantress. King Chang himself has asked, told, and finally ordered you to stop this."

It was about now that Joran noticed her eyes were a creamy, sickly-looking white. She fixed her sightless on Gunnarr as though she could see him.

She answered Gunnarr with a cackling laugh. "Those fools and their mortal fire can't hurt this one. There is a different fate that the universe has in store for her."

"Stop rambling like a brain-addled fool and get away from here. Don't come back either. Stop with the fate nonsense too," Gunnarr ordered. His voice was hard.

She cackled again. "This Hula sees what Hula sees from the universe. Your fate is still tied to you. Lord or not, fate has you. Remember what Hula says." She turned her head toward the sleigh. Her dead, sightless gaze seemed to pass over the driver with not one bit of interest. When she came to Joran, she lost the dark humor she had had with Gunnarr and gave him an awed, almost stunned look.

Then she dropped to her knees, her head almost bouncing off the packed snow as she bowed to Joran and solemnly greeted him. "Welcome, lord of all lords. When Hula meets you on the other side of life, she begs you remember her as the first who welcomed you to this world."

Gunnarr bellowed and came at her. Before he could get to her, though, she was on her feet and scampered off, her staff tapping a path before her.

"OK, what was that all about?" Joran asked as Gunnarr reseated himself on the sleigh and donned his coat again.

Gunnarr grunted. "Just a crazy old hag." He said dismissively, although his face said there was more to it than that. "If the king had any sense, he would have banished her long ago. Or better yet, lit her up at the stake. All she does is terrorize the good folks who pass here, rambling her nonsense at anyone gullible enough to listen to her." He nodded at the driver, and they were off again.

A glance over his shoulder told Joran the old woman was gone.

Chapter Thirteen

The castle of the King of the Northmen was massive, solid structure near the heart of the city. While massive, it was clearly ancient. Many parts of the castle were run-down. Broken windows, missing doors, and in a few cases, collapsed roofs and walls were in abundance. The main building seemed to be the only part that was cared for and maintained. It also seemed to be the original castle, the rest added on at the whim of whatever king ruled at the time. No real reason seemed to be behind the additions. That was probably why they were falling into ruin was Joran's silent reasoning. He was still curious though.

"Gunnarr, how come the castle is in such bad repair?"

"Eh? Oh, not all kings like what those before them built. So they let it fall apart." Gunnarr hadn't said a word since they had run into that old hag. His mood had been angry and cold ever since they had left the temple.

In front of the castle, the rest of their traveling band waited. "Seems the great Gunnarr has gotten hit in the head one too many times. He forgot his way home," Mouse said with a laugh.

"I wasn't the one driving, if you didn't notice," Gunnarr replied coldly. "We were stopped along the way."

Before anyone could ask about what had happened, the huge oak-and-iron-banded doors opened silently. After the doors had stopped, a regal woman walked out. Her long, raven-black hair flowed over one shoulder; delicate silver bands were evenly spaced along it, holding it from blowing around. Her deep-blue silk dress was intricately quilted and embroidered with silver thread. The fur trimming it was a deep black. She stopped at the head of the stairs and addressed them formally. "I welcome you, Lord Gunnarr. Regent of Mountfurt. Father of our children."

Gunnarr's face grew even more gloomy, if that was possible. "Lanna," he said with a curt nod at her.

"As is my right and duty, the king has allowed me to be the first to greet you to the castle," she said, her tone still formal.

"Always one to stick with your duty." Gunnarr grunted. "Since you are here to greet me, why aren't my children here as well?"

"They are in Mountfurt. With this bitter weather, I felt it best they not travel. For their health." No one could miss the almost cruel undertone to her voice.

"Of course, you did," Gunnarr replied quietly.

"Did I do something wrong, my lord?" Her voice was innocent.

"Never mind," Gunnarr said.

"Now then, if you and your traveling companions are ready, I will bring you to the king's chamber."

Gunnarr finally ascended the stairs, where he somewhat woodenly hugged his wife. The couple then walked through the massive doorway into the depths of the castle.

As they followed the couple into the castle, the Lord of Valmore muttered under his breath, "Sad."

"Oh, I wouldn't say that," Mouse replied. "Gunnarr has what he wanted, doesn't he?"

"You, sir, are a cold-hearted man," the lord replied.

"I don't think so. Gunnarr spent years trying to get her affections. Now he finally has her. Wouldn't you agree it is nice to see that kind of dedication rewarded?"

The lord just shook his head in reply.

Just after passing through the main doors, a royal guard appeared and led them through the seemingly endless confusion of doors, staircases, and halls. Their chain mail shirts softly rattled against their scabbards and sword handles. Sladvick noticed that each handle was beautifully made, yet the wrappings were worn and stained with what appeared to be more than just sweat. He bet that under their gloves, these men had heavily calloused hands from hours of training and actual combat. Some bore obvious scars of the latter.

After going down one narrow staircase that suddenly opened into a vast hallway with vaulted ceilings, Mouse commented on the design. "I don't see why others don't appreciate Chanese building styles. They are so full of unexpected surprises." His tone barely hid his sarcasm.

King Anderson either didn't hear the sarcasm or chose to ignore it in his reply. "Adding on to a castle or some other silly public works project has given the feeble rulers over the years a sense of worth and of doing something important. It is common in almost all kingdoms. Well, those that don't remove the feeble ones in short order. For example, there is one kingdom I have heard of that has impeccable sewers. Seems they had a string of sad excuses for leaders, and all they did was add to whatever the previous one had already done. Pretty soon they had sewers laid out into the country, where there weren't even subjects living."

Mouse chuckled. "This is true. Giving them some silly hobby like that keeps them from getting into trouble elsewhere. Sort of like giving a puppy a bone to chew instead of letting him chew your boots."

King Anderson didn't seem to find this so funny. Looking at Mouse sideways, he said, "While I like your king and hope he has a long and happy life, I do wonder what pet project you would come up with if you were under the crown."

Mouse feigned a horrified look. "That is a hateful thing to say. How could your mind even conceive of such a thought, much less let your mouth voice it?"

Picking up where Anderson left off, the Lord of Valmore commented too. "Oh, I don't think we need to go as far as making him king and all that. I would agree Mouse could use a wife. And maybe a mistress or two. Just to keep him on his toes."

With a chuckle and wink, the king replied, "On? That many ladies wouldn't keep him on his toes. More like off them." Sladvick and Gunnarr laughed heartily with the king. Mouse just looked stunned and a little worried.

Any further conversation on Mouse's love life or being a ruler came to an end as they entered the king's royal reception room. Joran was surprised it was so different from the other kingdoms' throne rooms. This one looked more like a grand taproom. Sure, the ceilings were vaulted and high with tall windows to let in light. And yes, there was a throne in the room. Several actually. That was about the end of the similarities. There was a large fire pit in the middle of the room; a huge slab of granite hung several feet over it. Under it, a fire happily burned away at the wood. Sladvick caught Joran's confused look at the granite. Leaning over he quietly explained that the fire heated the large slab of stone, and once the fire died down during the night, the heated stone would continue to keep the room warm until morning, when a new fire would be lit. Evenly spaced along the walls were more hearths; all had fires going as well. There were thick-handled torches set in holes bored into the stone at angles; all were lit as well. Not one candle was seen, nor were there a bunch of fine tapestries hanging to cover the walls. Instead of a bunch of dainty, primped-up men and ladies wandering around, there were big men, most with shaggy beards and long hair. All had some form of armored shirt on, whether chain mail or hardened leather with disks sewn to them and laced shut in the back. Not one was unarmed. They all carried large knives, not the cute little fashion accessories that other courts' members passed off as daggers. In addition, they carried a range of weapons. Joran saw everything from swords to battle axes on these warriors.

After taking it all in, he turned his attention back to the thrones. Hanging behind each one was the only real decoration in the room: a large flag. Sitting on the great chairs were royal-looking men. One chair was empty though.

Joran's observations were rudely interrupted when one of the royal guard slammed the iron-capped end of his spear into the granite floor and roared in a clear voice, "I present King Anderson."

Standing, one of the men on the thrones called to King Anderson, "Welcome. Come and join us. Your seat awaits you." He gestured toward the empty seat. Behind it were the king's colors and crest.

Joran was surprised that the king who stood to greet Anderson wore such a shabby crown. Calling the banged-up ring of three ropes made from gold and set with what looked like rubies that was around the man's head a crown was being sort of charitable in Joran's view. After all, it was clearly missing a few rubies.

The standing king continued in what sounded to Joran like a very old and overly formal form of address. "The rulers of the north welcome the king of the southern kingdom of Brassel. Please come join us and share your counsel with us." With that, the king motioned to the empty throne and then sat himself.

Sladvick was trying to follow it all and finally decided to just ask Mouse who was who.

"Well, let us see. The big, fluffy one on the end is my relative: King Oordah. Next to him, the starved-looking one in the ill-fitting robes is Lu-Ning of Cha-zin. He is probably hoping Oordah had a snack before this meeting. Now that odd one on the other end, the one with no crown, he is from Sykavik. His name is Drath."

Joran cut in at hearing the name from the old stories. "He is the same Drath from the stories?"

"Looks pretty good for a thousand-year-old man, doesn't he?" Mouse said seriously, then clarified it just in case Joran missed the joke. "No, every representative from there is named Drath."

By now, King Anderson had finished the formal greeting of each king or representative in what appeared to be the traditional manner, then took his seat.

Once Kind Anderson was seated, they all turned toward the old man and Elsa. In a formal, almost awed voice, King Chang addressed the pair. "Greetings, almighty Orrlick. Madam Elsalia. Welcome to our humble dwelling."

The old man cut in, "We really don't have time for this foolishness. What is it you want? You insisted I come and see you. What is so important?"

With a chiding voice, the fat one on the end spoke up, "Come now, let us enjoy our traditions, ageless one. Seems we won't be able to enjoy them at all soon."

The old man just eyed him, the frustration and impatience clear on his face. Joran started worrying about dungeons and cells.

An elegantly dressed woman entered the room from a door hidden in the stone work behind the thrones. Her silky hair looked blue when the firelight caught it just so. The deep-red silk gown she wore seemed to change from blood red to a pinkish red as the flame light danced over it. Walking to King Anderson, she knelt and briefly touched her lips to his boots. She then sat back on her heels and addressed him quietly. "King Anderson, the great journey you undertook to attend this gathering gives us much happiness. Thank you." She then leaned forward and kissed his other boot.

In reply, the king simply inclined his head toward her.

Mouse quietly filled in Sladvick and Joran; both were clearly lost. "That is Mrs. King Chang. Queen Jura. Things will get interesting when, well if, she greets Elsa."

Queen Jura stood smoothly and turned to the old man. Bowing deeply and averting her eyes, she said, "Holy and eternal Orrlick. Welcome to our humble home."

"Oh, I wouldn't go that far with things," the old man said.

Entirely ignoring the comment, she continued, "My humble dwelling is greatly honored to have a sorcerer of your power beneath its roof."

"Well, that was certainly flattering. Thank you," the old man said politely.

The queen then turned to Elsa, not only with her body but her whole demeanor. "Welcome, sister." Her tone was flat.

"Elsa has a sister?" Joran hadn't seen that coming.

Mouse hid his laughter and filled Joran in. "Oh, she's not really Elsa's sister. The queen plays at magic. Illusions really, more like parlor tricks— poorly done parlor tricks at that. Doing that makes her think she is a true witch or even an enchantress. Bet she has some trick planned to impress Elsa. Well, try to impress her anyway."

As though the queen had heard him, she made some movements with her arms and hands. A large pearl appeared in her hand, and she held it out to Elsa.

"And that was hidden in her dress," Mouse said with almost childlike happiness.

"Such a precious present. It is a pity I only have this to return the kindness," Elsa said formally and held out a black orchid to the queen. It looked like it had been freshly cut that morning.

"How did she get an orchid fresh cut up here?" Joran asked, awe in his voice.

Mouse just smiled and patted Joran on the shoulder.

Taking the delicate flower from Elsa, the queen suddenly went white and looked like she was about to fall. Elsa just looked at her passively.

Before she had a chance to fall, a smiling redheaded woman stepped forward. Clearly, she was another queen. Her thick, silky red hair was worn in a simple braid down her back, held at the end by a simple yet elegant silver ring and carved ebony pin. In sharp contrast to the first queen, this one simply smiled and walked right up to the old man and kissed his cheek. Then she went to the king and did the same. When she came to Elsa, she wrapped her in a warm hug.

"That, my little friend, is Queen Helena." Joran thought Mouse's voice sounded a little…funny. Catching a sideways look at him, Joran saw a sad yet almost longing look pass over Mouse's face. Even as young as he was, Joran suddenly understood Mouse's odd way of behaving at times. It saddened Joran to know this about his friend.

Finally, a third woman emerged to greet the travelers. She quietly yet regally walked up to each of them, formally embraced them, and said a few quiet words in greeting. Her voice was quiet and almost sweet.

Sladvick did a quick count of men versus women and noticed one was short a wife. Quietly, he asked Mouse, "Drath isn't married?"

Without taking his eyes off Queen Helena, Mouse answered him. His voice was sort of back to sounding like his normal self. "He was married for many years. Happily. His wife gave him three sons before her death some years ago."

Sladvick looked a little embarrassed. "Oh" was all he could think to say.

Sladvick was saved by Gunnarr just then. He stormed into the chamber, his face set in a look that would scare a bear away. Stopping at the foot of the king's throne, he bowed slightly to Chang.

"Good day, Gunnarr," he said. "I wasn't sure if I should send the dogs out looking for you. It wouldn't be the first time someone got lost in the maze of this place. I just never expected you to get lost here." He chuckled lightly.

"I was dealing with my wife," Gunnarr said coldly.

Chang let it drop and moved on.

Gunnarr moved on to a better topic. Looking around, he asked, "I see you have met my new traveling companions."

"I wouldn't say we have met them per se. Just had a look at them." King Oordah grunted good-naturedly. "We have been going through the tedious formalities of court. Now that we are over those, would you mind introducing them?" He smiled at the group.

"Of course, m'lord," Gunnarr said and gestured to Sladvick first. "This big man is Sladvick: a master journeyman not only as a blacksmith also as a bladesmith, and brave fighter." Joran couldn't remember ever seeing his friend turn that color red before. He found it amusing and did his best to keep a straight face. "The lad there is Joran, a good and brave boy and under Elsa's supervision. As much as he doesn't like it at times."

King Oordah chuckled. "What boy doesn't chafe at his guardian's rules from time to time?"

"And finally, you all know the fine Lord of Valmore," Gunnarr said and Valmore bowed formally.

"Okay, I have been polite and waited for all the fluffy introductions. Can we get on with things now? Starting with why you dragged us all here?" the storyteller cut in, the impatience clear on his face and voice.

Drath spoke up, "Orrlick, the reason you are here is well known to you. Unfortunately, my carelessness led to their making off with what you have been looking for lately."

"It wasn't your carelessness. I know the sneaky little crook, and nothing you could have done would have prevented him from getting in. The worrying part is, how did he make off with it without it killing him? Even I can't pick it up. Besides, it is supposed to take care of itself," Orrlick said.

"All we know is the name of the man who took it. The God told us no more than that," he said. "The rest we figured out on our own. One night it was resting where it had been for years. The next morning it wasn't there."

Mouse quietly coughed into his hand.

"Yes prince?" King Chang asked.

"Do you think it is entirely smart to discuss this in public like this? Vibaions are known to loosen a good number of mouths with gold or other ways. Add in any Jahagi who may be around, and they won't need any gold. Just a few minutes with the person, and any secrets they had will be known," Mouse said.

Gunnarr grunted. "These fighters don't sell their honor like that. As for Jahagi, there are none in the kingdom."

Mouse countered, "That may be true about the warriors. How about the servants? The chamber maids? The cooks? As for no Jahagi, I have found them in some very unlikely places. Never a good surprise."

King Oordah tapped his throne, a thoughtful look on his face. "I believe he has some valid points. He does have years of experience in espionage. If Mouse thinks our talks could reach unwanted ears, perhaps we should listen to him."

"Many thanks," Mouse said.

Leaning forward, King Chang fixed a cold look on Mouse. "Do you think you could get information from inside this castle?"

"Yes. Many times over" was his modest reply.

Oordah couched his head a little embarrassedly into his hand. The look from King Chang was making him a little uncomfortable. He finally said, "I didn't want to bother you with it, and it was more from curiosity than anything."

"Simply asking me would have gotten the same information."

"This was more entertaining anyway." He smiled.

"Let's get back to the what brought us here today. I think it best we take Mouse's suggestion and retire somewhere more private."

"Gunnarr, please go clear out the old king's hall and secure it for us," King Chang said.

Without a word, Gunnarr motioned to a group of warriors, who quickly followed him out of the hall, their alert eyes constantly scanning their surroundings.

Once the warriors were gone, the men rose from their chairs, all save Lu-Ning. Stepping forward from the shadows, a man with a slight yet strong build and a hairstyle matching Lu-Ning's moved to help Lu-Ning stand. Gently, the younger man helped him to his feet, then walked with him to where the others were patiently waiting.

Guessing Joran's thoughts, Mouse leaned over to Joran's ear and quietly told him about the sickness that the king had suffered as a boy and how it had crippled his legs. While he could shuffle along well enough, the king couldn't stand without help. Either a cane or an assistant. The royal clothier would order the kind kings shoes with thicker soles so they wouldn't wear so fast. The clothier knew having to get new shoes more often than others would only serve to remind the king of his difficulty in walking. While in other kingdoms, this would be seen as a weakness in a ruler, in Lu-Ning's kingdom, people rode more than they walked, and once on a horse, Lu-Ning was better than most.

Joran nodded his understanding. Then he asked who the lean warrior was who was helping the king. "Is that an appointed position, or is he forced to help him like that?" he asked Mouse.

"Oh no, that is a coveted position, one that his adopted son would rather die than give up. That who is helping him now. Angensen has been a loyal body guard and assistant since he finished the training and selection process."

"Have you met him? Angensen, I mean?"

"Oh, we have met a few times. After all, haven't you caught on yet? Everyone worth knowing, I know." Mouse winked. "He is a good man. Just don't tell him I said that."

Joran smiled and nodded.

One of the queens came over to where the two were standing out of the way. Joran was pretty sure it was Queen Helena. He was starting to have a tough time keeping all the titles, names, and kingdoms straight in his head. "We queens are going to the queens' sitting room while you men talk about matters of state."

"I understand, Queen Helena," Mouse said, bowing his head slightly.

The queen winked at him. "It is too bad, really. I wanted to spend some time talking with you. I doubt we will get that opportunity now. Could you tell me if you delivered the message I asked you to deliver?"

"Yes, I did. The lady said she would write you right away. It is a shame I didn't know you and I were going to meet so soon. I would have brought her response with me."

"Oh, this wasn't my idea. It was one of Jura's ideas. For some reason, she had this idea it would be nice to have a gathering of the queens while the rulers of the kingdoms were meeting. I believe she invited Sabrina as well. We all know she doesn't like to travel very far, and since she hasn't learned to swim, she detests sea travel."

"Yes, we are well aware of her dislike of the sea," Mouse said with a smile. "What have you ladies been cooking up among yourselves?" he asked with an exaggerated tone of conspiracy.

"No," she said flatly with a roll of her eyes. "All we do is sit around doing needlepoint while that wannabe sorceress does parlor tricks with overlong sleeves on her dressed and shuffles cards with old pictures on them and says they predict the future. Enough of that though. Do you think the queen can help me?"

Mouse smiled and nodded. "I am sure she can. Please don't be offended by her reply though. Without a doubt, the letter will be filled with great detail and be rather blunt. You know how down-to-earth she is. No overinflated views of herself there."

Blushing slightly, she replied, "Oh, I am sure it will make for very stimulating reading. And I am not an innocent little girl anymore either."

"M'lady!" Mouse said in mock shock.

"Shush. Like you didn't know better." She lightly slapped his arm and laughed.

"I would never think anything short of pure innocent and royal thoughts of a queen," Mouse said while trying not to laugh.

They were interrupted by Queen Jura. "Are you going to be joining us anytime soon, Helena?"

"Yes, coming," Helena said, then quickly moving her fingers, she signed to Mouse, "She is so mind-numbingly dull." With that, she followed the other queens out of the room.

Joran caught Mouse's odd look as he followed the queen out of the room with his eyes.

"Um. Mouse, we are getting left behind." He lightly tugged at the man's shirt and gestured at the door across the room.

"Oh. Yes. We best hurry up then." With that, the two slid in to the end of the king's procession out of the room.

Joran was happy being at the end of the group; something in his head told him that if Elsa saw him, she would send him out to polish the saddles or something rather than let him stay with the kings and other grownups. Keeping that in mind, he quietly kept up with the group, only staying close enough to hear them and not lose them while they wended through the castle.

It was while he was dawdling along behind them that he caught movement out of the corner of his eye while passing a hallway. It wasn't just someone going about his usual business. It seemed like the person was trying to hide yet still hear and see the group. Stopping and walking back, Joran had a brief look at the man. He was wearing a long dark-maroon coat that blended into the shadows surprisingly well. Other than being a normal-looking man from Chanese, only his manner made him stand out to Joran. Then the man was gone.

Joran hurried to catch up with the others, only to be caught at the door of the king's private hall by Elsa. "And what have you been up to?" she demanded.

"Elsa, I was just looking around. It is a big castle," Joran replied, keeping his tone somewhat awed.

"I am sure you were," she said, not believing him entirely. And for good reason. "Gunnarr? Is there something Joran can do while we hold this meeting? I am sure it will take a long time, and I don't want him getting impatient while we talk."

So much for slipping in at the end of the line, Joran thought bitterly.

Gunnarr scratched his beard and thought for a moment. "Yes, I think he would find the armory very...educational." He winked at Joran, making sure Elsa didn't see it.

"And what am I going to learn there?" he demanded in a bitter tone, clearly missing Gunnarr's wink.

"I am sure this castle has a kitchen as well. Would you prefer that? I know you can wash pots and pans well enough," Elsa sniffed.

"The armory should hold something I can learn about," Joran grumped in reply.

Gunnarr chuckled. "Go down this way to the end. There is a black door with a silver shield set in it. That is where you will find the armory."

"Now get," Elsa said. "And don't break anything or shoot yourself in the foot with an arrow or something."

After Elsa had closed the door, Joran set off, grumbling under his breath the whole way at the unfairness of it all. He couldn't even sneak back and listen at the door. Four guards with heavily calloused hands stood guard. Having been banished from the king's hall, he took the only other option he had: the armory.

While he wandered off to follow the directions from Gunnarr, Joran's mind wandered over everything but the armory. He was having a hard time accepting even the remote chance that the storyteller and Elsa were anyone except who he had known them to be all his life. Part of it was just plain old stubbornness. He was smart enough to admit that to himself. The other part was that seeing them as anything other than who they had always been was very difficult, even with the way the kings and other royalty treated them. It was clear they believed the two were none other than Orrlick and Elsalia themselves. Then his mind tossed in the flower Elsa had produced for the queen upon their arrival. There was no way it had been transported in her sleeve the whole way here. It would have died long ago or, at the least, been damaged. No, the flower was like it had just bloomed that morning in a garden. He just couldn't admit it to himself that she had made it pop out of thin air. The thought made his head spin a little. He decided he had had enough of that line of thought for the day.

He started paying more attention to his surroundings after putting the thoughts of Elsa and the storyteller aside. It was a stone hallway, poorly lit with a scattering of three-wick candles set in alcoves along the way. Joran found the candles interesting; who would have thought to put three wicks in one candle? He did have to admit that the extra two wicks gave off more light. This flickering light was reflected out into the hallway by polished silver plates set in the back of the alcoves. Some of the hallways leading off the main one were lit with the same candles and alcoves; others were dark or only had a single candle in a hanger from the ceiling. Just ahead he could see the light reflecting from the shield on a door. He stopped, though; he had heard a rustling too big to be a mouse or cat down one of the hallways. He wasn't sure why he stopped at this sound; it just didn't seem right to him. Even after telling himself that it was a big castle and it must have people working throughout it, what was one more noise? No, he stopped and stepped into the shadows of a recessed doorway with no candles nearby. Then he quietly waited.

He was somewhat surprised when after a few moments he saw the same man in the dark-maroon coat cautiously creep into the hallway and look behind him. Joran watched him closely, getting a good look at the man this time. He had a short, well-trimmed goatee and had his hair pulled back into a short ponytail at the base of his neck. To Joran, he looked almost boring. *If he wasn't acting so weird, he would never have attracted any suspicion*, Joran thought as he watched the man. His body language screamed that he wasn't supposed to be anywhere in the castle at all. Instead, the man stopped for a moment, as though listening, then scurried down the hallway back the way Joran had come. Joran waited a few beats of his heart, then slowly peered around the doorframe to see where the man had gone. There was no sight of him or any indication what hallway he might have ducked into.

The little voice in his head piped up suddenly. It told Joran that if he was to inform Elsa or anyone else of what he had seen, he would be laughed at for just having a "bad feeling about the man." He would have to have something solid to hand them. For now, all he could do was keep an eye open for the man again.

Chapter Fourteen

In the morning, the city awoke to snow falling. The quiet flakes coated everything, giving the castle a fairy-tale appearance. That didn't change the fact that Joran was still not allowed to join the kings with the storyteller and Elsa. The only change this time was Sladvick was now in charge of Joran's entertainment for the day. After the first meal, the two wandered into the public throne room, sitting near a warm fire. It sputtered every so often when a clump of snow fell down the chimney. Sladvick looked around the room while Joran stared into the flames morosely.

"Hey, Joran," Sladvick said after a bit, his tone quiet.

"Huh?" Joran mumbled, not taking his eyes from the fire.

"Have you noticed that none of these soldiers are doing anything productive? Just look around. They are playing some board game over there. That group is just eating and drinking. Isn't it somewhat early to be downing steins of beer already? Then there are those against the wall there just sleeping. At least there are a few who are doing something productive." He gestured at the small group sitting on stools in a corner, polishing their armor and sharpening swords, knives, and axes.

Joran looked away from the fire and took in the room and the activities around him. Sladvick was right; they seemed to be rather unproductive soldiers.

"Aren't these the king's personal guards?" Joran whispered.

"Still, I haven't seen any Chanese do much of anything since we got here."

"I think they are supposed to wait for the king to tell them to break the enemies' toys and then kill them," Joran replied.

"I mean anyone here. Seems they don't do anything really."

"True. Seems kind of monotonous and uninspiring," Joran agreed. Then he changed the subject. "When we got here, did you see how Gunnarr's wife treated him and what she did with his children? Keeping them from him like that?"

A sad look came across Sladvick's face. "Yes, I did see it. She clearly hurt him and had planned it out that way."

"Why does she do that to him?" Joran asked, puzzled. "He is a good man; clearly cares for his children, and at one time I am sure he cared for her as well."

"Mouse and I talked about it late last night," Sladvick replied. "Seems Gunnarr fell madly in love with her when they were in their early teens. The problem was, he wasn't born from royal blood, and she was. That made her look down on him. She never looked at him as a possible husband—barely treated him like a friend even. Then when Gunnarr gained status, her family decided she should marry him and create another valuable tie in the kingdom. Of course, Gunnarr was thrilled he could finally marry the woman he was in love with." Sladvick paused, seeming to gather his thoughts. He continued, "Of course she protested loudly, not that it did any good. Gunnarr found out only too late how downright mean and superficial she is—only interested in status, clothes, and playing court games (also known as gossip). She has driven him to stay away as much as possible, and when he is home, she keeps his children from him as much as possible, just to get even with him for ruining her life. At least that is how she sees it."

"That is sad," Joran said. "How many children do they have?"

"Mouse said they have two. I think they are around six and eight. From what Mouse said, Gunnarr loves them more than anything and dotes on them whenever he can. That's probably why his wife keeps them away from him at every chance."

"That is wrong. I don't see why we can't help Gunnarr; he is a good man and our friend," Joran said.

"No," Sladvick said, his tone cold. "Joran, you do not meddle with a man and his wife. I don't mean just stay out of her bed when he isn't around either. You don't meddle with them. It isn't done."

Switching topics without thinking, Joran said, "Have you noticed that Mouse loves Helena?"

"The *Queen* Helena?" Sladvick sputtered in surprise.

"Yes."

"That is a scandalous thing to even hint at, much less say aloud, and in the king's throne room to boot," Sladvick replied.

"Even if it is, it doesn't change the fact that it is true," Joran said, some stubbornness coming into his voice.

"Joran—" Sladvick tried to cut him off before he said more.

It didn't work; Joran just kept right on going. "I heard she isn't really his aunt, just his blood uncle's wife after his first wife. So it really isn't that scandalous, is it? It's not like she was his father's sister or something."

Sladvick was sputtering by now. His face was red, and though he managed to keep his voice slightly above a whisper, the tone still came through harsh. "Joran! Listen here! It doesn't matter if it is his blood aunt or not. The basic fact she is married makes this conversation wrong. Wait, where did you hear he was in love with her in the first place?"

"You didn't notice it? Just watch how he changes whenever she is in the room with him. Or even just walking by in the halls." Joran shrugged. "I thought everyone saw it."

Sladvick looked at Joran a moment, clearly turning it over in his head. Finally, he said, "You aren't old enough to know about these things. How Mouse looks at Helena, *Queen* Helena, is just something you misinterpreted." He waited for Joran to respond to this. Getting nothing except a sour look, he gently slapped Joran on the back and suggested they go look around. Joran agreed, thinking sheepishly it wasn't nice to cluck about their friends like women at a sewing circle.

"How about we start with the kitchen?" Joran suggested. "I could use a snack. Bet they have some of those sweet bread rolls left from breakfast."

"Good idea. I could use one too. Then let's go look at the blacksmith shop," Sladvick added.

After a few wrong turns, they found themselves in the scullery. Well, sculleries was more how it felt. Neither of them could see all the way across the kitchen. The far walls were obscured between the steam and smoke from the meat of entire cows being slowly turned on spits through a trough of gravy as they cooked. Rather than having all the cooking fires and pits on one side against the wall, here they were spread out throughout the kitchen. That wasn't the only difference. There was no order at all. None. People scurried here and there; the head cook screamed and shouted at everyone, but no one paid him any mind. A pot maiden grabbed another chef's hat, tossed it in a pot of boiling water, and laughed hysterically as he tried to fish it out and not burn himself.

Joran looked at Sladvick. Sladvick looked at Joran. Without saying a word, they both slipped quietly back out the way they had come. Joran had grabbed a handful of cookies off a tray as they passed. He shared these with his friend as they went in search of the royal blacksmith.

Passing a cleaning lady in the hall, Sladvick stopped and asked her, "Could you please point us in the direction of the blacksmith's shop?"

Instead of simply answering him, she eyed him up and down, clearly happy with what she saw. Then she said, "Never saw you around here before. I would have remembered a fine-looking man such as yourself."

"Thank you. We are simply visiting," Sladvick said politely, clearly uncomfortable with her look and compliment.

"Looks like you have come a long way. Where did you come from?"

"We come from Brassel," Sladvick answered politely, trying to keep his eyes from wandering to the maid's ample bosom that seemed to spill from her dress.

"I've never met anyone from there," she said. "I would like to spend some time learning about that kingdom; I am sure you could entertain me very well. The boy could take care of your business while we got to know each other." Her tone was suggestive.

Sladvick reddened and coughed. "Um, the metal workers' shop, please?"

She giggled. "Down this hall. If you get done early with your errand, I am around until after supper tonight. If you would like to…talk and show me things from your kingdom."

"Thank you for the directions," Sladvick said awkwardly and left. Joran trailed along behind him, trying his best not to giggle like an idiot.

Once they were out of earshot of the maid, Sladvick burst out, "Can you believe that woman? She had not one grain of decency about her! Making such suggestions to a total stranger like that. I should have gotten her name and reported her to Gunnarr."

Joran just couldn't help himself. Keeping as straight a face as he could and his tone innocent, he said, "Shall we go back and ask her for her name?"

Sladvick shoved the door to the courtyard open—a little harder than he had meant to, judging from the look on his face as the snow fell from the trim work over the door, down his shirt, and on top of his head. Between that and Joran's suggestion, he just spitted and sputtered for a moment.

"She seemed to like you. I am sure if we went back and asked her, she would give you her name and maybe more." Joran had barely said the words when he found himself floating through the air. *Guess that last one was a little too far* was the only thought that went through his head. He landed softly in a pile of snow near the door. Aside from the snow down his shirt, he crawled out of the drift uninjured. Sladvick was standing there, his massive arms crossed in front of him and an angry look on his face. The look went to laughter, though, once he saw Joran crawl out on all fours, covered head to toe in snow. Joran had to laugh too.

Once they had settled down and knocked the snow off each other, they continued to the blacksmith's shop. Joran was still amused by Sladvick's response to the maid. He kept his mouth shut, though; he didn't see any soft piles of snow around to land in this time.

Upon arriving across the courtyard, the two introduced themselves to the small giant of a man who was the master journeyman blacksmith of the castle. Joran had thought he had seen some big men. Gunnarr, for one, was huge in his eyes. The blacksmith who stood before them, though, was massive. The man's legs, covered in thick and well-worn leather pants behind a thicker leather apron, looked bigger than Joran's body. Behind the thick brown beard, though, was an easy smile that lit the man's eyes up like coals in his fire. After shaking hands with them both—Joran's hand had completely disappeared in the smith's—he welcomed them to his smithy. While he and Sladvick talked about tempering metal and good-naturedly argued over the best wood for a hammer's handle, Joran wandered off into the shop. No stranger to blacksmith shops, he was amazed at what he saw in the castle's shop.

The shop was filled with everything metal, it seemed. From razor-sharp felling axes to three-furrow plows, the shop seemed to have everything. Behind each man's forge was a wall that contained what looked like the man's best work. Each smith had at least three items displayed. One clearly specialized in ornate buckles and bits for horses. He had at least a dozen different buckles hanging from wood pegs. Another made the beautiful folded metal that Joran had seen only once in a knife. Looking closer yet staying out of the man's way, Joran saw different patterns in the metal. One was a flowing pattern, like waves on a pond in a breeze. Another looked like dozens of small boxes stacked together. The smith saw Joran admiring his work, smiled at him, and continued working at his anvil. Wandering deeper into the shop brought him to what he knew was the heat treat area. It was kept dark here so the men could accurately gauge the color of the metal. A man with fewer fingers than what he had been born with was working a hatchet head through the process. He never took his eyes off the glowing metal.

While Sladvick talked the morning away with the royal smith, Joran wandered around the rest of the courtyard. He was surprised at how similar the castle's work resembled that of the farm he had grown up on. Men were working on everyday things from making harnesses for the plow horses to butchering animals for the castle's kitchen. He saw men splitting wood for the fires and others carefully making torches or the three-wick candles. Most were teaching their skills to apprentices. All the while, though, he watched for the strange man he had seen in the hallways on his way to the armory. He didn't think the man was a tradesman; still, it didn't hurt to keep looking.

When the sun was high over the castle, Gunnarr came wandering out into the courtyard. He was greeted by many with a smile and a wave. Some called out greetings as well. Gunnarr replied to all of them, regardless of the man's station. Whether from a master journeyman or young apprentice, the greetings were all returned with a smile. Walking up to where Joran and Sladvick were talking with the castle smith, he heartily thumped the big man on the back and greeted him. Then he turned to Joran and Sladvick. "It's about food time. Let's go find something to eat. Preferably something good." They thanked the smith and said their goodbyes, then followed Gunnarr into the castle.

Once in the dining hall, Mouse waved from where he was lounging against a wall. They all walked over to Mouse. A cat sat happily in his lap, purring while Mouse gently rubbed its ears. Joran thought it was sort of funny that a "mouse" was petting a cat.

Gunnarr said, "I will be going out this afternoon and was wondering if you would like to come with. The kings are having a closed counsel after the noon meal. No point in staying here all afternoon." Mouse agreed and waited for them to finish their noon meal. He had already eaten his.

Once they were done eating, Mouse gently sat the cat on the floor and stood. Stretching, he said, "I think a walk outside would do me some good now. Even if my new friend here disagrees." He looked down at the big cat who was rubbing on his legs.

Gunnarr looked down at the cat. "After that meal, I agree with you. As for your furry friend there, I am sure he will forgive you later. It might cost you a few fish, but he will forgive you."

Picking up his thick cloak from the table, Mouse put it on and followed Gunnarr and the rest out the main doors of the castle. The wind immediately caught his cloak, and he was glad the snow had stopped. Wind was bad enough.

After a few blocks, Sladvick broke the silence. "I have been trying to figure out why you all seem to have so many titles or names. The old storyteller — whose real name I can't remember, now that I think of it — is called Orrlick by some and just the storyteller by others. Why is that?" he asked no one in particular. Joran was glad for the question, though; maybe someone could clear things up now since someone other than himself had asked.

"I think I can answer that," Mouse said. "Think of names as tools. You use this hammer for certain things, yet you use a very different one for other things. For us, names are the same thing. Tools. We pick them up and put them down as the task or situation at hand changes."

"Thank you. That doesn't really help though. I use my name whether I am at my forge or at a wedding," Sladvick persisted.

"Not everyone is so…sincere with their lives. Some of us are less than candid with those around us."

"I find it somewhat distasteful of you to lump Elsa in with that definition," Sladvick said.

"No offense was meant. It is just the way of the world that some of us sometimes have to hide our true selves from those around us at certain times to protect ourselves and others from those in the world who aren't good people." Sladvick let it drop at that point.

Gunnarr motioned to a smaller side street. "We can get there down here."

Mouse looked at him oddly. "It is faster if we go down the street we are on."

"Well." Gunnarr scratched his beard, an embarrassed look on his face. "This street continues past the shrine we passed when we came in. I have sort of slacked in my holy duties since getting here."

"So?" Mouse asked.

"Well, would you give your wife a chance to scold you in public if you could avoid it?" Gunnarr asked.

Even Joran knew the answer to this one, so he moved off down the street Gunnarr had indicated.

Joran looked all around him. The ancient city was made mostly of gray stone. He had heard it was mined locally and used as the primary material for building and paving the streets. He saw some buildings made of wood; most were stone though. The people were all dressed in heavy wool or furs to keep warm against the winter winds. This didn't keep them from yelling to one other across the streets or tossing good-natured insults to one another.

Turning the corner of one street, Gunnarr was caught square in the face by a snowball. They all stopped as he shook the snow from his beard and face. Two very well-dressed men were standing on opposite sides of a cart. One was in the process of standing up and packing a snowball to throw at the other when he noticed the crowd had grown quiet and his opponent had stopped stone still. He looked surprised and a little frightened.

"M'lord," the first man stammered. "I did not mean to hit you. No offense was meant. We were just—" Gunnarr raised his hand, cutting him off. Gunnarr then bent to the nearest snow pile and constructed a large snowball. He stood and tossed it at the man, who was still wrapping his mind around the fact that he had just hit one of the royal family in the face with a snowball. His thoughts of this came to an end when the massive snowball his face.

Gunnarr for his part roared in laughter. "I thought you would at least try and duck it." The crowd erupted in laughter mixed with a little relief, calling insults to the man as he wiped the snow off his face. Gunnarr laughed and waved at the two, then continued on his way.

"They meant no harm—just two friends having some fun in the cold," he said, seeing Joran's and Sladvick's surprised looks. "No reason I can't have a little fun too. Besides, once those two have their hands go numb, they will find a warm tavern, share drinks, and throw darts-more thank likely at the dart board- until they can't stand anymore. One can never be sure though. They might play cups with darts instead of throwing axes."

"The summers don't have snow here. What do they do then?" Mouse asked.

"They throw rocks, then go to the taverns and share cold lagers and throw darts. Again, usually at the dart board," Gunnarr said, shrugging.

A few blocks past the snowball fight, they passed a two-story building with a small balcony built off the second-floor rooms. Standing on the balcony were a few ladies who were scantily dressed under thick fur robes that seemed to fall open quite often, especially considering the temperature outside. Gunarr ducked his head and pulled the hood up higher to hide his face. He found he was just a moment too late when from above one of the ladies called out to him. "Gunnarr! Don't you want to come up and have some hot tea with us again? We have some sweet treats to go with it." Looking up, Joran caught one of the women smiling broadly while winking down at the red-faced Gunnarr.

"Gunnarr, do you know them?" Joran asked.

"I think he does," Mouse piped up happily.

"Yes, I have spoken to them from time to time," Gunnarr replied shortly, throwing a quick smile up at the ladies before hurrying along. "They speak with lots of people though. As do I," he hastily added.

Turning down a main street, they encountered a procession of men all wearing the same thick-furred cloaks. Their walk was all in step with one another as well. Sladvick wondered what they were, as people seemed to be in a big hurry to get out of their way. Entire groups of people scurried to clear way for the men.

The man who seemed to be the head man raised a hand in greeting to Gunnarr. Gunnarr in turn bowed and stepped aside for the men to pass. He didn't straighten until the procession of men had passed. Then he straightened and continued on his way. The others followed him.

Sladvick fell in alongside the big man. "Who were they?"

"Religious fanatics. They worship the great snow beasts. The white bears of the tundra," Gunnarr said.

Mouse piped up behind the two big men. "More like fanatical trouble. They have sects all over the neighboring realms. Their members spend their days divided between weapons training, hand-to-hand combat, strategy, and their religious rituals. While this makes them fierce and fearless fighters, they only fight for themselves and their goal. This leads to them poking into various politics with sometimes with large sticks. Just making a mess of things usually." He sniffed at the last part.

"Why do they mess with all the kingdoms like that?" Sladvick asked.

Gunnarr swept his hand around them. "This all used to be one big kingdom. Then a certain something happened, and the kingdom was made into several smaller ones. The men you just saw are part of a group that would like to make it all one kingdom again."

Sladvick scratched at his beard a moment. "Why is that bad to want the kingdom reunited?"

"The realm was broken up for a reason. Something came along that needed hiding and being kept secure. That was what brought about the breaking up of the one big kingdom."

In response to Sladvick's questioning look, Mouse picked up the story. "The item is probably the most important object in the world. The fanatics tend to ignore that part of things."

Before he could think about what he was going to say, Joran quietly blurted out, "That object is what the storyteller is looking for. Someone got ahold of it who shouldn't have it." His little voice in the back of his head had made the

connection quickly enough. It wasn't as quick with its word of warning about saying anything about it out loud. Maybe next time it would be best to reverse the order of things it said to Joran. First keep mouth shut, then make the connections.

Mouse and Gunnarr looked back at him. "He isn't as dumb as he makes out to be sometimes, is he?" Mouse said somberly.

"Yes, he does seem to have the beginnings of a brain upstairs," Gunnarr agreed.

"Since you worked it through yourself, yes, something was stolen and someone is running away with it. Yes, we are trying to get it back. It is of such importance that, if it comes right down to it, the kingdoms will join and take entire cities down to get it back. Stone by stone they will tear them down until it is found and returned safely," Mouse said, his voice serious.

"They would start a war over this?" Sladvick said, surprised.

"War would be a small price to pay to return this. Besides, it could turn into a good opportunity to finally remove the Mulsins from the earth permanently," Gunnarr said.

"Perhaps we should take this conversation up in a more private setting?" Mouse said.

They all fell silent as they covered the last little ways to their destination: the port of the city.

Joran looked around wide-eyed at the swaying masts of the ships. They looked like a timberland of trees, with a breeze making them rock back and forth. Walking across a footbridge, they came to the shipyards themselves. Several ships lay in their dry docks, either being built new or being refitted.

A small door opened in the side of a large warehouse, and out hobbled a short little man wearing a thick, work-stained canvas apron over his clothes. He looked older than the city itself. Even so, his eyes were bright and alert.

"Good day m'lord," he said, raising a hand in a friendly wave. His voice was dry yet carried well in the cold air.

"Good day to you as well, Almeric," Gunnarr said, clasping the man's hand in greeting. "You look as healthy as ever."

"Good of you to say, m'lord. I keep busy. This weather isn't good for it though. I can't get much work done until spring. My apprentices are busy casting the cleats and brackets. Others are carving the pulleys and such for installation this spring."

Gunnarr walked over to where a partially built ship was partially buried in the snow. He gently put a hand on the rib nearest him, almost like petting a newborn puppy. "Almeric has agreed to build a me a boat."

"A ship" was the old man's smiling reply.

"Yes, yes, a ship." Gunnarr laughed. "She will be the finest ship built by the finest builder."

"Awfully big bo—ship," Sladvick said, looking at the huge framework already assembled. "Are you going to be able to move that much weight?"

"I will get big oarsmen." Gunnarr laughed. "Powerful men to make her race across the ocean."

From behind and above them came a yell that caught Joran's attention. Looking back, he followed a hill up to its crest, where he saw several children having a snowball fight while others were flying down the snow on what looked like miniature horse sleds. Joran looked back to where the men stood. He figured they would spend the rest of the day talking about what in Joran's opinion were just oversize boats. They wouldn't miss him if he went to talk with someone near his age for a while. He thought it would be a nice change. He walked over to where the miniature sleds seemed to run out of speed and stop at the base of the hill. He leaned against a tree and just relaxed for a bit, enjoying the scene before him.

Not long after leaning against the tree, Joran took note of a girl with long blond braids flowing out from under her rabbit-fur-and-quilted-wool hat. She was as tall as a boy, even though she clearly wasn't. Even under her bulky winter clothes, Joran could see she was a young woman. A very shapely young woman. The dress she wore just made it that much clearer.

He watched her sliding down the hill; her clear laughter carried to Joran. He decided he liked hearing her laugh. As she got closer, he saw her delicate face had been turned a dark pink from the winter wind. She came to a stop on her sled near Joran. Gathering his courage, Joran smiled and gave her a little wave. When she smiled back, he said, "Looks like you are having fun." He was embarrassed to find his voice seemed pinched and nervous.

"Haven't you ever been sledding?" she asked happily as she stood up and shook the snow from her dress and knee-high boots.

"No. We didn't have hills like this where I grew up," he said, feeling somewhat like an idiot. He wasn't sure why he was feeling like this. It wasn't the first time he had spoken to a pretty girl.

"Would you like to try it?" she asked.

"It looks like it would be fun. I don't have anything to sled on though," he said.

"Well," she said with an angelic look, "I might let you try it with my sled — if you were willing to trade, that is."

"I really don't have anything to trade though," Joran said kind of nervously.

"Can't think of anything?" She eyed him up and down.

Joran shook his head sadly.

"Let's start with something easy," she said. "Then maybe we can think of something more fun to trade." Her look reminded him of the one the maid had given Sladvick earlier that day. "Where are you from that they don't have hills for sledding?"

"Brassel. We have rolling hills; nothing like this though," he said gesturing toward the hill she had just come down.

"Never met anyone from there. What is your name?" Her gaze was steady on him now, and it made him slightly uncomfortable. Not in a bad way though. He wished he had access to the kitchen like he did back home. He could trade sweets for sweet things like he used to with Geeta.

"Joran," he said.

"Odd name. Is that a common one in Brassel? My name is Anneliese," she said without waiting for an answer.

"It is nice to meet you, Anneliese," Joran said and bowed slightly toward her.

"Now that we know each other, Joran of Brassel, would you like to trade for a ride?" She let it hang for a moment. "On my sled I mean?" Her smile was almost coy.

Joran turned red, and it had nothing to do with the crisp wind. "What would you like?" he asked, almost afraid of the answer he would get.

She smiled at him, chewing one corner of her lower lip. "If you pull my sled up to the top of the hill, I will let you ride it down. Only if you give me a kiss at the top."

Before Joran could stammer a response, another sled came to rest not far from them. The boy riding it stood and looked at the two of them. His face was not friendly at all. In an angry and commanding tone, he yelled at Anneliese, "Get over here."

Ignoring the boy, Anneliese smiled at Joran. "Well, what about it? Fair deal?"

"Um, Anneliese, I think he was talking to you," Joran said, nodding toward the big boy, trying to buy time to come up with a good answer. Saying yes just sounded too pathetic to him.

"So? I don't want to talk with him," she said.

Deciding that the girl wasn't going to do as he told her, the big boy turned his attention solely on Joran. "Who said you could talk to her?"

"No one. I didn't think I needed to beg for permission to talk to a girl," Joran said, then realized maybe this was one of the times that he should listen to his little voice in his head before talking. Too late.

The bigger boy stalked up to them. This was when Joran realized this boy was much bigger than him. Not just a little bit bigger.

"You really want a beating, don't you?" he said as he closed his eyes and rolled his head from shoulder to shoulder.

The little voice in his head said that there was no way he could talk his way out of this or even just walk away. Not that he wanted to walk away from the pretty girl he had just met. Joran knew that the blustering would work into insults and then to blows. Once they got to that point, Joran knew he couldn't win a fight with the bigger boy and would probably take a pretty good pounding — all for just wanting to talk with her. Well, and now that she had brought it up, a kiss would be nice too. So Joran took the advice that he had received from Sladvick long ago. No fight is fair; they aren't supposed to be fair. Winning is the only objective. Keeping all of that in mind, he punched the bigger boy just below his throat. In Joran's view, the bigger boy had it coming. Why close your eyes when you are picking a fight with someone? Can't see, can't fight very well. Dumb idiot.

While the carefully aimed blow wasn't all that hard, the result was about what Joran had expected. Several things happened almost simultaneously, none of them exactly pleasant in the bigger boy's view. His eyes flew open in surprise, and he teared up instantly. While the tears streamed down his face, he grabbed his throat and started to wheeze while trying to breathe. Finally, he fell to his knees and bent over, his face in the snow coughing and wheezing.

Squatting down on his heels and resting his arms on his thighs, Joran looked at the big fella. "Relax. Turn your face out of the snow. Deep slow breaths. You aren't going to die. It feels like it, I know. You won't though. Breathe slow and deep. It will pass." He caught the stunned look on Anneliese's face. He hoped this didn't take her offer of a kiss away. She really did have beautiful lips. Really beautiful, full, and soft lips. He didn't let himself start thinking about her thick hair.

After a few moments, the bigger boy sat up on his knees and looked at Joran while wiping his eyes clear with one mittened hand and rubbing his throat with the other. "I will feel better soon?" he coughed out.

"Yes, it will pass in a little bit. See, you already feel better now. The more you control your breathing, the sooner it will go away," Joran said evenly.

Coughing a little more, he looked at Joran. "What did you do that for? All I did was talk."

"Oh, you were going to hit me, probably a lot harder and in more places than I just did you." Joran smiled.

"I still can't breathe," the boy wheezed.

"Then I guess you will just choke to death," Joran said dead-faced. He remembered the time his friend on the farm had been on the table in the kitchen. He knew that the boy would be fine—sore maybe for a little while—OK though. He was talking, which meant he could breathe, so he was fine.

The bigger boy got to his feet and walked over to where his sled was.

Anneliese seemed to overcome her surprise about that time and turned to Joran, who had just stood up as well. "Is everyone in your kingdom trained like you?" Her tone wasn't angry. Joran had a hard time deciding how she sounded really.

"I don't know many from my kingdom. Very few, actually. I grew up on a farm out in the country," Joran said politely. He was saddened, though, with how things had gone. He had only wanted to spend some time with other people his age for a little while, and it had gone sour. He smiled a little smile at her, turned, and started to walk away.

"Hey!" Anneliese said.

Joran stopped and turned back to her. She was quickly walking over to him. "Never had anyone turn down a kiss from me before."

"Um, I didn't hold up my end of the deal though," Joran stammered.

"I think you earned a little kiss nonetheless," she said. With that, she grabbed the back of his head, pulled his face down to hers, and gave him a good long kiss.

If that was a little kiss, I would love to know what a big one is, Joran thought while he enjoyed her soft lips on his and tried to keep his knees from falling out from under him.

"You're good at that." She giggled, then spun on her toes, grabbed the chord on her sled, and took off up the hill, her silky hair flying out behind her.

Walking back to the boat builder's shop, Joran heard laughter from the men. Wondering what he had missed, he looked up and saw that they were all looking at him. Turning a little red, and not from the cold crisp air either, he realized they had seen the girl kiss him.

Mouse was hanging on Gunnarr's shoulder, laughing. "Such an innocent," he managed between laughs and wiping tears from his eyes. Joran turned a little more red. He hoped that would be the end of it.

Nope.

Gunnarr's deep good-natured laughter stopped long enough for him to say, "Why didn't you go after her?" The twinkle in his eyes said he meant no harm; he was just amused.

For lack of anything better to say, Joran looked at his feet as he shuffled them in the snow. "Why? I don't know her."

Laughing harder, Mouse said, "Oh, she wanted you to know her. In many ways, I would say." As with Gunnarr's, his eyes said he meant no harm; he was just having fun at Joran's expense. Granted, Joran wished they would have fun at someone else's expense.

Standing up and wiping his eyes on the back of his hand, the boat builder slapped Gunnarr on his broad back. "You have fallen short on his learning. You clearly taught him to fight well. Why haven't you taught him the gentler things in life?"

Gunnarr looked down at Mouse. "You, my good friend, are smooth of tongue; why don't you let Elsa know she has missed a chapter in our friend's learning? A rather large and important one."

This brought Mouse's laughter to an abrupt halt. "Me?" he squeaked. "I would no sooner do that than go swimming in the whirlpool we passed to come into your kingdom." He looked like he meant it.

"Come now, she likes you," Gunnarr said.

"Wait here. I know how to settle this fairly," the boat builder said, then disappeared into his warehouse. Reappearing a few minutes later, he held out a pair of dice and a dicing cup. "Roll to decide who addresses this Elsa, who — from how you two talk — can level mountains with a single look."

"I have seen my little friend here throw dice, cup or no cup," Gunnarr said.

"Well, if you don't wish to do that, there is always the option of sending Joran back to the hill and letting his new playmate fill in his education, as it were. She looked quite willing and eager to study with him."

Joran's face was now redder than the wine at dinner the night before. He didn't like finding himself in an uncomfortable stop like this. All he had wanted to do was spend some time with someone his age. "I am not as uneducated as you are making me out to be. We don't have to tell Elsa about this either" he said as he kicked at a chunk of scrap wood. He winced when it didn't move. It was frozen to the ground. This just caused the others to laugh more. He knew it wasn't mean laughter; he would have laughed as well in their shoes. Which is where he would have liked to be at that moment; then his foot wouldn't be the one hurting.

He stood with the others while Gunnarr spoke to the shipmaster about his boat until the shadows grew long with the coming of night. Then they said their goodbyes and headed toward the castle for the evening meal. Joran was still a little moody after being laughed at, so he hung back a little. To top it off, he realized he never did get to try sliding down a hill like that. He looked up, trying to take his mind off the afternoon and noticed he could see stars through the clearing clouds. He sadly noticed that the star clusters appeared different than the ones he had learned the names of back on the farm. How far he had traveled, he thought.

Realizing that walking with his eyes to the stars was a good way to either get lost or slip on something underfoot, he brought his head back down to pay attention to where he was walking. That was when he saw a couple of men going into what looked like a tavern. He wouldn't have paid them any real mind; after all, men come and go from taverns all the time. It was their manner and the way one of them was dressed that caught his attention. One was the man from the castle, the one sneaking around the halls the other day. With him was an equally shifty-looking man. He was different, though, somehow. More confident in his movements was the best way Joran could think of to explain it. He was also familiar. Joran was sure he knew the man, even with his deep hood hiding his face. As though to confirm it, Joran felt a shiver, starting in the base of his brain and going down his spine. It was Ala Maona. Even though he knew that the man's being here was more than a coincidence, he couldn't get his mouth to work. Instead of speaking, he decided to make use of other things that did work: his legs and feet.

"Mouse, do you know of any Vibaions being here?" Great, now his mouth worked, he thought.

Before Mouse could answer, Gunnarr cut in. "They are forbidden from these lands. Any found here can be executed on sight, according to the law."

"Oh," Joran said. He wanted to say more, but his mouth had returned to the numb and useless state it had been in before.

Mouse just eyed him curiously yet remained silent.

Later that day they were at the great table in the dining hall when, much to Jorans dismay, Mouse and Gunnar decided to entertain the king and his friends with the story of Joran and the fair maiden at the sledding hill.

With a dramatic voice, made more so with the many steins of beer served with the meal, Gunnarr told of the bravery Joran had shown — how he had not only stood up to a larger opponent, but that he had done so with cunning to protect a fair maiden. And while Joran had struck first, it was such a calculated and decisive blow delivered with such power and speed that it brought the mighty opponent to his knees, coughing, spitting, and gagging for breath. Yet Joran showed compassion as well as courage by helping the fallen opponent get to his feet and leave the battle with his pride intact. Well, mostly. After all, Joran had brought him to his knees in one blow. As any man knew, that could be a little humiliating.

Up to this point, Joran was enjoying the story, as were the others at the table. He hoped that his friend would stop there.

No such luck.

Continuing in his deep voice, Gunnarr told them how the beautiful young damsel in distress had shown her overflowing appreciation for her savior. How she passionately kissed him, her eyes filled with adoration — which Joran found odd, since he remembered her eyes being closed — and locking her slender arms around his neck, never wanting the passionate kiss to end. She crushed her ample and firm body against her champion's chest as she rewarded his bravery and courage with a kiss. Joran was certainly shining right about then. Shining ripe-apple red. He kept his eyes firmly on his food as though it were the most interesting thing in the world at that moment. He cringed inwardly as Gunnarr continued. He knew Gunnarr meant no harm and was complimenting Joran in his own drunken way. He just wished Gunnarr wouldn't compliment the whole story. Having received his kiss, the noble and courageous knight in training politely accepted his reward and departed before accepting her other clearly offered gifts of thanks and adoration for defending her. At this, Gunnarr flopped heavily back down into his chair, took a long pull off his stein, and merrily slapped Joran on the back, making him choke on the meat he was chewing. *No need to chew the meat, really; just have Gunarr pat your back.*

Everyone from the kings to the hardened warriors at the table laughed heartily at the story. Some banged the table with their hands or stamped their feet under it. Many raised their steins of beer to Joran for being such a fine knight on the field of battle — and a gentleman off it. Even the queens were amused. Well, all except Lanna. She sat in her chair, her back as straight as ever, and didn't even crack a smile. Instead she glared at Gunnarr as though angry he was having a good time. Her look was ignored by the serving maidens, who giggled at the story and eyed Joran with doe eyes as they passed him. Somehow the top buttons on several dresses seemed to magically open around him as well while they bent over to fill his stein and his eyes.

Joran's ears felt like they would burn off his head if this kept up much longer. They only got redder when the warriors started yelling suggestions to him for what to do next time. Again, they were suggestions for the battlefield — and for after. The voices were all merry and good-natured, though, which made him feel a little less embarrassed. These smiling warriors and even kings were enjoying his company, treating him as one of their own. That felt really good. He looked up and smiled at them all, raising his stein to salute them in return. This brought another round of table pounding and shouting.

Standing, King Oordah tried to control his laughter. Taking a silk scarf, he tried to stop the flow of tears from his eyes as he looked at Mouse. "Come now, Mouse; that can't be the total story, can it? Tell us true."

Almost choking on his beer, Mouse nodded. "Gunnarr there has told it well. I can only think of a few liberties taken as a storyteller," he added.

The king roared in laughter. "Someone find a court musician. We shall have a song about this."

"Come now. I think Joran has been embarrassed enough by this," Queen Helena said gently. Right then Joran could have kissed her in thanks.

"It is all right, m'queen. If the king wishes a song from it, then he can have one," Joran said politely. "He is king after all." People laughed at this. Those on either side of him slapped him on his back.

Elsa cut through the merriment with a cold tone. "There is something wrong when two noblemen and a master journeyman can't keep a boy from fighting."

"Oui, m'lady, it was barely a fight. One mighty blow, and it was over. Joran showed great restraint and honor in not landing more," Mouse protested. "I say he should be commended for his actions today. Not only did he stand his ground against a much larger opponent, he showed great maturity and restraint afterwards. With both his opponent and the maiden. He surely earned the accolades he is receiving."

Gunnarr added, trying not to laugh, "He showed even more restraint and honor by accepting only a kiss."

Elsa was not to be swayed. "Next time it will be what, daggers in an alley and two maidens who show their thanks in less-than-chaste ways?" Joran had to admit, he liked the idea of two maidens and less-than-chaste ways. He was smart enough to keep that to himself though.

Sladvick, who had been quiet till now, came to Joran's defense as well. "Elsa, we both know Joran has been in worse fights on the farm just among the other boys there. This was hardly a fight by any definition, and he came to no harm. Neither did the boy he fought. I remember one time very well that things went much worse for the other boy. I am sure you remember it too. It didn't lead to daggers behind the barns though. Let him have his victory; no one was hurt. It was barely mischief that he got into." His tone was gentle yet carried his point well. It was answered by more whoops and pounding on the tables.

Elsa was clearly surprised by Sladvick taking Joran's side. Once things quieted down again, she turned on Sladvick. "Of all the people, I would have expected you to have seen the problem here."

"Elsa, if I were worried that he was going to start getting into knife fights over girls behind the barn or in alleys, I wouldn't have made him the knife he carries," Sladvick said evenly. "He is a fine young man, and today proves it. He handled himself with restraint, intelligence, good strategy, bravery and honor. I don't see how you can be mad about that." Sladvick paused, then continued, his voice rising somewhat. "You of all people should be proud he stood up not only for himself, but for a young lady as well — and he didn't take advantage of her appreciation afterward. Instead, he was a true gentleman."

Joran had slowly been going from embarrassed to angry. While the joking of the warriors and kings had made him blush and avoid people's eyes, he knew they were praising him as they would a grown and battle-tested warrior. He liked being acknowledged as one of them. Now, though, Elsa was putting him down. Again. Not only was she putting him down, she was doing it in front of those who had accepted and praised him for the very thing she was now using against him. This brought bitterness and anger. He couldn't seem to do anything right by her. If Elsa didn't give him direct orders or explicit permission to tie his boots, he seemed to be in trouble. He sat there and glowered at her.

Elsa looked at him, seeming to feel his angry look. Seeing him looking at her, she raised an arrogant eyebrow at him in challenge. He just looked down in disgust and ignored her. Leave it to Elsa to ruin what had been a good night.

Chapter Fifteen

A cold yet dazzling morning greeted them the next day. After a hearty and warm first meal, the old storyteller let them know that he, Elsa, and the kings would be spending the day in private conference again.

Gunnarr, looking none the worse for the beer he had consumed the night before, brightly smiled at his cousin. "It is far too pretty of a day to stay inside and muddle over things in a drafty, dreary castle. I, for one, am glad I am not a king and can enjoy the outdoors freely."

King Chang tried to give his cousin an angry look. Failing miserably to pull it off, he just laughed and continued his meal.

Thinking for a moment, Gunnarr looked at his cousin again. "If I remember right, the snow goats come out of the mountains this time of year."

"Yes, they do. They destroy the farmers' fields near the woods as well," Chang replied.

"Today would be a good day to help those poor farmers then. Don't you agree?"

Chang smiled. He liked hunting as well as his cousin, only he had other responsibilities to attend to as king. He scratched at his wild beard. "Planning on taking some of the castle warriors hunting?"

"It would be in service to the king and kingdom, don't you think?" he asked with a mischievous smile on his face. "Not only would I be helping those farmers, I would be working with the warriors on their bow, spear, and horsemanship skills. I would also be filling the castle's larders, minus what I give to the farmers for the privilege of hunting on their lands of course."

"I believe he has several good points there," King Oordah said. He was clearly thinking of a feast of freshly killed meat already. If Gunnarr didn't give it all away. He was known to do that from time to time. Usually during an especially cold winter or if the previous year had produced a poor harvest.

"Yes, he does," King Chang replied somewhat sourly. He was really starting to wish he could go with the hunting party.

Slapping his more-than-ample belly with both hands, King Oordah laughed. "Fresh meat it is then."

Gunnarr turned to Mouse, who looked like he was trying to hide from them all behind his water glass. "Feel like hunting today?" he asked happily.

Taking his hand away from his eyes, Mouse looked at him through bloodshot eyes. "You are joking, right?"

Queen Helena, who had just walked in and caught the last bit of the conversation, added sweetly, "You have to go. Someone from your kingdom should really be there as well."

"Not you too," Mouse moaned.

"Of course. You can be my knight at the games." She giggled.

"You read too many novels, m'lady," he said coldly. He knew he was going; he just didn't want to admit it yet.

"Oh, you will go. As a queen, I can make it a court order for you to go." She smiled innocently at him while she batted her eyes.

Standing and bowing, which his head didn't appreciate, Mouse replied, "As my queen commands, so I shall obey." He then stood up, a little slowly it seemed, and continued, "I can always hide in a snowbank if things start getting out of hand."

Gunnarr laughed. He looked at Sladvick, the question on his face. Sladvick answered him, "I only know about hunting birds or small game. We didn't do much large game hunting on the farm. I would like to come with, though, if you are OK with an amateur tagging along, that is. I do know how to butcher large animals; we killed beef cattle on the farm."

"Of course. It isn't just about hunting; it is about spending time with friends as well," Gunnarr said happily.

Gunnarr continued asking around the table. The royals politely declined until he reached Lu-nings son. "Would you like to come with?" Gunnarr asked.

Clearly the man wanted to come with. Rather than answer, he looked at his father. Lu-Ning smiled kindly, touched by the man's devotion to him. "I am sure Chang has a strong warrior who would be able to help me shuffle around. Or maybe he will let me ride through the castle instead? Go and enjoy yourself today."

"Nonsense. I will gladly help you myself, as it is my honor to do so," Chang said.

"That is settled then," Lu-Ning said with a chuckle. "I wish you luck in your hunt today, my son."

"I would be honored to accompany you today, friend Gunnarr," Angensen said happily. "It was very kind of you to include me. Thank you."

Joran had been sitting quietly at the end of the table, trying to keep out of Elsa's way. He was still angry about the night before, yet he desperately wanted to join his friends on the hunt that day. He had enjoyed hunting on the farm when he had time, and Elsa had always been eager to cook whatever he brought back. Maybe he wouldn't get in trouble for going with them.

Gunnarr looked down the table at him. "Oui, Joran," he called. "What about it? Feel like joining us today? I am sure the armory has a bow and some arrows laying around you can use. Unless you just want to use your knife," he kidded kindly.

Joran somehow knew Elsa wouldn't go along with this at all. Sure enough, she cut in before Joran could even ask her if it was OK or just say he wanted to go and not ask her permission. "Are you completely empty-headed?" Elsa yelled at Gunnarr. Now while Joran was still new to royalty, he was pretty sure that yelling at them like that first thing in the morning was considered rude. "You three let him get into more than enough misfortune yesterday. I can only imagine what would happen today with those mean-tempered animals and sharp objects around with horses tossed in for good measure."

Hearing her talk about him as though he weren't even there — and putting his friends down to top it off — pushed Joran over the edge. He looked her right in the eyes, never wavering, and said evenly, "I would be honored to go with the men today. Hopefully they won't mind my inexperience at this sort of hunting though. I think it would be a valuable learning experience."

Elsa's look went through a few changes very quickly. First it was stunned surprise at his open defiance, not only in what he had said, but also in his unwavering eyes. The surprise gave way quickly to anger and then settled on hardness.

The old man, who was sitting beside her, caught her look and laughed. "Seems the puppy has lost his baby teeth."

She didn't take her eyes off Joran. "Shush."

"Don't you 'shush' me, young lady," the old man shot back. His voice was no longer laughing or soft. Kiln-dried oak would have split if placed before his voice just then. "You embarrassed him last night bad enough. He is no longer a small boy who is expected to hide behind your skirts and do everything you bark at him without question. He is a free man and was offered a great honor today, much like the one he was given last night by these warriors and nobles. There is no reason he shouldn't accept this fine gift today. It is well past time that you stop tying him to you with guilt or just force of will. Today is a good day to start loosening your control over him. He is going hunting with some fine warriors and men; I am sure they will watch over him like a beloved brother. Now stop treating him like a little boy and give him the respect he has earned as a young man."

"Yes, you are right." Her soft tone made the old man know that she wasn't going to let it go and he would probably be cornered later about this. Mentally, he shrugged. Why should this time be any different? Oh well. What he had said was the truth. If she didn't like it, so be it. What he didn't shrug at was her next comment directed at Joran. "I hope you have a good day, and we will discuss this when you get back." Joran would have to be deaf and very stupid not to catch the cold fury that was behind that. From the look on Joran's face, he not only didn't miss the meaning, he simply didn't care.

Lanna stepped forward a few steps and addressed her husband. Her tone was flat, as it usually was around him. "Is there anything I can do to prepare my husband for the day afield?"

"No. Thank you" was his short reply. He didn't even look at his wife.

"Husband, I would be remiss if I didn't help you," she persisted.

"I said no," Gunnarr said, turning to her. "If it makes you feel any better, you haven't been remiss in anything today. You may go."

"Thank you, husband." She turned toward the other women and invited them to join her in attempting to see how the hunt would turn out. She had been reading about a new way to see the future that involved crystals and chants.

Hearing that invitation, Queen Helena made a face that showed just how much she would like to do that. The other queens and ladies caught Helena's look and giggled behind their hands quietly. Clearly, no one wanted to join her in reading crystals, no matter how pretty the crystals were.

Gunnarr missed the look and giggles, having already started walking out of the room. "The game won't be there forever."

The men followed Gunnarr out the door, thumping one another on the back and downing one last stein of beer. They couldn't hunt thirsty now, could they?

The men proceeded down the hallway to the armory, where they were met by a man even bigger than Gunnarr. His legs looked like they had been hewn from the giant redwood trees of ancient tales. The leather leggings he wore seemed to barely contain his muscle. Around his waist he wore a thick leather belt, scarred and worn soft from ages of use and fastened with a plain iron buckle that was blackened to keep it from reflecting the sun. A pouch made from some sort of hide—the hair had been left on during the tanning—hung from one side of the belt. A heavy knife hung off the other side. Its finely carved handle, which was made from the tusks of a boar, was worn smooth from use and had yellowed with age. Its sheath matched the pouch. A thick beard hid his face; what little skin still showed was weatherworn and tanned. His bright blue eyes, though, shone with delight.

Gunnarr walked up to the huge man and clasped his massive, hairy hand in friendly greeting. "Everyone, this is Bardawulf. He is the royal game keeper. I think he knows all the trees by name, as he always comes back with meat for the table. I think the trees tell him when game is hiding behind them."

Smiling, Bardawulf bowed his head to Gunnarr. "M'lord is kind. Thank you. However, I only know a few of the older trees by name. The rest haven't learned to talk much." He winked at Joran.

After introductions were over, Sladvick asked an important question. "Bardawulf, this is my first time really hunting animals such as these. How is this done here?"

"Ah, you are in for a great treat today then." Bardawulf chuckled. "What we will do is take the men who we call drivers or beaters to one side of the woods while you and the other hunters set up on the opposite side. Then the beaters will beat the bushes, making as much noise as they can to chase the game toward you and I and the rest of the hunters. Then it is your job to kill the snow goats as they run from the beaters."

"That sounds easy enough," Sladvick said.

"Oh, the snow goats are not like the little goats you had on the farm," Bardawulf said, not smiling now. "They are about the size of a cow — much quicker on their feet though. Speaking of their feet, their hooves are very sharp, and they like to kick things with them. I have seen a snow goat put a hoof halfway through a man's chest. That was after the goat punched its hoof through the hard leather chest piece he was wearing. Their horns are nothing to laugh at either. They look good on the wall, though, with those twists that they have. They don't run away either. If they see you, they are likely to put their heads down, point those long sharp horns at you, and charge." Sladvick didn't look so good at this point. His usual tanned face was a few shades lighter.

Seeing his friend's look, Gunnarr said, "That is where they are very stupid. They are looking at the ground, and they think you are going to stand there all nice and still while they poke holes in you. They don't think you will move and poke holes in them. That is why we use the spear or bow and arrows."

Bardawulf smiled. "Well, I know some who just jump on the snow goat and stab it with their knife until the goat stops kicking at them." He eyed Gunnarr as he said this.

"I would not suggest trying that," Gunnarr said sheepishly. Joran guessed there was a good story behind the game keeper's comment and Gunnarr's clear embarrassment. That tale probably started something like, "After several steins of ale…"

One of the men handed Sladvick a mail shirt. He took it gratefully, noticing that the rest of them were putting similar shirts on and picking their weapons for the hunt.

Mouse noticed them putting on the mail. "My dear, lovely friend Gunnarr. Why are they putting on armor?"

"Oh, we wear them just in case someone falls off his horse or slips in the snow. Rarely does anyone die during our hunt. I think the last time, it wasn't even from a snow goat. We scared up a boar, and he got ahold of a hunter," Gunnarr said lightly.

"That sounds like it happens all too regularly to me," Mouse said, picking a double-thickness mail shirt and sliding it over his head. The links sounded like small bells.

"Come now, little fella," Bardawulf said. "There should be some level of harm, otherwise it wouldn't be so entertaining."

From inside the shirt (Mouse was having a little trouble getting it on) came his reply: "I do believe you should try cards or darts."

Gunnarr and Bardawulf laughed.

The beaters carried out bows, quivers of arrows, and long spears while the hunters finished getting dressed in chain mail and picking horses.

Joran was less than happy with his first time wearing armor. The chain mail dug into him, no matter how he moved to make it comfortable. Even with his soft wool undershirt and the thick wool shirt over it, things just didn't seem to want to play nice and get comfortable. He finally gave up on the armor and decided to concentrate on the rest of the day. His excitement made him soon forget the uncomfortable and heavy mail. Along with the others, he pulled his thick fur cloak and gloves on, mounted his horse, and followed the beaters through the city.

Much to Gunnarr's unhappy surprise, the crone from the front of the temple seemed to pop out of thin air as they passed an old stone building. "Ah, m'lord," she called in a dry, cracked voice. "The reaper of death follows you today. Before the sun sets, you will feel his cold touch."

Gunnarr's horse didn't break stride as he stood in the stirrups, pulled an arrow from his quiver, knocked it, drew, and fired all in one smooth motion. The old crone simply stepped to one side, the arrow embedding itself in the doorframe where her head had been. "Lord Gunnarr. Killing me won't change today. Besides, you should know that no arrow, spear, or knife will kill me." She looked at Joran then as he rode past her. "My king of kings." She bowed deeply. "The reaper of death will come to visit you as well. You will greet him, and he will let you pass. It will not be so with Lord Gunnarr." She then scampered off into the building before Gunnarr took another shot at her. To add insult to his missed shot at her, he saw she had taken his arrow as well.

Joran heard Gunnarr muttering something under his breath about her being a thief as well as crazy. He thought it best not to ask him to repeat it louder.

Sladvick pulled his horse up even with Joran's. "Why did she call you that?" he asked, still getting over his surprise of what she had said and done.

"When we first came into the city, she stopped us at the temple," Joran said. "I asked Gunnarr about her; she is just some old woman who is addled in the head."

"Why did she say you would greet the reaper?" Sladvick asked.

"I don't know; she said something like that when we first ran into her. Gunnarr wouldn't explain it."

Sladvick shook his head. "This is bad luck. Especially on a day like today."

Joran couldn't argue.

All thoughts of the crazy old lady left their minds as they passed through the gate and found themselves riding through farm country. Joran felt a little homesick seeing the farms stretch off into the distance around him. They let their horses take up an easy canter, the light snow flying from their hooves. The horses almost seemed to be happy about the snow. In the distance, the woods where they would be hunting in looked dark against the white snow.

Looking around him, Sladvick noticed the farms, their buildings, and how they were built. All the buildings were built back from the road, not near it. Even so, he could see their steep, angled roofs atop the thick logs used to build the barns and homes. It was a sharp contrast to the stone-and-mortar construction back home that he was used to seeing.

"Joran, have you noticed how they build their homes and barns here?" Sladvick asked.

"Yes, they are from wood from what I can tell," Joran replied.

"Don't they know wood burns? How can you sleep knowing your house is basically a big pile of kindling?"

"I don't know," Joran replied. "We aren't home anymore. I think it would be kind of arrogant of us to think that the whole world is like Brassel."

"You are right. I just miss home. Sometimes I don't think I will ever be truly at ease anywhere else."

"I agree. Sometimes I think it would have been best to just stay home and never leave. We had a good, honest life there," Joran said, his voice a little wishful.

"You are right. It wasn't exciting, but it was a good life."

"Sladvick, do you think we will ever get to go home again? I mean really go home?" Joran asked.

"I don't know, Joran." Sladvick sighed. They rode the rest of the way in silence, each with his own thoughts.

Arriving at the hunting grounds, Gunnarr was back to his usual good humor and old self. He eagerly assigned places for the hunters, checking each one to be sure he had all he needed: Arrows for those with bows. Extra spears for those using them. Turning to Joran, he clapped him on the back and walked into the fluffy snow to an old tree. Looking around, Gunnarr smiled. "This will be a good place for you. There are rubs on the trees over there, and this tree will provide you concealment and cover if you need to hide behind something." Joran wasn't thinking about hiding behind it at all. He was eyeing the branches just over his head instead. How dumb did Gunnarr think he was? Staying on the ground after putting an arrow into one of these angry oversized goats? Like that was a good idea? He couldn't imagine poking a hole in one with an arrow would make it any less eager to return the favor, with interest. Now up, that sounded like a smarter idea. No one had said anything about the snow goats being able to climb. Properly motivated, Joran could climb very fast.

"You are assuming I hit it," Joran joked nervously.

"Oh, missing will make for a very bad day," Gunnarr said. "I strongly suggest you make your shots count."

"It's not like I was going to purposely miss," Joran said. "Wouldn't they run away if they knew I was shooting at them or throwing spears at them?"

"Eh, sometimes they will. Usually they seem angry that you not only shot at them, you missed them. They almost take it personally," Gunnarr said. "Best to just shoot them or poke holes in them with the spear and not take any chances."

Joran nodded.

"It's OK. I will stay close by in case you need help," Gunnarr said. "Remember, if they see you and charge you, forget about using your bow. Their skulls are harder than stone. Use the spear. If you put the butt of the spear against your foot or at the base of that tree and point the end at the goats, they will run into it since they keep their heads down. Once they run into it, though, don't try and pull it out to make more holes in them. They don't tend to stand still after getting poked with a sharp stick. Just pick up the next spear and throw it at them; don't stab them with it or use your bow. Got it?"

Joran nodded again. He was still thinking climbing into the tree limbs and shooting down at the goats seemed like a better idea than hiding behind the tree.

Gunnarr gave Joran a pat on the back, walked back to his horse, and trotted off through the snow. Joran found himself alone in the quiet woods. After a bit, he started looking around at the rubs and footpaths the goats seemed to like using. He decided that calling anything that made hoofprints that size a goat was foolish. His hand couldn't cover one from end to end. The rubbings on the trees looked like a woodcutter had taken his ax to them in places. *Goats my butt,* he thought. He went back to looking at the tree branches. At first, he went back to his first thought: it would make more sense to climb up and either drop the spears on the goats or shoot them from the tree with his bow. No, that was

the coward's way, he decided. These men met the animals on the ground. They had honored him with their invitation, and he wasn't going to act like a scared little boy in return.

About that time, the little voice in the back of his head decided to wake up and point something out to Joran. It didn't matter what he did; no one would consider him a grown up until he was fully grown. What difference did it make what he did as a boy? It did nothing to help him appear more grown in their eyes. He stopped listening at that point and decided to take in the quiet of the woods.

After a bit, he found it strange that he didn't even see or hear a squirrel chattering in the trees. The woods were quiet and dense. The snow seemed to absorb most of the sounds. The only sounds he heard were the rubbing of tree branches in the wind and snow landing on more snow as it fell off trees from time to time. This left his mind free to wonder about things. Of course, it had to wander onto the conversation he and Sladvick had on the way out here. This made Joran feel empty and sad. Why was he here in the first place? His life on the farm had been good. Hard work at times, yes. Those were offset easily by the kisses he traded for sweets. He smiled sadly at that thought. He really had no reason to be here. He looked at the spears leaning by the tree, their shafts collecting snow. He idly wiped them off, knowing the spears would be slippery if he left the snow there. After wiping off the spear shafts, he double-checked his bowstring and arrows. What had possessed him to want to hunt a man-killing goat? Who had decided to call something like this a goat in the first place? Goat meat wasn't even a favorite of his. Now beefsteak? He would gladly butcher cattle all day knowing he would get steaks at the end of it. Goats though? Not really his favorite meal. Even with Elsa's homemade mint jelly on it.

With that, he tried to clear his thoughts and settle himself in to wait for the goats. After all, he was here now. He'd better make the most of it. He pulled his fur cloak around him, tucked his hands deeper into his gloves, and again made sure his bowstring was protected from the snow and his arrow nocked. He then checked the spears again.

After some time — he might have dozed off a bit; he wasn't sure — he heard something moving through the woods. It took him a few minutes to realize it wasn't the hurried sound of the goats being driven toward him. Rather it was the calm, even sound from earlier when he rode out into the woods. Horses' hooves, not wild snow goats. Wondering if he had missed all the excitement, he slowly peeked around the trunk of the tree.

He was surprised at what he saw. Rather than seeing anyone from the hunting party, as he had expected, he was greeted by three men. They came to a stop in the middle of the trail that the hunting party had used. Their horses stamped at the snow and snorted, blowing large clouds of fog into the crisp winter air. The men all sat quietly, warm in their heavy fur cloaks. The men on the outer horses seemed to defer to the man in the middle. The two outer riders wore heavy beards and long hair pulled back into leather hair binders at the bases of their skulls. The one in the middle wore a finer cloak that looked ermine to Joran. Ermine was what nobles or very successful businessmen wore. The man was smooth-shaven, and he wore his deep-blond hair up under his fur-trimmed hat, where the other two men wore no hats. He also seemed less comfortable on his horse, almost like it was beneath him to ride.

Joran had forgotten all about the hunt at this point. He focused entirely on the trio standing in the woods not far from him. He had the presence of mind to put a handful of snow in his mouth and to wrap his scarf around his mouth and nose to keep his breath from giving his place away. He would have to remember to thank Sladvick for teaching him that trick. Not long after the trio arrived, Joran heard another horse coming. The direction was difficult to tell in the woods, and it wasn't until Joran saw the horse plodding through the snow that he knew it was coming from the direction the rest of the hunting party had gone.

Watching the fourth rider come through the woods, Joran thought he looked familiar. Then it came to him: it was the man's cloak. He was the same man Joran had seen in the halls slinking around a few days past.

The man from the castle lowered his hands to his horse's neck, letting the reins rest on the saddle. "Good day, sir," he said formally as his horse came to a stop a few paces from the trio.

"You are late," the man in the middle snapped.

"I am sorry, m'lord. Gunnarr got the idea that today would be a good day to go hunting. Unfortunately, his hunting land was the same land we had agreed to meet on. I did not want to be seen, and it took me longer to get here," he replied.

"What would a hunting party care if they saw you out riding today?" the blond man asked. "Come now, what do you have to report?"

The man from the castle seemed to squirm a little uncomfortably on his horse. "It has been impossible to hear what the kings are discussing with their guests. They stay in a locked and guarded chamber. I can't get near enough to hear anything. The servants aren't even allowed in to bring food or wine. It is all set up prior to their arrival. If something is requested, the servants are to set it on the table outside the door, and someone from inside takes it in."

"Nothing? You are taking my coin and giving me nothing in return? Lots of my coin," the middle man roared. "I suggest, strongly suggest, that you find a way to hear what they are saying in that private room. Soon."

"I understand, m'lord." He bowed and then nudged his horse to turn and leave the way he had come.

"We aren't finished," the well-cloaked man said. "Did you manage to at least meet the other man I asked you to meet?"

Stopping his horse, the man answered him. "I did meet with that fowl little man. We spent some time in an ale house. He had lots of words, very few of even any small value. I expected as much from that kind of rat though."

Ignoring the comment, the blond-haired man pressed him. "Did he agree to meet with us, as he led me to believe?"

"Yes. He agreed to that. Now if you choose to trust what he says, that is your choice." He almost sneered as he said it.

Ignoring the man's tone again, the man in the ermine cloak continued his questions. "When the King of Brassel arrived, who was with him?"

"He came with six others that I saw."

"And?" the man demanded.

"There was the storyteller and some female with him. Another noble from Brassel, if I am not mistaken. A small man from the Snow Granite Kingdom. There was some commoner who looked like he was from Brassel as well." The man recited the information quickly.

The man thought this over a moment, then asked, "No one else? A page perhaps? A boy of early manhood?"

The man cocked his head in thought, then answered, "Yes, he is just some common boy from somewhere. I haven't been able to place where he is from though. I don't think it is Brassel. I didn't see him worth mentioning."

"This boy, he is in the castle?"

"Yes. Just some lowborn commoner. I think he is indentured to the woman with the storyteller. Or possibly her nephew," the man said dismissively.

"Good. Now figure some way to hear what is going on inside those closed and guarded meetings."

"Very well, m'lord. I still say that will be near impossible, the danger aside."

In reply, the man in the expensive cloak looked to the men to his left and right; he then looked back at the man from the castle. The meaning clear, he jerked his horse around and returned the way he had come. His bodyguards followed closely, taking turns looking back at the other man until they were lost from sight. After a few minutes, the man from the castle turned his horse again and left as well.

Joran slowly turned back behind the tree, letting his legs slide out from under him as he released the tight grip he hadn't noticed on his bow. He set the bow aside as he sat there and thought over what he had heard. He realized he had to share this with someone. This was serious.

Just then, muted by the snow, he heard the whistles and steady beating on shields of the hunting party. Joran knew that meant that very soon just about every animal in the area would be charging toward him. All thought of the meeting he had just watched fled Joran's mind.

A flash of reddish brown caught his attention off to one side. He guessed it was an elk or a deer. He never saw enough of it to know. Next a bunch of rabbits and squirrels bounded through the underbrush at him. He debated shooting them with his bow. He did like fresh-roasted rabbit. Before he could grab his bow, though, they were gone. So much for that idea, he thought.

What he heard next made any thought of harmless, fluffy little bunnies flee his mind like the rabbits had. The grunts of running mixed with what sounded like a boulder rolling through the trees made Joran's blood turn cold.

He grabbed a spear, doubting his bow was heavy enough to kill something that could knock over trees as it ran. He could see the tops of trees shaking in the distance — the same place the sound was coming from. To top it off, the sounds were coming at him.

What crashed through the trees into his little clearing wasn't some little goat. *Whoever thought to call this beast a goat never saw a real goat before,* Joran thought, stunned at the massive creature that was clearly angry at the world for being disturbed in such a manner. Goats were nothing like this bull-size — forget cow-size — piece of muscle and long horns. No, make that long, pointed, spiraling horns. The wild eyes weren't scared. They were furious. Crushing trees was nothing to this animal. Then it saw Joran. Good. Something to take its anger out on.

About this time, when Joran should have been feeling terrified, something else happened. He felt a calmness wash over him. He had felt it before only a few times. One was the alley fight on their long trip here. He surprised himself to some extent when he found himself lowering the spear at the massive animal. He braced the butt of the shaft with his foot, making sure it was planted in the hard earth and stood his ground to meet the very angry boulder on legs.

The snow goat accepted the boy's challenge. Lowering his head on its massive neck, it charged Joran. A loud roar came from its throat, spraying snot from its nostrils. The hooves he had been warned about shot through the snow, making small snowstorms with each pounding stride. Time seemed to slow for Joran. He noticed the whites of the animal's eyes as it looked down. He saw the thick coat move over the muscle as it charged. He was aware of the cold seeping into his hands from the spear shaft. None of this seemed to matter to him though. He remained focused on the coming battle.

Then it hit. Joran had placed the spear well; it hit the center of the charging animal's chest. Piercing the thick hide, it buried itself deep. Joran felt himself sliding back in the snow, the spear sliding along the frozen ground. About then he remembered the pointy horns and realized they were inches from his face. *I knew I was forgetting something important*, he thought, more than a little panicked. The end of a spear buried to the shaft in an angry snow goat was not the place to be forgetting things. About then both of his feet hit a buried tree root and shot out from under him. As he tipped over backward, the horns caught up with him. He felt them shoot under his arm, glancing off the armor he wore. The next thing he knew, he was in the air. Then back in the snow, with the wind knocked out of him. He didn't think he had been pierced by the horns; he didn't see or feel any blood. His arm was numb, though, and his back hurt badly.

He rolled to his side; he had to know where the angry and now-wounded beast was. He saw it a little way away. Blood was mixed with its saliva, and he could see red mixed with the mist as it breathed out. That was where the good news ended. Seeing Joran move, it charged him, determined to kill the thing that had hurt it. Clearly the spear in its chest didn't bother it that much. Joran saw it coming and knew he couldn't get up and run away, so he did the only thing he could: he rolled at it, hoping to get under the beast's horns and avoid at least some of the hooves. As he rolled, he pulled his knife and slashed at its legs, hoping to cut the tendons and immobilize it. Or at least slow it down. He had no idea if he had accomplished that, though, as a hoof caught him with a glancing blow to the head, and the world went fuzzy.

The next thing he knew, Gunnarr was there, crashing through the snow. Joran blinked his eyes, trying to focus. He could have sworn that Gunnarr's head was on a snow bear's body. Nah, that wasn't possible. Must be the blow to the head. Which brought him back to the rather important topic of, where was the angry snow goat?

Ah, Gunnarr knew where it was. That was good. He saw bear body–Gunnarr head hurl his spear into the beast's neck. A deep-red fountain erupted from both sides of its neck. The spear had punched through to the other side. Then Gunnarr was on the dying-yet-still-fighting animal. Pinning it beneath his body, he pulled his hunting knife and opened its throat. This time the blood flowed freely, yet it lacked the fountain effect of the spear's wound. Bear Gunnarr then stood and bellowed in victory. That was the last thing Joran saw before passing out.

Later, Joran found himself bouncing around in the back of a sleigh and feeling cold and wet all over his head and neck. He slowly opened his eyes and saw Mouse holding a scarf filled with crushed icicles to the side of his head. Well, that would explain the cold and wet feeling.

"Ah, my little friend," Mouse said happily. "You have decided to stop napping now that the hard work of loading the spoils of the hunt are done."

Holding his head gingerly, Joran asked where Gunnarr was.

"Oh, he is riding alongside the sleigh behind us. Why?"

"Does he seem OK?" Joran mumbled, still dizzy.

"Gunnarr?" Mouse laughed. "Why wouldn't he be OK?"

"Um. He doesn't seem to be…changed?" Joran tried to think of a way to find out if he still had a bear's body and Gunnarr's head.

"Gunnarr is his usual Gunnarr self." Mouse laughed. "You, though, should rest. I think you might have some hurts inside you that we should worry about," he said seriously.

"Where is it?" Joran asked, half wondering if he had really seen it die.

"The snow goat? It's strapped to the last sleigh — took six warriors to hoist it up there." Mouse smiled and handed Joran his knife. "It's kind of a big goat to be taking on with just this, don't you think?" he teased gently.

"Thank you," Joran said, taking his knife and sheathing it. "That wasn't the original plan though." He half smiled. But even that seemed to hurt.

"It wasn't?" Mouse teased. "Could have fooled all of us. If you wish to live much longer, perhaps you should think about the advantages of hiding. No? That animal messed you up pretty good."

Joran just smiled, lay his head back on the folded cloak, and drifted off again.

When Joran next awoke, he was on a stretcher being carried into the castle by Gunnarr and another warrior. He noticed the prideful smile that the warrior behind him wore. Seeing Joran was awake, the warrior looked down at him, nodded, and winked, a big smile on his face.

The next face he saw wasn't smiling. Just the opposite.

Elsa took one look Joran, who was covered in blood and mud, and paled.

Seeing her look, Gunnarr quietly reassured her, "No need to worry. It's mostly the goat's blood. They were having a little roll in the snow after Joran stuck his spear in it. You know, arguing over the whole thing. The goat got a lucky shot in, and Joran got bumped on the head a little. I am sure he will be fine."

Elsa just motioned to Gunnarr and the other warrior and led them to Joran's quarters in the castle. Joran caught the warrior who was carrying the foot end of the improvised stretcher he was on. The big man smiled at him again, nodding his head reassuringly as though to say Joran would be fine.

Later, Joran had been bathed, his head and ribs wrapped in clean linen and poultices. He had choked down a cup of hot medicine as well. Overall, in his opinion, the bath had done the most good. He felt sore yet content and proud. He had stood his ground against dangerous big game. He knew it was mostly the sickly tasting tea mix making him feel a little dizzy, yet he couldn't help thinking it was mixed with pride.

Elsa, clearly still very angry, looked down at him unsmiling. Without warning, she turned on Gunnarr, who was quietly, if proudly, standing near Joran. Elsa was anything but quiet when she started in on the big man. "How stupid can you be? Leaving him alone on his first hunt when he is little more than a boy! Have you been hit in the head one too many times to think straight? Or is it from too much drink?" she yelled at him.

Joran very quietly giggled; the medicine was making him light-headed, and everything seemed funny. *Oh, she is mad,* he thought as he listened to her yell at his friend. *She so angry. Listen to her chatter like an angry squirrel. She even has a tail like one today, with her hair like that. Maybe she should have some of that nasty tea. Make her no mad no more,* he giggled to himself at that as he seemed to float over the bed.

"Elsa, there is no reason for that now," Gunnarr said evenly. "The young man acquitted himself very well today. Not many grown men would stand and face a charge like that, much less make their spears hit true," he added proudly.

"That is all that matters to you?" she shrieked at him.

"He did very well; you should be proud of him," Gunnarr said again. He seemed distracted though. Like he wasn't really thinking of Joran and the fight with the goat.

Elsa caught it and stopped her next verbal assault on the man. She looked at him closely. Then she reached up and gingerly rested her hand on his forehead. She closed her eyes and opened them a moment later. They were no longer angry. They looked almost sad. "I am sorry; I didn't know," she whispered.

"I had hoped this would never happen," Gunnarr said sadly. "It took me over. I never felt it coming. I didn't know how to direct it," he whispered mournfully.

"I understand. Things will work out just fine," she said reassuringly, holding the big warrior's hands in hers.

"No. Nothing will be right again," he said and gently pulled his hands from hers. He looked at her sadly, then turned and silently left the room. His steps didn't even make a sound. All Joran could hear was the soft creaking of Gunnar's leather belt against his sheath.

Joran had stopped thinking everything was so funny. Somewhere in his drugged mind, the little voice murmured that they had been talking about the odd thing he had seen in the woods that day. Trying to turn his head to ask Elsa what had happened, he was met only with peaceful sleep.

Chapter Sixteen

Joran woke up the following morning thinking maybe Mouse had been right. If he hadn't been so courageous and stood his ground, his body wouldn't be so many colors this morning. While the colors were OK by Joran, it was the lack of flexibility—well, the lack of being able to move at all without pain—that bothered him. His knee had swollen up like an oversize tomato during the night-different color than the tomato, same size. He didn't remember banging it on anything. Elsa wrapped a poultice on it and made him stay in bed. He was less than happy with being confined to bed.

On the bright side, all the kings paid him a visit. Each made a point of coming by his room and offering praise on his bravery and shaking his hand. Each brought a little something to keep him occupied while confined to bed. One brought a gaming board with several sets of pieces for various games. Another, a number of books, all on great battles and hunts of past kings and knights. The intricately detailed illustrations alone were enough to keep Joran captivated for hours. The king joked that Joran should take notes on what the others did to avoid this in the future. Another brought Joran a fine set of stones to hone his knife with. The king said it would bring the edge to a mirror finish, fine enough for a surgeon. Joran was pleased to find his knife setting next to him on a bedside table. Many of the warriors who had been on the hunt stopped by as well. Some brought friends who had missed the hunt. They all clapped him on the shoulders and offered their congratulations. To Joran, this was the best of everything people had done for him while he was healing. Some of the warriors brought little things as well to keep Joran's mind off his bed rest. He was pretty sure Elsa would take the crossbow and bolts away, even though they had brought him a target to shoot at. The one who had carried Joran's stretcher looked around dramatically, then leaned over and quietly said, "I would have brought you a girl or three from the village to keep you company, but I'm pretty sure Elsa would have had a fit had I done that. Even if it would make you feel better." He laughed and patted Joran's shoulder. Joran just turned red and grinned.

Not to be outdone, the queens came by as well. One brought a cart full of silk pillows filled with fine down. Another arrived with satin quilts. All brought him desserts from the kitchen, from molasses cookies to sweet apple turnovers covered in vanilla frosting. There were trays of them neatly placed around the room. Bottles of milk in ice-filled silver buckets chilled next to the treats as well. Joran happily shared all of it with the visiting kings and warriors. Several of them said they would be back to play him in one or more of the games he had been brought. The queens continued to fawned over him, checking his dressings and patting his head gently. After a few of those visits, Joran began to wonder if they thought him the royal pup. He took it all in stride though.

By day's end, Joran felt wonderful. He felt like he belonged. It was a feeling he had not felt since leaving his boyhood home. He felt good, if a little full from the desserts. They also made him sleepy.

As the shadows crept across the floor, one last person quietly knocked and then entered his room. The storyteller came in and sat on the stool near Joran's bed. The old man's cloak still had snow along the bottom, telling Joran he had just been outside recently.

Joran pulled himself up a little more in the bed. He was happy to see his old friend. "What did you think of my goat?"

"You made a great kill." The old man's mind seemed to be elsewhere. "I would like to point out that it is best to poke the animal, then get out of the way and make more holes in it, not hang on for the ride."

"It didn't really cross my mind at the time. I thought it would be weak of me otherwise."

"You were concerned the goat would think less of you if you sank a spear into it and then jumped out of the way?"

Joran looked down at his hand and shook his head.

Looking at Joran thoughtfully, the old man said, "Joran, while I still think it was good for you to go on the hunt, there are some things we should talk about. Okay? Good. You are much too young to have lost all sense of survival. Usually men take many years to get overconfident instead of smart. You are an overachiever, it seems. In the space of a night you have joined their ranks." Turning to Elsa, who had slipped in quietly while the old man and Joran had been talking, he asked, "Are you sure he isn't Gurnish? Not one little twig of the family tree?" She shook her head no. "Well, let's see," the old man continued, "First you decide to ride the whirlpool like it was an old draft horse. Then you decide to impress a snow goat with your bravery, almost getting gored in the process. I am sure you impressed the goat, by the way. He will be happy to tell the other goats in the

afterlife that a brave hunter killed him." Joran smiled a little at that. "Elsa, are you sure he didn't drink bathwater or lick one too many raw fish as a small child?"

Elsa smiled and shook her head.

Looking back at Joran, the old man kindly said, "Get better soon. While you are laying around, maybe think about what we have talked about here tonight. OK, my friend?"

Joran wasn't smiling as the old man stopped to say good night to Elsa before leaving. All day he had been praised by royalty and battle-hardened warriors. Yet one of his oldest friends thought him a fool. That hurt more than all his current physical injuries combined.

Wiping at a tear in the corner of his eye, Joran spat out, "He had to ruin everything, didn't he?"

Clearing up some of the trays of desserts, Elsa asked, "What did he ruin?

"Everyone else today has praised me for what I did. Then someone who is supposed to be one of my oldest friends" — he spat the word out — "tells me I am being stupid and foolish."

"Darling, I don't think you should pay all that much attention to royalty," she said. "They are taught to say things like that."

"You're saying I wasn't brave too?"

"No, I'm not saying that. I am sure you were. Perhaps I will hold a prayer service and ask the goat what he thinks about it," she said lightly.

Joran's look at her said he thought she was as hurtful as the storyteller had been.

"Now, now," she said after seeing his look. "I know it isn't what you want to hear or enjoy hearing. It is the truth though. Enough of that. I will get you something for supper. Then you can sleep. What would you like?"

"Nothing," Joran muttered.

"Hmm. You must still be ill. I will make something for you to make you feel better then," she said thoughtfully, moving toward the door.

"Stew," Joran blurted out before she had made it two steps. It was the first thing he could think of besides the desserts all around him.

"I see you are feeling better. I thought you were," she said as she turned and looked at him. The next thing Joran knew, she had wrapped him in a tight hug. Her breath was hot on his ear when she sadly whispered, "I am very happy you are OK."

One minute she was threatening medicine, and the next she was hugging him and looking sad. Taken aback, he stammered, "Elsa, I am fine — just bruised up some."

Sitting back on the bed next to him, she looked at him fondly. "Joran, showing bravery is all fine and good for a man to do. Being foolish about it, though, shows he is braver than he is smart. Could you be smart a little more often, for me? Please?"

Shifting on the bed a little in his discomfort, Joran looked at the quilt and answered her. "OK." It slowly dawned on him that she was worried about his well-being. Maybe there was something still there, even if she wasn't a blood relative. The little voice in his head said things would never be as they had been when he thought she was really related to him. It would be better than nothing at all though. This thought made him feel better, and he leaned back into the pillows. After he ate, sleep found him quickly.

In the morning Joran felt much better. He could get out of bed and around on his own. Only the injuries to his ribs really bothered him. Otherwise it was just soreness with ugly colors. The soreness seemed to lessen the more he moved around. Around noon he and Sladvick decided to take their meal in the main dining hall together. About then the Lord of Valmore found them and joined them.

After a friendly greeting to both, the lord turned to Sladvick and asked if he would be so good as to join the kings in their private rooms.

Surprised, Sladvick replied, "Are you sure they want me to join them in their private council?"

Smiling, the lord replied, "The kings would like the input of an upstanding and level-headed man. You see, what we are dealing with affects not just royalty; it affects every man, and you have made quite the good impression on the kings with your practical thinking."

"Well, thank you m'lord," Sladvick said, practically jumping off the bench. "If you lead the way, I am honored to help if I can. I don't think I shall have much to offer, though; I am just a simple blacksmith."

Joran had remained quiet during the exchange. He was happy for his friend to have such praise from the kings. He knew it felt good.

The lord turned to Joran, a great smile on his face. "I would like to congratulate you on your great showing during the hunt. Very few men can claim to have killed a snow goat at your age. Very impressive." Joran smiled, a little embarrassed, and thanked him politely, saying it was really Gunnarr who had killed it. The lord acknowledged Gunnar's help, pointing out that it would have died soon enough from the spear Joran had stuck in it. Joran smiled and thanked the nobleman. With that, the two men left, leaving Joran to sit by himself.

Joran sat at the table, lost in his thoughts. While he had been paid a great compliment by the Lord of Valmore, his ego was a little bruised when they hadn't asked him to join them. He was more than a little affronted by not being asked to join the council himself. He wasn't sure why. After thinking about it for a bit, he finally got up and decided to go see someone who had taken him seriously: the dead snow goat who was hanging to cure in the castle's ice room. This cheered him up somewhat.

After a while, though, even he had to admit that spending too much time in an ice room with a dead animal can make you feel down and cold, no matter how thick your boots were. He also got his first good look at the snow goat. He had to admit that he hadn't gotten that good of a look at it when they were rolling in the snow. As he looked at the gutted carcass hanging there, he didn't think it was as impressive as it had been while he was leveling a spear at it. The horns, while still sharp and curled, didn't look that long or thick now. On the whole, the dead animal didn't look that big or intimidating at all. He decided after a bit to go warm his hands. The only question was where.

His first thought was to go find Gunnarr; maybe they could play one of the games of strategy that the kings had brought him or go shoot targets or throw axes out in the practice yard. He dismissed that idea as soon as he thought of it though. Gunnarr had gone to his rooms. To Joran, it seemed like his friend was mourning the death of a loved one. He wouldn't speak to anyone. He wouldn't even answer his barred door if someone knocked. This left Joran with no other ideas. Feeling depressed again, he began wandering the vast castle. With no real plan on where he was going, he explored the winding maze of hallways and stairs that seemed to have no real floor plan. At times, he would turn a corner and run into a brick wall. After the first time he banged his nose into a wall in the dark, he learned to take a candle with him when the passages were unlit. Other times he would follow a winding passageway only to come back to where he had started. One staircase led up for what felt like five floors, only to come to an abrupt halt at a block wall.

From the outside, the castle looked big. From the inside, it was huge. Joran had the impression that the entire farm he had grown up on could fit under the roof of this castle and still have room to get lost. Turning one corner brought him to a portion of the castle that had clearly been abandoned long ago. The roof was mostly gone, and birds filled the rafters. Grass and small trees had started to grow on what Joran assumed was the third-story floor. The ruins seemed to reflect his current mood. Or maybe he reflected the ruins in his mood. Either way, depressing thoughts of death and hollow feats of bravery filled his mind. The rooms he explored were mostly covered in white snow crossed with small animal tracks that looked like fine stitching on a well-made quilt. The abandoned furniture stood silent sentry to a long-gone age of royalty. Turning another corner, Joran saw something new. In the snow were tracks, only these were fresh. And not from a small animal. These were made by a man. Taking a second look at them told Joran they were probably made that morning. There was no sign of frost on them, and the edges showed no sign of melting like they would had they been made the day before. The sun had been out all day. His first thought was that he had just wandered through another one of those halls that circled back, and he was someplace he had been already. This thought quickly changed when he noticed the prints had a distinct heel-to-toe impression. His boots had flat soles. And he didn't recognize anything around him.

All his previous thoughts fled his mind and were replaced with new ones that were no less depressing. While his rational mind knew there were lots of different explanations, he kept

coming back to three. The first was the man he had seen skulking around in the hallways. The second was the highborn man he had seen in the woods on the hunt. The third thought came to him after going through the first two a few times: the Vibaion, Ala Maona, was also wandering around somewhere.

None of these men had innocent intentions. Joran suddenly felt vulnerable; he only had his knife with him. He started looking through the rooms he had already been to for some sort of a weapon. The third room he came to had a set of swords mounted over the hearth. While they looked like they had been there since the age of Gods, Joran reasoned one of them was better than nothing. He took down the better looking of the two. Once he had it in his hands, a feeling of confidence swept over him — so much so, he decided to follow the new trail rather than head back to tell the others what he had found. Never once did it occur to him the sword might be giving him a false sense of security.

He was thankful for the fresh snow. It made following the man simple: just look for the boot prints. Things became slightly more challenging after the man had walked into a section that still had shelter from the snow. Joran was thankful for the hours he had spent in the fields tracking small game on the farm. It made picking up the signs of the trail easier—small drops of snow here, a disturbance in the dust there. Since no one had been in this area of the castle for ages, there was plenty of dirt and dust on the floors. While he was skilled in tracking, he was also still sore from the goat hunt. After only a short distance, his injuries decided to remind him that they were there. The constant bending over and kneeling soon took a toll on his already-abused body. Aside from the confidence it gave him, the old sword wasn't really helping any either. Not long after he had started tracking the man, he started thinking about a long soak in the royal baths. Turning back was looking better and better. He could always come back tomorrow if he wanted to.

He had just decided to return the way he had come, replace the sword, and then treat himself to a very hot and long bath when he saw a slight movement down the dark hallway. All thoughts of a bath vanished from his mind. He hugged the wall, hoping the bright snow behind him hadn't silhouetted him to whoever was ahead. He closed his eyes for a moment to let them get used to the darkness. When he opened them, he saw a shadow, darker than the rest, almost glide across the hallway. He recognized the man's movements from before in another part of the castle. Squeezing the sword tighter in his hand, he forgot all about the weight or his injuries. Joran slowly an silently crept ahead toward the man, making no noise with his leather boots. If it hadn't been for the familiar voice—Joran knew it was the Lord of Valmore—Joran would have probably poked the man with the tip of his sword. He froze. He listened, barely daring to breathe.

"As a sorcerer, Orrlick, you should know, can the Evil One be brought forth ahead of the signs?"

Straining his eyes and ears, Joran could barely make out who the man was. The voice they were both listening to came from below them. Seeing that the man wasn't going anywhere, Joran decided to slip back into a doorway for a better hiding spot.

"That is a very good question." The reserved voice of Lu-Ning seemed to float up to them.

The old storyteller's voice was the next one Joran heard. The other man heard it too. "That's most insightful of you both to think of that. While he currently holds the power, I doubt he will use it. Not from lack of desire to though. More from fear of messing it up and killing himself in the act. He will research the proper way to do it, if he is going to do it, and that gives us a little bit of time to get it back."

Joran heard Mouse's voice next. "What if he doesn't want to give it over to his lord? Holding that kind of power in your hands can be intoxicating. Maybe he has other plans. Making himself ruler over all the Arrahs might appeal to him more than bringing forth his lord and surrendering all that power."

Joran heard King Oordah's voice next. He sounded like he was smiling. "The followers of Jahagi don't seem like the kind who just turn around and walk away from a newcomer. Their leader holds great power as well, from what my spies tell me."

King Chang spoke up at this. "I mean no offense. With that kind of power in his hands, and once he learns to use it, he could just destroy their temples without even breaking a sweat. Like a man kicking over a child's blocks. Then, if they still chose to resist him, he could simply kill off all the worshippers in Gorikail. From there, he could easily go where he chooses. I am sure he will choose to come here sooner or later. I don't see that anyone will really care if it is the thief or his master who holds the power; they will follow him. It is all in the research I have done on this topic."

A thoughtful voice floated up; this one Joran recognized as belonging to Drath. "Would it not be a good idea to avoid being taken by surprise, like we were last time? Warning the Gurns and Thysions that it has been stolen would go a long way in preventing that nasty surprise again."

"I don't see it being in our favor to poke that hornets' nest right now." The old storyteller was again speaking. "Traveling through a kingdom that has been alerted for battle only makes traveling more difficult. The fact that they keep their armies on alert for war already is bad enough. If something were to happen, they would be able to respond quickly. They are highly skilled soldiers with experienced leaders. I see no reason to cause more panic than needed." Elsa was heard to agree with him. Joran was surprised she was in the meeting; he thought she was with the queens. The old man's voice returned. "All those soldiers would just become unneeded obstacles for us. I still think we can catch my old student and put the stolen item back where it belongs. I still say there is no reason to rouse a hornet's nest just yet. It's always easier to get the hornets to come out than it is to get them back in. The other side of it becomes the issue of a ruler with all those fun armies to play with. He just has to do something with them, and that something is usually something not smart. I say we tell the rulers of the lands south of here only what they need to know — just enough to get them to let us move freely and quickly. But the Oslugs should be given notice. This time of the year, it will be difficult to get a messenger to them."

"I believe I can get one through, even with the mountains covered in winter snow," Lu-Ning said thoughtfully.

"Thank you," the storyteller said. "For now, I don't see much else to do. Keeping this among us would be the wisest decision for now. We can always alert others as needed. We can't take back the warnings, though, if they aren't warranted. If things decide to go badly, we should have enough time to warn the rulers of the north and give them time to prepare."

The concerned voice of King Anderson came next. "For you to speak of battle in such light terms is easy for you; your people are trained almost from birth for battle. My country is almost the exact opposite. Our castles are more for looks than for holding off a siege. My subjects are craftsmen. They raise crops. They train and breed horses. They are bankers. Very few are trained solely for fighting, and most of them are pit fighters, not soldiers. We are peaceful. Fighting for us is the last resort. History has shown that picking Stutgath for the front line of a war was a tactical error. I don't see the Arrahs being that stupid, as dumb as they are at times. Coming across the unpopulated lands and taking Brassel, and take it they will, would be a much smarter move for them. Not only are we lightly defended, we are almost entirely self-sustaining when it comes to food, clothing, and pretty much anything else. Yes, we would lose some luxuries that we import from other lands. This would mean nothing to an invading army though. They would value our lands as a staging ground for further invasion of other countries. We are a ripe and easy target for an invading army."

To Joran's surprise, he heard his friend Sladvick speak up then. His voice was firm and hard. "I mean no offense to you m'lord; I say this with respect to you. You are mistaken, however, in not giving the men of your country enough credit. While it is true we aren't trained in sword fighting or poking spears into soldiers while charging on horseback, the men of your kingdom will fight. It most likely won't be a traditional fight, with two armies on a battlefield. There would be hit-and-run tactics. Traps laid here and there for the enemy. Fields empty of crops. Silos emptied of edible grain. Horses suddenly gone from the pastures. This would not only rob them of necessities such as food, it would also destroy their spirits. They never know when an arrow from that clump of bushes will kill them. Or if that pile of dirt hides a pit filled with sharpened stakes and covered with a tarp. We may not be a well-trained army. I know the men I used to live around, though, and they wouldn't hesitate to fight an invading force."

Sladvick's little speech—Joran couldn't remember him ever speaking so much at once— left a still quiet hanging in the air for a long while. Finally, King Anderson broke the silence. "My good man Sladvick. I seem to have lost touch with my subjects, and I feel ashamed of that. Thank you for reminding me what kind of man I rule over." His tone was almost awed.

Joran was proud of Sladvick for not only standing up for his fellow countrymen, but for doing it to a king of all people.

Angensen was the next to speak. "I think you are overlooking the mountains. There are only a few passes that can be used for transporting that many men. If it happens to be a bad year and some rocks fall down into the roads, it would make them unusable. Perhaps those rocks would accidently come loose while the army is on the roads. They would either be knocked into the gorges or trapped between the two landslides. There is no food on the road, which would leave them to either starve when their wagons ran out or to try and climb out in small groups and escape. Another possibility would be, with nowhere to go, they might get shot full of arrows."

Mouse laughed. "I think that is a rather entertaining thought: all those poor invaders stuck between two rocks, a gorge, and a company of bowmen. We could even save those poor men some sore backs if some barrels of oil happened to accidently spill over the rocks onto the road. I hear their God likes to have his offerings lit on fire."

"You are right, Mouse. It would also help keep the poor men who happened to be carrying those barrels warm." Drath chuckled.

Joran realized he hadn't been paying attention to what was going on when he heard the heavy footsteps coming from down the old hall. About the same time he heard them, the man he had been watching heard them as well. At first Joran thought they were coming from the way he had come. Then he realized the coming men were marching toward him from the other way. The spy quickly stepped from his hiding spot and, much to Joran's horror, started to lightly run toward where Joran was hiding. Holding his breath and taking a tighter grip on the all-but-forgotten sword, Joran watched the man run past him while looking over his opposite shoulder back down the hallway. He never saw Joran hiding in the doorway.

For a moment Joran thought about just waiting for the royal guards to come and find him. On second thought, it would be rather sticky to explain why he was snooping around in the hallways with a sword. He chose to quietly disappear as well. While he did think about trying to follow the man again, he decided it best to find someone whom he could tell what he knew. It had to be someone whom the kings would listen to though. That left only one person whom he knew he could trust. The trick would be getting that person to open the damn door.

Chapter Seventeen

Joran found himself talking to a board. Well, more accurately, several boards. "*Hey! Gunnarr! Open the door!*" he yelled at the boards again. He had spent the previous five minutes banging on the door. *Stupid carpenters, making these things so solid*, he muttered in his head as his hand got sore. He did have to admit the grain of the wood looked nice though.

From the other side of the door came the slurred reply, "Are you going to ever go away?"

Finally, progress, Joran thought. "Open up; it's really important."

"Leave me be" was the response. It was still slurred, just louder.

"Gunnarr, this is really important. Open up. You have been in there too long already."

Silence at first answered Joran. Then he heard something hit the floor and break, followed by a muttered curse and then footsteps. A scraping sound and a dull thud proceeded the door slowly opening.

Joran was surprised by how bad Gunnarr looked. To say he looked like a walking dung heap, as Sladvick had said of some of the farmhands before, would be an understatement. Gunnarr was naked to the waist, and his pants were stained in places from what Joran would guess was vomit. Gunnarr's usually well-kept hair was a mess. Birds could nest in it as far as Joran was concerned. Gunnarr's beard was just as unruly and had patches that were matted and crusted. All of it was surrounded by the cloud of unwashed man, mead, and vomit. Joran took a step back, trying to find clear air. It was then he noticed the look in Gunnarr's eyes, which were filled with terror. Some self-pity might have been mixed in too.

Gunnarr looked at Joran without really seeming to see him. "You know," he said, his voice dead. Joran really was confused. What could make a man like Gunnarr scared and fall into such a state? And what did Joran know? As far as he was concerned, he knew very little, thanks to those around him who were trying to keep him in the dark like a kid.

When Joran didn't reply, Gunnarr yelled at him, "I know you saw what happened out there!"

"Out where?" Joran was still bewildered by this.

"When you speared the goat, and I came to help you. You saw what I turned into!"

It all fell into place for Joran then—what Gunnarr feared. Joran answered him quietly, "Gunnarr, all I saw was snow, an angry goat, and then darkness when I hit my head."

"You saw my death."

"Death? You are still alive, even if you smell like you're dead. Unless you have decided to haunt us in that state." Joran hesitantly poked Gunnarr with a finger. "Nope, you are alive."

"No. You didn't see me die. You saw my fate. My fate of death." Turning, he walked back into his quarters and dropped into a chair. Aside from the bed, it was the only thing standing upright yet.

"I know you saw it. My death destiny," he said morosely, hanging his head and letting his hair fall over his face.

"Death? I don't get it. We could compromise and go with walking corpse. That would give you the dead part and cover the smelly part too." Joran smiled.

"Death destiny isn't mean the person is dead right then. It is something that he is destined to have happen in his life," Gunnarr said flatly. "A death destiny can be death, or it can be something worse than death. Or something other than death. I only wish mine were death itself."

Joran thought for a moment. "Gunnarr, some woman who has her brain half-baked has really gotten inside your mind. That isn't good."

"I wish it were only her. When I was born, my parents summoned a seer. In my country, this is done for all men on their birthday. Usually, nothing special is foretold. Most men live quiet, unremarkable lives. I am sure it is the same in your homelands. Most men are just that, simple men. Once in a great while, though, the seer foretells something so big in the man's life that all he can see in the man's destiny is death. All that the half-baked woman was doing is repeating what the city has been talking about since I was born."

"What garbage," Joran scoffed. "I never would have expected you to believe something that some blind old fortuneteller with a deck of odd cards said would happen. A while back, a traveling one stopped at the farm. She couldn't even predict what cake Elsa was going to bake. She baked a pie the next day, not even a cake of any kind. Sladvick even went to her. She told him he would be born twice in life. Can you see a woman trying to give birth to him now?" Joran chuckled.

"The seers here have much more skill and ability. Over the years, many of them have said the same thing. I will turn into a snow bear. Since the hunt, I can feel my hair getting thicker and longer. Even my eyes are looking different now." His tone was flat, almost dead.

Joran took a long look at him in the dark. As far as he could tell, Gunnarr was still big old Gunnarr. He said so.

"I know better. It is nice of you to say that though. Even my tongue feels different. Soon I will either be taken out into the snow mountains and left to live with the snow gnomes, or the king will lock me in the cells in the basement of the castle. If I am lucky he will just put me in a cell, not chain me as well," Gunnarr said sadly.

Joran wasn't going to give up on his friend that easily. "No one can turn into an animal. Smell like one, yes. Turn into one? No."

"Oh? You know that, do you? What did you see when I came toward you and the snow goat?"

"We have been over that; all I saw was snow and blackness from getting a blow to the head," he said, hoping his voice sounded truthful.

"Tell me what you saw. It was a snow bear, wasn't it? I have to know if the seers were seeing the truth all those years ago." Gunnarr was almost on the verge of tears. Seeing this, Joran thought to try and cheer him up.

"Are you worried that you will turn into what I saw you as that day? OK, you are right. I didn't see you as Gunnarr; I saw you as a beautiful princess, full of bosom and long of legs with long, thick black hair and sparkling green eyes and soft, full, kissable lips, wearing nothing but ribbons in her hair and a smile on her face," he said with a straight face.

Gunnarr looked up with a bewildered look.

"What? Women can be bears. I hear men say it all the time about their wives," Joran said innocently. He somehow managed to keep the laughter from his voice.

"You are no help," Gunnarr said flatly.

"Look, I was busy playing with the snow goat and getting my head banged around. You were there; don't you remember anything about what you think happened?" Joran replied, trying to take yet another tact with his friend.

"I was there in body, yes. I don't remember anything between hearing the fight through the woods and then standing over a dead animal with you half under it and all covered in blood," Gunnarr said. Joran took his look of intense concentration as a positive improvement.

"I do remember the smell of the snow bear," Gunnarr said, still trying to remember more.

"That was just the snow goat and the horses. There was no bear there. You just got caught up in the moment. Nothing more," Joran said with more conviction than he really felt.

An optimistic look started to come across Gunnarr's face. "You mean blood drunk? That could..." His voice trailed off before finishing the sentence. He shook his head then. "No, I have been blood drunk in battle before. This was definitely something else."

Joran realized that coming at it from a different way wasn't working either, so he went back to a blunt head-on attack. "Gunnarr. You are not turning into some snow bear. You certainly smell like an animal though."

"The seers all agreed. It will happen. It is happening," Gunnarr said doggedly.

Before Joran could argue or reassure his friend, depending on how you looked at how things were going, Gunnarr's wife barged in through the still-open door.

Gunnarr muttered something under his breath that Joran didn't catch at the same time Lanna said, "Ah, my husband has decided to stop sulking."

"Go away, Lanna," Gunnarr said.

"I only wish to take care of my loving husband."

"No, you are here to play games of some sort," Gunnarr shot back.

"But husband, it is my privilege to care for my noble husband when he is sick."

"You are only worried about appearances and privileges. Stop being so concerned about all that nonsense, and leave me alone."

"I see. When you returned from your latest adventures and travels, you were very concerned about the rights of a husband. Three times concerned, as I remember it. Even though I was more interested in sleep."

Gunnarr flushed a little at that remark. "I thought things between us were improved, and you were just playing more of your games. Clearly you weren't playing games this time." Then he added under his breath, "For once." Joran was pretty sure she hadn't heard the last two words.

"M'lord, I would never play games in that respect. It is a good wife's responsibility to please her husband whenever he chooses to enjoy her in the bed chamber. Whether she is tired or he is drunk and aggressive should make no difference to her. I will not have rumors flying round the kingdom of me not submitting to my husband when he wants me."

Gunnarr looked at her out of the corner of his eye, clearly irritated with her. "Oh no, you could never have that. It wouldn't look proper to your friends. Now stop playing games with me when I am not feeling whole."

"Games?" she asked innocently, yet there was a hard cut to her voice as well.

"You want something. What is it?" Gunnarr said shortly, fixing her with a hard stare.

"What any good and dutiful wife wants. To care for her husband in his time of sickness. I only wish to —"

Gunnarr cut her off before she could finish. "You honestly want me to believe that? I am neither drunk nor sick enough to believe that load of horse dung." He leaned forward in his chair, rested his massive forearms on his knees, and looked at her coldly. "I doubt you would like me to order you to stay here to "care" for your husband once the change fully starts to take hold. You could be immortalized as the dutiful wife who was killed by her cursed husband as he fulfilled the seers' prophecy."

"I would simply have the royal guards take you to the cells, should you grow that violent," she said tartly.

Joran decided things between the two had gone on long enough, and it might be best to change the subject. Besides, it was the reason he had come to see Gunnarr in the first place.

Clearing his throat, Joran said, "I did come here for a very important reason, Gunnarr."

"I am busy right now," Gunnarr shot back without even looking at him.

"Um. No, this can't wait," he said nervously.

"What is it then?" Gunnarr turned to look at him, clearly still angry.

"There is a man in the castle who is poking around the king's meeting rooms. His private ones."

"Eavesdropping?"

"Yes, more like spying though. He wears heeled boots," Joran said, remembering the boot prints in the snow.

"Pffft. Many men here wear such boots," Lanna scoffed at Joran.

Gunnarr turned on her in an instant and roared, "Get out! This is none of your affair!" For a second Joran thought maybe Gunnarr was right; he was turning into a snow bear. Then Gunnarr turned back to Joran, and asked, "You said spying. Why do you say that? He could have just been curious or passed by and heard a bit of a conversation."

"I have watched him skulking around the castle halls several times. Today I tracked him in the abandoned part of the castle, where the roofs have fallen in. He purposely stopped over the king's private meeting chambers and listened intently to the conversation. He heard every word. That is, until the royal guard came. Then he ran from them."

"You were spying too. If you knew he could hear everything, then you could too," Lanna shot at him.

"Yes, I was there. I was wandering around the castle when I saw fresh footprints in the snow in that part of the castle. I followed and found him over the chambers. Before he could see me, I stepped into a doorway and watched him. We could both hear everything said in that meeting. It was like standing in the room with them," Joran said.

"Besides his boots, what can you tell me about him?" Gunnarr said, ignoring Lanna.

"He wears the same maroon coat all the time. His hair is pulled back into a short ponytail at the base of his neck, and he wears his beard in a short-trimmed goatee," Joran said.

"Anything else?" Gunnarr asked.

"I have seen him several times since we arrived here, once in the city. He was going into an ale house with a Vibaion."

"See, he knows nothing of what he is speaking. There are no Vibaions in the city," Lanna said with a condescending tone.

Ignoring her, Joran focused on Gunnarr. "Yes, there is. This isn't the first time I have watched this Vibaion either." He kept trying to pick the right words to get his point across before his mouth betrayed him and stopped working when he spoke of this one person. Already his lips felt like he had been out in the winter night too long without a scarf.

Gunnarr didn't help with that. His next question made dancing around the topic pretty much impossible. "What is his name?"

Damn, Joran thought. *So much for getting around that topic carefully.* Instead of answering the question, he went back to the man in the coat. "I saw him in the woods when we were hunting too."

"The Vibaion?" Gunnarr persisted.

"No, the man I saw in the castle spying," Joran replied.

"What was he doing in the woods?"

"Meeting with three men," Joran replied evenly.

"What makes meeting people in the woods suspicious? There's no law against that," Gunnarr said.

"Two of the men were warriors. They looked like bodyguards or mercenaries. The third man looked almost like a nobleman. He wore a cloak that looked like ermine, and he had a clean-shaven face and dark-blond hair. He did most of the talking, and then they left. I saw them while I was waiting for the drivers to chase the snow goats at us. They didn't see me; I was hiding by the tree."

"Joran, many men travel with bodyguards. What exactly makes you say they were spying?" Gunnarr persisted.

"They weren't friendly toward one another, for one. The man in the maroon coat kept referring to the other man as m'lord. The one with the bodyguards kept giving him orders and reminding him he had to get close to the king's meeting and get the information he wanted because he had already paid the man for it," Joran said.

"OK, you have a point. That is important," Gunnarr said. He seemed to have shaken the foul mood that he had had for the past two days. "Is there anything else?"

"Yes. The one with the guards ordered the man in the maroon coat to find out about all of us: the storyteller, Elsa, Sladvick, Mouse, me. All of us."

"The dark-blond-haired man?" Lanna asked.

"Yes, the one the man in the maroon coat kept referring to as m'lord," Joran said.

"His hair was long, like a woman's almost? Dark blond?" she persisted.

"It was dark blond, yes. I don't know how long it was though. He had a hat on, and his cloak's collar was turned up against the cold. It looked like he might have had his hair pulled up under his hat. That is all I can say on its length," Joran said.

"He was about my husband's age, yes?"

Joran looked at Gunnarr and thought a moment. "Yes, I think Gunnarr is younger though. Maybe five years or so?"

"And he was clean-shaven, no beard at all?" she asked again.

Before Joran could answer her, Gunnarr cut in. "I don't think it is who you are thinking of. King Cherek exiled him years ago. There is not only a bounty on his head if he comes back, there is a death sentence too."

"Husband, you are naive. If that man wanted to be in the kingdom, he would be here," she said arrogantly.

Looking at her, Joran asked, "If you know him, I am guessing you know he doesn't think very highly of Gunnarr. He said some rather nasty things about him."

"Oh, I wouldn't doubt that at all. Gunnarr offered to run a knife through the man's organs once. He said he would do it in order from bottom to top, to be sure he got them all before the man died."

Gunnarr had decided to get up and do something. Joran watched the big man stomp into his boots and go looking for his other clothes.

"Gunnarr, would you please at least put on fresh clothes and tie your hair back?" Joran was surprised to hear no condescending tone from her directed at her husband for once.

"There's no time to bother with looking all primped up and pretty right now. We must talk to the king as soon as possible," Gunnarr said, pulling a mail shirt over his head and moving toward the door, where he grabbed his sword belt.

While Joran was glad to see his friend back to normal, his aches and pains were less than happy that he would almost have to jog to keep up with Gunnarr's fast walk. Lanna was having trouble keeping up as well. She was holding her skirts up so she could hurry along with them. Gunnarr barged through the main hall, with the two trailing behind him. The look on his face made the royal guards hurry to get out of his way.

Once they reached the royal private meeting quarters, a guard greeted Gunnarr with a smile. "Good to see you out and about, m'lord."

"Good to see you as well." Gunnarr returned the greeting without slowing and practically knocking the door off its hinges as he came into the room.

All those assembled looked up, startled at the intrusion.

"Well, hello there, Gunnarr. Nice of you to join us. Perhaps your next stop could be the royal bath?" Chang commented with a smile.

Ignoring the greeting and the joke, Gunnarr bellowed, "There are spies sent here by the Lord of Starn. He has defied you and returned to the kingdom."

"Starn? No," Chang said.

"Yes," Gunnarr said.

"He can't be that stupid," Chang replied, doubtful as he waved his hand dismissively as though shooing a fly away.

"Well, he is stupid then. He was spotted in the woods not far from here and was overheard plotting against you."

"Pardon me, for those of us who don't know this Lord of Starn, who is he?" Drath asked politely.

Chang sighed. "I banished him about a year ago after finding a letter to a Vibaion on one of his couriers. The message was from him; it even bore his wax imprint. While a letter to a Vibaion is one thing, this one had detailed state secrets in it. We searched his home and offices—both had more bags of gold coins from Brassel than he had from our kingdom. Gunnarr wanted to do interesting things to his organs. I wanted to simply cut his head off and hang it from the gates. Instead, I gave in to his wife's begging and banished him from the kingdom. She is related to me as well. Seems I should have let Gunnarr play with him instead. We could always have found someone else for her to marry."

The old man looked at Gunnarr, then asked, "How did you find out about this? You locked yourself in your quarters last I heard and were trying to drink the castle's entire mead supply by yourself."

"You doubt my husband?" Lanna shot back at him.

"No one said we didn't believe him. All I asked was where he got this information," Chang said calmly, a bemused look on his face.

Gesturing at Joran, she replied, "That boy said he has seen him with his spy in the woods. I heard him share what he saw with Gunnarr, and I believe him." Her tone suggested that she was challenging anyone to doubt Gunnarr or her. Elsa looked at Joran with surprise.

King Lu-Ning turned to Joran, who at this point was wishing he could turn into a mouse and disappear out the door with no one noticing. "Joran, would you please tell us what you told Gunnarr and his wife?" he asked kindly. "A tale such as this deserves to be heard from the person who experienced it. Especially when a banished lord with ties to the Vibaion spy network decides to risk having to play with Gunnarr."

Everyone turned to look at Joran. He was glad to see puzzlement or curiosity on their faces rather than anger or disappointment. When he hesitated, Gunnarr caught his eye, nodded to him, and made a little gesture with his hand as if to say, well, come on now. Let's go.

Joran straightened his shirt and bowed stiffly to the kings. "Your Highnesses, since I have arrived here, I have seen a man wearing a maroon coat sneaking about the castle. He does everything he can to either look like he belongs wherever he is or to avoid all contact with anyone. Not only have I seen him in the castle, I saw him in the city. He was going into an ale house with a Vibaion. I know I have been told that there are no Vibaions in the kingdom. I know what I saw, though, and he was a Vibaion."

"Joran, why do you say he is a Vibaion?" Chang asked.

Joran looked at him, perplexed, as he wanted to tell the king what he knew, only his mouth wouldn't work. Everyone saw him visibly struggling to talk. His mouth moved, and his tongue stuck out once or twice, yet not a sound came forth.

Mouse saw Joran's distress and decided to come at things in a different way. "Joran, do you know this man?" Joran was relieved he had help. He quickly pointed at Mouse and gestured yes.

Mouse leaned back in his chair and looked at Joran thoughtfully. "You haven't had the chance to really meet many Vibaions. Let me think. There was the one we met while traveling here, first in Broonard. We bumped into him later in Elexadra." Joran's head was bobbing up and down at this. His mouth still didn't seem to be able to work. If it hadn't been so serious, it would have been rather comical.

"Is there a reason you failed to share this with us back then?" Gunnarr asked.

Still fighting to get words out, Joran replied, "C-C-Can't talk a-a-about him."

"Huh?" Gunnarr looked at Joran like he was addled.

"I try to. Something happens to my mouth though. And my lips and tongue. It doesn't make sense to me. I don't understand it. Whenever I want to talk about him, I can't."

"This has happened before?" Mouse asked.

"Several times," Joran said.

Mouse looked over at Elsa, concern written plainly on his face. "Elsa, I am out of my depth on this. Some help here, please?"

"While I know it can be done, it is very spotty at best. The results aren't consistent. I don't use it myself due to the lack of dependability. That doesn't mean it can't be done or doesn't work from time to time." Her face showed great concern. Joran had seen that look on her face before. He didn't like it. It usually meant some nasty medicine was coming next. Yuck.

"Well, there are people who aren't as worried about reliability as they are in the awe factor. Jahagi are big on making their followers say wow," the old man said.

"I will have to deal with this," Elsa said, standing and looking at Joran.

Great, and here comes the fowl-tasting teas, Joran thought miserably.

"Not so fast, Elsa," the old man said.

She turned on him, her face growing dark. "And why not? I must take care of this."

"Yes. And you can deal with it after Joran tells us everything else. All you would be doing is closing the gate after the cows get out."

Grateful to be spared any medicine from Elsa, even if for just a little while, Joran picked up where he left off. "The man in the maroon coat was with us in the woods when Gunnarr took us after the snow goats. I was hiding behind a tree in the woods, waiting for the drivers to chase the snow goats to me, and I saw him meet with a man who had dark-blond hair and a clean-shaven face. The bald-faced man demanded that the man in the maroon coat find out and report back to him everything that you were saying in this room. All of it."

King Chang broke in, "You are only telling us this now?"

Joran continued as though no one had spoken. "If you all remember, I took a blow to the head while hunting. I didn't remember much of that day until today. With Sladvick summoned here, and Gunnarr locking himself in his rooms, I didn't have anyone to really spend time with, so I decided to wander around the old parts of the castle, back where it has started to fall apart. While I was there, I came across some tracks in the snow that were fresh. The trail led me to the man in maroon, who was standing over this room, spying on you all. When I saw him, my memory started coming back."

"This is very important, Joran. Do you know what he heard or how long he was there?" Lu-Ning asked.

Joran gathered his thoughts before answering. "Well, when I got close enough to hear what you were talking about, you were discussing a man using the power he now had. You didn't know if he knew how to use it without killing himself. A couple of you were worried he could awaken his master, while others thought the man would keep the power for himself and use it to conquer entire kingdoms. Sladvick said that the men back home would fight any invaders who came in. The storyteller advised you not to warn other rulers about this threat of power so that he could travel easier between these kingdoms." Joran stopped there and looked at each of them.

What he saw was surprise and concern on all their faces.

He continued, a little worried now. "The man in the coat had been there longer than I had, and I know he could hear everything you said as well. We weren't that far apart. He fled when the royal guard approached. I left as well and went straight to Gunnarr's room to warn him."

"The ceiling is crumbling over here," Mouse said, holding a candlestick near the corner of the room. "That is how he heard us."

"You are a resourceful young man," King Oordah said, looking at Joran. "Have you given any thought to what you would like to do as a profession? You seem to have a talent for this sort of thing. I could use someone like you, and the intelligence field can be very fulfilling."

Before Joran could open his mouth, Elsa cut in, "He certainly is talented. Talented at going somewhere he shouldn't be. And doing other foolish things as well."

"Well, that wasn't nice," King Chang said. "I would think you would be pleased with him finding this out. I am not sure how or if we can reward him for bringing us this information."

Sensing that silence and a hasty retreat might be the best course of action, Joran bowed as best he could to the kings and backed away from the center of the room. He was trying to figure out how exploring the abandoned portion of the castle could be called going where he wasn't supposed to be. He didn't ask though.

"Gunnarr," Chang said, "Would you be so kind as to go find this gentleman in the maroon coat? It isn't polite to snoop around like that on kings. It would be good to have a talk with him about his manners."

"Of course, m'lord. I will take some warriors and see what rats we can find in the halls," Gunnarr said as he stood.

"Um, Gunnarr?" King Chang called before Gunnarr had gotten too far.

"Yes?"

"Please don't break him too badly. I would like to be able to talk with him for a while. Then I might give you some time to play with him on your own as you would like."

Gunnarr smiled. "Of course."

Chang smiled back at his cousin. The smile didn't reach his eyes though.

King Chang then looked at Lanna. "Lanna, it was good of you to help bring us this information. I am sure you had an important hand in this. Thank you."

Bowing her head, she replied, "No thanks are warranted. I only did my duty as a wife."

"Lanna, can't you just accept thanks for once? You always say everything is your duty," Chang said. A hint of frustration crept into his voice.

"There is nothing else for a good wife, only duty," she said.

"It is a shame you feel that way. There is much more to it than that. If you don't know that, you will have to figure it out on your own."

Elsa provided a polite change of topic. "Please come over here," she said, gesturing to Joran.

So much for hiding, he thought. He walked across the chamber, showing his unease in his walk.

"It's OK, Joran. I am not going to beat you," she said as she gently laid her palm on his forehead for a moment.

"And?" the old man asked quietly.

"It is very faint. Without Joran telling us, I would never have known it was there. Please forgive me, Father."

"Joran, come here," the old man said.

Joran walked over to him, and the old storyteller repeated what Elsa had done. "Well, at least it isn't something critical or life-threatening."

Joran was beginning to feel like a puppy that everyone wanted to pet. He doubted it was because he was cute.

"No, this time it isn't. Still, I was supposed to keep watch on him, protect him. I failed," Elsa said stiffly.

"OK, you messed up. Now deal with it. Berating yourself constantly is a waste of time, and it doesn't fix the problem. Speaking of which, fix this," the old man said, gesturing at Joran's head.

"Um. Excuse me? What is wrong with me?" Joran asked nervously.

"Oh nothing, sweetheart," Elsa said lightly.

Joran didn't believe that one bit. The old man had just said to fix whatever it was that Elsa had found. That usually meant fowl-tasting tea or some oily ointment rubbed all over him.

"Come over here, and I will fix this," Elsa said. Joran almost pointed out that if there was nothing wrong with him, what was she going to fix? He wondered where she was hiding the tea or ointment. He went over to her anyway. No point in putting it off.

To his pleasant surprise, Elsa simply took his hand and rested it between her own hands. Then she brought her hands and his to her forehead. The instant his hand touched her head, he felt light-headed, and his heart began to pound like he had just sprinted a mile uphill. Memories seemed to flash across his eyes in little flashes. Then his knees gave out, and he collapsed to all fours, breaking into a cold sweat.

Once his breathing came back to normal, the old man knelt down beside Joran. "Deep breaths. You will be OK."

Joran looked at the old man for a moment. Then he nodded and stood. The old man stood, facing him. "Joran, do you remember a Vibaion from your past?"

Without hesitation Joran answered, "Yes."

"And what is his name?" Elsa prompted.

"Ala Maona."

"How do you know him?" Elsa continued.

"Since I can remember. He watched me when I was young. At the farm," Joran said.

"OK. No more for now. Let him get his breath back. We can come back to this later," the storyteller said.

"He was sick?" King Lu-Ning asked, concerned.

"Not really. It is more like a head injury, where someone can't remember something that happened until later," Elsa said. "He is OK now." The she turned back to Joran. "Are you OK to walk on your own?" He nodded. "OK, go back to your quarters and sleep. In the meantime, I will make something to keep this from happening again. Understand, Joran?" He nodded again. "I mean it. Straight to your quarters and to bed. No wandering off to the kitchen or playing with puppies if you find one in the halls. Understand?"

"Yes, I will go get some rest," he said. *She said I shouldn't play with the puppy in the hall if I found one. She never said I couldn't take it with to bed though*, he thought.

"Before you fall asleep, I want you to think back to every time you have seen him. This Vibaion. What he said each time. Understood?"

"That is easy. He never spoke. He would just stand and look at what was going on, then disappear," Joran said.

Seeming not to have heard him, Elsa continued, "In a while I will come and check on you. Then you can tell me everything you remember. Everything. This is very important. Think back to every time you saw him. What he did. What he wore. If he rode a horse. Everything. Write it down if you have to."

"I can do that," he said.

Elsa gave him a long hug and then shooed him along to bed.

Joran turned and walked out the door, his knees still a little shaky. His head felt better, though, and his heart had returned to normal. He decided that overall, he was good.

After closing the door behind him, he saw Gunnarr and his men. They were finishing up putting their weapons on before going to look for the man in the coat. Joran noticed several of them carrying long poles with nooses on one end. He wasn't sure what they were for, and he decided he probably didn't want to know. He walked through without speaking to them; he just nodded to Gunnarr and kept walking toward his room.

As he walked through the hallways, he felt groggy—like he had drunk too much sweet wine at the winter festival. Yet his little voice in the back of his head seemed totally sober. He smiled to himself. That would be a neat trick, getting drunk while his little voice stayed sober. He wasn't sure why this was amusing to him. What wasn't so amusing, though, was how Elsa had somehow fixed his head. He could now clearly think about the Vibaion and speak of him, while in the past, that had been something that seemed intimate to him; only he and the other man knew of it. Now, though, it was out in the open. It left him feeling somewhat distant now. Softly shaking his head, he mounted the stairs to his quarters. Elsa had the right idea; sleep sounded really good. Even if he did come across a puppy, he doubted he would really bother playing with it.

Reaching the top of the stairs, Joran realized Elsa might be mad at him for not following her directions. Not that he didn't mean to or want to. This time it would be because he couldn't. Standing outside his rooms were eight men. They were all dressed as the other warriors he had seen in the castle and out in the city. It just felt off to Joran. Why would they be looking here for the man in the coat? There were too many people around this part of the castle. Why would he be in Joran's room in the first place? Rather than stick around to find out, Joran decided to go back to the king's meeting room and tell them what he had seen.

No sooner had he started to back down the stairs than a finely dressed man emerged from Joran's room. At first, he didn't see Joran, who was quietly and slowly backing down the stairs. Then the man turned and saw him. A cold smile spread across his face. "And he is found." His voice was soft, yet it sent chills down Joran's back. "You, boy, are a tough one to find. Now come here."

Joran's head seemed to spin for a moment, then it cleared. He looked right at the man, yet kept stepping backward slowly, making sure of his footing before taking another step. His knees still felt a little shaky. Falling now would be bad, he thought.

"Come now, you aren't going to run away from your old friend now, are you? Besides, you know you can't ignore my commands. Now come here." His voice wasn't so quiet now.

Something happened in Joran's head. He felt like he was trying to remember a long-forgotten memory, and it kept disappearing whenever he almost remembered it. He took another step backward.

"I told you to come here," Ala Maona yelled at him.

Joran took another step back.

Ala Maona glared at Joran. Suddenly Joran's head felt hot, like he had been soaking too long in the royal bath. Then he felt dizzy again. He looked back at the man, defiant. He stepped back again.

The man's eyes grew wide with surprise, then narrowed into a cruel look. "Do not try and fight me, boy."

Joran took another step back. Just a little farther, and he would be back in the hall that led to the king's meeting chambers. Suddenly his head felt like it had taken a glancing blow from an ax handle. He shook his head and looked back at the man.

"How? Who?" Ala Maona was confused for a moment. "The old man? Or his witch of a daughter? Who removed it?" he hissed. "Never mind; neither is here to protect you now. You are too young and don't have the power to refuse me. Once you were mine, and you will be again."

"Maybe I don't have the power you speak of, but I am sure you're too old and fat to catch me," Joran shot back at him.

Pointing at Joran, fury etched on his face, Ala Maona yelled at the men with him, "Bring him to me!"

The man to his left had his spear raised and half thrown before Ala Maona knocked it off its intended course. "Fool! I didn't say bring me his body!" The spear sank into the doorframe off to Joran's right. Joran took that as a hint to run.

And run he did.

Chapter Eighteen

Joran's plan had been simple: get to the bottom of the stairs, run back to the king's chambers, tell them Ala Maona was in the castle, and let the royal guard deal with him. Simple.

Like most things in life, though, simple didn't stand up to reality. Instead of an empty hall, like the one he had left not long ago, Joran was greeted with royal guards fighting what he could only think of as invaders. Instead of just bringing the men Joran had seen with Ala Maona, the man had brought in an entire invading force. It didn't take Joran too many steps to figure out how he had gotten them inside either. The crumbling wings where he had been exploring would easily let an entire army in, and no one would know.

For Joran, this brought more than one problem. First, his original plan went out the window. He couldn't just run down a hallway filled with men hacking one another with everything from axes to daggers. Seeing the battles going on around him brought to light another very serious issue. Joran hadn't yet learned the subtle differences in dress or armor to tell one Chanese from another. For all he knew, he would be running to the enemy for help. That wouldn't do him any good. He kept moving away from the men chasing him. At least he knew they weren't allies.

That pretty much ended what he did know.

What he didn't know was where he was. When his plan of running straight to the royal chambers fell apart, he had taken off running through any open hallway, door, or stairway he could find. While it kept him away from Ala Maona and his men, it also kept him from knowing where he was. Lost was OK if it kept him from bumping into Ala Maona again. Joran knew that if he was captured again, whatever Elsa had done to untie his mind the Vibaion would redo. Only much stronger this time. Joran decided hiding would be his best option. After all, the castle was huge, and there had to be lots of hiding places.

His chest was heaving when he stopped to put his plan together a little more. Leaning against the cool stones of the wall, he looked around. A torch burned down at the end of the hall he was in. Realizing that the fighting was all on the first few floors, he decided going up would be the best idea. The higher he went, the fewer people there would be and the easier it would be to hide. It made sense to him. He ran past the torch and started up the stairs that lay just past it. After a few strides up the stairs, he realized he might not have thought this out all the way. The stairs offered only two choices: up or down. Well, three choices, if you counted just stand there and do nothing. There weren't any doors or hallways leading off them once you were on them. There weren't even any recesses for torches for Joran to hide in. He continued up. A harsh yell behind him told him going up was a good idea. The man who had thrown the spear at him was coming up the stairs behind Joran. He continued up, his lungs burning from the hard run.

Just as he was coming to the top of the stairs, Joran skidded to a stop. While there was a man with a spear chasing him from behind, there was a man with a wicked-looking sword at the top. Not seeing any other option, Joran slammed himself back against the wall and drew his knife. After taking a second look at the sword the man above him carried, Joran felt a little foolish. Like his knife was going to stand a chance against that.

The man with the spear caught up to Joran at that moment. He saw the man with the sword standing above him and seemed to forget about Joran. The two men bellowed cries of rage and sprang at each other.

A whistling swing of the sword missed its intended target, instead clanging off the wall. Ducking, the man with the spear jabbed it upward and hit the swordsman just above his belt, sinking the spear into the man's belly. He dropped the sword and drew a heavy knife from behind him. As he fell forward, he drove the blade into the other man's lungs. The momentum of the swordsman falling forward knocked the spearman from his feet as well, and they half slid, half bounced down the stairs past Joran. He was amazed to see the two carving each other up with their knives, even as they fell down the stairs.

Joran was stunned as he followed the carnage down the stairs. A thick trail of blood was left in their wake. To Joran, it looked like a red carpet had been rolled down the stairs. The stomach-turning sounds made him change his mind. Carpets didn't sound like that. Or smell like that. The coppery smell filled his nose, reminding him of the times he helped with butchering cattle back on the farm.

Joran's stomach rolled again. He could feel the saliva start to build in his mouth — not the good kind, like when he smelled Elsa's baking. The bad kind, like when he had a sick stomach. He fought down the bile he could feel coming up his throat. He won, for the most part. Spitting out the little bit that he couldn't swallow back down, he turned and sprinted up the last few steps. He tore through the castle as fast as he could run, randomly taking this hallway or that staircase, until he could run no more. Gasping for breath, he staggered into a long-abandoned room. Dust mites floated through what light there was, hanging in the stale air of the room. He slammed the heavy wood-and-iron-banded door shut behind him. The solid feel of the door raised his spirits somewhat. He dropped to his knees and leaned his head against the door. After a little bit, his breathing slowed, and his heart wasn't pounding as much.

He stood and turned, taking in his surroundings in the dim light that filtered through the dirty window set up in the ceiling. What looked like a couple of stools and a broken desk were piled together in the corner opposite where he stood. A mattress lay on the floor in front of him — at least it looked like it was, or had been, a mattress. Its frame had long ago rotted and collapsed. A chest, once finely carved, was at the foot of the mattress. Its top was open, hanging off by one hinge. The sides were worm-eaten and falling apart. Once he saw where he was, it dawned on him that this probably wasn't the best place to be. On one hand, while there weren't any men falling down stairs while carving one another, if any of them poked their head in here, Joran had nowhere to go. Looking at the fitted stones of the floor confirmed his new worry. The dust plainly showed that someone had been in here. He fought the growing panic and took a deep breath. He carefully looked around the room, taking stock of what he did and didn't have.

Ruling out hiding, he started with fortifying his little stronghold by pushing the chest against the door and piling the old furniture on it. He knew that wouldn't stop anyone for long, but it did make him feel a little better. Next, he walked over to the embroidered curtains hanging against the wall. He hoped that they hid a window that he could crawl out of. No such luck. There was a doorway behind them. At first, he thought it opened into another room. Once his eyes grew accustomed to the dark, he saw it was a dark corridor a little wider than his shoulders. He could barely see past the end of his arm when he put it out. He took a quick look around again and realized this was his best (and probably only) option to get out of the room and not go back into the hallways. A chill ran down his spine when he realized he would have to choose between the known and unknown. The known: the hallways he had just come from, where he knew men were looking to kill him; or the unknown: this small corridor, where he doubted anyone had been in years.

Joran really had no idea where he was, and that wasn't helping him make a decision. He looked up, hoping the window in the ceiling would give him some idea where he was. What little he could see through the dirty skylight were just more parts of the castle roof. No help there. As he stood there, it came to him that if he went out through the hidden hallway, anyone who opened the door would know the footprints were that of a child, not a man. He quickly grabbed a half-rotted cushion from the floor in the corner. He walked to the door and then backed up slowly, banging the dusty cushion over his footprints. The light dusting from the cushion obscured his footprints as he went. *It's not great, but it's better than nothing*, he thought as he looked at his handiwork. He threw the cushion back to the corner, turned, and steeled himself for what lay ahead in the darkness.

He closed the door and pulled the curtain over it as best he could. He couldn't see anything. The darkness enveloped him. After a few tentative steps, he walked into a spider web that covered his face, making him panic to get it off. He stopped walking and started almost running. He learned to hold his hand in front of him to avoid the experience with the spider web again. It would also keep him from running into walls face first. His only thought was to get away from what he had seen and heard in the hallways behind him. The first time his foot caught on a loose stone and he started to fall, he slowed his pace considerably. His overactive mind brought images of holes in the floor or trap doors. The dust he was kicking up was making it hard to breathe. He realized that falling and dying in here with no one ever finding him was a very real possibility. He slowed to a steady walk, sliding one foot ahead, keeping one hand on the blocks of the wall and the other one in front of his face.

A strange thing happens in the dark; all sense of time is lost. It can be a few minutes and feel like hours. Or it can be a few hours and feel like minutes. For Joran, it was the former. He began to wonder if he would ever come to the end of the corridor. Then he felt a wall in front of him. On one side, he just felt solid blocks. He started to panic again. Had this part collapsed? Did he have to go back where he had started and try something else? He reached out to the other side and, to his relief, felt nothing. He turned and joked with himself, *Of course corridors turn; how can you be so thickheaded?* After a little way, he saw a glimmer of light. At first, he thought his eyes were just playing tricks on him. Then he saw that the light was getting brighter.

When he got to the source of the light, he saw it was a small hole about knee high in the blocks of the wall. He crouched down and took a long deep breath of fresh air. It smelled almost sweet to him after all the dust he had inhaled. After another deep breath, he looked out the hole. It took him a few seconds to recognize what he saw. The large room had a fire raging in the fireplace. This and the dozens of candles showed Joran that it was the king's royal reception hall. It looked very different from where he was now versus the first time he saw it. He saw his friends, Mouse, the old man, and Elsa with the kings: Oordah, Lu-Ning, and Anderson. He could see their wives as well. Even Gunnarr's wife was there. They were all standing around quietly talking, except Mouse. He was trying to wear a path in the floor. He kept striding back and forth between the closed main doors and the throne. The royal guards didn't seem to notice him; their attention was on the doors. Finally, Joran thought he was safe.

Before he could yell at them that he was up there, he saw the huge doors fly open. King Chang practically marched in. His black mail shirt clinked softly as he moved across the chamber, his sword held at the ready. Gunnarr and Drath followed close on the king's heals. Each had hold of an ankle of a fourth man, who had his hands tied behind his back and was being dragged belly-side down across the floor behind the two. Taking a second look at the man, Joran realized it was the man he had overheard in the woods.

Well, look what Gunnarr dragged in. Literally. Joran half giggled to himself. Then he brought it under control and listened to what was being said below him.

"You do remember what the punishment is for betraying the kingdom, don't you?" Chang said calmly as he sat on his throne and laid his sword across his captive's legs.

Elsa stepped forward. "Your Highness, we are safe now, yes?" she asked.

"Oh, maybe not yet. I am sure there are still some of his mercenaries being rounded up by the royal guards," he replied. "I am not sure things would have gone in our favor if there hadn't been a warning."

Joran swallowed the yell that was about to leave his mouth. For some reason, he thought it best to keep quiet and listen. Besides, this was how he had been able to warn them in the first place: listening.

"Now then, Lord Starn. We shall have a little chat now," King Chang said, looking at the man lying on the floor.

Lord Starn seemed to realize that kicking against the two big men holding his ankles was not only not going to get him free of them, it wasn't in his best interest for his physical well-being. He remembered how, as a boy, he had taken the wishbone from the turkey and made a wish with his father. He hoped the two men holding his feet didn't have similar memories from their childhood. If they did, he really hoped they didn't decide to relive them — only this time with him as the wishbone.

"Well?" Gunnarr said, looking at the man and shaking the leg he held.

If they could have seen his face against the floor, they would have seen his look of resignation.

"There is nothing to tell. I tried to take over your rule. It didn't go entirely as I had planned, or I would be sitting where you are."

"Well, that is the short version of the story, yes," the king replied. "Now let us have the long version, with the interesting bits and pieces included. Shall we?"

"No."

"Really now, is that how you want to approach this?" Gunnarr said.

"I'll tell you nothing. Torture me any way you want. I won't say a word," he said with conviction.

"Very well. I am sure Drath and Gunnarr will find things to do to — and with — you. I know Gunnarr can get very creative with kitchen utensils," the king replied.

"There is a much more effective way to get what he knows from him," Elsa said. After a long look at Lord Starn, she slowly walked toward him.

"True men don't fear the parlor tricks of a woman," he sneered at her.

"Oh. Now that just was plain not friendly," the old man said sadly from where he stood by the throne.

"You're right. It wasn't nice, Father," Elsa said, looking intensely at Lord Starn.

"Elsa, be careful. You like to...overreact sometimes. Be nice. We need him alive. At least for now," the old man cautioned.

"I will be careful, Father," she snapped back at him.

Joran watched from his hiding place as Elsa stopped short of the tied man on the floor. The two men holding his ankles had let go of them, and Lord Starn had rolled over and sat up. He was watching her as she leaned forward a little, looking right into his eyes. About now, the lord realized he might be in trouble. A sheen appeared on his forehead head, reflecting the candlelight. His face went white, and his mouth fell open. A thin line of drool appeared at one corner of his mouth as his body shook. While she never touched him physically, he couldn't fight her will.

Suddenly, a shrill sound — not really a scream but not a yell either — came from him. It sounded to Joran like the man's soul was dying. Had he not already been on the floor, Joran was sure he would have collapsed.

"No, no, no, no, no," he started whispering. His voice was desperate. "Stop. Please. No more," he babbled on.

Mouse, who was leaning on the king's throne, wondered aloud, "Now what could such a sweet lady do to him to make him act like that?"

"My friend, you probably don't want to know," Drath said, shaking his head.

Joran had noticed Queen Jura had been watching Elsa very closely, like she was trying to figure out the trick to what she was doing. Much like she had tried to figure out the flower trick when they had first arrived. Her head jerked back, though, when the man seemed to break inside and emitted that odd sound.

The king leaned forward, resting his forearms on his knees, and whispered at the lord to start his story from the beginning and to tell it all. He then leaned back in his throne, ready to hear the tale.

"Yes, Your Highness," Lord Starn sputtered. "Just make her go away. Please, please, please, please." Elsa backed away, a satisfied smile on her face. He then started his tale. At the beginning, there didn't seem to be anything really wrong with what was being done. About two or three years ago, he had taken a trip to the Snow Granite Kingdom. The man he had gone to meet was a businessman: Orochi. He was a Cosllaan. He was a decent businessman. At least he seemed like one. Then one day, Orochi approached Starn with a business offer: transport him and a chest on one of the lord's ships. At first, he had said no; after all, he was a lord, not a common businessman and certainly not a lowly cargo-ship captain. Orochi had badgered him into it though. Besides, it was just a trunk and a nice fellow passenger. One that Orochi didn't want to have fall into the hands of pirates. What pirate would attack a lord's vessel? What, with all those armed guards? Never. Starn had never even asked what was in the trunk. What had pushed the lord over the edge was the purse of gold he was offered. A large purse of gold. After all, what man can say no to that much gold for something so simple? Just put the trunk on the boat,make up a bed for the passenger and drop them off at the other end, and collect the gold. Easy. So they made the trip Orochi had proposed. They sailed over to Broonard and met with Orochi's business associate, a Vibaion named Ala Maona. When Joran heard the name, he jerked back a little from the hole in the wall. He then leaned back toward it, eager to hear the rest of the story. Even if it wasn't as good as one of the old man's stories.

Lord Starn was now telling them how even after getting that first purse of gold — and it was more than he had ever had — he seemed to need more. "That is the nature of their gold. It seems to infect people with a hunger for more and more. That is why the Arrahs are so free with it; they know they are buying people's lives with their gold," the old man said.

Hanging his head for a moment, Lord Starn agreed. He then continued telling them how he had gotten to where he was today. Orochi had told him to look him up if he ever wanted more gold. He was sure he could find another business arrangement for them. Lord Starn looked him up. What man wouldn't? Not long after the first purse had been received, he had found a reason of some sort to go to Broonard. This time, though, he spent his time with Ala Maona. Lord Starn told of how he sat for hours in an ale house telling Ala Maona about his homeland. Ala Maona was curious about White Straights, since no Vibaions were allowed inside the kingdom. The more questions he answered, the more gold Ala Maona handed him. At the time, it seemed way too easy. Talk about his home and get piles of gold? Who looks the gift horse in the mouth? He came home, putting the new gold with the old. Again, it didn't seem enough. Still, nothing seemed wrong. Where was the crime in talking about home? After all, sailors do it in ports far from home every day.

He continued his story, telling how after a few days, he had become obsessed with seeing and touching his new wealth. He spent hours just sitting in his vault, looking at the candlelight sparkling off the gold. When that wasn't enough, he began carefully buffing and cleaning the coins. One by one he carefully inspected them. He was mesmerized by them. Even the sounds they made as he stacked them became music to his ears. Still, it didn't seem to be enough. Like a drunk sobering up and not liking it, he went to get another drink.

It was here that Lord Starn hung his head in shame, knowing what was coming next. In a sad, quiet tone, he shared how this time Ala Maona had wanted more than just stories of home or help carrying a chest across the water. This time he asked for how things were decided on the ruling assemblies. How did the kings and their appointed heads of state think? What was their thought process? The lord's shame was clear as he recounted how he had said no at first. This was treason. Yet when he was shown the bag of gold, bigger than any he had seen before, he said yes.

A man would sell out his entire country for a bag or two of gold? Joran thought, high above the proceedings. He had a hard time understanding that, especially here, where it seemed men were made of better morals and pride than that. His thoughts seemed to be reflected in the faces of those below him. Some showed empathy; others showed unmasked disgust for this traitor.

After a brief pause, the lord composed himself and continued. His spying hadn't lasted long. Shortly after he had agreed to take the gold, one of his messages was intercepted. That led to his being tossed out of the kingdom. At first this was OK; it let him enjoy his time sitting among his treasure. Like any drug, though, it wasn't long before it wasn't enough, and he wanted more. So he devised a way to get more. It started with a message. The message he had sent to Ala Maona brought the man to Lord Starn. After long hours and many tankards of beer, they came to an agreement whereby he could get more gold.

King Chang interrupted him there. His eyes burned with anger. "Let me get this straight. You spied on the assemblies and then went back after being removed from the kingdom and begged to betray us more?"

Lord Starn didn't look up. He just shrugged his shoulders and looked at the ground.

"Not only that, you broke a sacred law of this kingdom? You brought Mulsins into this country? That is the same things as bringing in terrorists! That is breaking probably the oldest law of this kingdom. Not one has ever set foot on our lands since the beginning of the kingdom. Not one from any clan! It has let our kingdom and people grow and prosper. Unlike kingdoms that have let them in. Then you bring one into the kingdom, and there is a battle in this very castle! How stupid can you be to bring them in?" His voice was getting heated by now.

Lord Starn just looked at the ground. "Honestly, I was past caring by this point. They had a plan — a sound and well-thought-out plan to bring them in by ones and twos. What harm could one or two do? I found hiding places for them until they were needed for the attack. Once all the kings were assembled, I would sneak the Mulsins into the castle and let them loose on the royals. After they were all killed, I would become king."

"King? After killing all of the rulers?" the old man said. "I doubt you were just going to be handed the crown just like that. What was the hook in that bait?"

"Compared to everything else I had done so far for him, he was asking for nothing. To him it was worth an entire room full of gold. All I had to do was to bring him some kid, barely a teenager. He was traveling with you." He nodded at the old man. "Just that: bring him the boy, and I would not only become king, I would have an entire room filled with gold."

Hearing this, Joran thought that if he was worth a room full of gold and a kingdom, maybe Elsa should be a little nicer to him.

King Anderson eyed the man on the ground. "Why would they want a simple farm boy so badly they would give you all that?"

Before he could answer, Elsa let out a muffled scream. Sladvick was running across the room. Mouse was following close on his heels. It wasn't the two men that Lord Starn was staring at in horror; it was Elsa. Her eyes looked like they glowed; there were two big white balls of fire where her eyes had been. That was what terrified the man.

"If you hurt him. Even bruised him. They will be telling stories for generations of the horrors you faced before you died," Elsa hissed at him.

"Guards, take him and execute him," the king said quietly.

The tied man didn't resist as the royal guards picked him off the floor and led him out the door.

After the initial shock wore off, Joran felt a little embarrassed by what he had been doing. Here he was hiding and eavesdropping while they were all scared for his safety. Look at how upset Elsa was. She had practically raised him, and here he was, making her worry more.

Taking a deep breath, he yelled out the little hole in the wall, "Everybody! Up here!"

If it hadn't been a serious matter, Joran would have thought it was kind of funny how everyone looked up. The surprised looks on their faces were mixed with confusion.

Sladvick was the first one to get past the surprise from the heavens. "Joran? Is that you?" His deep voice carried easily.

"Yes, it's me."

"Where are you?" Mouse called.

"Um. Aside from in the ceiling, I'm not sure."

"Fair enough," the old man said, chuckling. "Do you remember how you got in there?"

"Down a hallway."

King Anderson laughed. "That was very helpful. We should find you sometime before I die then."

"It's true, Your Highness. I was running away from the attackers; they wanted to kidnap me or worse. I didn't stay around to ask. Then I got lost. I found a hidden hallway, took it, and wound up here. Well, up here. I think some stairs were involved too."

Gunnarr, Sladvick, Mouse, and Drath were trying not to laugh when Joran had finished. You had to admit, it was rather funny.

Elsa wasn't seeing the humor in it at all. "Young man! You get down here right now."

"I would like to. I won't fit through the hole up here though. And there is no rope or stairs," Joran said.

Taking a breath and getting ahold of herself after the surprise of finding Joran, she told him to stay where he was. They would figure something out.

"Um, won't that take a long time? Like the king said, there are lots of hallways in the castle." His voice was a little worried.

"And stairways," Drath added, chuckling and avoiding Elsa's angry look.

Chapter Nineteen

Squinting up at the ceiling and trying to find the hole Joran had mentioned, King Chang said, "Go back down the hallway that you took to get there. Then just keep taking stairs down until you are on the first floor. After that, go outside and walk around the castle until you either come to the front again or you wander into familiar settings."

Elsa looked at him as though he had grown a second head. "Wander around? You don't know if the castle has been cleared yet. What if he walks, excuse me, wanders, right into the Vibaion? No, he should stay where he is until we can get someone to him."

"Bah. The terrorist Vibaion has fled the castle and is fleeing the kingdom now," the king said.

"Fleeing? Fleeing from a kingdom he isn't supposed to be in in the first place?" Elsa snapped back.

"Elsa, be nice," the old man said. "He did have a good idea, and it was the simplest of them. If not for the Vibaion, I would say go ahead with it. It would work."

Drath called up to Joran, "Can you point us in the general direction of where the hallway goes? Back toward the doors of this room? The opposite way?"

Gunnarr added under his breath, "And the stairs." Drath fought a smile.

"It seems like it goes toward the wall to your right," Joran said. "I can't really tell if it is a straight hall or if it curves. It is pitch black in here."

"Joran, we will get you some candles. Light them and set one at the hole. Then walk down the hallway with the other until you can't see it. That will tell you if it is a straight hallway or not," the old man called up.

Mouse looked at the storyteller. "Now if only I were older than the oceans, I could have thought up something like that."

Sladvick had been looking at the ceiling for a bit. "Why not just knock a hole in it?"

Chang looked a little unhappy with that idea. "While that is a good idea, maybe we can save that one for later if nothing else works. I do like my throne-room ceiling."

"As you wish, m'lord." Sladvick looked a little embarrassed.

"And how do you suppose we get the candles and matches up to him?" Elsa asked.

"Joran, is there room enough for you to move to one side of the hole and not be in direct line of it?" Drath called up.

"Yes."

Elsa and a few others were looking at Drath a little confused. They let him go on with his idea, though, even if they didn't know what it was.

"OK, good," Drath called up again. "We can't see the hole from down here, though; could you mark it somehow? Hang something from it?"

"OK, I can do that," Joran said. Then he slipped his belt off, careful to keep his knife in his waistband so he wouldn't lose it in the dark. He then pushed the end out the hole, letting it fall until he just had the buckle in his hand.

"OK, good, we see it. Hold on a bit, OK?" Drath said. He then walked over to one of the royal guards and whispered something in his ear. The guard ran off and came back a few minutes later. He handed Drath a large spool of yarn, several candles, and matches.

Drath took them, thanked the guard, and walked over to the middle of the floor. He carefully unspooled the yarn on the floor, making neat figure eights with it that were slightly offset from each other. He then went over to one of the royal guards and asked for his bow and quiver of arrows. The guard handed them over quickly.

They all figured out what he was planning now. Or at least the general idea. Elsa stopped him. "You plan on shooting arrows at him?"

"M'lady, if you will let me finish, I think you will see this will work with little to no danger to the boy," Drath said politely to her. "May I?"

Elsa looked at the others, none of whom seemed too worried. So she backed off.

Drath took one of the arrows out of the quiver and carefully cut off the broad head at the tip. He then made a notch where the arrow head had been and tied the yarn to it. Then he stood and called up to Joran. "Move back from the hole. Be careful to stay on one side of the hole, and don't put your hands or anything you value in front of it. Understand?"

"Yes," Joran called back.

"Ready?" Drath yelled up.

"All ready!" Joran yelled back. His voice sounded farther away this time.

Drath drew the bow — not to full draw, though —
and let it go. The arrow arched through the air
and fell short of the hole. Undaunted, he
retrieved the arrow and did it again, pulling the
bow a little closer to full draw this time. On his
fourth try, the arrow shot through the hole that
Joran's belt was hanging from.

"Are you OK?" Elsa called up, worried that
Joran had just been shot with an arrow.

"Yes," Joran called back.

Gunnarr had picked up the other end of the yarn
and tied the candles to it. "OK, pull it up Joran,"
he called.

Joran pulled the candles and matches up and lit
them. He poured a little wax onto the stones to
set the candle near the hole and then started
walking away from it.

"From where that hole is, it looks like he will
come out back there," King Change said,
pointing at the back of the room.

"Aren't those where the king's personal rooms
used to be?" Gunnarr asked.

"Well, based on our centuries-long tradition of
battles, it could just be an escape tunnel no one
remembers," King Chang said.

"Yes, nothing at all to worry about," King
Oordah said dryly.

For his part, Joran was walking back down the passageway, only this time he could see what was around him. He kept looking back as well to keep the other candle in view. After a bit, he saw a door set flush with the stones in the wall. He had walked past it in the dark. Knowing the other opening of the passage, he decided to explore this way instead. He opened the door, and the draft from it blew out his candle. The next thing he knew, he was falling and then landed with a splash. Thrashing in the water for a moment, he found he could stand. Wiping the water from his eyes, he found himself in a bath. He climbed out of the cool water and sloshed his way out of the bath chamber. It was attached to a well-decorated room. Being wet and hungry, he didn't bother admiring the fine decorations. He just walked over to the nearest door, opened it, and walked out into the hallway.

Joran didn't recognize where he was and, with a shrug, set off to the right. It looked just as good as the left did. After a few minutes, he saw men coming down the hallway at him. Leading them was Bardawulf. The chief huntsman recognized Joran right away. Laughing, he winked at Joran. Then he said, "You seem to have a habit of getting all wet around me. First it was blood, now it's bathwater." He laughed and slapped Joran on the back.

Joran just smiled, glad it was over.

"I am sure Elsa will be happier to see you covered in bathwater this time," the big man teased gently as they walked to the throne room.

"I am sure she will still yell at me," Joran said morosely.

"Eh, I wouldn't worry about it," the huntsman said gently. "Women are mad at the men in their lives most of the time. Men rarely know the reason; we just live with it. You'll see when you are grown and have a woman of your own. Or two." He winked at Joran when he added the last part. Joran just smiled and blushed.

Much to Joran's surprise, Elsa didn't yell or lecture him when she met the party at the entrance to the king's royal reception room. Elsa simply grabbed him and hugged him for a long time. Then she released him and led him to the rest of the group.

As they approached, they could hear Chang talking with Bardawulf. "He fell into my mother's bath? That is where the tunnel came out? Her bath?" He laughed. "She was never anything other than a grouchy old woman who used to try and hit me with her walking stick."

"Oh, I am sure she aged poorly. She wasn't born that way though." Bardawulf chuckled.

Queen Helena smiled at the men, a mischievous twinkle in her eyes. "No reason to start rumors."

"Aye, that may be true," Bardawulf said. "From the appearance of the dirt and dust in the passageway, I doubt it has been used in generations. She may not have known it was there."

"Still, what an interesting revelation," Chang mused, half to himself.

The rest decided to let things lie, even though King Oordah had a little grin on his face that made those who saw it wonder what he was thinking.

"Joran, I believe you have quite the tale to share," Lord Valmore said. "Would you be so kind as to share it with us?"

Elsa eyed Joran. "I am sure he does have a tale—one that should be short, since he was told to remain in his quarters," she said.

Joran looked at her calmly. He was getting used to her criticizing everything he did, especially when it was something that she hadn't told him to do. He looked at her evenly and replied, "I went to my quarters like you told me to. The men who were at my door had other ideas. Telling them to leave me alone and let me go to my room because Elsa told me to go there didn't seem to be something that would work." Joran then looked at the rest of the group; several of them were trying to cover smirks. "Ala Maona was there with hired fighters. At first, he tried to do something with my mind to make me go with him. He said he had controlled me before; he would do so again. When that didn't work, his men tried to capture me. After one threw a spear at me, I decided to run from them. They almost caught me on a set of stairs. A warrior—I don't know if he was one of the royal guards or not—fought with the one who almost caught me. That was when I hid in one of the abandoned rooms and found the passageway where you found me."

Drath was openly laughing at this point. "Well, Elsa, he did try to do what you told him to do." Even with her angry stare, he laughed. "If I went to my quarters, saw a Jahagi at my door, and had a man throw a spear at me and then try to kidnap me, I would run too."

Mouse wasn't finding it quite so funny—amusing perhaps, after listening to Drath put it that way, but not funny right now. "Joran, this is very important. You know it was Ala Maona? No doubt at all?"

Joran looked at him. "Yes, he has been around me since I was a child. I just didn't know it." His voice was barely more than a whisper. "He not only recognized me, he knew my name."

"This man has been causing a great deal of trouble in my country. It would be nice to discuss this with him," King Chang said. "Maybe convince him to stop it."

"I wish you luck with that, Your Highness," the old man said. "Once, a while back, I felt his mind. It wasn't entirely natural."

"Nonetheless, I will make every effort to catch him," King Chang said. "I doubt he can swim like a fish, so I will hold all ships in port and send the guardsmen and huntsmen into the city and surrounding forests to look for him. If nothing else, it will be good practice for them— and it will keep them from getting bored and throwing snow at one another in the streets."

"Chang, pushing your men into the bitter weather of winter here might not make your men overly found of you," King Oordah pointed out.

"Money," Mouse said. "Offer a bounty on his head. Whoever brings him to you gets a sack of silver. Or something like that."

Chang brightened at that. "What exactly would you put up as a bounty?"

"Whatever his weight is, you will match it in silver?" Mouse offered. "We want to make sure even the oldest and crankiest of your men have the motivation to leave the warmth of their hearths or mistresses' beds."

Chang made a face. Not a happy one.

"OK, it sounds like a lot," Mouse offered after seeing the king's reaction. "Look at it this way. First off, he is a Jahagi. What are the chances they actually find a Jahagi who doesn't want to be found? Very slim. While your bag of silver is safe, your kingdom is safer as well. Your men will be tearing the kingdom apart looking for him, and he will be much too busy trying to keep his head attached to the rest of his body to be causing any more trouble. You'll get all of this and a reputation for being a fair and thoughtful ruler who rewards work well done. If you are too worried about the silver, offer a fine stallion as the reward, complete with tack and weapons."

Chang looked at Mouse thoughtfully for a moment. He then said, "You, sir, are a very creative little man. I like it. I will offer the horse and weapons instead of the silver. Any man in the kingdom worth anything would just spend the silver that way anyway." He laughed.

Mouse gave a theatrical bow to the king. "I am at your service, Your Highness."

"You are?" Chang said. "Then when can I expect you to start working for the kingdom?"

"Wait! What?" Oordah blurted out.

"Sadly, I am bound by not only oaths to my king. I am bound by relationships as well," Mouse said sadly. "I am interested in your proposal though. I may be able to use it in future negotiations with my current employer." He winked.

The laughter from Queen Helena covered the moan from Oordah as he shook his head. "How is a chubby, crippled, gray-haired old king supposed to rule when he is surrounded by mercenaries like this?" A couple of laughs greeted his moaning troubles.

The heavy footsteps drew everyone away from the kings. A royal guard strode through the doors. He walked up to King Chang, saluted, and said, "Do you wish to see what is left, m'lord?"

"No, thank you."

"Very well, m'lord. Shall we dip him in tar and hang him in the city square?"

"That won't be necessary. At one time, he was a good man; let him have peace in his death," the king said sadly.

"Yes, m'lord," the man said, saluting him.

"Please do it with some respect. Don't just drop him at her door off the back of a horse," the king added before the guard could leave.

"No, m'lord. I hadn't thought of doing such a thing. I was going to prepare his body for burial and put it in a coffin, then take his body to his wife. Let her give him a funeral as is right," the guard replied, somewhat surprised that the king thought he would just roll the body off a horse at her doorstep.

"Thank you."

"Yes, m'lord." The guard saluted again, turned on his heel, and strode out of the chambers.

Queen Jura looked at Elsa and asked, "Sister, isn't there a way you and I could find this Jahagi?" Her voice sounded arrogant.

Before Elsa could respond with what the old man was sure was going to be a rather short and biting response, he answered her, "That is a courageous idea. Unfortunately, it is overly dangerous. While my daughter would be safe, you would be unprotected, and if he thought you were a threat to him, he would destroy your mind. Think of a ball of snow held over a fire. That is what he would do to you. We can't risk the queen living the rest of her life sitting in a corner, drooling and eating broth until she dies." The queen gasped and brought her hand to her mouth, her face suddenly ashen. She missed the clever look the old man gave her husband.

"The storyteller is correct," Chang said firmly. "You are not to do anything so foolish as that," he said, leveling a hard look at his wife.

"As my husband commands," she said, bowing slightly.

"Good," he said as she skittered back from the throne.

The old man's look became less amused as he stepped before the kings. "Your Highnesses, this talking has gone on far too long. The battle and slying has proven that fact today. Time to make some decisions. Where can we talk and not be overheard? It seems the throne room has ears, as does your private quarters. Or not-so-private, I might say."

"There is one place I know where no one can sneak up to or listen in on us, though it might prove challenging for King Lu-Ning to get there," he said gently.

"I appreciate your kindness. Thank you. In this instance, however, I think my discomfort or inconvenience should not be a factor in where we talk," he said. "May I ask where this place is?"

"At the top of one of the towers."

"Ah, I see. Some exercise may do me some good. Don't you think?" He smiled. "Just give me a head start, and I will meet you all there." He smiled. "It is better than having our conversation spied on."

Sladvick patted Joran on the back. "I will keep an eye on our young friend here while you all talk. Make sure he doesn't get into any more mischief."

"No," Elsa said. "I want to keep an eye on him myself until this is resolved."

Sladvick shrugged. "As you wish." He then looked at Joran. "Sorry, friend. I tried." Joran just smiled at his friend and shrugged. He did try.

"Then it is settled. Let us get to this room you told us about and get things decided," the old man said. "I would like to leave early tomorrow and get back to tracking this man."

Jura was standing off to the side as her husband walked across the room. She watched his hands as he passed her.

"We can talk later," he said.

"As you wish, husband," she signed back. Her face was still ashen. Her fingers, though, showed her anger at being excluded.

"Here we follow their ways. Now compose yourself as you should," He said with his hands. If hands could have an arrogant tone, hers were dripping with it as she signaled her unladylike reply.

Even with the help of Angensen, Lu-Ning had a rough time with the stairs. His determined spirit was at odds with his not-so-determined body. Wheezing, he stopped and tried to catch his breath. He then straightened and motioned for Angensen to continue with him.

Chang had six of his royal guards stand at the base of the tower. Their orders were that no one was to come up the stairs or near the tower. He then climbed the stairs himself. Once at the top, he barred the thick oak door behind him.

"Gunnarr," he said, "it's kind of chilly up here. Would you mind getting those logs burning?" Gunnarr smiled and took some of the wood from the box near the hearth and piled it on the grate. He then held a torch to it until it blazed and started to warm the room.

They all took a seat. While the room wasn't as big as the king's private chambers, there was plenty of room for them all to sit comfortably. The old man was looking out one of the windows. The city spread out before him. The city lights looked like hundreds of fireflies in the winter air. "When I was a pupil, I studied in a tower. The time I was there is very dear to me. Since then, I have always enjoyed being in a tower," he mused, more to himself than anyone else.

Still, King Lu-Ning heard him. "Old man, I would gladly give everything to spend an hour with your master." He then whispered to the old man, "Did his hair really glow like snow in the night?"

Chuckling, the old man replied, "I've never heard that rumor about him. Not to disappoint you, but he was a rather plain man. I studied under him for years before I knew what he really was."

King Chang joined them. "Storyteller, was he really as smart as the stories say?"

"In that aspect, I am sure the legends fall short," the old man said. "Back then I was a foolish and bull-headed young man. Did you know he found me at the base of that tower of his in a snowstorm? I was almost totally blue, frozen. He took me in and taught me much. He had the patience of a saint, since it took him a couple of generations to get me under some form of control," he said, his voice far away. "OK, enough of the old stories. We have things in the present to get done with."

"True. When you leave here, where do you plan on going?" King Anderson asked.

"Before we came here, I felt it in Tarathon," the storyteller said.

"Good. I will assign an escort of royal guards to accompany you. After what we have dealt with, I think it best," King Chang said.

Shaking his head, the old man said, "No. Absolutely not. Not only can they not fight what we are dealing with, they would also bring much too much attention to us. Traveling through other kingdoms with a battalion of your guards will be difficult to explain to other kings. Besides, they will slow us down. Thank you for the kind offer though."

"Now father," Elsa said. "You are forgetting it isn't just us to think about. These men live in this world as well and have been nothing but helpful to us. Be nice now."

"I don't think he was thinking of sending that many," King Oordah said. "I believe he was just going to send a couple, maybe half a dozen at most. It would be the smart thing to do."

"I appreciate your thoughts. However, the larger the traveling group, the harder it is to blend in. There is nothing I can think of right now that Elsa and I can't take care of. Besides, we have these fine men with us to take care of the more day-to-day issues we might cross," the storyteller said, gesturing at Sladvick, Gunnarr, and Mouse. "The only addition I would like to make to our little band of merry travelers would be Angensen. If you would be OK with him traveling with us, I believe his training could be invaluable to us someday."

Angensen shook his head no. Before he could say anything, though, his father answered the old man, "Yes, it would be good for him to go with you. He has the right to a life besides carrying around a fat old man."

"Father, it is my duty to stand by you. There are many others with my skills and training. Let them go in my place," Angensen said firmly.

"I understand your devotion to your father. How many Dietmarsan are there though?" the old man said.

Angensen shot the old man a hard look, clearly trying to make him stop talking.

"My son?" Lu-Ning said, confused.

"I don't know. I never mentioned it. I never saw how it would change anything," he said.

Lu-Ning looked back and forth between the old man and his son. The old man nodded to him and said, "It was clear to me as soon as I met him. He had to find out for himself though."

Lu-Ning's face shone with overflowing pride. He hugged his son tightly; tears of joy streamed down his face.

Uncomfortable with the sudden and unbridled affection from his father, Angensen blushed. "I don't see it as important. Standing with you is what is important," he said.

Joran was standing in the corner, more than a little confused by all the goings on. He gently tugged on Mouse's sleeve. "Do you have any idea what they are talking about?"

Mouse nodded and quietly answered Joran. "Yes. This is something that borders on sacred to Angensen's people. They have a belief that some people are born to communicate with dogs and horses with just their minds. They are called Dietmarsans. Every generation has one or two of these people. If someone is found to have this gift, they become royals. For Lu-Ning, he will become very rich when he returns home. That is, if he doesn't burst from pride first."

"It is that special to them?"

Mouse nodded. "They think so. They have a meeting that lasts almost two months just to find out if anyone might have it. If they find someone, they present that person with not only royal titles, but also elaborate gifts. Being related to him, Lu-Ning will become extremely wealthy as these gifts are often shared with in the family. Then again, maybe not. He doesn't seem the type to want wealth like that."

"So just dogs and horses? Not cats or birds?" Joran asked, a little confused yet.

Mouse smiled. "Have you ever been able to teach a cat tricks or get one to work?"

"No."

"Then why would they bother talking to humans?" Mouse asked. "And birds are easy. Anyone who can whistle and listen to their songs can talk to birds."

Joran had to agree; he had whistled with the birds many times while doing chores or just walking in the fields. Mouse was right about cats too. They were plain old lazy — nice to play with or pet at times, just lazy.

Lu-Ning's booming voice, full of pride, brought them back to the other conversation going on in the room. "My son, you must go. This is a great honor for us."

"Yes. As you command, Father," Angensen replied with a sigh.

"Now that we have settled that, when can you get to Mopta with some of your fastest horses?" the storyteller asked.

"That depends on the weather. The passes are usually difficult to get through this time of year. Maybe three weeks, if we are lucky," he replied.

"Good. At daybreak we will all leave then," the old man said. "If King Chang would be so generous as to loan you a ship, you can get on your way. Once you have the horses, bring them to a place a few miles from Tarathon. Across the river, near some ruins. We will meet you there."

Angensen nodded his understanding.

Continuing, the storyteller said, "Later, we will have a few more additions to our group. One will be a Tra, the other a Gurn. These people will help us as we move through the kingdoms."

"They will also assist in making the foretelling come to pass," Chang said mysteriously.

The old man smiled. "Oh, that isn't a bad thing. As long as it doesn't interrupt the drinking of good mead or wine." His eyes seemed to glimmer with the thought.

"I don't suppose there is anything we can do besides sitting here," Drath said.

"Oh, I don't think you will be just sitting here." The old man chuckled. "Regardless of the outcome of our travels, you will be getting ready to deal with the Mulsins. They may have stories that we don't know about, and they are already working themselves up for something big. Whether they choose to do something foolish — and they are prone to do that — or if they decide to calm down if we are successful in our search is yet to be seen. They tend to be overemotional about things. My guess is they will do something foolish. With that in mind, if I were you, I would spend that time preparing for the worst."

King Chang smiled. It was not a pleasant smile; it was more like the kind you would see a mountain lion give a mouse just before it eats the mouse. "My people have been getting ready to deal with that sickness known as Mulsins for hundreds of generations. This time we will wipe that garbage from the earth."

"I wouldn't slaughter the victory calf just yet," the old man cautioned. "It's best to do that after the war is actually won. I would suggest building things up without making any more fuss than necessary. Remember, they have sent Jahagi to spy on you. I would like to avoid riding into a horde of angry Vibaion along the way."

Mouse noticed that King Oordah had a contemplative look on his face. "What is going through your fine mind?" he asked.

"I was thinking that I can do things to make their lives difficult, much the way they are making my life difficult. I think I will be much more effective at it though."

"You have our attention now. Care to share?" the storyteller asked.

"Well, I can send wagon trains out from my country. You see, the Mulsins will require help moving themselves. That help will come from here or nearby," the king said. "An extra purse of coins to the right people can make workers suddenly lose interest. I can drop a few kegs of good beer here and there at the pits, and one can never be sure what mischief will suddenly start. Leave a coin or two with certain ale house owners, and we might get a little bird chirping in our ear long before an advancing army shows up here." He smiled and sat back in his throne.

"You are correct—and devious," Lu–Ning said. "While you are spreading happiness around your kingdom, I can do something similar around mine. Rackians are far from the brightest candles in the room, even if they are the only candles. I will send my scouts out to watch things. If they are planning on advancing, they will prepare forward posts and operating bases. This will give us an idea where they are planning on invading." The king looked at the storyteller. "Can you think of anything more we can do?"

The old man stared into space for a bit, thinking. Then his face lit up. "The person whom we are pursuing has a spell cast that will alert him if anyone mentions his name. As careful as we are, sooner or later someone will make a mistake. When that happens, he will know where we are and what we are saying." He looked around the room. Some were nodding. "I think it would be much more effective if we mentioned his name on our terms. Could you persuade your storytellers, singers, and anyone else you can think of in your kingdoms to begin telling the old legends and songs again? It will sound like a herd of stampeding horses to his ears. He won't be able to make out any one person in all the noise. He will stop listening to all of it, and we will be free to speak without worry."

"Yes, I think we can get our entertainers to start doing that," King Chang said.

Lu-Ning agreed, adding, "I think the soldiers would like to sing those old songs again too."

"Good idea," Mouse said.

"Now that we have that settled, it is getting late," Elsa said.

"True," the storyteller said. "This is a very dangerous situation we are in. While our side of things is dangerous, the enemies carry just as much danger with them, whether they know it or not. As much as I would like to say I know what the outcome will be, I can't do that. No one really can. Keeping that in mind, please begin taking quiet steps toward the worst case and hope for the best. Be careful whom you confide in. Above all right now, keep level heads. Don't get goaded and throw a torch on a dry straw field. Right now, there are only two people who can do much of anything: Elsa and me. We are asking you to believe in us, even when we do things that might seem a little odd. This means leaving us to our task. No more poking around in our business. If we need your help, we will ask. From time to time I will send updates on what is going on and how we are doing. Do you all understand?"

He looked each king in his eyes as he in turn nodded his agreement.

As they began to leave, King Chang approached the old man quietly. "I know it is late. Still, there are a few things I think you, Elsa, and I should briefly discuss before you leave. Would you please meet me in my personal tower before turning in?"

"Of course, Your Highness," the storyteller said.

Elsa turned to Joran, who seemed a little overcome by the meeting. "Joran. It's over. Time for us to prepare for tomorrow morning." Joran nodded tiredly and followed her out of the room.

Chapter Twenty

To say the king's tower room was untidy would be charitable, not to mention unkind to rooms that were untidy. Leather-bound books were stacked all over. Some lay up, open to pages held down with various things, notes scrawled in their margins. Others were stacked precariously on stools or in stacks so high they looked like they would tip over if you walked past them quickly. Mixed in with the books were maps, blueprints, mechanical drawings, sketches, and scribbled notes. Not to be outdone by the paper, oddly shaped mechanical things made from brass, copper, iron (even one that looked like gold), were littered all over. Old nooks in the wall had been filled with dripped candlewax from countless candles. A plain yet well-made draftsman's table stood along one wall, where it would catch the sunlight during the day. In front of it was a matching swivel stool. This is where they found the king, reading a scroll that looked to be from ancient times. It looked more like dried onion skin than parchment.

The storyteller and Elsa were allowed past the guards at the door without hassle. They quietly walked up to the king. "Your Highness, you had something you wished to discuss with us?" the old man said politely.

King Chang looked up from his scroll and brushed the hair from his face. "Thank you for coming, even though I see you brought a guest." He looked past Elsa and the storyteller to Joran, who was awkwardly trying to hide behind a bookcase near the door.

"I said I wasn't going to leave him anywhere. I meant it," Elsa said coldly.

Chang smiled at Joran. "It's all right. You don't have to cower in the corner like that."

Looking around, the old man said, "You have quite the collection of books and, well, things."

"Yes, I do seem to have let it get away from me." Chang chuckled. "There is so much I don't know and so much to research. You know, I have you to thank for this. You brought this thirst for knowledge to me," he said, looking purposefully at the old man.

"Well, I do seem to remember that someone asked me about something first. I didn't just drop it in your lap like a puppy and then run away," he said.

"Well, it wasn't like I had to twist your arm to get started. You could have walked away." Then, turning his attention to Elsa, he changed the topic. "I know you said not to meddle. Ala Maona just isn't acting right in my view."

Joran got the impression he wasn't really supposed to be hearing any of this, so he quietly wandered off to explore. He was careful not to bump into anything. A set of copper gears and levers caught his attention. He began trying to figure out what it was supposed to do — without touching it, of course.

"It isn't anything for you to worry about. We will deal with it," Elsa said airily.

King Chang wasn't put off so easily. "I don't think it will be as easy as you think. For many years now there has been talk that you two are here to keep a certain item" — his eyes went to Joran, then back to them — "safe. Many books and scrolls speak of this."

"You should get out more. Not spend so much time reading such nonsense," Elsa said. "And have this place cleaned," she added while making a face.

Chang sighed. "Reading is good for the mind; it keeps it sharp. Besides, the alternative is sitting around in the great hall telling tired old stories with the boring royalty hangers-on. Aside from the hollowness of it all, the wine would make my stomach sick, and the food would make it fat. No, I prefer being here than with the bragging and drunk lords down in the hall. The books and things here are much more to my liking. Plus, they don't sick up all over my robes."

"Stupidity," Elsa sniffed. "You should know better than to listen to such gossip."

"I have no doubt that we are all stupid from time to time," King Chang said. "Enough of that though. If what I have said isn't just gossip, you two are taking a very big chance. This isn't just a walk in the wildflowers on a sunny day."

"You are right," the old man said. "The thing is, nowhere is really protected when it comes to this."

"This is true. However, you seem to be poking fate with a sharp stick just to see what it will do — and a short stick at that," the king replied.

"Aren't you the clever king?" the old man said as he chuckled.

"Oh, I don't know how clever I am," Chang replied. "I would think it would be safer to leave that item someplace safe rather than wandering around the countryside with it out in the open. Put it somewhere safe, go accomplish your task, and then go back and pick it up. Banks have made this a cornerstone of their business."

"I see your point," Elsa said. "Where would you suggest we deposit the item? We have seen that their gold manages to find its way to all corners of the world. Even here. Do you think Lord Starn was the only one they bought? Can you be sure there aren't any more like him? The old man and I are very capable of taking care of this item," she finished.

Not wanting to leave it on such a bad note — he was a king and a friend, after all — the old man added, "We appreciate your offer and worry. Thank you."

"This concerns all of the world," Chang pointed out.

For his part, Joran sensed they were talking about him even though they didn't want him aware of it. Yes, he was young and none too bright — even downright foolhardy at times. He wasn't stupid though. He could tell that whatever it was they were discussing in hushed tones involved him. If it involved him, he might be able to learn something about where he was from. Or anything about his past, for that matter. To cover that he was straining his ears to hear every word, he unrolled a dusty scroll. His intent was to look like he was reading something, hoping they would forget he was there or think he wasn't listening. The problem was, rather than words, the scroll had what looked to him like someone had dipped a bunch of chickens' feet in ink and let them walk over the paper. If it was supposed to be art, Joran thought it was a poor attempt. He found it foul. *Foul made by fowl*, he thought and chuckled a little.

That brought Elsa's attention to him. As if it weren't bad enough that she seemed to have a sixth sense about what he was doing, he had to help her by laughing. "Joran, what are you messing with?"

"It's just an old scroll. It looks like an attempt at a picture. I can't read anyway," he grumped.

"Joran, put the king's things down. Right now," she snapped.

Joran carefully sat it back down.

King Chang smiled at Joran. "It's all right. It is just an old scroll from ancient times. The writing is all but dead. It is ancient Mulsin script."

Elsa gasped. "Why of all things is that here? It is prohibited, and you know it."

"Elsa," he said patiently, "That is just parchment with ink on it. Nothing more. It only becomes something more if people give it meaning." He ignored her look. "Reading what the enemy writes helps us understand their thought process and helps us understand them."

"Chang, with all your research, you must have learned by now that Arrah can twist and control your mind without you knowing it. All he has to do is wait for you to release even a tiny bit of control," Elsa said.

"Elsa, I am sure that Chang's mind is just fine and under his control. After all, Arrah's little tricks are clumsy and easy to spot. No one ever said Arrah was all that clever," the old man said.

Chang didn't seem to be paying much attention to Elsa and her father. Instead, he was thoughtfully looking at Joran. After a few minutes, he gestured for him to come over to him. Joran walked over and waited for the king to speak. Or do something else.

"Joran, for your age, you are very bright and alert," the king said solemnly. "Because of your recent actions, I am still ruler of this kingdom, and a great many people are still alive and safe. You did a great thing for me and my kingdom. I want to thank you for that. If you ever need my help, please don't hesitate to ask for it. I would like you to think of me as your personal friend." The king then put his hand out for Joran to shake. Joran simply reached out and took it, as he had been taught to do since he was a small boy. He firmly shook the king's hand while looking him in the eye.

Because Joran was looking him in the eye, he saw the king's expression change the instant they shook hands. King Chang's face turned almost sickly white and his eyes grew large. He looked down at Joran's hand, then let his gaze work its way up over Joran's wrist, then to his arm where his gaze stopped when he saw the scar like mark on Joran's arm.

Joran was surprised when he felt Elsa's hand on his and the king's. She gently removed the king's firm handshake from Joran's.

The king shook his head as though to clear his mind, then said quietly, "It has happened." Although to Joran it seemed the king was speaking to no one in particular.

"Don't start mixing your books and stories with reality," Elsa said, keeping her hand firmly on Joran's. "It is late. We still have to get ready for our trip tomorrow." With that, she walked out. Joran's hand was still in hers as he rushed to keep up with her.

In between almost falling over Elsa's skirts and trying to keep up with her, Joran let his mind think on what had just happened. Why would a king be so surprised to find a mark like his? Elsa had once told him that it was passed down through his family. It all had come to a boiling point. His curiosity had become a need: a need to know about his family, where Elsa fit into things. Everything. If finding out the answers made him suffer, then so be it. He would suffer; at least then he would know.

Getting the answers, though, would have to wait. First, sleep.

He awoke to a crisp and clear day. Everyone was up and ready to leave for the docks as the sun was coming up. While they were mounting horses and climbing into sleighs, Gunnarr's wife strode out of the castle wearing a fine white fur cloak.

"Lanna, why are you out in the cold? There is no reason for you to be out at this hour," Gunnarr said.

"It is my obligation to see my husband off on his next voyage," she sniffed arrogantly as she stepped into a sleigh.

Gunnarr just signed, a resigned look on his face. The procession set off with the king and queen leading them off to the docks. The fresh snow crunched under the horses' feet and the sleigh's runners.

Joran was quietly riding between Mouse and Angensen. Mouse looked quizzically at Joran. "You are awfully talkative today," Mouse said.

Joran just shrugged a little. In truth, he was still trying to wake up and stay warm. It seemed doing both at once was beyond him this morning.

"Something is on your mind; maybe I can help," Mouse said.

Joran thought for a moment before answering Mouse. He was trying to get his sleepy thoughts together. "Since we got here, I have been confused about most of what has happened," he finally said.

"That is part of life, Joran," Angensen said. "Not even great scholars have a grasp of everything in the world."

"Well, that is one way to look at it," Mouse said. "Chanese tend to react viciously to things from time to time. It seems to depend on their mood at that time. Their moods seem to change with the wind too."

While Joran appreciated the fact that Mouse and Angensen hadn't dismissed his comment out of hand, their responses didn't really help him. Trying to work his thoughts around into clearer picture in his head, Joran tried again. "I sort of have them figured out. It is the entire time since we left the farm. Elsa, the storyteller, Ala Maona. I can't figure out what is happening. It's like being stuck on a runaway horse, and you can't see where you are going so you know how to get back." Even as he said it, he knew that wasn't the best way to explain his feelings. It was just the best he could come up with right then.

"I can understand that, Joran," Angensen said thoughtfully.

Joran looked at him, surprised.

Seeing Joran's look, Angensen continued, "If you look at life overall, it can be likened to riding a horse. At first, it is young and fast, running everywhere, ears up. Everything is a wonder to be explored. Sometimes they get spooked and run really fast for a long time. If you hang on long enough, even the best horse will finally slow to a walk. That is when you can look around and make sense of where you are and what has happened. Later you get to laugh about the wild ride and share it with friends over a tankard of ale."

"Thank you," Joran said quietly. Then he retreated into himself and tried to make sense of things.

Eventually they came to the large church they had passed when they first came to the city — the one Gunnarr had avoided when they had gone to the shipwright's warehouse. Sure enough, the same woman was there again. Joran was almost relieved she was there. He expected them to drive on past her, since Gunnarr didn't seem to like her and from the sounds of it, the king didn't either. Instead, all the horses came to a dead stop. No amount of whistling or shouts from the riders or drivers would make them move.

The blind woman turned to face Joran. "Greetings, Holy Lord!" she shouted. "Please remember that I give you my prayers for a safe and good journey today."

Remembering his manners, even in his confusion, Joran returned her greeting. "My thanks, kind lady. I am no lord though. Why do you refer to me as one?"

She continued as though he hadn't said a thing. "My Lord, just remember me and my kindness when you come into your birthright."

"Why do you say that whenever you see me? What birthright? I have no parents," he asked, frustrated. It was just one more thing to add to his confusion about what was going on.

That was as far as their conversation went. Gunnarr and the king were both getting to the ground in a blind fury. Gunnarr was raging with anger and ripping his cloak off to get to his sword while the king's face was deep red with rage.

Elsa cut them off. "Stop it! Both of you!" she shouted at them. "Let me deal with her." Elsa stood and looked directly at the blind woman. "Listen, seer in darkness. You apparently see far too much in darkness. It is time that darkness no longer bothers you."

The blind woman turned to look at Elsa. Her face showed no fear. "Burn me to ash, Elsalia. It won't change what visions come."

"Oh, come now. Why would I want to burn you to ashes? That would just be mean of me. Besides, it would take hours, and we have somewhere to go. Instead, I wish to give you a present." With that, Elsa made an odd movement of her hands and muttered a word that Joran couldn't understand.

While he didn't understand what she had said or did with her hands, he did understand what he saw happen to the old woman. He watched her eyes go from the color of winter-frosted glass to bright green. It was like someone had held a candle near the cold glass, and the frost had melted away. The sickly, milky color just seemed to melt away, starting at the center of her eyes and working outward. Even if he wanted to say he didn't see it, he knew he couldn't do that.

For her part, the formerly blind old woman blinked at the bright sunlight a few times, then covered her eyes and wailed as though she were in great pain.

Jura looked at Elsa. "You took her blindness?" she snapped.

Elsa sat down and busied herself with arranging her cloak. "If you look at it that way, yes," she said. "Or you could say I returned her sight. Either way works. One just sounds nicer."

"How did you do that?" Jura demanded, even though her face was now as white as snow and her voice quivered.

"It is something you haven't figured out? Really, it is such an elementary thing to do."

Ignoring the jab at her, Jura asked, "Without her blindness, she won't be able to have any visions now. Will she?"

"I doubt it. Wouldn't you agree, though, that it is a fair trade? Being able to see the world around you?" Elsa asked simply.

"You took her abilities. She is no longer a seer? A sorceress?" Jura persisted.

"Jura, I gave her her sight back. I took her power at visions in trade. We can agree she wasn't all that great at them. At best, she was haphazard with them. This way she isn't pestering good folks with her naysaying and foolishness." Elsa then looked at the king, who was standing still, as though he had been frozen to the spot. "Your Highness, I believe our boat's captains are hoping to sail on this tide."

The horses jumped ahead as though they were just waking up from a deep sleep and trotted off toward the docks.

Joran turned and looked at the old woman. She knelt in the snow. Weeping.

"Remember today, Joran. We were blessed to see a wonder from the Gods," Angensen said, his voice grave.

"I think that blessing would depend on what side of that wonder of the Gods you are on. The giver seemed happy enough. The receiver though, less than happy," Mouse said.

Joran nodded in agreement. It seemed that Elsa's gifts had two sides to them. One good. One bad. Depending on how you looked at it.

Chapter Twenty-One

The cold black waves seemed tipped in jewels, sparkling in the early-morning sunlight as the small procession reached the docks. The travelers came to a stop at the tarred beams of a slip. The large ship pulled at the ropes, making them creak each time it rose on the waves. To Joran it reminded him of a horse wanting to run. The ship next to it also seemed to be eager to set sail.

Angensen, Lu-Ning, and Queen Victoria all moved off to one side and spoke in low tones. The serious looks on their faces made it plain they wanted privacy.

Jura was sitting stiffly in her sleigh. Her color had returned somewhat to her face, and she wore a painted-on smile. Anyone could see was trying to hide her unease. Her husband had gone off to talk with the storyteller, leaving her alone in the sleigh. Elsa walked over to her.

"Jura, we all know you have at best a very limited ability in the area of magic. Why don't you find something else to occupy your free time? It isn't wise for someone to poke around in things they really don't know much about. Things can go wrong in big ways."

Jura just looked at her, clearly trying to keep the anger off her face.

"One more thing," Elsa continued. "It is very bad form for a wife to be so close to her husband's enemies. Especially when her husband is a king. Stop all your dealings with a certain religious order. The one that runs the big church we passed?"

That brought a reaction from Jura. The shock crossed her face in a rush. "Please tell me my husband doesn't know," she begged.

Elsa just looked at her with disdain. "Don't you think it would be surprising if he didn't know? He is the king, after all. While you think you are the smart and devious one, he is far from stupid. The fact that you are practically a traitor and he hasn't openly accused you says much. Stick with something you would be good at. Have some children; raise them to be good rulers or wives. That is something that will be useful and beneficial to the kingdom and the king. I am sure it would be much more beneficial than you trying to play at being a sorceress. Thank you for the enjoyable time here." Elsa then pulled on her mittens and set off toward the ships.

Mouse was discretely watching and listening to the two women. Once Elsa had walked off, he hummed a few bars from a sad tavern song. Joran looked at Mouse, the question plain on his face.

"Oh, I just had a number of things fall into place," Mouse said.

"Things fall into place?" Joran asked.

"A certain religious member of Vangarth has been playing in Chanese affairs recently. I had no idea they had started playing at being a spy too. Certainly not in the royal court," Mouse said.

Joran took a second or two to put it all together. Then blurted out, "Jura?"

Mouse smiled a little. "She is infatuated by sorcery. Anything that even remotely appears to be magic, she is drawn to and blindly believes it. There are some ceremonies that some religions perform that appear to be magical, especially to those who want them to be magic. These people are usually foolish and easily deceived." Mouse then looked around and spotted Queen Helena standing along on the pier. He led Joran over to her.

"Queen Helena," Mouse said with a little bow.

"Mouse, you know you don't have to bow to me," she said with a smile.

"Only being polite to royalty." He smiled in return. "I was wondering if you could pass some information along for me."

"If I can, I will help you out," she replied. "Whom would you like to get a message to?"

"Thank you, m'lady," Mouse said. He then turned serious. "If you could, pass along to King Oordah that Jura has been a very bad wife. It seems she has been attending certain religious ceremonies to learn their illusions. Or as she thinks, their magic. She has been active with them in Chanese."

"That is a very poor choice of things to do. Even for her," Helena replied, the surprise written on her face. "Does her husband know?"

"I would be surprised if he didn't at least know a small part of what she has been doing. He probably wouldn't say anything about it though," Mouse replied quietly. "A little bit ago I heard Elsa tell her to stop wasting time with her obsession of magic and to stop spending so much time with that certain religious group."

"Well, if Elsa told her to stop it, that should be the end of that nonsense from her," Helena said. "About time too; we were tired of trying to look surprised at her clumsy attempts at magic."

"Oh, Elsa was about as about as subtle as a hammer between the eyes when she told her to do something worthwhile for the kingdom and her husband." Mouse smiled. "Jura seemed to take the warning to heart. Just in case, please pass it along to my uncle. He likes to know about things like this."

"I will pass it along."

"Thank you. While you are at it, you might want to remind him that these things seldom happen alone. Other sects are more than likely in on something like this too. It has been a while since we had to remind them where their boundaries are," Mouse said.

The queen nodded. "You are right. I will do that. When I get back home, I will also ask my spymaster what he knows. I am sure his people in the local sect will know something."

"Your spymaster? My, you have progressed nicely. At this pace, you will surpass me. Perhaps I should be keeping an eye on you, just in case you find a way to twist me to do your bidding as well." He winked at her and smiled.

"My kingdom is brimming with spies. Not just the religious nuts. The capital city alone is a major hub for traders and businessmen from all over the world. I would guess that half of them are spies as well. One has to protect her king and kingdom," she said.

"Well now, m'lady," Mouse said. "Does your loving and doting husband know what his lovely wife is up to?"

"Now Mouse, you know I don't keep secrets from him. He knows. He was the one who introduced me to my spymaster and told him he was to work for me," she said with a smile.

"Well, how thoughtful of him," Mouse said with a little sarcasm in his voice.

"Now Mouse, it is a smart thing to do. Look at it from the standpoint of a king. He is concerned with what other kingdoms are doing. It only makes sense to have someone he trusts keep abreast of things in his kingdom. That way he isn't distracted by all the smaller yet no less important things going on at home. I admit, my network is not nearly the size of yours or other masters of the game. I still keep up with what is going on though." She smiled demurely at him. "You know, if you ever decide to settle down, I can think of lots of work for you at my kingdom."

Mouse blushed slightly while he smiled and bowed to her. "M'lady, I will keep your very generous offer in mind. It seems I have many offers all of a sudden."

When Mouse stood, the queen wore a serious look again. "It would be nice for you to finally stop playing at meandering businessman and come home. You would do much more good as head of relations or as an instructor of spy craft."

Mouse avoided her direct gaze and looked out over the harbor. "I am flattered. Right now, though, working with Orrlick is more important—not just to me; to the world in general. Maybe when I have more gray hair, the enjoyment has left the game, and my joints aren't happy with me riding all day, I will take you up on that offer. I really can't say right now though."

The queen sadly looked at Mouse. "You know there are people back home who really do miss you," she said softly. "Like me."

Mouse looked at her, an impish smile on his face. "You're so ignored in the castle?" he chided her playfully.

The little woman shoved him with her tiny hand. "You just can't be serious."

"Oh, I do try though. Very hard," he said, smiling.

Not far away on the dock, Angensen was saying his farewells to his mother and father. He hugged his mother tightly, then moved to his father. Standing tall and looking his father in the eye, he offered his hand for a farewell shake. His father returned his look, took his hand, and then pulled the hard warrior into a fatherly hug. Releasing him, he smiled at his son. Angensen then jumped onto the sturdy ship, turned, and waved to his parents. A big smile was on his face, and his eyes were alight with happiness at the coming adventure.

His parents watched as the ship moved away from the docks and disappeared into the horizon. Then they turned, took each other's hands, and made their way to the sleigh.

Across the slip, a gangway (just two boards nailed together, really), was set on the snow and ice-covered stones. The other end was anchored to Lothur's ship.

Mouse walked over, being careful to keep his balance on the slippery stones. "Lothur! It is good to see you. May Joran and I come aboard?" he called up.

"Of course, my little friend" was the friendly reply. Mouse motioned to Joran to follow him up the rickety gangway.

Before boarding, Gunnarr turned to his wife. "Tell my daughters I love them and miss them."

"Yes, husband. Is there anything else before you leave again?" she asked, her tone dead and overly formal.

"This will be a long journey. Make sure the north fields are left alone until fall this year, then plant winter wheat. The south and east acres should have hay and clover planted this year. Corn for the west — sweet corn, we have more than enough silage already. Work out something with the cattle man across the road to have his bull breed the cows this year. I know he won't sell you a bull; his sire fees, though, should be fair."

"As you wish. I will carry out m'lord's wishes. I shall watch your property carefully in your absence," she said.

Sighing, Gunnarr looked at her. "You understand they are ours, not just mine."

"If that is your desire," she said.

A sad look came across his face. "Will you ever get over it?"

She just looked at him, confused.

"Never mind," Gunnarr muttered.

"Would m'lord care for a kiss before he leaves?" she asked formally.

Gunnarr just looked at her sadly for a moment, then turned and jumped onto the ship. Without looking back, he headed to the rear berths.

Elsa was on her way to the gangway when she stopped Gunnarr's wife with a hard look. For a second, the other woman thought Elsa was going to say something. Instead, Elsa just giggled at her.

Surprised, Lanna looked at her coldly. "Care to share the joke, Elsa?"

"Oh, it will be shared with you soon enough," Elsa said mysteriously, a mocking expression on her face. With that, she walked up the plank gangway herself. A seaman helped her step onto the deck of the ship.

The old man finished his goodbyes with the rulers, shaking each of their hands firmly and then boarding the ship himself. He hopped onto the deck like a boy going on his first adventure. He then turned and took a last look at the snow and ice-covered city he was leaving.

King Chang raised his hand and waved a friendly farewell. "Safe travels!" he called.

"Thank you! Remember to send out the storytellers" was the shouted reply.

"I have already sent it out!" the king called back.

With that, the old man wandered off to the bow of the ship. Joran had been quiet during all the farewells; after all, whom did he really have to say goodbye to? Everyone he really knew was going with him. He watched the old man head to the front of the ship and decided to follow him. He still had a lot of questions rolling around in his head. Joran figured that if anyone knew all the answers, it would be the old storyteller.

Joran quietly stood next to him for a minute, not sure how or where to start.

"Something troubling you, Joran?" the old man asked kindly.

Chewing his lip for a second, Joran just decided to jump in with whatever came to his mind first. "How did Elsa make that old lady see again?"

"She used nature's forces and manipulated them to do her bidding." His hair blew around his face in the cold sea breeze. "Really isn't that hard to do," he said.

Joran was beyond confused. "She did what?" he asked.

"If you want to do something bad enough, have a strong enough desire, you can do what she did. If you know the ancient words for it as well, of course," he said.

"That is it?" Joran's tone showed how let down he was.

"Yes."

"The ancient language is magical?"

The old man chuckled, not unkindly though. He looked at Joran. "Words by themselves aren't magic. None of them are, regardless of how mysterious they might sound or what someone says. They are simply a tool for the forces of nature. Like Sladvick's forge. It isn't magical, yet it lets him form metal. He is using the forces of nature, in this case fire and strength, to achieve a goal. Does that help you understand?"

Joran thought that over a bit. "Is it something I can do?"

The old man looked thoughtful. "I've never thought about it, now that you mention it. I suppose you could. The first time I managed to do it I was a little older than you. I had been studying it for years already. I'm not sure if that makes a difference."

"What did you do your first time?" Joran asked.

"I was asked to move a log," the old man said, a faraway look on his face. "My teacher and I were getting ready to start cooking the evening meal. He wanted the log on his fire. I struggled to pick it up. I couldn't get my arms around it. I kept wondering why he wanted that log when there were plenty of smaller logs around. I finally stepped back from it and yelled at it. To my surprise, it flipped end over end onto the fire. My teacher didn't seem at all surprised by what had happened."

Joran looked at him, his doubt clear on his face. He wasn't sure if the old man was being honest or sharing a story with him. "All you did was yell at it. Nothing more?" Joran was thinking that he could have used that trick a lot when he was on the farm and told to carry in firewood or stack hay bales.

Nodding, the old man said, "Yes. I just yelled at it to get on the fire. At the time, I was stunned that it had worked. Then I was surprised at how simple it had been and wondered why I hadn't tried something like that before. Back when I was your age, I thought any man could do that. Many years have passed since then, and I think maybe men have changed too much. I can't say for sure."

"In the stories, magicians always use foul-smelling potions, strange words, and long enchantments," Joran said.

"Stories sometimes need some dressing up to make them more entertaining." The old man chuckled. "In reality, those things are just for showmen at fairs and frauds. Some do entertain their audiences; others prefer to cheat and scare people. All those chants and bottles of potions have nothing to do with it. They are just props. A true magician, one who can really control nature, needs nothing more than his mind and a word. Some find making signs with their hands helps them concentrate. Like Elsa. It really doesn't have anything to do with anything though. She refuses to stop doing it that way. I've tried to break her of that annoying habit for centuries. Come to think of it, maybe that is why she does it; she knows it annoys me."

Joran's mouth fell open. "Centuries? Just how old is Elsa?"

"Now Joran, you should have learned by now that it is rude to ask a female her age. Just go with the fact she is much older than she lets on." He winked at Joran.

Joran's face fell when he came to another realization. "She really isn't related to me at all, is she?" His heart felt empty and cold.

"Why do you say that?" the old man asked.

"If she is that old, how could she be one of my parents' sister? It would be impossible for her to have grown up with them if she is that old."

"Joran, you seem to enjoy that word. If you look at things, there is almost nothing that is truly impossible. Difficult, yes. Impossible, no."

"Then how can she be so old? She would be my great-great-grandmother — maybe a few more 'greats' in there, you know what I mean?" Joran said.

"Let me try explaining this a little differently," the storyteller said. "Elsa is related to you, in a manner of speaking. Try not to attach the traditional terms to her, like aunt or mother. OK? That will help." He waited for Joran to nod. He then continued, "Your father's great-grandmother was Elsa's sister. Therefore, she is related to him and you. She is sort of a really old aunt. Just don't call her that. She will probably get upset." The old man chuckled.

Joran smiled; a bit of his earlier despair fell away.

"What brought all the interest in this up in the first place?" the old man asked.

Joran shrugged a little and looked at his feet. "For a while now people have been saying I am not who I had thought I was. I began thinking that Elsa was saying she was related to me in some way just to make me feel better. I was scared I had no family," he half mumbled.

The old man looked at Joran, sadness and understanding on his face. "What were they saying to make you scared?"

"It's hard to put into words. I can't remember my parents. I don't know what I am. Mouse pointed out that I am not Brasselian, not a true blood anyway. Gunnarr said I remind him of a Sykavik. That was after I spent my life thinking I was like Sladvick. After hearing all those views, I tried to hang on to Elsa being the only family I had. No one has been willing to tell me anything about my real family: who they were, what happened to them. Nothing. Figuring out Elsa wasn't really related to me would mean I was alone. No family. Nobody. Nothing."

"You saw being alone in the world as being a horrible thing?" the old man asked gently.

"Wouldn't you?"

"I guess I would, yes. You feel better now? Knowing you and Elsa share the same family tree?"

Smiling, Joran looked up at the old man. "Yes, even if she is the roots of that ancient oak, and I am the leaves at the top."

The old man burst out laughing. "That was good, Joran. Just don't repeat that to Elsa." He laughed some more.

"I won't. Thank you for telling me. It has been keeping me awake at nights," Joran said.

The pair stood and listened to the sailors and ocean as they made their way out to open sea. A thought came to Joran's mind. "If Elsa really is my very old aunt," — he laughed, then continued — "would that make you my even older grandfather? I've heard people call her your daughter."

"Well, she is my daughter, even though at times I try to forget that part." He laughed. "Yes, I guess if you simplified it, it would make me your grandfather. I never looked at it that way." He put an arm around Joran and gave him a quick hug.

Joran hugged the old man back with both arms. He had tears in his eyes.

Caught off guard by Joran's sudden emotional display, the old man gently patted his back. "You are quite the smart young man. Sometimes." He chuckled.

After a long moment, Joran let go of the old man, his newly found grandfather, and stood next to him. He seemed a little embarrassed by his tears. The old man seemed a little embarrassed as well by the long hug. The two stood and watched the shoreline recede into the horizon.

Joran leaned on the rail of the ship and looked into the dark waters below him. "Grandfather, would you tell me how my parents died? The truth?" he asked without looking up.

Joran's newly found grandfather's face paled under his whiskers. "Joran, the truth isn't very pretty. Are you sure you want to hear it? Once you hear something, it is something you can't really forget."

"Yes, I want to know."

"All right." He sighed. "A fire killed them."

Joran's face paled. Fire was a very bad way to die. "How did it happen?"

The old man looked sadly at Joran's back without answering. Finally, Joran turned and looked at him. "Please" was all Joran said.

"Well, OK then. Come here and sit down." He motioned to the neatly coiled ropes near them. They both sat; the railing of the ship kept the cold wind off them. "If you are asking the questions, you must be able to hear the answers, as unpleasant as they are."

Joran arranged his cloak around his legs and simply looked at his grandfather, waiting for the answers he had been looking for.

"Where do we start?" the old man said, pulling his hair out of his face and pulling his hood up. "Well, the beginning is a good place. Joran, your ancestors reach back a long way. During those years, enemies were made. It happens to all old families."

"My family had enemies?" Joran hadn't thought of that before. Only rich and powerful families had enemies, not the simple folk he imagined his family to be.

"All families can have them, regardless of their social standing. If someone does something that makes someone else mad, that anger can build. If it is left alone too long, it will build into blind rage. If that rage isn't addressed, following generations will follow it. It can grow into something like a cult. The hatred the original person felt turns to hatred of everything about the person whom they felt originally wronged them. The followers, if you will, of this cult learn to hate not only that person. They hate everything about him. His family. His dog. His language. Left to grow long enough, it will encompass everything about that person's life." He stopped to see if Joran was following things. Seeing that Joran seemed to understand, the old man continued. "Well, centuries ago it got so bad that Elsa and I decided to protect what was left of the family. We hid it."

"Grandfather, what are you hiding?" Joran bluntly interrupted.

"You're smarter than people give you credit for, I see," the storyteller responded irritably. "You are right. I am not sharing everything. Right now, it isn't safe for you to share everything. I am more or less setting the scene for what happened to your parents, giving you some background. In time, you will learn what I have left out."

"Why not just tell me everything now?" Joran demanded.

"Knowledge can make people act differently, and right now, I would like you to act just like you are now. Let me enjoy my newfound grandson as he is a little longer, OK?" The old man smiled.

"If you want an uneducated grandson, fine," Joran moped.

"I'll take that for now. Are you going to let me continue? After all, I am a storyteller. You asked for this story."

Joran nodded.

"OK." The old man ruffled Joran's hair. "Being related to your family, we naturally wanted to see your family safe. The best solution to things that we could come up with was hiding everyone. So that is what we did."

"You can hide an entire family?" Joran asked.

"Well, your family has usually stayed small. That made it much easier. Plus, we realized that in order to keep your blood line unbroken, all we really had to do was hide three people. A husband, his wife, and their child. Cousins, uncles, or anyone else really didn't need to be worried about all that much." The old man paused and wiped some salt spray from his face. "We actually became very good at it. Practice makes perfect, or if not perfect, better. Over the ages we moved them from country to country. Sometimes just to a different village was all it took for a time. They worked at trades, never drawing attention to themselves. Usually they were farmers, cabinetmakers, things like that. One was a simple woodcutter. Over the years, things had been going very well. They had no real issues or emergencies, just nice, quiet, simple lives. That brings us to your father. I told you once he was a very hardworking and talented craftsman, didn't I?"

Joran nodded. "He was a master journeyman in several trades, you said. He was a very kind man too; you would visit him from time to time," he said.

"Yes, that he was," the old man agreed.

"Where was my mother from?" Joran asked eagerly, happy he was finally getting some answers about his past.

"She was from Mopta. She was one of many daughters of a tribal leader. Elsa played matchmaker with the two, then left things take their course. Things went as they typically do, and you popped out not long after they were married. On a similar note, be careful of Elsa dabbling in your love life." The old man chuckled. Joran didn't remind his grandfather that she already had—and clearly not in the same way she had for her parents. He wasn't interested in that right now.

"How did the accident happen? The fire?" Joran persisted.

"Patience, Joran. That will come along soon enough," the old man chided Joran. "Let's get back to the enemies of your family. For centuries one of them had been hunting them."

"He was a wizard?" Joran blurted.

"Why do you say that?"

"Only wizards and magicians live for so long. Right?"

"Well, I guess you could call this enemy a wizard. He at least had some basic skills in that area," he admitted, then tried to get back to the story. "A term like that, though, is kind of broad. It is sort of deceptive, in fact. Elsa and I don't look at ourselves as being a wizard or a sorceress in the way most people think of them. Let's get back to your parents though. One night, while your parents were sleeping and Elsa and I were gone, this enemy finally found them. While your parents were sleeping, he sealed up the house. Once that was done, he burned it."

"Wasn't it made of brick though?" Joran asked.

"You are right; it was stone and mortar. Even that can burn if heated enough. You just have to really work at it. Your parents knew there was no way for them to survive the fire. Your father, though — he knew he could save you from their fate if he could break a small hole in the wall. Once he had managed that, your mother wrapped you in some thick blankets to protect you and pushed you out of the house. You know, now that I think of it, I sometimes wonder if you didn't land on your head." The old man chuckled at Joran's look. Then he got back to his story. "What they hadn't planned on was that the one who had set fire was waiting for them to get you out of the house. Once he found you, he simply picked you up and left. To this day I don't know why you were taken. Was he going to kill you? If so, why bother taking you when he could have just left you in the fire that killed your parents? Did he have a different reason? Something he planned to use you for? I just don't know. Whatever his reason, I managed to get there in time to put out the fire. Sadly — and I am very sorry for this — it was too late to save your parents. I really am sorry, Joran." Joran reached over and laid his hand on the old man's. Then his grandfather continued. "After finding you missing, I set out to find you. It wasn't hard to track him. The trail was fresh. It didn't take me long to catch up to him. He wasn't expecting any pursuit, and he had you to worry about."

"I hope you burned him to death, like he did my parents," Joran said through clenched teeth.

"Well, I had other thoughts for him. Burning him would have been much too quick and nice for him. Regardless, I am not allowed to do things like that unless absolutely necessary. It tends to make a mess of things down the road."
"I am glad you punished him," Joran said.
"Well," The old man said sheepishly. "I had to make a quick decision: catch you, or catch the man who had burned your parents to death."
"I thought you did catch me. He was carrying me, wasn't he?" Joran was a little confused.
"Oh, he had you all right. Right up until he threw you at me so he could get away. I could keep chasing him or catch you before you went over the edge into the river."
"I seem to have issues with rivers," Joran muttered, thinking back to a time he'd raced a cart down a hill and wound up in the water.
The old man waited for an explanation on that; when none came, he continued his story. "After I had made sure you were OK, I took you to Elsa. She has taken care of you ever since, while I went looking for your parents' murderer."
"Did you find him?" Joran asked.
"No. Not for lack of trying though," the old man said sadly.
"Good," Joran said.
The old man couldn't hide the surprise from his face. "What? Why?"
"I should be the one to avenge my parents," Joran said firmly.
"That is a grave and hazardous path to follow."
"I don't care. He killed my parents. I should be the one who holds him accountable for his past crimes."
"That is one way to look at it."

"Good. Tell me who it was."

"Perhaps I will wait some time before I share that. You are still young, and I don't think it would be wise for you to leap off the cliff before you are ready."

Joran eyed his grandfather, not sure if the old man was just brushing him off or if he would really share the information later. "When you think I am ready, you will share that information with me. Right?"

"Yes, when I see you are ready for it."

"Do I have your word on it?" Joran persisted. He wasn't going to let things slip away again.

"Yes, on my word as a traveling storyteller and a man, I will share that when I see you are ready. Happy?" The look on Joran's face said he was still skeptical and far from happy. "OK, if I don't keep my word, and I will, you can ask Elsa. She views it much the way you do."

The last comment surprised Joran. "You don't agree he should pay for what he did?"

"When you reach my age, you tend to see things a little differently," the old man said quietly.

"Well, I am still young and don't have your abilities to do things with nature. For me, killing him will have to suffice." He noticed he had been beating his fists into the coarse rope under him. He couldn't remember when he had started doing that. He only knew his hands were bloody from it.

The old man sighed, looking sadly at Joran. "You won't change your mind, will you?"

"No."

"Afterward I hope you will have a different view of things."

"I am sure you do. And I am sure I won't."

"Maybe I know you better than you think I do."

Tired of this from the old man, Joran decided it was time to change the course of the conversation. "I am glad you shared that with me."

As though he hadn't heard Joran, the storyteller went on. "In time, you would have figured it out or heard stories. I guess it is best you hear the unbiased and true version from me."

So much for a change of topic, Joran thought. "Elsa wouldn't give me the true version?" he asked, somewhat surprised.

The old man looked out over the water. "I can't say she wouldn't tell you the truth. She would. She was much…closer to the events than I was though. That makes her see things from a different angle than I do. She also tends to get tunnel vision as well. I try to look past what is right in front of my nose and see the entire forest, not just the tree in front of me." He sighed. "Especially in this situation. Things just aren't as simple and clear as some may think."

Joran sat quietly for a while. He rested his hands in his lap and let the blood on them dry in the sea breeze. He looked between his hands and the ocean, letting his mind wander over what he had learned while sitting there, aside from the fact that ropes on ships hurt your hands when you beat on them. Then he looked up at his newfound grandfather. He really looked at him this time. He studied the old man's face, the creases around his eyes, the weathered skin, and how the white hair seemed to have a light all its own yet still floated in the ocean wind.

"Grandfather?" Saying that still felt odd to Joran.

"Yes, Grandson?" the old man asked Joran in a gently teasing tone as he looked down at his grandson.

"How does it feel to have lived since the beginning of time?"

"Oh, I am nowhere near that old." He chuckled. "Why, do I look that old? Here I had thought I had aged pretty well." He dramatically straightened himself up and combed through his whiskers while tossing his head back. He then looked at Joran, and they both laughed.

"You know what I mean; you've been around forever," Joran said.

"I haven't been around that long, so I can't answer that for you."

"You're really old though."

"True. I am no longer a puppy curled up in old feed sacks with his littermates in the grain room." Then he paused, almost searching for a way to answer Joran. "While I don't wake up without some aches and pains nowadays, life hasn't changed much for me. I still like my daughter's desserts. A good pipe from time to time is a simple pleasure as well. What you should understand, though, is that we all die sooner or later. When our usefulness runs out — we complete the mission, so to speak — we fade off. I just got lucky and have been needed for centuries. Well, if you can call it lucky at times." He chuckled. "OK, enough talk about my age."

"What you are doing, what you brought us into, it is for the good of the people. Right?" Joran asked.

"Not just for people: for the world and heavens above."

"Why am I along then? I haven't been much help — more of a hindrance most of the time, it seems. I can't be much help in this, can I?" Joran said quietly, remembering the times he seemed to mess up or get in the way.

Looking solemnly at Joran, the storyteller answered him. "Life often has great surprises in store for each of us. Your surprise may yet come. Be patient," he said and gently put his arm over Joran's shoulders, giving him a reassuring hug. Joran looked up at his grandfather and smiled a little before following the old man's gaze out over the railing of the ship into the distance. Both let their minds clear. The men at the oars put them at ease with their rhythmic rowing as they carried them to what the future held for them all.

www.ingramcontent.com/pod-product-compliance
Lightning Source LLC
Chambersburg PA
CBHW021956050726
47498CB00001BA/26